The Mountains of Morogoro

By Anne Holderness

The European has the clock but the African has the time
 - African proverb

-o0o-

*This novel is dedicated to the people of Tanzania,
past and present.*

--oOo--

The characters and most of the events described in this novel are entirely fictitious

Contents

Part 1
Ch 1   Arrival in Dar es Salaam
Ch 2   Setting out and the Journey South
Ch 3   Landa
Ch 4   Meeting Father-in-Law
Ch 5   Meeting Mother-in-Law
Ch 6   The Journey Home
Ch 7   The Aftermath
Ch 8   The British Council
Ch 9   The Driving Test

Part 2
Ch 10   The Ad Agency
Ch 11   New House in Dar
Ch 12   What's in a Name?
Ch 13   Mosi starts school
Ch 14   Letter to Christine 2
Ch 15   Shortages
Ch 16   Hedda next door
Ch 17   The Wake
Ch 18   After the Krolls
Ch 19   The Women's Group
Ch 20   The Journalists
Ch 21   Decision Time

Part 3
Ch 22   Morogoro
Ch 23   Settling in
Ch 24   French lessons
Ch 25   Morogoro with the French
Ch 26   Branching Out
Ch 27   New Ventures

Ch 28	Small Beginnings
Ch 29	The Launch
Ch 30	Meeting with Gerhard
Ch 31	Christmas

Part 4
Ch 32	Moving On

Acknowledgements
Glossary

Ch 1: Arrival in Dar es Salaam (*1968)*

The oven-blast of air that greeted her at the door held her breathless for a moment. She clutched Mosi closer to her as she looked across the runway to the modest single storey building. '*Karibu Tanzania*' was written in large letters and, underneath, 'Welcome to Dar es Salaam International Airport'.

A gentle push at her back reminded Esme that she was holding up the passengers behind her and she muttered an apology. She carefully descended the metal staircase to stand on Tanzanian ground at last. She blinked in the overhead sun: it was like nothing she had ever experienced. Had she really left Edinburgh in a few inches of snow yesterday morning? For a split second she wondered why she was in this situation then Martin flooded back into her consciousness and, hugging the baby to her, she whispered,

'We're going to see Daddy!'

She pulled the brim of Mosi's cotton sun bonnet further over her face as she walked across the tarmac. Above the smell of the engine was an unfamiliar earthy note. Mosi's head was turning from side-to-side taking in this new environment, no doubt relieved to be out of that small space at last. Esme followed her fellow passengers into the arrivals area to queue before the immigration desk. The stifling heat was barely mitigated by the fans turning languorously overhead but, as she waited for her turn, she suspected the sweat running down inside her dress wasn't entirely due to the temperature. What if there was a problem with her passport and visa? When the white-uniformed officer handed back her passport saying '*Karibu* Tanzania,' with a brief smile, she felt dizzy with relief.

Sweat was beading on her face as they crowded into the next small area to wait for their baggage. Mosi began to cry. Esme scanned the faces of the throng of people beyond the barrier for a glimpse of Martin. Many pairs of eyes met hers – she scanned each face but none was familiar.

'Mosi look!' she tried in vain to distract the now wailing child. 'Daddy will be here in a minute!'

'Mrs Yusufu. Excuse me, Mrs Yusufu.' Her heart stopped: a young uniformed official beside her. Mosi wailed louder.

'Yes. Yes, that's me.'

'Please follow me.' His facial expression and tone of voice were impassive. She was aware of eyes tracking her progress across the hall to a door at the side. As she entered the small office a man seated with his back to her stood up. Even before he turned her whole body was electrified as she recognised him.

'Martin!'

'Esme, Mosi. I hope you had a pleasant trip.' He smiled at her as he touched her lightly on the arm then reached out to take Mosi. Mosi stopped crying immediately and looked intently at her father.

'She's grown a lot in a month.' Martin's tone was approving.

It had been two months but she kept quiet. Martin nodded towards the official who was standing beside them. 'This is Gerry, a cousin of mine.'

Gerry shook Esme's hand enthusiastically with both of his. He was shorter and slighter than Martin – but then most people were.

'*Karibu, Mama*! You are most welcome to our country. I apologise that I could not explain to you who I am in front of the other passengers.' His English was excellent. Esme felt the blood rush to her face, wishing she could remember a single word of the Swahili vocabulary Martin had written out for her before he left Edinburgh.

'I hope you will excuse our mistakes, Mama Mosi. It is only seven years since we got our independence from the British and we are still establishing our ways of running our poor country. He smiled then. 'Sorry, I hope you will not be offended. The British were much better for us than the Germans were, so the elders say.'

He indicated the chair Martin had just vacated. 'Please sit here, Mama Mosi.'

Seeing Esme's confusion, Martin said 'You will get used to being called "Mama Mosi", Esme. It just means Mosi's mother. Once a woman has a child that's how they are known among family and friends.'

Still holding Mosi, Martin said,

'My driver will take your suitcases through customs and put them in the vehicle. I don't think we will need to wait very long.'

Then he turned to Gerry and engaged him in a conversation in Swahili enabling Esme to sit and feel the cool air wafted towards her by the table fan on the desk. Her head was spinning with all that had happened since she had arrived. She looked tenderly at Martin. Like her, he must be feeling awkward after their period apart. If he had a vehicle and a driver to take them from the airport it must mean he was quite high up. His letters had explained very little but before he had left Scotland he had been concerned for his position; his friend Edward had returned home with his diploma a term before Martin although he had joined the course a year after Martin; because of the time Martin had spent with Esme, Martin had failed his finals and had to stay on to re-sit them – leaving the best job for Edward.

Half an hour later, in the white Combi driven by a young khaki-uniformed man she asked 'How far is it to the house, Martin?'

'The house? Oh, well that still has some work to be carried out on it. We're staying temporarily in a hotel.'

'Oh.' Esme didn't know what else to say. She had unintentionally created a picture in her mind of the house they would go to. The image was like a photo in her head she could admire at will. Now she had to construct a new image. Into her head swam the memory of The Railway Hotel she'd stayed in once when her father had taken her to some relative's funeral in Inverness: even she could tell that the building and furniture were cheap, flimsy and ugly, the staff indifferent and unhelpful. Her spirits fell.

As they drove from the airport, wood smoke drifted through the open van windows. Along the roadside rough grassland was dotted with coconut palms so easily recognisable from pictures. A buzz of excitement ran through her; she was here at last. Small rough dwellings increasingly cropped up between the palms and a whole variety of shrubs: one-storey, some roofed with corrugated metal sheets but most were thatched with palm fronds. She saw a bicycle loaded, with the same dried palm branches some ten feet long, being pushed by a man, dressed in long sleeved shirt and trousers. People milled everywhere, the women wearing bright blouses or dresses with coloured cloths around their lower halves. 'Don't people feel the heat? Everyone had so much clothing on!'

'People have respect for their bodies here, Esme. They don't go around half-naked. Women cover their legs, it's most important. No self-respecting man would ever wear shorts now. The British made men wear shorts in any job because it was their chosen style. Now we are our own masters, we wear the trousers.'

Esme continued to watch the passing sights with wonder and to ask Martin for explanations until they reached the centre of Dar es Salaam. The New Africa Hotel could not have less resembled the one in Inverness. Martin, with a grimace, said it was a relic from the German colonial era: an imposing grey building with balustraded balconies. In the lobby were vast spaces, vaulted ceilings, sombre heavy furniture. Europeans and Indian-looking men lolled in basket chairs, long drinks before them. The atmosphere was cool, hushed.

An elderly porter in a long white cotton suit and tasselled red fez laboured with her suitcases ahead of them up the wide stone steps to the first floor. The faint fragrance of incense, reminding her of church, seemed to emanate from the walls.

Mosi had fallen asleep in her arms. Esme lay her in the cot in the corner and lay herself down on the bed. She patted the coverlet beside her and looked meaningfully at Martin.

At that moment there was a rap at the door. Martin opened it to reveal a young black woman with a tiny baby in her arms. Esme sat up on the edge of the bed.

'*Karibu*, Dada!' Martin ushered her in. '*Karibu sana.*'

'Esme, this is my younger sister, Safina.'

Safina shook hands with Esme. '*Karibu*, Tanzania. Welcome, Mama Mosi.'

Esme's incomprehension got through to Martin. 'I suppose she's a cousin in your system.'

Martin took the tiny baby in the crook of his arm and shook hands warmly with Safina, speaking in Swahili. Martin sat in the wicker chair and Safina sat beside Esme on the bed. Esme gazed at the tiny baby bundled up in a white shawl that would have kept out an arctic chill.

'Safina doesn't speak much English. The baby is called Martin, after me.' Safina smiled but said nothing. She didn't look anything like Martin but was slight in build, quite tall, with high cheekbones and up-tilted eyes. She had an air of self-satisfaction that unnerved Esme.

Martin and Safina continued to converse in Swahili. There was some laughter. Esme felt increasingly confused and bereft. Visions of the last twenty-four hours swam in her head: the surprise of a white covering of snow to greet her on a May morning; the glamour of the new terminal building at Edinburgh airport, her first ever flight, her first trip outside the British Isles: her father didn't believe in planes - ships were risky enough - and he had declined to pay for her to go on school trips to Europe; the farewell with her parents. Then the anxiety of the transfer in Heathrow, embarking on the jet aircraft that was at least three times the size of the first plane; the difficulty of keeping Mosi entertained; the anticipation, excitement; the misgivings. And now ...

Martin went out saying he would order drinks and something to eat.

Safina turned to Esme. 'When you are going to Martin's village?' Esme felt stupid and racked her brains. After a pause she had to ask,

'Sorry, which village do you mean?'

'Where Martin is coming from. His home. Martin said he will take you.'

Martin had said nothing to her but so far they hadn't had much time to talk. She would ask him about it.

'I'm not sure,' she said to Safina and both lapsed into silence until Martin came back followed by the same elderly porter carrying a tray of refreshments.

After about half an hour Martin escorted Safina downstairs. He was gone for ten minutes by Esme's watch. The 'gold' watch he had given her when he had been courting her. When he came back Esme got to her feet, put her arms around him and put her head on his chest, saying 'I've missed you, Martin.'

He kissed the top of her head lightly. 'I've missed you to, *mpenzi*. But you must be exhausted. I'll leave you and Mosi to rest. I need to go and see a few people, get our accommodation sorted out.'

As the door shut behind him, she closed her eyes and imagined, as she had so many times over the past weeks, Martin enveloping her in his arms. She thought back to their first meeting in the university café where she had worked in the evenings. He had been charming and flirtatious towards her and she, not exactly having a queue of admirers, was utterly beguiled. She readily agreed to go with him to the film show on campus the next evening. Later he said it was her bottom he had first noticed and her voluptuous curves that held him; until then, she had never viewed herself as other than overweight. Their relationship blossomed; however, while Martin's payment had been an extra term to get his qualification, hers had been to go down early with a baby instead of a degree. She gently touched the sleeping child beside her: she would never wish Mosi away but Esme wondered now how things would have been had Mosi not been born.

Ch 2: The Journey South

She sat on the edge of the bed folding a pile of Mosi's square nappies into triangles, ready for use. The memory of what had taken place in this bed the night before surged back to her, sending a thrill through her body as she recalled their lustful pleasures. The small bedroom had been filled by their moans, body-heat and sweat, combining with the mugginess of the night as they had been driven by yet further desire and fulfilment. Her face burned as she hugged the nappies to her. Why did she still feel so guilty afterwards? It dawned on her that even though their union had been sanctioned by the Church, deep within her lurked the conviction that sex was not for enjoyment, but for procreation. The irony was, of course, that once Mosi had been born - even though she had not yet been a married woman – the family planning clinic allowed her contraception, liberating Esme and Martin from premature withdrawal and anxiety, to revel in hitherto unknown enjoyments, at least unknown to Esme. Martin had made no secret of his previous experience.

She heard herself sigh as she stowed the nappies in her overnight case and acknowledged the growing feeling of unease in her chest. So much to learn, so much to understand, but the few people she had met had been kind to her, patient with her faltering Swahili.

What would her parents-in-law think of her? Of their child? And what would Martin's mother, Leah, be like? *'Mama Mkwe'* Esme would have to call her. All Esme knew about Martin's father was that Alured had been the first family member to be educated and after working for the colonial government as a civil servant, had retired with a small pension at the age of forty. This, Martin said, was the normal retirement age for the miniscule number of native government employees – the same age as the average person lived - he had added with an ironic laugh.

She'd better hurry up with the packing before Mosi woke from her nap and the evening routine began: they were leaving first thing in the morning. Should she take some of the *kanga* Martin had given her?

She surveyed the pile of folded cloths, a phantasmagoria of riotous colours. She pulled out a cloth at random and found that it was still in its original form, the two matching halves printed on one continuous length of material. She exchanged it for another pair of *kanga* , already cut into two separate pieces and the raw edges hemmed by a tailor, and unfolded the cotton rectangles, wider than her arm span. She loved their imaginative patterns picked out in bold, contrasting colours and the cool smoothness against her skin. She draped one piece of fabric in purple and green, hues that moderated the pinkness of her skin, around her lower half, like a towel over a bathing costume, falling nearly to her ankles. Securing it round her waist was the tricky part, it took practice, but she looked better with much of her bulk hidden in folds.

Martin's sister hadn't worn a *kanga* over her dress when she had visited her at the hotel but it was a common style here in the outskirts of the city. Martin said it showed their village upbringing, feeling the need to conceal their lower legs, obscuring stylish dresses in the process. His response had seemed to contrast with his view on men wearing shorts.

Esme draped the matching *kanga* around her head and shoulders, slinging one end over her shoulder as many women in the market did. Now she looked ridiculous!

Martin had presented her with a pair of *kanga* that first day, when he'd got back from seeing Safina off, and again four days later when they'd moved into this flat, this horrible flat, last week.

'It's what men give women, to show their love,' he'd explained. Some women have cupboards full, to show how many admirers they have.'

How did Martin know that? Anyway, she would never have a cupboard-full so what was the point in saving them? And since they were, in effect, the national dress for women she felt it would symbolise some kind of solidarity if she plucked up the courage to wear them. Or would she just look foolish? Still ambivalent, she undraped herself and folded up the fabric, carefully following the creases, smoothed them out flat and put the two sets into the case.

Mosi's voice came from the next room, not so much crying as calling out to announce she had woken. How well she had coped with all the changes!

'Hi, Mosi, beautiful girl.' Esme lifted her child from the new blue metal-barred cot and held her close. Together they looked out of the small, high window. The sky was turning crimson, marking the time that Martin usually arrived home. Or at least he had at first but the last few days he had been delayed at work, getting home after seven, when it was already dark. In the morning he was gone before seven: it was a long day here with no-one save the girls and women in the neighbouring flats who spoke only Swahili, as Martin explained, with not enough education to get jobs in town.

'Daddy'll soon be home!' She stood holding Mosi in her arms watching the fruit bats soar and swoop and the sky darken to deep blackberry.

After the evening meal, over Mosi's determined calls for Martin's attention, Esme asked Martin if he had a route map. He laughed.

'A map! What would I want a map for? There's only one way to go. We get on the road south and drive down the coast for five hundred miles!'

He leaned over and kissed her on the cheek.

'Tell you what, have a look at that atlas of yours.' She'd brought her Collins' blue-covered atlas that she'd bought with her mother before she'd started Form One at St. Bridget's and had used right through to Sixth Form.

Of course what was now known as the United Republic of Tanzania was called 'Tanganyika' on the map and was depicted in pink.

'When did the mainland unite with Zanzibar? I should know but I forget.' Martin, his arm firmly round the squirming Mosi on his lap, replied,

'Nineteen sixty-four.' He pointed out Landa the nearest town to Mabalo, their destination, which lay twenty miles to the west but was too small to be marked.

'That's Mozambique,' Martin said pointing to a mauve area to the south of Mabalo. 'It's still a Portuguese colony and the freedom-fighters cross back and forth over the border all the time.' On the map Mozambique, and their destination, looked a long way away.

The journey was indeed long, and very dusty, once they'd come to the end of the tarmac at Kibiti, eighty miles south of Dar es Salaam – or just Dar, as everyone seemed to call it. Martin's car was ideal for well-paved roads but the sleek little coupé bounced around uncomfortably on anything less. So it had been something of a relief after two hours of the neck-wrenching, disintegrating tarmac when the road had petered out into an undulating earthen track. In parts, it stretched away into the distance, two sandy parallel lines, separated by a strip of dust-covered vegetation. The world seemed to contain only their small capsule, surrounded by the bush: as far as the eye could see thickly-packed shrub skeletons – interspersed with occasional mounds of green - trees which had devised strategies to keep their leaves throughout the parched months. Like the Highlands she remembered visiting as a child, there were no walls or fences, just a seemingly endless planet of untouched land.

'Do you know the names of the trees?' she'd asked Martin. Martin had laughed.

'Yes, but in which language? I know some in *Kiswahili*, some in English, and others in Latin from school. Or in *Kilanda* my tribal language – the ones I learned at home.'

'English would be useful.' She smiled. 'What are these then?' she indicated the spiky throng around them.

'Mostly acacias. We have a dozen different types, flat-top, toothbrush, apple-ring, hook thorn... They shed their leaves in the dry season.'

'What about the green ones?' Martin shrugged.

'Tamarind, maybe. That's *mlegea*!' he pointed to his right. 'The Fathers called it a sausage tree.' It was a large, wide-spread tree with dangling seed pods.

'Look, Mosi,' she pointed it out to the chubby child she held on her knee. Mosi smiled, the meaning lost on her but not the contact.

At times Esme was lulled into a semi-torpor, only to have it burst apart by Martin cursing at a scuttling rodent or an inconveniently situated rock. They passed red cliffs above and below the crumbling track, the air red with dust. She was uncomfortably aware of the prickling in her nostrils, the grittiness behind her eyelids, between her teeth and everything her hands came into contact with, even though they'd rolled up the windows every time a vehicle approached. Mosi had intermittent coughing spasms, eased by sips of water.

'This is where the East African Safari Rally passes.' Martin had volunteered, a couple of hours into the journey. She'd never even heard of the rally. Cars raced here?

They'd passed a wooden signboard: Maniki Boys Secondary School, Ministry of Education'.

'I spent seven years there.' Martin had said. It was rare for him to talk about his youth. 'Of course, it was the Anglican priests then.'

'Were you happy there?'

'It was alright. I got my education, didn't I? We wouldn't be here today without that; in this car.' His pride and joy, bought for a very reasonable price from an expatriate Martin had worked with who had returned to Britain. Martin beamed as he caressed the leather shelf below the windscreen, imprints of his fingertips remaining in the dust.

His education by priests would explain his ability to quote passages from the bible when it suited him, though he had not clung to the habit of church-going. Still, he'd insisted that they get married in the Church in Scotland. Mosi's christening had been the end of any pursuit of religion, thank God. That didn't deter him from spasms of hymn-singing throughout the journey, though, apparently oblivious to the fact that he was tone deaf.

They rarely met a vehicle. The road narrowed and she noticed at one point that the earth had changed from compacted red to sand. She wished she'd noticed whether it had been gradual or sudden. Occasionally the car faltered as its wheels stuck in deep mounds of soft, dry sand, but otherwise the car rose and fell, rose and fell in an almost soothing rhythm. Martin was a good driver when he was even-tempered. Long periods elapsed when he said nothing, others when he sang at the top of his voice. He was exultant. It seemed a good time to ask him if she could have a turn at the wheel. She had taken lessons in Edinburgh but because they'd had no car to practice on and she couldn't afford many lessons, she hadn't taken her test. Martin had promised her she could learn on his beloved car.

'Sure, *mpenzi*, next time we stop.' He'd rested his hand on her thigh for a moment and she covered his hand with hers. But when they did stop again, Martin said no more about her driving and such harmony existed between them, she decided not to broach the subject again. She suspected he didn't really believe women should drive; he was probably not alone - she could not recall seeing an African woman behind a steering wheel.

The landscape had changed as they'd descended to the Rufiji river, the plain spread with densely-packed *shamba* – with what she had soon learned were banana plants, interspersed by lanky coconut palms and rice paddies which, Martin told her, flooded with regularity.

'The flooding is good for the rice but destroys human habitation. You would think they would learn to live on the high ground and walk down to tend to the paddies, but no, they move back to the riverbanks as soon as the floods recede and the same thing happens all over again.' Perhaps the makeshift character of the houses was a reflection of their frequent demolition by the water and their hasty repair as the villagers returned year on year to reap their livelihood from the rich plain, dicing with the floodwaters.

They stopped to buy hard-boiled eggs and green oranges from vendors at the roadside. She came to expect that, wherever they happened upon small-holdings, young boys clad in tattered clothing would appear, bearing aloft round aluminium trays laden with whatever was grown locally. Martin bought some oranges from a mite no more than eight, who expertly skinned each with a small kitchen knife, the wafer-thin green peel dangling down in one unbroken piece, revealing a white translucent membrane. Then, the orange held in his palm, he sliced each fruit in two with a frightening chop of the knife. They sucked the sweet juice out of the halves of the orange flesh and tossed the pithy remains into the dusty roadside to join the rest of the detritus which was then pecked over by scavenging chickens. They bought a hand of small green bananas. Strange how green didn't always mean unripe. Esme had no idea so many shapes, sizes and colours of bananas existed, even dark red ones. All the while, a group of children jostled by the car windows, defying Martin's bellows, peering at this strange woman. Several times she heard them say 'half-caste' pointing at Mosi.

The visit to the ancient ruins at Kilwa was completely unexpected.

'I want to show you something,' Martin had said. They'd taken a detour down a narrow sandy track. The ruins were in open land, about half a mile from the sea, scattered among the coarse brown grass-stalks and the coconut palms. Nothing to draw attention to them but a small weather-worn notice reading 'Property of the Ministry of Culture of the United Republic of Tanzania'. An elderly man dressed in a white ankle-length robe, reclining against the trunk of a palm tree, heaved himself to his feet at the approach of the car. A bicycle was propped against a nearby ruin. The man smiled broadly as the car drew up in front of him: he couldn't have received many visitors.

'*Karibuni, wageni!*' By now Esme recognised the words "*Karibu*" and "*Karibuni*" as meaning "welcome" to one or more people respectively, everyone she had met had used one of these, but she didn't remember "*wageni*". She asked Martin to explain it.

'"*Mgeni*" is one, "*wageni*" is the plural,' Martin pursed his lips. Hard to translate because in English you have words with quite different meanings – guest and stranger. To us they're the same thing.'

The guide led the way round the ragged stone remains, giving a detailed commentary in Swahili, with an occasional English word thrown in. Martin, carrying Mosi, pointed to various features and asked questions. Esme soon grew tired of trying to follow the discussion and dropped behind, drinking in the melancholy aura. She gathered that this settlement had been built by Persians, starting from the ninth century. Later their trading activities had been hampered by the invading Portuguese and the end had finally come in the sixteenth century with a visit from neighbours from the south, a tribe of cannibals from Mozambique. Or so the story went.

The small rectangular ruins of coral masonry were apparently dwellings, a mosque and a palace. A few plain doorways and more elaborate portals were still intact. From some of the buildings rose tall, narrow stone pillars, echoing the columns of the headless palm trees behind. In a land where the only permanent buildings that Esme had seen had been built during the past hundred years, she'd been unprepared for this encounter with vestiges of a town started in the ninth century. She wished she knew more about the people who lived there.

After Kilwa the trees thinned out until the landscape was scattered only with scrawny bare shrubs and candelabra trees which she took to be cacti but which Martin said were Euphorbia.

Here and there a majestic, lone baobab -ugly trees but fascinating: enormous trunks and naked, stumpy arms culminating in extended fingers, suspending oval, husked seed-pods.

The last toilet they had encountered had been in their flat in Dar. Since then she'd had frequent cause to squat nervously behind bushes in the stretches between the hamlets, her eyes peeled for an approaching smallholder or charcoal burner, sack on head. She supposed her digestive system was having difficulty coping with the change of diet; at times she was in considerable discomfort and had to seek relief as a matter of extreme urgency. She felt guilty about the trail of toilet paper she left behind her but reasoned that every trace of her visits would be consumed by dung-beetles and others of the myriad of menaces skulking in the vast bush; according to Martin these included scorpions, snakes, spiders - all of which administered painful, if not deadly bites, though - he assured her - nothing larger roamed in these parts.

Despite her aversion to anything that crawled, they stopped at the roadside for a picnic of sorts. They'd brought nothing to sit on, and Martin simply paced around, holding his chin in the cleft of his hand and stroked his cheek with his index finger, a familiar indication that he had something on his mind. Mosi sat beside her on the parched, bare and cracked earth. They appeared to be the only non-crawling creatures out in the midday sun with scant shade from the leafless umbrella trees. Esme wore a cotton head-square over her thin, red hair but her pale skin soon began to pinken and, prompted by Martin's frown, she realised how inappropriate her short dress was for travelling.

Luckily no-one was around to see this immodest show of leg.

'Did you bring a pair of *kanga* ?' he asked after a few minutes. You could have sat on one cloth and worn the other half to cover up your legs.' She felt her face grow redder still. He could have reminded her since he had known what to expect. 'Yes, but they're somewhere in the big suitcase.'

'Well, never mind. You can get them out this evening.'

They'd had no means of keeping a packed lunch from spoiling in the heat and she'd been concerned to learn from Martin that they would have to rely on what they could buy along the road-side. But it had been fine: roasted maize cobs, a peeled and sliced pineapple, more hard-boiled eggs, some deep-fried rice cakes. Mosi needed all the food she could get, the energy she expended. She had shown no interest to date in walking, had no need to, scuttling on all fours as if on wheels. Now she fearlessly explored the terrain, zooming over littered stones and clumps of scratchy, straw-like vegetation, lion's paw plants towering above her. How different this was from Scotland. In all that brilliant vastness, no birdsong punctuated the incessant chatter of crickets. Not a whiff of a wild flower in the arid air nor the merest patch of lush green grass to lay her head on. Without warning, a sadness welled up inside her. Martin didn't see the tears that spilled down her face.

Ch 3: Landa

They had stopped for the night in the small, coastal town of Landa. As dusk fell, Martin gave them a tour of the tiny harbour. It was dreary and dilapidated, dominated by massive grey concrete structures whose purpose was unfathomable. Rusting twisted metal abounded. Difficult to imagine this had been an important port for the Germans during the first world war. Now two dhows were all that testified to the fact that it was a port. The sails that would have shone white in the daylight against the intense aquamarine of the ocean when glimpsed from the shore now looked shabbily grey bobbing in the harbour, adding to the general air of despondency.

'Cheer up, *mpenzi*!' Martin put his arm round her shoulders, this time reading her mood and lifting it. 'You should see this place when the ferry docks from Dar; a great rush of people who cannot wait to get off, especially if they have had an engine breakdown and the ferry has been stranded out there for a day or two! Sometimes the fresh water runs out on board!' Martin laughed. 'That's why we had to take advantage of the dry season to travel by road. It will be impassable once the rains start. For the next six months the ferry is the only link with the capital and the rest of the country. The threat of being posted to this region helps to keep us government workers on the straight and narrow!'

'So, if it's some sort of rustication for someone who comes from this region originally, what would it be like for someone originally from the north of the country? Esme asked.

'Oh, hell on earth!' Martin was amused at the thought. 'Cut off not only from the trappings of modern life in the capital but also from their extended family networks, their mother tongue and customs! Time to go and look for a *hoteli*.' Martin scooped up Mosi as she scuttled past on all fours. Esme barely noticed the use of the Swahili word for hotel, suddenly realising how ready she was for a rest from the road. They stopped in what Martin described as the 'centre of town' in front of a single-storey house with a corrugated iron roof, a style familiar to Esme from the suburbs of Dar es Salaam. It was only then that it dawned on her that '*hoteli*' held a different concept from 'hotel': she'd envisaged something along the lines of the New Africa Hotel where Martin had taken her and Mosi straight from the airport.

In their Landa 'hotel', the communal bathroom contained an oil drum filled with cold water and an enamel mug for 'showering'. In place of toilet paper, the Asian toilet was equipped with a knee-high tap and an empty tin that was still emblazoned with the name 'Kimbo', the ubiquitous imported cooking fat.

Martin took Mosi to see the chickens in the backyard while Esme washed a half dozen nappies in a bucket of cold water. She draped the clean, wet towelling squares round their room, it could hardly be hotter in an airing cupboard.

They were greeted in the eating area-cum-bar by a young woman displaying her ample bosom to advantage. *'Karibuni, wageni'*. She plonked the plates of rice and beef stew on the bare wooden table unceremoniously with a big smile in Mosi's direction and a long, flirtatious look at Martin from beneath her lashes.

'Welcome!' she said in English to Esme. Did she think Esme understood no Swahili at all? Despite its unpromising delivery, the food was hot and tasty. They shared a bottle of chilled Tusker lager with the meal. Esme felt all was well in her world till they finished eating and instead of Martin picking up Mosi to carry her back to the room said,

'You go ahead, I'll be in shortly, I'll stay and have another Tusker.' It was a statement of intent, no room in it for negotiation. She wouldn't mind if it was just one but somehow she didn't think it would be. She sighed as he carried his empty glass over to the bar to join couple of men who had been there for quite a while by the look of them.

In their room Esme settled Mosi in their iron bedstead, under the dingy mosquito net, undressed herself and lay beside the softly-breathing child. The mattress had been decidedly short-changed of its share of kapok stuffing, still containing its hard little seeds. The pillows, however, were overstuffed: they were like rocks.

It was some hours later when Martin crawled beneath their net, Mosi spread-eagled between them. Esme lay for a while, balanced on the edge of the bed listening to their breathing before falling into a fitful sleep.

Next day, just as she felt she'd reached her limit with the midday glare, burning heat and the monoLuka of the baked landscape, the car climbed onto the plateau. The air was cooler, fresher. Unfamiliar trees, many still in leaf even in this, the dry season, gave fleeting shade.

'I think we will call in on my Uncle Saul,' Martin announced. He continued looking ahead of him as he spoke, apparently unaware of Esme's surprised look.

'You've got an uncle round here? When did you get in touch with him?'

'I have not been in touch with him. I have only just decided that we will visit him. Is something wrong?'

She and Mosi could do with the break and besides, now that they were in his home district, her curiosity about Martin's family was steadily increasing.

'No, it will be good to meet him. I'm just surprised, that's all. You've never mentioned him before. How are you related?'

'Yes, well, he has had a difficult time and he keeps himself to himself but I was always a favourite of the old boy. I suppose you'd call him my mother's cousin.'

They arrived at Uncle Saul's home, off the main road at the far end of a scattered hamlet. His house was tiny but solidly-built. The sound of the car brought Martin's uncle to the open door. Recognizing Martin, he came out beaming broadly, chuckling and exclaiming, '*Lo! Jemani!* What a pleasant surprise!'

'*Karibuni, wageni!*' he said over and over, as he shook hands with each of them, clasping their right hand in both of his and pumping it up down. There was that phrase again: 'welcome, strangers; welcome, guests.' He slapped Martin on the back and laughed uproariously. He was so evidently delighted, Esme was pleased they had come. She could see no resemblance between him and Martin who towered over him. Saul was very slightly-built under the long white robe, similar to the one worn by the guide at the ruins. The little bit of hair that was visible under his white embroidered skull cap was grey. This was the first time she'd seen anyone in the country with grey hair. Was that because people didn't go grey as early, or because they didn't live long enough? His English was impeccable, and he seemed to enjoy using the language with his visitors.

'Uncle, since when did you start wearing a *kanzu*?' Martin gestured towards the robe. The warmth between them glowed, they kept patting one another on the shoulder and laughing. They seemed so close and yet she had never even heard about Martin's uncle till now.

As Saul ushered them into the small whitewashed room, Mosi pointed upwards. Esme looked up to the corner of the ceiling where insects were flying to and from a dark mass. As she gazed at it, the mass subtly changed shape: it took Esme several seconds to realise that what she was looking at was a multitude of bees! They were crowded onto, and into, a formation of grey mud adhering to the plaster wall and ceiling. Every second bees were flying in and out through the open window.

Saul, noticing Esme's concern with the hive, laughed. 'Do not worry, Mama Mosi.' His expression was kindly, his tone reassuring. 'They will not harm you. This is their home. The bees and I have lived together under the same roof for many years without any trouble. I find their buzzing soothing.'

Esme smiled, more out of politeness than conviction, and for the rest of their visit, she hardly took her eyes off the bees. Mosi, however was unconcerned and crawled happily round the rough cement floor, sitting back every now and again to watch the activity around the hive.

As they sat on an assortment of rustic chairs, a young woman came to greet them. Her head was covered by a *kanga* and she kept her eyes cast down. She extended her right hand, supporting it with her other hand, keeping her elbows tight to her body. Her '*Shikamoo*' was barely above a whisper, as if she really meant the traditional greeting, literally 'I hold your foot!' Uncle Saul introduced her as Selina, no-more. Esme wondered who she was. Surely too young to be Saul's wife. His daughter? Esme caught Martin's eye with a questioning look but Martin didn't respond.

A long while elapsed while muffled clinks emanated from behind the next room. The men were outside somewhere talking. Would it be rude to start walking around outside? Martin would tell her it was demonstrating her dissatisfaction with the hospitality. But it really was taking a long time. She entertained Mosi as best she could once Mosi tired of exploring the room.

Eventually Selina brought in a tray and placed three covered dishes on a small table as Martin and Uncle Saul came in. Saul picked up Mosi who, enticed by the prospect of food, had her eyes on the table. Saul bade Martin and Esme be seated while Selina timidly brought round a shallow plastic bowl, a jug of water, some soap and a towel over her arm and stood first in front of Martin then Esme while Selina poured water over their hands, waited while they soaped them and again trickled water to rinse them. Martin deftly balanced Mosi on his left knee and washed her grimy hands.

'*Karibuni chakula*'. Selina dropped into a curtsey and moved quietly on her bare feet out of the room.

'Welcome to food!' Saul said and he too left the room.

'Why don't they eat with us?' Esme kept her voice low. Martin shrugged.

'We are guests. It is respect. Normally, I would eat with Saul but he knows European families eat together. He's an educated man, you know. He is being very considerate of you, aware that you are a stranger to our customs.'

Despite the confusion of her thoughts, Esme was very hungry by now, well into the afternoon. The removal of an aluminium bowl revealed a smooth white mound exuding a steamy fragrance.

Esme pointed to it, 'What's this, Martin?'

'*Ugali*,' Martin answered. He sniffed at it appreciatively. 'This is made from freshly-milled maize-meal.'

He pinched off a bite-sized chunk of *ugali* with his right hand and deftly formed it into a ball, then created a well in the centre of it with his thumb and scooped sauce into it, without the slightest mess. He popped it into Mosi's mouth and patiently continued to feed her while he ate. Martin had such a confident, effortless way with her, when he had the time, Esme thought. Thank God Mosi had such a good appetite and would eat unfamiliar foods like this with gusto. And the food *was* delicious; these were fresh kidney beans, not the old, dried ones they had in Dar, and what Martin said were sweet-potato leaves, both dishes cooked in a sauce of tomatoes and onions with mild spices. But Esme felt frustrated that she needed to eat her *ugali* with the spoon provided, proving right the assumption that *Wazungu* can't eat with their hands. She vowed to herself that she would master the technique: she would practice it more at home. She still stung from the memory of her first experience, back in Edinburgh when Martin's friend Fintan had laughed heartily at her futile efforts. She hadn't understood then that laughing meant something different to Tanzanians but she still wasn't clear exactly what. Look at the way Martin and Saul had behaved when they'd arrived, as if they shared a huge joke.

Martin's words interrupted her reverie:

'You need to learn to make *ugali*. This is our staple food. Rice and cooking-bananas and even your potatoes are supposed to be for a change, a treat, but normally we live on *ugali*.'

'I see.' Something else she needed to master.

After the meal, Saul apologised to Esme for the lack of meat and rice.

'Your husband should have told me you were coming!' he laughed, 'And he refused to wait while we organised some meat. He's become a white man, always rushing around looking at his watch!' Esme protested that she had really enjoyed the food. She would have liked to thank Selina but they didn't see her again.

As they were leaving Uncle Saul gave them a Fanta bottle filled with viscous, amber honey, flecked with unidentifiable, black specks, stoppered with a wodge of folded newspaper. Esme couldn't envisage them eating it but appreciated the gesture.

Back in the car, she felt able to voice the question. 'Your uncle didn't introduce us properly to Selina. Who is she?' Esme felt unaccountably protective towards the young woman who, she recalled, had curtseyed before leaving the room on every occasion. 'Is she a servant or his daughter or what?'

Martin shrugged.

'She is his wife, though perhaps they are not married as such. What he does is his business. He fell out with his former wife. His kids are grown-up, working in Dar. You'll meet them some day.'

'But what about her? She's like a servant, she can't be happy.'

'She probably came from a very poor family. She lives in a decent house, everything provided for her. Why would she not be happy? I bet she does not plague Uncle with twenty questions every ten minutes.' He laughed.

'And what was all that with the hand-washing, I felt really uncomfortable.'

'Esme, there are always good reasons for what happens. Firstly, water has to be carried on some woman or girl's head from the river and that hand-wash method uses water as sparingly as possible. Secondly, guests are always treated with the highest respect. Things have changed a bit, of course, so while a visiting man will always be offered a meal and a bed for the night, it is no longer the custom to offer him the wife or daughter as well.'

Esme felt a shock run through her at such a notion and scanned Martin's face for a sign that he was joking.

'I can't believe that really happened!' she said.

'Believe what you want, Mama Mosi.'

They fell into silence after this. Esme reflected on Selina's situation. Surely this was no longer what was expected of girls. Well Mosi would certainly have a better future than that. She hugged the drowsy child to her.

Eventually the scenery seized back her attention; no other vehicles disturbed the dust of the track. A milky yellow cloud followed their passage. Their route took them through groves of trees, covered with red apple-sized fruits. She asked Martin what they were.

'Cashew apples.' Martin replied. He slowed the car from a fast running pace to one of walking, 'Look, you can see the nuts hanging from the bottom of the fruit.' Fat, green kidneys clung to the pinkie-scarlet fruit.

'Can we stop a minute and see? Please!'

'We need to get to the village before nightfall. Alright, just for a minute then.'

He pulled up in the middle of the track. Not a soul in sight. The sun was beginning to loosen its grip on the day. Cashew trees in fruit. She'd never considered before how cashew nuts grew although Martin had bought some from small boys near the market selling them by the handful wrapped in old newspaper. They were often broken, scorched in places, but tasty for all that. A few of the fruit had fallen to the ground.

'Can I eat them?' Esme reached down to pick one up. It was waxy, lighter and less substantial than an apple.

'Wait!' At Martin's sharp tone Esme withdrew her hand. 'Do not touch the nuts. The outer case has a sort of chemical, like petrol, it will burn your skin. You can eat the fruit but be careful. Here, give the child to me.' Esme carefully took one of the fruit and knocked the nut off the end without touching it. She took a tentative bite: a strange flavour, not sweet exactly, not unpleasant but one could acquire a taste she supposed.

'I haven't seen these for sale, Martin? They're not bad and it's food, after all.'

'They do not keep. These will be rotten in a day or two.'

'How do they get the nuts then, if they're so dangerous?'

'That is the problem. It involves a lot of work so only kids do it. The outer nuts have to be burnt first to get rid of the harmful toxin, obviously just for the right amount of time before the whole lot goes up in smoke, then you can get at the nut inside. Most of the nuts get exported for processing. The farmers get next to nothing. But the government has plans to build a processing plant here and to keep the profits in Tanzania by exporting the finished product. It should give better returns to the local people too.' Mosi squirmed and whinged in his arms to get down.

'No, sweetheart, you cannot get down.' Esme blew her a kiss.

'I'll watch her.' Martin said as he put the child down on the sandy ground and she scuttled off on all fours into the long spiky grass, fearless. She sat on her solid little bottom and, as Esme had known would happen, picked up a fallen fruit, her eyes squinting as she concentrated on forming her chubby fingers into a pincer ready to grasp the nut on the end.

'*Acha!*' in a stride, Martin was looming over her, snatching the fruit from her grasp. Mosi's face screwed up tragically as she began to howl.

Martin picked her up, holding her tenderly. '*Basi, basi.* That's enough.' he soothed. They resumed their journey.

Martin's mood had been ebullient since they'd left home, he seemed to be deriving a lot of pleasure from the company of his little family. Esme offered again to take over at the wheel but he said,

'You just relax and enjoy the view.' She supposed that, as on his daily trips to the office and any travel on duty only official drivers could take the controls of government vehicles, this was too much of a novelty for him to forgo and she decided against making a fuss. Probably just as well anyway.

They were well away from the sea now, on the high central plateau. The air was pleasurably fresh and there were sweeping views across to Mozambique in the setting sun. They passed several isolated homes in ruins, their *shamba* overrun by the bush.

'Part of the Villagisation campaign.' Martin said. 'The militia - shall we say - *encouraged* people to move into villages. Not far to go now.'

She was aware at that moment of a hollowness in the pit of her stomach which she knew wasn't hunger but a growing concern about how Martin's family would receive her.

Ch 4: Meeting Father in Law

Esme sat in the gloom of her father-in-law's hut, clutching the sleeping Mosi slumped on her lap. Irritation was gradually pushing out the incredulity that had filled her when, within minutes of her arrival in this room, she'd become the focus of attention for what seemed to be the village's entire child population. Since arriving in Dar es Salaam a few weeks ago, she'd got used to being regarded as an *Mzungu*, a white person, but people had gone out of their way to be courteous and welcoming. Nothing had prepared her for this. Martin had certainly come a long way from his ancestral village in more ways than one.

She surveyed, as best she could from within the gloom, the dozens of eyes peering through the chinks in the mud-daubed lattice that was the wall. Children of all heights were silhouetted in the bright sunlight. Her only point of reference for such adulation was a visit from royalty. She'd have been a child herself when, lined up among the crowd on the pavement in Edinburgh, she'd craned her neck, hopping from one foot to the other, to catch a glimpse of Princesses Elizabeth and Margaret waving and smiling from the cruising open-topped limousine. The difference was, she reflected, while that crowd had been almost reverential, these kids were noisy and intrusive - seemingly oblivious to her discomfort. She just wished they'd go away!

Esme sighed, shifting Mosi's dead-weight on her lap, the slats of the folding wooden chair biting into her buttocks. How long were they planning to leave her festering here? She flicked her handkerchief at the infuriatingly persistent fly that was attracted by Mosi's sweet breath and her gently perspiring brow. This simple action prompted excited whispers from the gawpers. How little entertained them! She mopped her face. The day was heating up. Presently wood-smoke drifted in. Preparations for the midday meal must be underway. She had the impression that the house contained four rooms: the one that she was in, one through a faded *kanga* which served as a curtain to her left and the one Raheli, Martin's sister, had disappeared through; logic dictated that a fourth room completed the square. She could hear metal clatters through the mud partitions, then the rhythmic thud of an axe cutting firewood. Beyond the excited chatter of the children, all that broke the monoLuka were the sounds of chickens squabbling, cockerels, goats, voices that died away and – once - a motorbike engine approaching and spluttering to a halt.

Had Raheli completely forgotten about her? She studied what little there was in the room. An unvarnished three-legged stool, hewn out of a single chunk of white wood, scorched with decorative brown swirls. Another chair, probably the twin of the one she was sitting on, folded flat: no wonder she felt as if she was caught in a pair of pincers! Two palm-frond mats rolled up in the corner, apparently considered unsuitable for royalty but how much more inviting they looked. For some twenty minutes she played out in her imagination moving from her designated throne. Would they be offended? Anxiety held her immobilised. Suddenly her body took over: she pulled her bottom out of the vice-like grip of the chair and was on her feet crouched over, the sleeping child in her arms, unfurling one of the mats to lay it on the floor. She set Mosi gently down on the mat, shoving a bit of *kanga* under her head quickly before it flopped with a thud. The floor might only be mud but it was rock-hard. Even so, it was bliss to lower herself to sitting with her legs stretched out in front of her beside Mosi and ease her aching muscles.

Esme's thoughts drifted to her meeting Raheli on their arrival. Enveloped from head to foot in a pair of crimson, tangerine and yellow *kanga* , she had curtseyed deeply while offering a limp handshake hand and breathing '*Shikamoo*'. Esme was at a loss as to how her seniority of a few years warranted such an excess of deference and hoped it wouldn't be a barrier to whatever friendship could evolve during her brief stay, given her embryonic Swahili. It was clear from the few pleasantries Esme had attempted that Raheli's English was little better.

'I'm coming', Raheli had said and had withdrawn into an adjoining room. That had been an hour ago. So this was the royal welcome Martin had said they would roll out for her. If she'd understood Raheli's explanation, Martin's mother had gone to the health centre that morning with a fever but she'd be back 'soon'. As Esme knew, Martin and his father had gone off on 'some business', leaving Raheli to hold the fort.

Esme looked down at Mosi, now deeply tanned, her soft dark hair, even in the obscurity, glinted gold. Esme crooked her neck awkwardly to brush her face across the baby's downy curls. No doubt that she was part *Mzungu*. Esme had plenty of time to reflect on her first meeting with her father-in-law before he and Martin had gone off. Alured was a smaller, wirier version of Martin, pent up energy driving his movements despite his age. But his eyes held a weariness, a pre-occupation not evident in his son. It was the first time the two had met since Martin had left for Scotland four years earlier to embark on his studies. For Alured, the notion of his son marrying an *Mzungu* would have had time to percolate through but was he fully reconciled to it?

He turned quickly towards her saying, '*Samahani sana.*' Then he seemed to catch himself and went on in perfectly accented but slightly hesitant English, as if taking it down and dusting it off as he spoke:

'I must apologise for not being here this morning to receive you properly, to welcome you. You are most welcome!' His smile was warm and courteous, a little too much so considering he was so much older than her, and a man, both of which - according to Martin - afforded him superior status in his culture. Was this an acceptance of her as his daughter-in-law? Or could he see no further than her colour, her resemblance to his former superiors' wives? Martin's generation had a pride and confidence in their national identity, but had Alured's?

'And this is my granddaughter! A fine child!' His voice rose up the scale and Mosi returned her grandfather's beam with a steady assessment. she allowed her *Babu* to hold her in his arms without protest. 'This is my first grandchild, you know! Look she has her father's cleft chin!' Turning towards Martin he added: 'And when are you going to give me a grandson?' She raised her eyebrows to Martin from behind Alured's back but if Martin caught the irony of her look, he didn't share it with her.

The older man's eyes had a grey film over them that seemed to affect his sight. His slight frame was clad in trousers and short sleeved shirt, very similarly to Martin, in fact, though Alured's clothes were loose-fitting and showed considerable signs of age. He drooped as he sank into a chair.

'A terrible business today. I was in court,' he addressed this directly to her. 'In the dock! That used to be my job - reading the charges out! I got fined a lot of money.' He shook his head slowly. 'So embarrassing. You know what my crime was?' His voice had risen again.

'No, I don't.' This was the first she'd heard of it.

'I was caught burning the weeds around my cashew trees. What do they expect an old man to do? Last year, I was living quite comfortably only about two miles from my cashew plot when militiamen came and ordered me out of my house. My own house, mind you! I was expecting it because they'd already done the same to other people in the area. Well, of course, I repudiated their suggestion, so what did they do? They destroyed my house! Half the wall fell on my back. We were forced to leave the house then, at gun point!'

'Why did they do that?' She was shocked.

'Villagisation, so-called! So that we can all be near the health centre and the school and so on. Yes, I agree it's a very noble idea but what about my cashew trees? How am I supposed to walk ten miles in the morning, weed around the trees all day in the hot sun, and then walk home again in the evening? I'm an old man!'

He did look old although Martin had told her he was forty-eight. He was one of the few people who actually knew their birth-date, having been born close to a mission station. But no wonder he looked old if this was what they had to cope with! She felt for Alured, and she felt honoured that he was pouring out his heart to her like this.

'So, I had no alternative. I had to set fire to the grass. I know I'm risking destroying all the trees but....' his face gathered into a scowl, 'They're my trees! The government is poking its nose into everything. They threatened to put me in jail!'

'That's terrible! Martin, did you know about this?' He had been quiet while his father spoke. Martin looked grave, but not angry. He didn't meet her eyes.

'Only when my father wrote to me, a few weeks ago. The problem is over-zealous local militiamen. The President doesn't wish to hurt people but he has a long-term goal for the common good. He leaves the implementation of his policies to his Prime Minister and then in the regions it's down to the local authorities. I don't think there are too many of these incidents. Of course, they expect co-operation.' He gave his father a sideways look. The two men began a heated discussion in *Kiswahili* or, for all she knew, *Kilanda*.

She wanted to accept Martin's interpretation of events. A few days earlier, President Nyerere had come to speak outside their district council office just as they were passing and they had stopped to listen. Although she understood nothing of what he said, she knew a little of his vision for a fair and equal society and that day his charisma and obvious passion completely won her over. Martin's father turned towards her now, and said apologetically:

'Mama Mosi, this is a very poor introduction to our home. No more talk of politics! You must rest. Martin's sister will take care of you.' Shortly after, Alured had excused Martin and himself saying: 'We have a little business to attend to. And the two men had gone off leaving her sitting here in a muddle of thoughts and impressions.

What was she really expected to do, to think? It seemed so rude to leave her alone all this time but she remembered the same thing had happened when they were at Martin's Uncles and Martin had remarked that this was a sign of esteem, that they were making special efforts to welcome them properly. How different Martin seemed now from back in Edinburgh. He so obviously belonged here. He was brimming with confidence and was clearly seen as a man of consequence. Had she fallen in love with him in Edinburgh partly because she felt protective towards him – a foreigner whose accent and, even more, skin-colour made him an obvious outsider? He'd been a target on several occasions for racist remarks and treatment. Like the time two youths across the street had started singing 'Black is black.' But surely he was the same person now and he still loved her, she was sure. He had explained that it was totally unacceptable to make a display of his affection in public but she wondered if he'd already got in the habit of self-restraint even when they were alone. She was suddenly overwhelmed by a wave of misery, a tear trickled down her cheek which she quickly wiped away with the corner of the *kanga* . 'Don't be so stupid,' she whispered fiercely. 'Martin's family are doing what they think is best. Just get on with it!' She recognised her mother's words and tone and this brought a grim smile to her face. Yes, that was exactly what her mother would have said.

At that moment Mosi stirred and opened her eyes. Looking round her at the unfamiliar walls of the hut her eyes rapidly sought Esme's face and as Esme kissed her child's soft, plump cheek she banished her melancholic ponderings. Mosi was due a feed.

Ch 5: Meeting Mother-in-Law

It must have been late afternoon when she heard voices right outside the house. Most of the kids peering through the chinks in the wall had grown bored with the *Mzungu*'s lack of performance after the spectacle of her drinking tea and had drifted off gradually; an authoritative voice now sent the remainder of them packing. Of course, she could make nothing out of the conversation that followed except for the words 'Mama Mosi': they were talking about her. A moment later, the door curtain moved aside and an upright, middle-aged woman entered. There was no mistaking those large, luxuriantly fringed eyes, the dark irises surrounded entirely by a startling white. As Martin's mother smiled diffidently, Esme noticed with a shock that she had a black disc inserted into the flesh between her nose and upper lip.

Her mother-in-law leaned forward to extend her hand to Esme who was still seated on the floor and the *kanga* draped loosely over the older woman's head slipped to her shoulders to reveal short cropped hair, with no trace of grey. Her body resembled Martin's in its solidity. Only the crows' feet, barely visible in the gloom, around her eyes gave a hint of her age. Her movements were of a young woman, though she exuded weariness.

She shook Esme's hand: '*Karibu. Karibu, mgeni.*'

'*Ahsante.*' Esme had rehearsed the basics many times now.

'*Habari?*'

'*Nzuri.*'

'*Mtoto hajambo?*'

'*Hajambo.*'

The barest form of the ritual completed, they fell into silence.

It was unclear as to which of them felt the more awkward. Leah wasn't anything like her eldest son who felt as comfortable in a bar with strangers, like the one in Landa yesterday, as he had in that swanky restaurant in Edinburgh where he'd taken her on their first date.

Mosi's behaviour didn't help. She refused to take her Grandmother's proffered hand or even look at her, covering her eyes with the backs of her podgy hands and kicking in her direction, catching Esme with the back swing on the shins. Esme wanted to sink through the earthen floor. She supposed Mosi was reacting to the journey, the strangeness of the environment and the constant looming of new faces, but Esme was unable to put this into words for her mother-in-law. Nevertheless, Leah tried to win her grandchild's confidence which at least provided a distraction for a while. Then Leah sighed wearily and as she spoke, she put her palms together beside her ear, tilted her head and closed her eyes for a second, making it clear that she was going for a nap. Much as she understood her mother-in-law's need for rest, Esme could not bear to be abandoned there a moment longer.

'Can I go for a walk?' she spoke in English, of course, and the words were out before she'd considered their propriety. Leah looked taken aback for a second. She called Raheli and after a rapid exchange between the two women, Leah smiled and gestured towards the door. Raheli adjusted her *kanga* around her head and shoulders and beckoned for Esme to follow. Esme's concern for having been undiplomatic gave way to relief at being out in the open and seeing her surroundings. She blinked in the bright sunlight and felt a delightful waft of air on her face. The sun was strong but compared to Dar es Salaam, the air had a fresh feel to it. Just to stretch her legs was bliss and for once she was content with the customary strolling pace she had already come to expect; this was certainly not the time or the place for the brisk *Mzungu* rate, impossible anyway since the *kanga* she had tied inexpertly round her lower half effectively shackled her ankles together.

As Raheli walked ahead of her along the paths worn into the earth, she took in the mud-daubed homes, very similar to that of her parents-in-law. The roofs were thatched from a different type of leaves than the palm fronds which proliferated in the coastal belt. She noticed that there were no coconut trees at this higher altitude.

'Which trees do you make the roofs from?' she asked Raheli. Raheli smiled and nodded agreeably. Esme sighed to herself, resignedly.

Smoke filtered through the thatch of several roofs - there were no chimneys. Esme loved the smell of wood smoke, so redolent of her childhood holidays with her grandmother in a thatched farmhouse in Ireland. Now the wood smoke mingled with the pungent scent of the bush which had been only partially quelled. It was evident at every turn that the bush was attempting to regain its territory, vying with the papaya, cassava and banana plants amongst which thorny shrubs and wild grasses grew in clumps.

Boys, kicking around a ball made of a parcel of banana leaves, stopped in their tracks to stare and she braced herself for the inevitable cries of '*Mzungu*' but there were none, presumably the sight was so unfamiliar as to render them speechless. Or had they not yet cultivated the loutish manners of their urban counterparts?

At the second attempt, Mosi consented to be carried by Raheli, tied in a *kanga* her on her back, surprising Esme as Mosi was no more accustomed to it than was Esme – though she had tried. It looked so effortless for the Tanzanian women, even the small girls they passed carrying younger siblings almost as big as themselves, but she knew the cloth cut into their shoulders and failed to understand how they could have got so used to it that they carried on with their normal activities, as if the child weighed nothing at all.

A few goats were tethered amongst bushes which they were busy devouring, thorns and all. Chickens scratched among patches of spiky grass.

'*Kuku*!' Mosi shouted, pointing at the chickens, her eyes bulging with excitement. It was the first word she'd said that Esme had recognized!

'She is speaking Swahili!' Raheli, herself speaking Swahili, was both pleased and surprised. Esme wasn't surprised at all. She just hoped that Mosi would speak English as well. Mosi meanwhile continued to point at every hen and repeat the word, chuckling with glee. Her glee was infectious, Raheli's reserve diminished a little and Esme's apprehension dropped a notch.

An intermittent stream of women and girls passed, the apparent ease with which each balanced either an earthenware pot or a galvanized bucket of water on her head belied the effort it must cost. On the drive down Esme had occasionally caught glimpses of women drawing water from shallow pools and streams. God, she hoped that wasn't the origin of Mabalo's drinking water! Had they actually drunk any water since they'd arrived? She'd had tea, Martin had had bottled lager, Mosi had drunk milk that morning. Could she ask Raheli where the water was being fetched from? But even if she managed to make herself understood, would she cause offence?

Just as well she'd said nothing: an instant later they came to a clearing between the houses and saw a queue of a dozen girls with an assortment of vessels waiting their turn for the tap on a stand pipe at knee height while the water spluttered clear and sparkling into clay pot or a large aluminium *sufuria*, the type of handle-less cooking pan everyone seemed to use. When it was full the girl filling it dropped a twig of fresh leaves onto the surface of the water. In fact, everyone in the queue had a similar sprig in her hand. Esme asked Raheli what they were for.

'The water not spill,' she said, looking pleased. Esme watched as each water-bearer in turn heaved the heavy vessel carefully onto some sort of cushioning material on her head, sometimes with the help of a friend, and watched as they walked steadily away. Not a drop spilled. How did the leaves work? And how did women discover that it worked? Perhaps she'd learn more science living here than in the countless hours she'd suffered through boring lessons at school.

Two girls, who could only have been about five, between them lifted a full *sufuria* onto the head of one of the girls. The pan was as wide as her shoulders. Esme's own neck ached as the girl braced herself, steadied her load with one hand and walked off, her eyes slid sideways to take in the *Mzungu* watching her, her expression was of satisfaction. This wasn't playing at being grown up, it was the real thing.

They crossed paths with several women carrying heavy hoes on their shoulders and usually a bundle of green, leafy vegetables or of freshly-uprooted cassava balanced on their heads, returning home from their *shamba*. A boy careered along a narrow path between tall, dried maize stalks, bowling a hoop - a rusty old bicycle wheel stripped of its spokes. Esme could feel the scratching of the rough leaves against the boy's bare arms and chest though he was apparently oblivious to it.

A group of small girls, squatted in the shade of a vast baobab tree, one of the few trees still in full leaf while the land thirsted for rain. As she passed, Esme recognised the game they were playing with pebbles in the dust as 'jacks' from her own childhood . A fair amount of bickering seemed to be going on, judging from the raised voices but there was also a lot of laughter. Several girls had a sleeping child tied in a *kanga* on their backs. Toddlers were crawling around in the soft dust or sitting happily amusing themselves with a soda bottle top or a bit of stick they'd picked up. Despite being engrossed in their own games, their guardians were ever vigilant – grabbing dangerous objects from small hands and issuing warnings to their wards. As these little tots played, snot ran freely down from their noses, their bottoms were bare. At what age did they start wearing pants? It seemed that what needed to come out was not immediately mopped up or stopped in its tracks but treated as natural.

In front of several of the houses they passed women, bent double from the waist with seeming ease, were sweeping with brooms of plumed grass the compacted earth around their houses which were plastered with the same earth they stood on. The women exchanged greetings with Raheli and then called out a greeting to Esme. She could tell when it was to her, rather than Raheli, because they adopted high, sing-song voices:

'*Habari, Mama*', in much the same tone as speaking to a baby. When Esme responded in what she believed was quite passable Swahili, the women laughed, whether in surprise or pleasure she couldn't tell. She was still baffled by people's laughter at such times; when she had quizzed Martin about it, had said with a shrug, 'It's not malicious! It's just our way.' Nevertheless, she was unable to raise more than a limp smile in response. She couldn't help but wonder if they were laughing at her.

One woman insisted, in a smiling, friendly way, that they come into her tiny house. Inside, clutching a baby on her hip, she drew up a low stool for Esme to sit on, Esme could barely see anything in the gloom after the dazzling sun outside as there were no windows. Through the smoke from an open fire that filled the room, Esme discerned a young girl squatting in the middle of the hut, stirring an earthen pot balanced on three stones in the middle of which burned the fire. Esme suppressed an urge to cough. The woman said something in Swahili and indicated the plethora of small children who could have ranged from a year to six years old.

'It is porridge for the children,' Raheli said, indicating the white gruel in the pot. 'From maize flour.' Surreptitiously, Esme glanced around the room through stinging and watering eyes: there was no furniture only rolled up mats and various packages and pots in corners and in the rafters above. The smoke drifted upwards and while some filtered out through the thatch, most of it still remained inside. The inhabitants seemed largely inured to it, though the girl at the fire occasionally wiped her eyes with the back of her hand. After a few minutes Raheli said their goodbyes to the woman who handed Esme three young cobs of maize, still attached to their soft green leaves, saying '*Karibu, mgeni.*' Frustrated at her lack of words, Esme grasped the woman's hand to shake it and smiled, repeating lamely, '*Ahsante, Ahsante sana.*'

The village seemed to have no focal point other than the stand-pipe. The rest of the dwellings were haphazardly scattered around the village, interspersed with un-cleared ground where tiny outhouses stood, surrounded by rickety screens of woven leaves. A young man's head and shoulders were visible above one as he poured water over himself. A few yards to their right, a canopy of thatch was set apart from the homesteads. A cloud of smoke and steam rose from a huge three-stone-hearth on which balanced a massive pot. An unfamiliar, sour smell hung in the air. A woman bent over the pot, stirring the contents. Beyond the smoke and leaping flames, Esme could make out groups of men lounging on benches, drinking, talking and laughing in the inviting shade. The bright colours of the women servers' *kanga* contrasted with the drab browns, greys and white of the men's garb.

'What is happening there, Raheli?' Esme asked.

Raheli, laughed.

'They, are, drink-ing *pombe*. Al-co-hol.' Raheli pointed towards the dried stalks which bore drooping sprays of grain growing on the other side of the path.

'*Bia*, beer. The woman is cooking from *ulezi*.' Esme was none the wiser. 'This is called millet. It is for eating. They also cook it for beer.'

'Oh, millet beer,' Esme said.

'You want some?' Raheli asked as an afterthought. Esme shook her head. Quite apart from the smell having put her right off, she had a hunch Martin would not approve of her going close to that throng of men. Perhaps he was actually amongst them.

The next day was very much like the first but, whereas that had been brimming with new experiences, the second time around the novelty was missing. Esme found it hard to bear the long hours with nothing to do. She eventually convinced Raheli that she should be allowed to help prepare food and was allowed to sit on a stool outside the kitchen hut, Mosi on a mat beside her. Her task was to slice a heap of onions but Esme was so slow and inept, having no chopping surface, failing to produce the wafer-thin slices required, that Raheli took it away from her after ten minutes. Raheli then showed her how to strip pumpkin leaves of their stems, bringing the veins with them, and Esme managed this better though was still painfully slow. She was defeated completely however in her efforts to bunch the leaves tightly together and slice through them to create ribbon-like strips ready for the cooking pot. Esme was dumfounded by the dexterity of her sister-in-law and the fact that she still had all her ten fingers. When Esme managed to convey her admiration she was rewarded by a shy smile from Raheli.

The only other relief for Esme from the hours of sitting was the frequent dropping by of neighbours and relatives who wanted to meet Martin's wife. Whether she would have attracted the same interest if he'd married a woman from elsewhere in Tanzania – as black as they were – she had no way of knowing. When she asked Martin – the once she saw him that day - he merely laughed.

Late that afternoon Raheli led her to a clearing amongst the *shamba*. Esme had found the weather delightful, sunny and warm without the cloying humidity of Dar which lay on the coastal plain. Raheli, nevertheless, frowned as they walked: 'Hot!' she complained as she wiped her brow with the edge of the *kanga* draped loosely over her head and shoulders. Esme was bareheaded as usual, torn between wanting to conform and being too pretentious; she felt self-conscious as it was, wearing just the one *kanga* .

A group of people, predominantly excited, chattering children - mostly boys - were seated in a circle on the bare earth, leaving a wide arena, the air of expectancy palpable. Raheli led the way to a couple of rusting, iron chairs for the guests of honour, which formed part of the perimeter. A man in shabby, ill-fitting brown trousers, half covered by his shirt tails, attempted to keep order amongst the audience with the aid of a cow's tail fly-whisk and harsh barks at any child entering the central space. Despite his efforts, as soon as he turned his back on one group the children would snigger and bottom-shuffle forward a few inches. He took the bait every time, spinning on his heel, catching sight of the culprits and chasing them back while they feigned terror. Esme and Raheli were well-entertained during the wait for whatever it was. Even Mosi caught on to the game, shouting and pointing gleefully.

Situated on the western side of the arena, they benefited from long shadows of the huts cast by the sinking sun. After a while, Esme allowed the babbling of the children's voices to float over her. How long had they been waiting now? Raheli had offered by way of explanation '*Mganga*' – doctor. She brushed her lips against Mosi's soft tresses which two of the little girls cousins had plaited into neat rows that morning. Where were the cousins now? Probably helping with the preparations of the evening meal. Childhood didn't last long for girls.

A hush from the assembly, brought her back to the present. A bundle of black rags shuffled into the circle. A hideous wooden mask and straw hair rendered it inhuman. The figure first cavorted around the arena then thrust its mask menacingly towards Esme. Mosi buried her face against Esme's bosom. The *mganga* retreated, spun round to face the spell-bound faces of the now-silent village boys, capered, wailed, chanted and exhorted the heavens in a cracked yet piercing voice. The writhing creature approached again. Mosi shrank down in her mother's lap but her gaze was transfixed. It was the waft of male sweat, stale smoke and alcohol that broke the spell for Esme. This was a very ordinary man, one who was not pleasant to have this close. Was the performance supposed to be humorous? No-one was laughing. Did it have some significance? For herself? Surely, if that were the case, more adults would have been present. She felt confused and uneasy. Why couldn't Martin have been here to explain it all to her and to reassure Mosi? He could have taken her on his lap and she would have taken it all in good part. As it was, she was taking her cue from Esme.

When eventually it was over, Raheli's cheerful dismissal offered little explanation of the event. 'It's just *mchezo* - a dance, a game.'

By the time Martin returned that night, Esme was in bed, the child asleep beside her. Esme and Martin spoke in whispers, not only to avoid waking Mosi, but because the rooms were separated only by mud and wattle partitions.

'Why do you think the witch-doctor put on a show for me, Martin?'

'Hey, that was not a witch-doctor! Be careful about associating our family with witchcraft!'

'Well what was he, then?'

'*Mganga*. A doctor, any kind of doctor is *mganga*. He knows about medicine and helps people when they're sick or have had a bad spell put on them by a witch or a witch-doctor - *mchawi*. No-one admits to being a witchdoctor, they pretend to be ordinary people but folk have their suspicions. They often suspect cats too of being witches in disguise. It's all just superstitious nonsense anyway. Forget about it. It's late.'

It took her a long time to get to sleep. Whenever she closed her eyes she saw a menacing figure with horrific features approach her. She missed Martin's body against her. Mosi's snores were intrusive as she lay between her parents. She tried to turn the child but she was obstinate in sleep and Esme gave up for fear of waking either her or Martin. Having a baby in the bed with the parents was a necessity for most people but it must also be an effective contraceptive, perhaps the only one for most couples. Not that she'd needed one lately; before this trip, she couldn't remember a night when she and Martin hadn't made love, and this was the third night in succession they had abstained. He had always been passionate and loving; there was no doubt in her mind either that he was an expert, even if she had no grounds for comparison. He'd told her once that he'd been taught the art – or science – at bush school, she supposed not far from where they were now, during the preparations for his initiation.

She fell asleep eventually, dreaming of goggle-eyed young teenage boys, seated cross-legged under a mango tree, while an elder in an academic gown and mortar board labelled diagrams of the female body drawn on a battered backboard, propped against the trunk of the tree.

Ch 6: The Journey Home

Breakfast was the one meal Martin shared with Esme and Mosi during their short stay in Mabalo before he and one or other of his male relatives wandered off about their *shuguli* – the nebulous 'matters' that took up so much of his time. Martin's plan had been to stay a week but during breakfast on the fourth day Martin's father burst unceremoniously into the room. He wiped his brow, now more furrowed than ever, with the back of his hand and his whole manner was agitated.

'The rains are coming, they will be here by tomorrow, you will have to leave at once.' He spoke loudly and Esme felt the urgency of his announcement.

'Are you sure, *Baba*?' Martin's tone was respectful but he was clearly sceptical. The rainy season isn't due for a few weeks yet.'

Esme was inclined to believe her father-in-law, not that she had the faintest clue about the seasons here, but that morning, in contrast to other mornings, she'd woken up, bathed in sweat under the light blanket. Not a breath of breeze ruffled the heavy, cloying air.

'The *Mganga* has just warned me! I'm telling you, you need to go today or you'll be here for weeks – months even. And you have to get back to your work!'

Alured was not interested in discussion and, for once, Martin took no further convincing. It was probably what he wanted anyway, Esme thought, he soon became restless in any situation. Esme's immediate reaction was relief to be going home but then a stab of regret passed through her. That flat, that place didn't feel like home. Once back in Dar, Martin would be setting off for work early each morning, returning late in the evening, leaving her and Mosi on their own. Here, despite Martin's absence during the day, Esme felt he was never far away and with some member or other of his family. Although she knew that Leah would soon return to her daily work wielding a hoe on the family plot on the outskirts of the village, since her visit to the clinic with malaria she had been going to her room each afternoon to rest for several hours, but they had also sat for several hours together with Esme and Mosi at the front of the house in the shade of the thatch, mostly in companionable silence. Raheli had been spending most of her time around the house; Esme gathered this was in her honour as normally she too would have worked in the *shamba*. In the last two days Esme had begun to tag along with Raheli to fetch water, to collect fresh sweet potato or cassava leaves and to sit with her at the back of the house watching her preparing food, helping when she could. But there had been times when Raheli had said, '*Nakuja.* I'm coming,' and disappeared for an hour, returning with a load of firewood or a bundle tied in a *kanga* on her head. So much was still unknown and unfathomable and yet a kind of familiarity was beginning to creep in.

'OK, pack the things – we'll have to get moving.' Martin said, already on his feet his plate of eggs abandoned. ' We need to get to the river before the ferry stops for the night.'

'Can you give me a hand please, Martin. It'll be quicker.'

Martin handed her the car keys. 'Here, I'll take care of the child.' Esme looked at Mosi who was crawling around happily on the sandy ground outside the open door and could easily have been left under they eye of Raheli or her grandmother but, she realised, he probably wanted to spend the last few minutes with them.

A few hours into the journey, the towering white clouds gave way to a dark, leaden sky. Martin's expression matched. Trees waved giddily as the strength of the wind increased in anticipation of the rain. Then the sound of the engine was almost drowned out by the approaching roar of raindrops drumming on the bone-dry earth. As the water penetrated the soil a pungency was released, filling Esme's nostrils. The beaded curtain of the deluge swept over the car and they were soon under a waterfall. The windscreen wipers couldn't keep up with the torrent. The rain came in sheets.

A crack of thunder startled them with its intensity, then rumbled on. The air was filled with the aroma of the parched earth soaking up the water. Martin, grim-faced, kept on driving. They rode in silence, even Mosi was awed. Esme couldn't understand why Martin didn't wait it out.

'We've time enough for the ferry, Martin, haven't we?' she asked. 'It only took us about four hours on our way here. What time does is stop?'

'It stops at dusk, and with these clouds that will be early.' He shook his head. 'You don't know this soil – black cotton-soil!' The grey dust looked harmless enough. Within the hour, though, she understood. The track ahead transformed into a treacherous black slurry. It was like nothing Esme had ever seen. Martin had no choice but to drive in first gear, the engine revving, the wheels spinning. They came upon several stranded trucks and then a bus, most of the passengers sitting dejectedly, soaked through and shivering. Where they could find them, people held banana leaves over their heads as improvised umbrellas. The more able passengers laboured with tree branches, rocks and brute force – levering, pushing, pulling the bus or truck from the quagmire.

Esme's head thumped: she was weary with the combination of the humidity, the constant pounding of the rain above them, the increasingly foetid odour, and constant anxiety. Though their tiny car seemed to skid across the surface of the mud, it faltered from time to time. Occasionally, Martin guided it off the deeply rutted track to skirt round the debris in their path. The engine steamed. Martin poured half their precious drinking water into the radiator. As the storm intensified, he displayed none of his earlier grimness, but seemed to be relishing the excitement. Esme realised, however, that whereas she had initially completely underestimated the menace of the early onset of the rains, as Martin's spirits rose, she felt hers sinking into the morass. 'Martin,' she said, as he got back in the car. 'Do you think we're going to get through this mess?'

'Hey, don't worry! We're doing fine. Great little car, this!' He was beaming. 'Alright, Mosi?' Mosi babbled a response as he restarted the engine and eased the car forward onto the slithery track.

'You see what a beauty she is?' he said, patting the dashboard. 'Passing everything on the road!' Mosi, taking her cue from her father, waved her podgy arms about and jabbered every time they passed a lorry or bus, oblivious to their passengers' distress.

Half an hour later they came upon a truck marooned in a narrow cutting, completely blocking their passage as loose rocks lay scattered close to the track. Martin turned off the engine and got out to survey the situation. The rocks varied in size from ankle- to knee-height. Esme, carrying Mosi, got out of the car and gingerly trod a couple of steps through the goo to perch on a rock on the hillside while Martin approached the lorry driver. Soon the two were joined by a dozen or so men - turn-boys and passengers; a lengthy and animated discussion ensued. Eventually, Martin handed some money over to the driver and the group ambled over to the car. With Martin orchestrating, about ten men grasped the car from underneath and the next moment they lifted the car bodily. Stumbling and staggering the men raised the car above the strewn rocks and deposited it in front of the truck. Martin grinned from ear to ear. He shook hands with each of the sweating men, all laughing and congratulating each other, clapping one another's palms. Martin beckoned Esme and Mosi back to car. After that, it was relatively easy and they came across no more vehicles. Nevertheless, the going was slow and Esme kept a nervous eye on the time.

'You see how the mud is completely virgin?' said Martin. 'No other vehicle has got this far since the start of the rains.'

'No, and we haven't met any oncoming traffic – since I don't remember when.'

'Yes, you are right. Any one planning to drive south has thought better of it at the ferry.'

They journeyed in silence for the last half hour, Esme willing the car forward and the sun to slow its descent in the sky. She knew – from her beloved atlas – that they were somewhere near the ten degrees south latitude and as the equinox had passed only a week or two ago, and dusk would be not be the long drawn-out affair of Scotland.

They arrived at the river-crossing just as the sun was setting, flushing the cabin of the ferryboat rose-pink. It was securely moored on the opposite side of the fast-flowing river, tantalisingly close, the cabin's long shadow cast behind it on their homeward path. No sign of life stirred. Martin switched off the car's engine. Only the rushing water sounded above the thudding of the rain. 'So what do we do now?' Esme asked. Martin must have a contingency plan.

'What do you think we do? We sleep in the car!'

A chill travelled up through Esme, lodging at the base of her skull. Surely it wouldn't come to that.

'Isn't there a hotel – at least a *hoteli* - somewhere near?'

'Where would a hotel be? This isn't Scotland, you know, with country hotels for the idle rich. Hotels are in towns, not in the middle of nowhere!'

She closed her eyes in an effort to compose her anger and disappointment. Opening her eyes and seeing those of Mosi switching apprehensively between her parents, she held back from voicing any of her jumbled thoughts and said quietly, 'OK, Martin.'

It had all been an adventure to him till now. She felt too anxious to be hungry but she knew that Mosi must be famished by now and indeed, just then, she started grizzling.

'But, Martin, we haven't got anything to eat.' It hadn't occurred to her – nor, apparently, to Martin - to bring emergency rations. On the way down to Mabalo they'd bought fresh produce at the roadside. No sign of any road-side vendors now, of course.

A tiny *duka*, a shop that was no more than a kiosk, abutted one of the scattering of mud houses. Esme, her clothes just beginning to feel half-dry, got soaked to the skin once more, as she carefully picked her way across to the shop. Its stock seemed to consist of little more than tiny packets of tea-leaves and matches. She bought up the entire stock of edibles: two packets of cassava-flour biscuits. Back in the car she snapped one of the biscuits in half and found it had the taste and texture of cardboard but, fortunately, Mosi gnawed on it with obvious relish. Martin made a moue and shook his head to the offer of one. Mosi and Esme washed down the scanty meal with their dwindling supply of water. They still had one packet of biscuits in reserve for breakfast.

By then it was completely dark. The drone of mosquitoes filled the car. Martin and Esme covered themselves and Mosi as best they could with *kanga* before attempting to sleep. Esme did her best to slap away the mosquitoes that droned around her and Mosi's heads but they were still sitting targets for the wretched creatures.

During the night the drilling of the rain gradually lessened and finally ceased. The croaks of hundreds of frogs took up their rule of the airwaves and, at various junctures, a truck roared up and shuddered to a stop. It was the longest night Esme had known. Cockerel crows joined the refrain well before the first gleam of light.

At last, in the grey dawn, Esme heard the throaty strains of a tractor-like engine starting up in the distance. For a brief waking moment, she was back on her parents farm in Kirkcudbrightshire, till she awoke, stiff, damp and cramped, to Martin's voice telling her the ferry was on its way. As it approached she saw no vehicles were on it no-one being mad enough to head south at this time. She had barely time to squat in the bushes to relieve herself before the ferry reached the river bank while a small group of local boys gathered to watch its arrival. Once their little car was on board the tiny platform of the ferryboat, there was not enough space for any of the lorries. They chugged back across the river as the sun streaked the sky red and gold. Gradually the clouds dispersed, leaving only fluffy remnants banding the blue. A silky breeze blew. Esme began to relax, to believe that soon they would be out of this nightmare. Today they'd be home.

They disembarked as the sun rose higher and she noticed a dry crust forming on top of the mud. However, the journey continued in exactly the same way as before. The lorries and buses that had crossed the river going northwards early the previous day had been caught in the downpour on this side and were now mired in the bog. Time after time their way seemed blocked but somehow Martin always negotiated a way through.

Martin and Esme were by now splattered with grey mud from their frequent sorties from the car, Martin steering through the open window with his left hand and pushing the car with his right while Esme had pushed from the rear with all her might, Mosi on her hip, aided by the weary travellers whose vehicles the little red car was about to bypass. She was constantly grateful and amazed at how those who were stranded made an effort to help her family on their way. What motivated them? Was it because Europeans – *Wazungu* - were in trouble or would it be the same for anyone who had a chance of forging ahead? At home, wouldn't it have been more of a sink-or-swim-together philosophy?

And then the petrol ran out. The engine, running for all those hours in first gear, revving with wheels spinning, had guzzled up the fuel. Esme could only guess at the meaning of Martin's expletives in Swahili as he thumped the steering wheel repeatedly. She glanced at Mosi's fearful face. How much more of this could they all take? Finally, conquering his exasperation, Martin gave the order:

'You take the jerry can. I'll stay with the car. Mosi can stay with me.'

'Why me, Martin? Why don't you go?'

'Because someone is bound to give you a lift – a white woman in distress.'

Esme could see the logic in that though the notion of striking out on her own filled her with a cold apprehension.

'How far is it to the petrol station?' She must remain calm in front of Mosi. She remembered filling the tank on the journey south, before the tarmac had run out.

'Maybe twenty miles.'

'Twenty miles!'

She looked back over the way they'd come. The track, which looked as if it had been ploughed by an escaped maniac, was steaming now in the overhead sun. Not a vehicle in sight as far as the horizon. Martin handed her a crumpled ten shilling note.

'Will that be enough, Martin?'

'It's all I've got!' He laughed mirthlessly.

Esme didn't like leaving Mosi but she had to trust Martin's judgement. She set off, ignoring Mosi wailing at her departure. The fact that they had a jerry can was a matter of course, rather than part of any contingency plan. Running out of petrol, she had already learned, was an everyday occurrence in Dar. The philosophy of drivers seemed to be that it was risky to invest too much of your limited cash in the fuel tank of a car which might (a) break down (b) crash (c) be stolen; in any of these situations the fuel would be wasted or at least necessitate it being siphoned out of the tank. Plastic tubing was also standard equipment for a motorist.

She'd never hitch-hiked in her life, it wasn't something you did in the wilds of Kirkcudbrightshire, but she needed to concentrate all her attention on putting one foot in front of the other. The going was treacherous. She was additionally hampered by the *kanga* over the lower half of her short city dress. She slipped and slid and struggled to free her useless flip-flops from the clutches of the bog. Every few steps she'd find her foot leaving the sandal behind in the mud with a wrench across her toes, until one of the thongs gave way under the strain. She abandoned the pair there in the sludge. It was easier barefoot, though she hated the slimy feel of the mud on her feet and every few paces she would step painfully onto a sharp stone.

It started raining again. She was no stranger to rain and mud, it had been part of growing up, but then she had been protected by a raincoat, sou'wester and a pair of wellingtons. The rain fell relentlessly. Now she understood the expression 'coming down in stair-rods'. Her hair was plastered to her head, water was running into her eyes, her cotton dress clinging to her skin. The ten-shilling note tucked into her bra would be soaked too.

After what seemed like an hour of this she glanced at her wrist watch: it had stopped, drowned. A watch was superfluous here anyway as no-one gave a hoot about being in time for anything. The sun came out again at this moment, the grey clouds scudded away with astonishing rapidity and the rain gave way to the powerful rays of the sun. Esme judged it to be mid-afternoon. Steam began rising from the earth. Although the air had been cleansed of the mugginess that had dogged them in the last couple of days, the sun burned her scalp through her sparse hair and she could feel her face and arms reddening. Why hadn't she thought to bring along an extra *kanga* ? At this rate she'd be too sore to sleep tonight. And where would they be spending the night?

Would they really be back on the road and able to reach home by nightfall?

A band of panic gripped her chest. Her throat, already parched, felt constricted as panic mounted. No-one but a fool ever travelled at night in a small vehicle, Martin had said: too many hazards lurked along the way - the drivers of buses and lorries with only one head light who nevertheless drove as if they owned the road; lorry drivers from Somalia who, kept awake by chewing qat in order to keep their vehicles on the road day and night. Added to which, in the not infrequent event of an accident or break-down, there were no phone boxes and, in any case, there were no break-down services, no AA or RAC. She couldn't ever recall seeing a police patrol car beyond Dar. No, driving after dark didn't bear thinking about but neither could they spend another night in the car. They needed water and food and clean clothes and nappies. Tears welled in her eyes and ran down her face, mingling with the rain. The sound of a labouring engine behind her brought her to a standstill and wiped all thoughts from her mind. She turned to see, in astonishment, the unmistakable shape of their own little mud-bespattered car. Martin, his arm resting on the open window, looked tired but smug. Mosi's beaming face came into view below her father's as the car roared up and sashayed to a standstill.

'What happened? How did you get here?' Relief flooded through Esme: her daughter was apparently none the worse for her most recent experience. In fact her resilience throughout this nightmare amazed her. Martin shrugged.

'A relative of mine from the Regional Commissioner's Office came along in a Land Rover. He was staying in a village near here and his driver had brought spare petrol. Get in, let's go!'

Half-an-hour more in the mud and they came, at last, to the paved road. The pot-holed surface was a welcome relief this time around. She gladly bore the lurching in and out of the miniature craters. After the rain the air was fresher, lighter and as the sun slid lower in the sky its heat gradually diminished. The road wound into a forest punctuated by extraordinarily tall trees whose smooth pale trunks soared gracefully up to the canopy. At first the sunlight flickered between the tree trunks but, the deeper into the wood the car penetrated, the less of the fading daylight seeped through.

'Will we make it home before dark, do you think?' Esme asked.

'No problem.' Martin's confidence was still intact. She tried to let the exhaustion take over, to relax. The nagging hunger pain was strengthening. They hadn't had a proper meal since breakfast in Mabalo the previous day. Then a relatively smooth road stretched ahead; the going was the easiest they'd had the whole journey. What was the first thing she would do when they got back home? What was there to cook? She'd have to prepare something fast, Mosi must be starving, poor thing. She was dozing now, thankfully.

'Shit! The water's boiling again!' Martin's voice sent a shock through her. This was the last straw for her, she wanted to curl up in a ball and weep. But Mosi woke up and started to cry and Esme had to put her own feelings aside to hug and kiss the child till she merely grizzled miserably. Martin was out of the car and investigating under the bonnet, soon calling out: 'We need a fan-belt. A stocking would get us home.

What was he saying? Don't tell me we're not going to get home! She said nothing. Martin strode off in the direction of a lone, insignificant dwelling, tiny compared to the homes in Mabalo. The occupants seemed to be back from their *shamba*, smoke was filtering through the thatched roof. But what help could they offer? Martin surely didn't expect them to have a phone or car-mechanic tucked away.

In the meantime, Mosi must have something to eat. Again there was no swarm of boys, laden with fare to offer the travellers. In fact, looking around, she saw no other houses, it was eerily quiet. There mustn't be a village close by. With little expectation, Esme searched through the parting gifts Raheli and Leah had given Esme before their hurried departure: rice, maize meal, a large quantity of dried yellow beans tied up in an old *kanga* . Nothing in edible form. Then she remembered the honey that Uncle Saul had presented to them. The bottle was wedged upright behind their luggage. She pulled it out, tilting it as little as possible; she had noted earlier that, when disturbed, the numerous black specks deposited on the bottle floor sluggishly floated upwards.

'Look, we've got some lovely honey!' She proffered the bottle.

Mosi reached out for it and while Esme held it to her mouth, she drank almost the entire bottle. The intense sweetness brought a broad beam to her face and Esme took an experimental swig: it was strong stuff! Martin, she knew detested honey and by the time he had returned the honey was down to the dregs and Mosi and Esme were chortling.

Martin, carrying a battered jerry can of water, was accompanied by a sinewy man dressed in once-white shorts and vest. In his hand was a roll of plaited palm leaves, the same leaves as those handed out in churches at home on Palm Sunday. Esme had seen the women of Mabalo plaiting inch-wide strips such as these. After dyeing them emerald, magenta, and violet, the strips were stitched together into beautiful floor mats. She had also been given one as a leaving present.

The two men's heads disappeared behind the car bonnet and a great deal of discussion went on. The shadows cast by the trees deepened and lengthened, contrasting with the luminous pallor of the trunks. Under the dense canopy, a chill crept in.

At length, Martin called out: 'Esme, switch on the engine!' She judged from various exclamations and flapping sounds that the repair hadn't been successful. More waiting while the two men struggled with their improvisation in the engine. Mosi was in tears again. She'd been so little trouble on the journey but her resilience was wearing thin now.

'Let's go for a little walk.' Esme said, hefting Mosi onto her hip. Night wasn't far off. A solitary bird-song was audible above the crickets. Esme sniffed the air: dank smells of rotting foliage.

She glanced back towards the car. The man she had left with Martin was walking rapidly towards them. He gestured urgently towards the car. Esme stopped and turned towards him. As he approached, she saw his expression of fear and as soon he was near enough he said in a strained, lowered voice:

'*Hatari – simba*! Very danger - lions!' Esme's heart thudded. She'd heard what lions were capable of in this country. Mosi, no doubt feeling the adults' tension clung tightly to Esme as she followed the man back to the car. Martin said they'd have to spend the night in the shelter of the good Samaritan's hut. To Esme the prospect of the three of them sheltering in that tiny, smoke-filled house, together with the occupants, was preferable to spending another night in the car in the midst of lions' stamping ground, but only very marginally. As they turned towards the house, the whine of an approaching vehicle, the first since their breakdown, caused them to pause. Lumbering towards them in the direction of Dar es Salaam was a battered pick-up, dangerously over-laden with dozens of bulging sacks of charcoal tied on in a gravity-defying fashion. Martin eagerly waved the driver down and, through the open window, a discussions took place.

'OK. He'll take you home,' he said turning back to Esme. 'You and the baby.'

Esme dubiously regarded the dilapidated vehicle, its charcoal-blackened driver and young companion who showed great interest in them. A series of doubts flitted through her mind – were these men trustworthy? Was this creaking vehicle safe?

'Are you sure it's a good idea, Martin. Shouldn't we all stay together?'

'But I need to stay with the car, and we need to get it fixed.' Martin had obviously decided this was the best option. 'He was only going as far as Magomeni, this side of Dar, so you'll have to give him that ten shillings I gave you for petrol to take you up to our flat. Tomorrow morning I want you to phone Dominic and get him to bring me a new fan belt.'

'You think it's safe, Martin?'

'Esme, yes, I told you before, you're safer than anyone, *Wazungu* are treated with great respect here.'

Esme, heart thudding and clutching Mosi, wide-eyed, squeezed into the passenger seat beside the young charcoal-blackened boy, feeling the grating of charcoal particles on whatever part of the door and seat of the cab she touched. In the darkened cab, she could make out nothing of the two men's features just the whites of their eyes and teeth. They responded to her greeting with little more than mono-syllables, not even speaking to one-another. In the dark, the only sounds were the labouring of the engine and the grinding of gear changes, she battled to quell her imaginary fears. How would anyone know if she never got home? Or what if these men forced their way into the flat? The men might think she had money, people always thought Europeans had money. Her body ached with weariness, her eyes stung, but she kept alert. A three-quarter moon rose, lighting their way and giving her glimpses of the men's unremarkable profiles. The driver's expression was impassive. The youth had nodded off, his head lolling forward. They must be as weary as she was. She settled into the journey, Mosi had already fallen asleep.

It might have been two hours later that they approached the scattering of electric lights seeping from shuttered windows and the occasional illuminated kiosk or bar. Esme's mood began to lift: they were entering the suburbs of Dar. The road broadened slightly and they met other traffic as they skirted round the centre of the city. She caught sight fleetingly of cyclists and pedestrians before they disappeared into the shadows. She guessed in must be about ten o'clock as they approached the already familiar landmarks of their suburb: the market place, the district office. The driver stopped on the almost deserted main road near the flats. She clambered out of the cab stiffly and awkwardly, carrying the sleeping child, and fished out the ten shilling note, warm from its resting place of many hours, and proffered it to him.

For the first time he made eye contact with her and smiled wanly, shaking his head.

'*Hata*. No. No need. Safe home.' He engaged first gear and turned to check the road. What an idiot she had been!

'*Ahsante sana*. Thank you so much. I'm very grateful.'

'It's nothing,'

Shame at her suspicions flooded hotly through her as she watched the pick-up drive off. She trudged through the cool, deep, white sand the hundred yards to their block, third from the road, six more stretched towards the skyline. The setting amongst the sand and the coconut trees couldn't compensate for the fact that they had no garden, no space of their own. A tiny flat on the third floor had been such a far cry from the farm she had grown up in and the weeks she'd spent there before the trip south had not made her any the more fond of it. She had barely seen her neighbours who all seemed to be out at work during the daytime, leaving their children with young ayahs with whom she could only exchange smiles and a few struggling pleasantries. But now she felt elated by the buildings' familiarity, their solidity.

'We're home, Mosi!' she whispered.

At the bottom of the stairwell she fumbled for the light switch and found that, once again, there was no light bulb. She wearily climbed the stone steps to the top floor in the eerie glow of the moonlight seeping through the lattice-work wall.

The flat door opened directly into the living room, and this time the light switch worked and Esme stood blinking in the brightness. Everything was as they'd left it but then it had seemed cramped, the amateurishly-made furniture and bare cement floor had seemed meagre but now the room looked spacious and almost luxurious. A rush of pleasure flooded through her. Mosi woke with the brightness and demanded to be put down. She started crawling round the room crowing in excitement while Esme went to find something for them to eat.

The counter in the tiny kitchenette had been colonized by a multitude of tiny black ants. Martin must have spilled some sugar when he'd made that cup of coffee after she'd already cleaned up. He didn't notice these things, said she was lucky to have a husband who went in the kitchen at all. That's not how it had been in Edinburgh: part of his charm was that, despite his a very masculine manner he had been a good cook – had actually taught her. Not just how to cook exotic dishes like rice and curries but fairly basic ones too. Her mother had always given Esme the menial tasks of peeling potatoes and washing up, and Esme – eager to escape the kitchen as soon as possible - had never bothered to try her hand at the stove. It was still a chore to Esme but one she had no choice in these days.

Deciding what to cook now was made easy by the lack of alternatives and Martin's absence for the night at least allowed not having a full-blown meal. It had been the same on the rare her occasions when her Dad had been away from home: the three of them would be happy with a pile of pancakes that would never have passed muster with him. She measured out a cupful of rice from the stout brown paper bag, grimacing at the stale odour so different from the aromatic fresh grains of Mabalo. Having made a hasty attempt to remove any bits of gravel as well as the odd un-husked grain and live weevil from the rice, she rinsed it in a sieve under the tap. She dwelled for a moment on the contrast with the village, how they would respond to the sight of water running from the tap right into the kitchen?

While the rice was cooking, she put a large *sufuria* of water on the other gas ring to heat for Mosi's bath. Another miracle, she reflected, a cooking fire ready in an instant, and no need to feed it with wood or even charcoal. She grunted a half-laugh to herself looking at Mosi, covered in charcoal dust, she really was black for once and Esme wasn't too far off it herself.

'Mosi come on, you need a bath before you eat. Let's get you ready.'

She half-filled the plastic bath and undressed Mosi, by now laughing one minute, crying the next. It was at the moment when she was carrying the *sufuria* of boiling water through the living room that the electric power chose to cut off. Mosi, alone in the pitch-black, windowless shower-room screamed as if being murdered.

'I'm coming! It's alright!' Esme called out, gingerly making her way to the shower-room. The next thing Esme tripped over something soft and, in horror, realised it was the child. The pan became light in her hands and there was a splat as the water hit the floor.

'Mosi, are you alright?' Esme screamed. If the boiling water had fallen on Mosi ... She threw the empty pan behind her and groped by her feet till she could touch Mosi – she felt dry and her cries subsided a notch as she felt her mother's hands. Thank God, the water had missed her.

By the time she had lit candles, Mosi was bathed and dressed for bed and they'd sat down to eat, Esme had lost any interest in food. Mosi, was so hungry that she devoured enthusiastically the concoction of tinned corned beef mixed with rice. Over the past few days, Esme had got used to the tasty home-grown, elaborately-prepared fare which, moreover, had been cooked by someone other than herself.

In her own cot once more, Mosi fell asleep quickly. Esme felt as if she could have slept on a clothesline. In the event, although she wasn't waiting for the sound of Martin's key in the door, neither did she have the reassurance of his warm, solid body beside her, the familiar scent of his skin. And she couldn't help but wonder how his night was. She slept fitfully.

Next morning, not able to think of any other telephone she could use, she had to go to Martin's office in order to phone Dominic,

Martin's younger brother, at his place of work. According to Martin, after Dominic's recent graduation he had been employed in the Prime Minister's office as a junior, but very ambitious, administrator. While she stood at the bus stop, Mosi, on her hip, a bus went past without stopping, passengers bulging out of the door, clinging on perilously. This was the rush hour. Mosi was for once content to stay put, awed by the traffic – cars, lorries, buses, bicycles and handcarts – passing within a few feet of her. Waiting in the dusty, exhaust-filled air, Esme, still tired, couldn't get out of her mind the previous night's dream of Martin in his refuge in the forest: a lion had pushed in the flimsy door with one blow of his paw then mauled and devoured Martin. When she had woken herself up, she recalled having recently read a newspaper report describing just such a scenario. Falling asleep again, she'd gone on to dream of Dominic coming with the news that Martin was dead and comforting her by embracing her then announcing that he was inheriting her as his wife. The thought of it made her shiver in the already hot sun. The couple of times she had met him she had found him entertaining and genial but physically he held no appeal whatsoever, being short and overweight. He wasn't even Martin's real brother, in her terms, but here they counted as brothers because their mothers were sisters. Martin had said that in former times a man usually automatically inherited his brother's widow, or widows. She reassured herself that Martin wasn't the type to be eaten by a lion but even so it must be terrible for him, being stranded out there. Everything depended on her until Dominic took over. She hoped he would see this as his chance to pay back his big brother, Martin having contributed to Dominic's up-keep while he was at Makerere University in Uganda. It was only recently that Martin had absent-mindedly revealed to her that all the time he had been studying in Edinburgh, he had been sending money from his meagre allowance to his younger cousin; apparently a few pound in sterling went a long way in East African shillings.

At last she reached Martin's office, where she was treated with great courtesy by the Martin's deputy. On hearing Dominic's voice over the phone – at first brusque and officious relief flooded through her. She explained as best she could and was taken aback by Dominic's response – a cackle of laughter.

'We'll soon sort him out, *Shemeji*!' Dominic chortled. 'I will need another half an hour here, then I'll come and pick you up.'

'Er, Dominic, *Shemeji*, just to let you know, I've got Mosi here with me and I need to get some things for her to take ...'

'Ah – we can't drag the child up-country with us, don't worry we'll take her to my sister's house, there are a lot of children there.'

Esme's hand shook as she replaced the receiver. Poor Mosi, the disruptions she had encountered in the past few days! Mosi looked unfazed at this moment, as long as she was with Esme and her basic needs were met, she seemed to adapt to the continuous changes in her little life.

Getting the new fan belt involved a tedious round of small suppliers clustered in Kariakoo, a thronging shopping area, which although at first appearing to be a confusing maze with its chaotic traffic, turned out to be built on a grid. Then, at last, they were speeding down the road to Kibiti with barely another car on the road, Dominic driving with total contempt for the pot-holes. About an hour into their journey, a pick-up approached, crammed with standing passengers and Dominic was forced to slow down, to give way to the larger vehicle. As they passed the pick-up, with a shock of recognition, Esme found herself looking at Martin's face. He was gazing ahead, as if focused on his destination, and their eyes did not meet.

'That was him! It was Martin! Turn back, we'll have to follow him and get the driver to stop.' But Dominic shook his head and doggedly kept going.

'It could not be Martin. Anyway, we would not catch up with the pick-up.' Esme, incredulous, looked at Dominic and put her hand on his arm.

'Dominic, please! You have to stop! You'll easily catch up with it. Anyway, Martin's got the car keys.'

'We'll get in somehow, don't worry.' Dominic kept his eyes on the road and his foot pressed on the accelerator. Panic filled Esme.

'Dominic, please turn back. We need Martin. It's his car. I don't think we should do anything to it without him.'

'Why didn't he stay with the car, then? What does he think he's doing?' Dominic's face was thunderous, spit flew from his mouth as he practically shouted. ' I'm not going to waste my time, my petrol? No, we've got this far, and we're going to do the job we set out to do!'

Esme couldn't believe what was happening. The situation seemed to just get worse and worse. She turned and watched the cloud of dust that was the pick-up until it could no longer be seen and she knew it would be useless to plead with Dominic to turn back: the gap between them and Martin was widening with every second and once the pick-up reached Dar they would never find it in the traffic. It seemed that to Dominic the task of recovering the car had become a mission in its own right and had nothing to do with her or Martin.

What on earth was Martin doing? He must have found the waiting intolerable but, had he thought it through, he would have worked out that even if she had reached his office the moment it opened and that Dominic had been able to drop everything the minute she'd phoned, they could not have reached the car by the time Martin had abandoned it.

Dread filled her stomach as they entered the forest. When she had left the previous evening, the car had been pushed off the road and now she had to scan the undergrowth as they passed until, just as she began to think she had missed it altogether, she spotted the gleam of red paintwork in the gloom. Martin's host was not in evidence, presumably he had gone to his *shamba*, leaving the car in the safe hands of its owner. Now, ignoring her protests, Dominic forced open the side window, opened the driver's door and then the bonnet. With much muttered complaint about the dustiness of the engine, he fitted the fan belt. He then fiddled with the ignition wires. Was he really as knowledgeable as he claimed with car mechanics? Surely, Martin would be glad when they got the car back to Dar. Then she'd have to try and get in touch with him. He'd make for his office to use the phone. Or would he go directly to Dominic's office?

Eventually the engine flared into life, Dominic grinning with his success. Esme manoeuvred herself awkwardly into the driver's seat. Her hands on the steering wheel. She'd barely ever driven though she had persistently asked Martin to teach her. She stilled the tremor in her hands by gripping the steering wheel and tentatively followed Dominic's car. Within a few minutes, Dominic was out of sight on the winding road and, as she strained to catch sight of him, she thought she detected an unfamiliar sound to the engine. She sniffed as a new note mingled with the dankness of the forest – yes, she could smell burning, maybe a charcoal kiln? But a few minutes later the smell was still with her and much more acrid. It was coming from the car! Dominic's car was not to be seen. She pressed the horn repeatedly and then gave up and turned the engine off. She waited for the boys with hard-boiled eggs and sure enough, within minutes, they were there in their tatters, their aluminium dishes balanced on their upturned palms, their large, sad eyes fixed on her.

Ten minutes later Dominic returned – she could almost see the steam emanating from him. '*Shemeji*, what's the matter?'

'I can smell burning rubber, it's definitely coming from the car.'

He laughed. 'It's just these local people,' he waved his hand dismissively in the direction of the forest. 'They're always burning tyres and such like.'

'*Shemeji*,' said Esme, standing her ground, 'The smell has been with me for the last ten minutes.' He sniffed the air, 'Well it's gone now. Don't worry, we'll try again, drive slowly this time.' He shook his head regretfully, 'I should have brought a driver from the office with me.' Esme threw a glare at the back of his head as he re-entered his own car. She was rapidly revising her opinion of him as an ally. As she drove on, sure enough, the fumes returned and a few miles further on the engine died. Dominic scratched his head, but it did little to bring him inspiration. After lengthy poking around, he shrugged.

'I'll just have to tow you. It's not going to start.' It was clearly a failing of the car, not to respond to his ministrations.

'You've got a tow-rope?' Esme brightened a little at this prospect. But rummaging in the boot of his car revealed that he didn't. By this time a sizeable group of interested onlookers had joined the young vendors. Esme remembered the strip of plaited palm leaves provided by their Good Samaritan the previous evening. She explained her idea to Dominic who immediately turned and issued a series of commands to the bystanders. She was open-mouthed at how arrogantly he, a total stranger, addressed these people who were, after all, in their own neck of the woods. She longed to be out of this place and out of this man's company.

Esme lost count of the number of times the palm rope snapped and had to be retied in the few miles to the petrol station at Kibiti. There Dominic bought a dishevelled sisal rope for an exorbitant price and thereafter the number of breakages dropped slightly. Nevertheless, the distance between the two cars had diminished alarmingly by the time they reached the outskirts of the city and it was still a long way from home. Dominic towed the car into the first car mechanic's outfit they came to – recognisable simply by the large number of cars parked around a ramshackle shed. Of course, Dominic had never had any dealings with this *fundi* before and Esme suspected that walking in off the street to an unknown car-repairer was probably not a good idea but – like everything with Dominic - it was out of her hands and, even if he had been prepared to continue their pathetic crawl through the city, she knew that she could not have negotiated the hectic traffic nearer the town centre. Given the chance, she would have tried to establish a rapport with the *fundi* but, as it was, she feared he was instantly turned sour by Dominic's lofty attitude.

That evening Martin arrived home as she was preparing their meal. He stood in the middle of the living room, muscles flexed.

'Where's my car, Esme?' I went all the way to Dar and back to the forest with a new fan belt and the car was gone! What have you done with it?' His voice was raised, his eyes boring into her. Esme wiped her hands on the dish towel and didn't answer immediately as she dealt with a series of emotions: he was safe, thank God, but no enquiry about her and Mosi's welfare and now he was ready to blame her for everything. She squared up to him. She felt the blood rush to her face and her whole body tensed with anger and disappointment.

'Martin, why didn't you wait for me at the car? I went back with Dominic and the fan belt but you didn't wait.' Martin didn't answer. Mosi had crawled up to him and was tugging at his trouser leg, babbling insistently. He suddenly became aware of the child, or it suited him to acknowledge her at that moment, and stooped to pick her up. Esme took a deep breath and explained the rest in calm, measured sentences.

Martin fumed but he stopped short of blaming her. He confessed he'd quickly grown tired of waiting by the car. On contacting Dominic's office he had been informed by a clerk that Dominic was out of town and Martin had assumed that Esme had been given the same information. He had then secured an advance on his salary and eventually succeeded in commandeering a driver and vehicle from his office. Then came the difficult part: Esme had to explain that the car was with a *fundi* in the southern outskirts of the city. He must have passed close to it on his way back. He spent the rest of the evening on their tiny balcony in the company of the current affairs station of Radio Tanzania and spoke not another word to Mosi or Esme. Some hours after she had gone to sleep she felt the dipping of the mattress as he lay down on his side of the bed, a wide gulf between them.

Ch 7: The Aftermath

'Martin. Martin! Mosi's dreadfully hot. Sorry, Martin, please wake up!' Martin rolled over onto his back. He smelled strongly of beer.

'What time is it?' He was only half awake, screwing up his eyes against the light from the living room.

'Two o'clock. Two in the morning,' she added, not sure how clear his head would be.

'What?' What is the matter?'

'Mosi's burning hot. She was covered in bites when we got back from Mabalo and she's never stopped scratching. I'm sure she's got malaria. We've got to do something!'

Esme was sitting on the edge of the bed, placing a cold, wet flannel onto Mosi's brow as she lay impassive in her arms. Rather than this prompting her usual robust yells, all Mosi could summon was a weak whimper. Martin put the back of his hand on Mosi's bare torso and sat up, fully awake. Mosi coughed deep in her chest and whined with the pain.

'She was grizzling all afternoon and evening,' Esme said, 'She wouldn't let me put her down for a single minute. I had to carry her round from the moment she woke up after her nap, even while I was cooking. Where *were* you?' She was angry with him now, she felt all those lonely, anxious hours weighing on her, unsupported.

'I had to meet someone. Let's deal with Mosi now.' Martin's answer was gruff, probably more to do with a hangover than contrition, she thought.

Mosi began to cry again, and Esme stood up and paced around the tiny space between the bed and the door, Mosi's head on her shoulder, her body hanging limply over Esme's shoulder.

'I've been awake with her for the last three hours, Martin. I heard you come in and I haven't slept since – Mosi woke up just after you went to sleep.'

If Martin took this as a rebuke he didn't react.

'You could have put her in that ... pram thing?'

He was referring to the once bright yellow corduroy carrycot on folding wheels given to them by the wife of Martin's departing English boss. The 'pram thing' had been a godsend: she had tied an arm's length of string to it, moved aside their flimsy furniture in the living room and, holding the other end of the string, sent the carrycot back and forth by pushing it away with her foot and pulling it back towards her. For a while it had lulled Mosi into an uneasy sleep.

'I did. For hours!' Esme strove to remain calm. Martin sat up and gently took Mosi in his arms.

'My God, she *is* hot! Have we given her anti-malaria medicine this week?'

'Yes, Martin.' How could he have forgotten the ritual, the battle they went through every week, Martin patiently but firmly holding the child clamped in one arm while she struggled with all her might, Martin's other hand forcing Mosi's jaw open while Esme attempted to slip a spoonful of the bitter, cerise *Nivaquine* syrup down her throat at the same time holding her nose.

'Good girl' Esme would say.

And they would wait. Then Mosi would gag and wretch and bring the whole lot back up.

'We can try and give her some more now,' Esme said.

Mosi put up no fight this time but immediately, painfully, vomited the entire contents of her stomach: the colour of the semolina pudding mixed with blackcurrant jam that Esme used to have at school.

'We can't wait till morning to take her to the doctor. What shall we do? I'm really scared.'

'Give her some paracetamol,' Martin said.

'I did and she brought that up too.' Nevertheless, they repeated the performance, with the same result.

'She's been like this since midnight, Martin.' Esme's voice contained a tremor she couldn't still.

Martin stood up and quickly put on his discarded clothes from the floor. Martin never got dressed without showering first and *never* wore clothes twice.

'We will have to go to Muhimbili Hospital. The local health centre will not be open now.'

'Muhimbili! That's right across town, isn't it? How will we take her? We have no car.' The car was still where Dominic had towed it.

'I *know* we have no car .....' Esme was dimly aware that Martin was making an effort to keep his voice level and that her own was becoming shrill.

'Are there ambulances?' Now she thought about it, she couldn't recall ever having seen one. 'How can we call one - we have no phone?'

'I will get *Baba* Vero to take us.' *Baba* Vero lived in one of the flats below, the father of one of the many young children who teamed in the wide entrance hall, open to the air but shaded from the sun. She hardly knew the man.

'Do you think he'll mind?' Martin paused in the middle of doing up his trousers.

'Esme, why would he mind? He won't even think twice about it: a neighbour's child is sick and needs to go to hospital, that's all there is to it!' Martin left the flat immediately to see their neighbour. It seemed an eternity while Esme paced around the flat carrying Mosi. Then Martin returned, out of breath.

'OK let's go. Here, let me take, Mosi.' He lowered his voice as he addressed Mosi:

'It's OK, *kisura*.' Mosi barely reacted as he lifted her out of Esme's arms.

Baba Vero's stocky form was already seated behind the steering wheel of his battered car outside the entrance to the flats, the car engine running, somewhat erratically. As they entered, the car creaked alarmingly. God, would they make it?

'*Ahsante sana*, *Baba* Vero,' Esme said.

'It's no problem, Mama Mosi.' His tone was lugubrious as he met her eyes in the rear view mirror. 'These kids choose their own times to be ill. I lost my first-born to malaria. Have to be quick.'

A shock travelled through Esme's body. His child *died!* She shuddered at the notion of Mosi's little body cold and lifeless in her arms. Esme began to shake and tears ran down her face in the gloom. Over and over in her head she repeated, *please, please God, don't let her die*.

Their neighbour leant over the steering wheel, making frequent crashing gear changes, as if urging his car to its limit and yet, despite the absence of the normal throng of traffic, their pace was agonisingly slow. The deserted streets, suffused with moonlight were a melancholy blueish hue.

In Accident and Emergency, they had to wait their turn. Esme knew that Mosi was no more important than anyone else's child except to her and Martin but every minute they were kept waiting dragged like an hour. To keep her mind from imagining the worst, Esme read every sign in sight. Most of them were in English and she asked Martin about this.

'English is still the official language, we inherited it, didn't we? But Swahili is being taught in schools around the country and will replace English in due course. And probably the hundred and twenty odd tribal languages as well.' He shrugged and pulled a face of resignation. Looking round at the rows of shabbily clad patients and their relatives, she wondered how many of them could actually read English, let alone understand it.

'What do the different grades mean, one to four?'

Still lightly stroking Mosi's arm, Martin explained that treatment was the same in all grades and was free to everyone, only *The Standard* of accommodation differed the higher the number the better the grade. Civil servants of officer rank, like Martin, and their families were entitled to subsidised Grade Four accommodation, the level of entitlement descending with the employee's position, the grades descending with the floors of the hospital. Accustomed to the indiscriminatory National Health Service, Esme felt a twinge of guilt at belonging to the elevated few.

She felt Mosi's chest again, it was still burning hot. She held her forehead in her hand and closed her eyes in an effort to control her anguish. At last a nurse called out 'Mosi Yusufu' and they were led to the duty doctor. The fatigued young man prescribed an immediate chloroquine injection and instructed Mosi be admitted to the ward. The injection produced barely a moan from Mosi.

The three of them, Martin still carrying Mosi, followed an orderly, an elderly woman in a green uniform along a covered pathway, away from the lifts.

'Why aren't we going up to Grade Four, Martin?'

'The hospital has only one children's ward: it's here, in Grade One.'

'But surely we're entitled to the best treatment!' She was panicking now.

'I told you before, the treatment is the same in all the grades, only the accommodation is different. All the children's doctors are here, in this ward. And it's free to everyone.' She was partly reassured as they reached a set of double doors.

Tenderly, Martin handed Mosi to Esme. 'I can't go in. No men allowed.' Esme looked at him in incomprehension.

'Only women and children are allowed, except at visiting time.' He was patient with her.

'I have to stay here by myself? When am I going to see you?'

'I'll come at visiting time, at four.'

'Four o'clock this afternoon?' The orderly interjected impatiently at this point,

'Jemani, twende! Ninakazi inaonisubiri,'

Martin nodded towards the orderly who had been standing watching them wearily, one hand poised on the swing door.

'She's waiting to show you where to go, Esme.'

'How am I going to understand what's going on?'

'She said she's got other work waiting for her. The doctors and nurses speak English, don't worry.'

Entering the ward, Esme recoiled as her senses were beset: a vast room, jammed with beds containing *kanga* -clad forms. Women and children were milling everywhere; the cries of babies, the wailing of older children, a buzz of chatter, voices calling: it was a marketplace! At the same time the air hit her – heavy and warm, laden with bodily odours mingled with that vile smell of antibiotics, a faint overlay of disinfectant, fused with food and children's soiled clothing.

The orderly guided her to an empty bed, made up with a freshly-laundered but stained sheet and bearing a gigantic pillow. Several backless benches were placed between the beds around the ward; recumbent women with *kanga* over their heads lay on most of the benches, apparently sound asleep.

Esme felt dizzy, her head buzzing as the blood drained out of it. She sat down on the edge of the inflexible bed, gripping Mosi. Was being in this hell-hole really going to benefit the child? Dozens of eyes were trained on her – a number of women and young girls were clustered at each of the neighbouring beds and were quite obviously discussing her with clucking tongues, shaking heads and the occasional guffaw.

'*Habari, Mzungu?*' This greeting was from one of the two teenage girls at the bed opposite. The pair giggled. Esme scowled in response. She closed her eyes as she felt the tears prickle. *Don't cry now,* she told herself severely, *everyone is watching!*

A nurse approached, her head held so high it was tilted back at a ridiculous angle, the expression of disdain on her face seemed to encompass the room at large. Martin often complained about people who thought their positions put them in a class above the rest of the population. The nurse assessed Esme for a moment.

'We must drive her fever down. Come!' Her tone was imperious.

Esme, carrying Mosi, followed her through the crowded ward, gratitude and resentment vying with anxiety within her, leaving little space for discomfiture at the dozens of eyes following their progress. They entered a white-tiled bathroom. While Esme watched uncomprehendingly, the nurse filled the bath with cold water and added a huge lump of ice.

'Take her clothes off,' she commanded.

'What are you going to do?' Esme asked while removing the cotton dress and nappy from Mosi who was as flaccid as a half empty sack of rice. The nurse took Mosi from Esme before answering,

'We will give her a bath!'

Esme watched horrified as she plunged the barely conscious child into the freezing water. Mosi screamed, her voice hoarse, convulsed in coughing but somehow found the strength to struggle.

'Hold her down!' instructed the nurse. Esme's tears ran unchecked down her face. The nurse laughed.

'What's the matter? Don't you want her to get better.' She sucked air through her teeth derisively. Whether it lasted five minutes or an hour, Esme couldn't tell. Finally the nurse took Mosi sobbing and shivering out of the water but, far from wrapping her in a towel, kept the child naked while she pinned Mosi's arm to her side with the thermometer under it. The treatment had worked: her temperature had dropped below crisis level. As she carried the still howling Mosi back to the ward, Esme was trembling with relief that the extreme danger had passed and that this ordeal was over.

During the next few hours, Mosi was put on a drip and given further injections. Because of the drip, Esme couldn't carry her and, though she whispered to and stroked the child, Mosi would not be comforted. She continued crying weakly, tearing at Esme's heart.

All the other sick children had large extended family groups of women and girls encamped around them, some lying width-wise across the foot of the beds, others sleeping on mats on the floor as well as on the nearby benches. As Esme watched, she realised that they took shifts in tending to their patients, some bringing freshly-cooked food from home, others going home to rest and bathe. If only

Martin would come! She hadn't brought her watch and she couldn't see a clock. Eventually she plucked up the courage to ask a neighbouring woman wearing a watch, '*Saa ngapi?*'

'*Saa nanne kasor' robo.*' Esme smiled her thanks and first translated it and then transposed it, picturing the face of a clock: eight o'clock less a quarter, that meant a quarter to two. Two more hours till visiting time. The woman said something to Esme in rapid Swahili which Esme figured out was enquiring about Mosi but was so exhausted and the woman so unable to adjust her conversational language to Esme's level that their efforts quickly petered out. Still, for a while, the woman's friendliness left a small glow in the midst of Esme's misery.

Without knowing the time, Esme could tell that Martin was late. In all her previous experience of living in Tanzania, the general populace had shown a complete disregard for punctuality – they kept 'Swahili time', as Martin termed it. Today, however, when the ward doors were opened, a surge of male visitors had poured in, everyone adhering to '*Mzungu* time' – except Martin. By the time he arrived, she had convinced herself he would not be coming, that Mosi would die and that she would have to deal with everything alone.

When he came up to the bed all she wanted was for him to put his arms around her and to rest against his solid chest but, of course, propriety forbade any public form of physical contact or expression of intimacy. Martin stood beside Mosi, touching her gently, concern evident in his face.

'You can go and have a walk round outside if you want to, Esme. You must be tired of sitting in here. Mind you, it is very hot out there.' He wiped his brow with his handkerchief.

'It's hell in here, Martin! If it wasn't for Mosi being on a drip, I'd take her home now! I don't know how much longer I can stand it!' She couldn't keep from crying and noticing people looking at her only increased her wretchedness.

'I'm exhausted, Martin.'

'But Esme, what can I do? If we had one of my relatives living with us, like every one else does, she could have taken over from you. Why don't you lie down and sleep?' Martin's face showed unease as he nodded in the direction of a prone adult shape swathed in *kanga* on a nearby bed also occupied by a small sleeping child.

'I can't sleep, it's so noisy and Mosi's crying most of the time.'

He turned his attention back to Mosi. She had, in fact, quietened down now and her eyes were half closed. Though she wasn't looking at

Martin, she seemed aware of his hand on hers and the sound of his voice.

Without the car, she couldn't make the trip home to shower and change before the end of visiting hours and one look at the basic, over-used facilities had decided her against using them – not that she had a towel or change of clothes. Instead, she went outside the building, breathed in lungfuls of warm air.

The night was endless. She did try to sleep, curled up at the end of the bed while Mosi dozed but every few minutes Mosi tried to pull the drip needle out of her arm. In the darkness and subdued hum of the ward, constant heart-rending cries from one lone child rang out. It was the families who did the actual nursing – the nurses themselves only came with medicine, injections, to change the drips, and had then, like now, disappeared. Tears rolled down Esme's cheeks as her heart ached for the abandoned child.

As daylight seeped into the ward, Esme saw that the awful pallor under Mosi's tan skin had been replaced by a tinge of pink. She was hot but no longer burning and she had enough strength to make it known how wretched she felt. Esme fretted that she couldn't pick up the child but could only caress her and tell her everything would soon be alright.

The young male doctor doing his round mid-morning made agonisingly slow progress round the ward, disappearing altogether for about half an hour. Eventually he reached Mosi, checked her chart and after a brief discussion cheerfully discharged her. Esme wanted to kiss him as he instructed the sister to remove the hateful drip.

'She's doing fine now, Mrs Yusufu. Take her to your local health centre for injections for the next three days,' he said, handing her a prescription. Mosi was far still far from well but her eyes told Esme she had come back from the brink. Now all the child wanted was to cling to her mother and be carried. Esme felt wretched with exhaustion, only sheer effort of will was keeping her going. She asked a nurse where she could find a phone. The nurse shook her head, and shrugged but her face showed some sympathy. 'We don't have any phone for patients.' There was nothing for it but to wait till Martin came at visiting time so that she and Mosi could go home with him.

Ch 8: The British Council

Esme sighed heavily in the stifling, windowless bathroom as she wrung out yet another bucketful of nappies. It seemed to her that the daily routine – though only a few weeks old - was more tedious and lonely now that she'd had a break from it while on their trip south. But at least, she thought, I do have running water most of the time and electricity. And, thank God, mosquito screens on the window. She shuddered as she relived for an instant their recent stay in hospital.

Mosi whinged from the adjoining living room where she was playing with her few toys. 'I'm coming, Mosi,' she called out. Mosi raised the level of her protests. Esme left the nappy-washing and went to pick up the child and hug her. 'What are we going to do with you? Are you hungry again? Or are you just fed up like *Mama*, stuck indoors? Let's put some music on and we'll go out soon.'

She turned on the radio of Martin's prized radiogram. He had tuned it into the English language station which seemed to consist entirely of political discussions so she quickly changed it to the Swahili entertainment station. She liked the popular music - the Tanzanian and Congolese jazz bands with strong melodies and dance rhythms, far more uplifting than Martin's droning LP's of the likes of Jim Reeves.

Esme offered half a banana to Mosi who eagerly grasped it. Esme was relieved that the child had recovered her appetite after that awful illness. What could she give her to eat at lunch time, in fact what could she and Martin eat? Evenings were the highlight of her day, a shame she couldn't produce a more appetising meal. With Mosi on her hip she rummaged through the few remaining carrots and potatoes. All rotten. When would she learn that nothing kept in this climate?

She took down the small clay pot from the top of the kitchen cabinet which served as the household kitty – fifteen shillings and fifty cents. That would buy them meat once in the week. Should she get some today, she wondered.

'Looks like beans again, Mosi,' she said with an exaggerated smile and an attempt at joviality. 'What kind would you like today? Let me see. We had small green ones yesterday, middle-sized brown ones the day before so, yes, you're right we'll have big red ones today. Clever girl!' Mosi chortled back at Esme. She felt a twinge of guilt at talking nonsense to the child and went on to describe what they were doing as she tidied them both up for the trek to the market. She wished she could get the hang of carrying Mosi on her back. Only the evening before she had asked Martin to help her.

'Hold Mosi in front and swivel her round the back – no, lean forward first! I won't let her fall,' he had said. 'Now throw the *kanga* over her - no, you have to fold it first.'

'Couldn't you demonstrate, Martin?' Martin laughed.

'Me? I've seen it done a million times but I've never done it before. OK, let me try.' With a few deft movements, Mosi was secured on his back and Mosi beamed, fully aware of the novelty of the situation. Martin had also looked pleased with himself. Esme had succeeded in the end but she was too fearful of dropping Mosi while on her own and anyway she had found the *kanga* cut into her shoulder with the weight of the child after only a few minutes.

Nothing for it but to take the 'pram-thing'. Awkwardly, despite much practice, Mosi on her hip, she manoeuvred the pram round the corners and down the six short flights of stairs. All the flat doors she passed today remained closed. Most days she met young girls in faded *kanga* and flip-flops, carrying children or loads and occasionally glimpsed them through doors left ajar. She hardly ever met any of the adults, and the only time she saw them was from the balcony as they left for work smartly dressed in the morning and as they returned in the evening.

As she pushed the pram over the sandy path and along the dusty verge of the main road to the market she responded with unfelt smiles to the amused stares of adults and cries of

'*Mzungu!*' from children. She hated the attention she and Mosi attracted, even though they had made this trip numerous times before. She wished she could just feel grateful that she had the pram - it was certainly the only one Esme had seen since her arrival in the country and, judging by the reaction it caused, it was the only one everyone else had seen.

She had to steel herself to go into the gloomy covered market, with its musty, spicy, sometimes fetid, smells. She would rather have bought from the women seated outside on the ground and felt guilty walking past them with their meagre mounds of produce, and their wheedling calls in Swahili. Mostly their undersized onions or tiny dried fish didn't look appealing but she knew that the real reason she passed them by was because they didn't speak English to her. Her Swahili was still hopeless and to avoid making mistakes she never spoke it unless she had to. Here inside the market it seemed the traders, all men, spoke enough English to ply their trade. They seemed happy to practice on her; the only time she had seen other *Wazungu* was when Martin had brought her that first Saturday – then there had been some expatriate couples. Martin had said in the past there would have been the colonial wives, accompanied by their house-boys to carry their baskets. Most week-day mornings there were very few customers at all.

As she approached, the stall-holders would call out in exaggerated sing-song tones, '*Habari, Mama*? *Mtoto hajambo*? Very nice ladyfingers, very nice potatoes. Good price for you.' She would make the effort to smile back pleasantly, feigning an outer confidence, and conduct the transaction in English. She never bargained like Martin and the occasional Asian men and women did. She just wanted to get it over and done with and how was she to know what a fair price was anyway?

The vegetable section was at least pleasant on the eye with carefully arranged mounds of tomatoes, rice, kidney beans, sweet peppers of every hue, carrots and great hands of green bananas, but the meat stall was what she really hated and was glad they could only afford to buy meat once a week. In a far corner where neither air nor light penetrated was a cage with a small opening through which the butcher served his customers. The stench was overwhelming and swarms of flies buzzed excitedly around alighting on any surface they encountered – including her and Mosi's faces and arms. The airlessness was almost overwhelming as she waited in the queue. Sweat ran down her face, offering a feast to the flies. Mosi began to cry until the young woman, draped in *kanga* , ahead of them turned to Mosi and distracted her by chattering incomprehensibly with a cheery grin and little waves of her hand. Esme gave the woman a grateful smile.

Esme's turn came at the hatch. She didn't recognise the glowering face in front of her. Martin had explained in somewhat sarcastic terms – that butchery was not a widespread skill and that there were basically two cuts of meat: '*steki*' and '*kawaida*' which was the rest.

'Half a kilo of steak, please.' The man behind the hatch shook his head and gabbled at her. '*Kiswahili*' was the only word she could pick out. He turned away and chopped viciously with his enormous machete at a carcass of beef – bones and all - on the slab. He threw a lump into a piece of newspaper and plonked it in front of her. '*Shilingi tano.*' He growled. Esme handed over the coins and, feeling as though she'd been slapped in the face, took the flaccid, soggy bundle; as she tipped it into her basket, splintered bones stabbed her hand. All she could think of as she negotiated her way around the stalls and between the shoppers was that she would show the bastard. She would learn to speak Swahili and till then she would just buy vegetables.

As she struggled up the last flight of stairs to their flat, Esme saw a young woman standing on their landing, a tiny baby peeping out from the *kanga* on her back. The infant was mewling softly, quite unlike Mosi's lusty yells. The young woman dropped a quick curtsey.

'How are you? How is the baby?' she said in English.

'*Karibu,*' Esme put down her basket and opened the door. 'It's nice to have a visitor!'

The woman picked up Esme's basket and brought it into the flat. The two women sat down and the visitor introduced herself and the still grizzling baby, now on her lap as Rose and Jacob. Now that she could see him properly, Esme was taken aback by the baby's huge eyes staring out from his little pinched face. Mosi looked in fascination at the baby.

'I am sorry to disturb you,' Rose said. 'I have come to ask you for advice. I have seen you from our window. Your baby looks very strong and my baby is not growing well.' Esme felt a twinge of gratification that her opinion was being sought but mainly she felt concern for the desperately unhappy little might.

'Have you taken him to the doctor?' It seemed a silly question but she had to ask it.

'Yes, I took him today. The doctor said Jacob is not sick but he needs to drink more milk. I don't understand because he always finishes his bottles.' She took out a tin of formula milk from the brown paper bag she was carrying. Esme had seen the tins in the local kiosks, it always seemed to be the same brand on sale. 'Do you think this milk is bad for him?'

Esme took the tin from her. 'I haven't used it myself, I'm still breast-feeding, but it's a well-known brand, even in Britain, it should be fine if you follow the instructions.'

'People at work said it was better to give formula milk than to breast feed, it's more nutritious, and I am usually at work during the day so I have to leave the baby at home with my young sister.' Esme, read the directions on the side of the tin.

'The amount depends on the age of the child - how old is he?'

'Three months,' Rose replied. Esme controlled her features with effort. She thought the baby no more than a few weeks.

'Six scoops of milk in six fluid ounces – this is what you give the baby every feed?' It seemed that it was Rose's turn to be startled:

'Every feed?' the woman widened her eyes. 'I don't understand. You mean every day?' Esme shook her head slowly.

'This is how much you should give the baby every time he has milk, it should be five times each day. 'She held up her hand with the fingers outstretched. 'Is that the total quantity he has been getting in a whole day?'

The two women fell silent as the implications sunk in.

Esme made them both a cup of tea, wishing she had some Fanta or Coca Cola to offer like a proper Tanzanian would have, and tried to console her tearful neighbour as best she could, trying to suppress her own feelings of condemnation for such neglect. The visitors left soon after and once again it was just her and Mosi.

With the usual persuasion, Mosi eventually submitted to her need for an afternoon nap. As always, Esme initially felt a sense of relief at having some time to herself before the loneliness set in. Today she decided, as she hung up the nappies on the balcony overlooking the car park, she really would write to Christine, her friend from university. Even though Esme had stayed only a year, their friendship had continued and gone from strength to strength over the distances and years. There was nothing they couldn't tell one another, even by letter. Esme had written to Christine along with her mother and brother after arriving in Tanzania but, though the other two had both replied, she still hadn't heard from her friend. Only yesterday she had asked Martin if any letters had come for her to his work address.

'Esme, I will give your post to you when there is any!' he'd replied.

'I know, Martin, it's just in case you might have forgotten. I can't help asking, I'm used to letters being delivered through the door. I don't get anything these days, even bills!'

'Just as well, you wouldn't be able to pay them!' She hadn't known quite how to reply to that and felt it had been left hanging in the air.

By the time she had finished with the nappies, she had lost the resolve to write to her friend, seeking instead an hour of oblivion in sleep.

That evening, as she sat Mosi on a cushion on the chair between them and began spooning the food into the child's eagerly opened mouth, she gave Martin a condensed version of the incident at the market:

'Couldn't you bring some decent meat from town some days, Martin, like you did when we first moved in here? I had to boil this for hours and it's still as hard as old boots.' She chewed on a chunk of grizzle and picked out tiny splinters of bone from Mosi's gravy, 'Why is it so tough, do you think?'

'It's because the cattle have to walk to market from half way across the country. Be grateful we can afford meat at all, Esme. Most people never have it.' She pushed around a lump of bone with indeterminate adhesions.

'I think I'd rather not bother with this any more.' Esme could hear herself beginning to whine but couldn't stop herself. 'If only we had a fridge with a small freezer compartment, we could store proper meat and eke it out.'

'Esme, *mpenzi*, that filet is expensive and I have already said I cannot afford a fridge on my salary. I wish I could. I understand that you have needed time to get settled and get Mosi settled but, really, we cannot manage any more on just one salary.' Esme felt tears welling; she knew Martin's opinion, he had hinted at it enough times.

'You have noticed all the other mothers go out to work. It's normal for anyone who has been fortunate enough to have an education to find employment, so many people have no choice but to dig the land or work as a servant, doing menial housework.'

'I know what you're saying, Martin, but whenever I think of leaving Mosi with some stranger, I can't bear it.' She remembered the mix up made by Rose and told Martin about it.

'How could she have made such a mistake, Martin?'

Martin looked thoughtful. 'I suppose it's not surprising with the way things are changing so quickly in the country. Women used to work in the fields and keep their babies on their backs – there was no such thing as formula milk. But this young woman would have gone to boarding school where I don't think they teach them about such things.' He shrugged. 'Who would advise her? Even if her mother was around she wouldn't be able to read and she would know no more than her daughter. Everything is changing, sometimes too fast.'

'Aren't there mother and baby clinics?'

'I'm sure there are some, but if she has been working she would only get a month's maternity leave so maybe she didn't manage to go.'

'Now can you understand why I don't want to leave Mosi with someone who doesn't understand my way of doing things?' Esme felt on the verge of tears.

'You will teach them your way. You can have her for a week before you leave her alone with Mosi.' Martin sounded weary. 'Let me make some enquiries about a *yaya* - you could at least meet some women.' He popped a forkful of food into Mosi's mouth, and pulled a face at her making her chuckle. Esme didn't trust herself to speak. She pushed her plate away, her appetite gone.

'As a matter of fact,' Martin went on, there's an advertisement today in *The Standard* for a secretary with the British Council. They would give you the job – English being your mother tongue and with your training. Have a look at it.'

Three weeks later she started the job, working as secretary to Mr Taylor, in charge of the newly-created masters' scholarship scheme. The offices were on the main street of Dar - the tree-lined Independence Avenue, at the quieter end where the sea breeze ventured, in a two-storey colonial building, set slightly back from the road and surrounded by a beautiful garden filled with bushes of frangipani, purple, scarlet, pink and orange bougainvillea and many other flowering shrubs whose names Esme didn't know. Inside were high-ceilings with creaking fans, stone staircases, and arched portals. Despite the cool atmosphere and the courteous colleagues, Esme's palms were sticky with sweat the whole of her first day.

At lunch time they took their sandwiches out onto the spacious, balustraded balcony overlooking the garden, a row of Royal Palms screening them from the road. She followed Julia out onto the balcony to sit in wicker armchairs with the other secretaries round one of the two coffee tables. There was already a group of people at the other table: everyone nodded and smiled politely at each other across the space and then carried on with their conversation. The four girls at her table were pleasant enough, including her in their inconsequential chit-chat but she was too anxious and self-conscious to join in.

At the end of the following morning she was taking dictation from her boss, an inoffensive, weedy little man. When he had finished, he looked at his watch and said: 'Time for tiffin' and began rummaging in his desk drawer. Esme collected her meagre rations from her desk and, as the other girls weren't in the room they shared, she followed Mr Taylor out onto the balcony. No one else was out there so, hesitatingly, she sat down with him. He didn't say anything but he kept clearing his throat looking as uncomfortable as Esme felt. When Julia and the others came out, she thought they smiled strangely at her as they sat at the next table. Then 'The Representative', the head of the British Council, joined Mr Taylor, followed by some other English chap who looked at her as if she was selling fish as he said 'hello' without moving his lips.

Feeling more and more uncomfortable, she began to realise that she was at the wrong table. It must be only for men, she thought. She could feel her face going red and broke into a sweat. Her appetite was gone, the bread stuck in her throat. But, then to add to her confusion, a tall blonde woman she vaguely remembered being introduced to earlier as the librarian, came sashaying over to their table and arranged her diaphanous skirts as she took her seat while undisguisedly glaring at Esme. Then completely confounding her, Narendra, the Asian filing clerk, emerged from the gloom of the office and, nodding deferentially in The Representative's direction, joined the secretaries. Now each table had a mix of sexes. She had no idea what the topic of conversation was at her table – her head was buzzing loudly drowning out their voices and any thought other than that she had committed an unforgivable faux pas.

From that day on she stuck with Julia at lunch time and over the weeks observed that when the gardener, toiling away in the noonday sun, saw the office staff taking their seats above he downed tools and took himself off to the garage round the back to join the other African employees – the fetchers and carriers. And she realised what it was that divided the office staff: on the one table were the 'London Appointed' and on the other the locally-hired: apart from Esme, the second group were wives of expatriates and a few local Asians; whereas the London Appointed employees are on fat contracts, carrying the work of Her Majesty's Government to the far flung corners of the British Empire, the support staff were on a fraction of their pay and conditions. They addressed the 'LA' staff as 'Mr' or, in one case, 'Miss' who, in turn, addressed the more lowly mortals by their first names.

As it turned out the job lasted only two months. Although Esme was vaguely aware of what was going on between governments, it came as a shock to find herself at the end of a chain of events. Ian Smith had declared independence for Rhodesia from Britain which, in its turn, gave recognition to the minority white regime; this incensed the Tanzanian government who consequently severed diplomatic relations with Britain. So the short-lived scholarship scheme closed and she was given two-week's notice – a whole week more than in her contract.

By the time she left she had begun to settle in and almost to enjoy her days there; like most non-government offices in Tanzania, the office closed at four in the afternoon which had given still given her a couple of hours of daylight once she got home. She missed the company. If not exactly a friendship, a sort of camaraderie existed between the secretaries. None of them was ambitious – for the others it was a way of keeping busy while their husbands were out earning the real money. For Esme, of course, it was about keeping their heads above the breadline. And that was the real issue: Martin's pay was even less than Esme's had been. It was, she knew, all to do with President Nyerere's socialist ideal of a classless society. But people like Martin needed an incentive to study for years and she was not sure that it was sufficient simply to hold out the prospect of being able to work in an office, keeping his hands and clothes clean, rather than wielding a heavy hoe in the burning sun day in day out. She knew he aspired to the lifestyle of the expatriates he, and until recently, she had worked with.

In the meantime, they couldn't afford to keep the ayah they had taken on to care for Mosi in Esme's absence and she was back to the old routine which of course had it's compensations, being with Mosi all day. However, Martin had left her in no doubt that she would have to try and find another job soon.

Ch 9: The Driving Test

'Shall we turn left?' It was definitely a question. Not an instruction. Why was he asking a question?

'No.' Esme's tone was confident. 'There's a "No Left Turn" sign.'

'Very good!' he smiled.

She sneaked a glance at him. The examiner's profile was aquiline. He was impeccably turned out in his taupe safari suit, cucumber cool in this mugginess. She felt the dark sweat patches under her arms though she'd worn as little as possible, within the bounds of decency. He politely put her through the final manoeuvres in the empty supermarket car park and asked her to park. He smiled, turning towards her. His glance travelled fleetingly down her body, taking in her too-large breasts and bare knees, before meeting and holding her eyes. Her stomach tightened. He seemed to like what he saw but it was, as always, a puzzle to her. It couldn't be her thin, frizzy red hair, her pasty, freckled face or her plump, sun-reddened arms. Well, they'd probably never meet again if she'd passed her test. He seemed to pause for an age before he said,

'Congratulations, Mama Yusufu. You've passed.'

What a relief!

'Oh, thank you! *Ahsante sana!*' She wanted to hug him but instead put out her hand to shake his.

Martin was waiting outside the test centre, pacing up and down. At the sight of him, his broad-shoulders, bent head and impatient frown, she felt a surge of the old attraction he still held for her.

Martin's expression changed to one of enquiry as he caught sight of her. Then softened into the smile that had ensnared her from their first encounter.

'Congratulations, Sweetheart!' His smile expressed his desire to fondle her. She felt the familiar stirring but knew better than to even put a hand on his arm.

The moment he'd come back from Scotland, Martin had adapted to the taboo on public demonstration of affection between men and women. Walking along the street that first day together in Dar, she had spontaneously clasped his hand and he'd snatched it away. Effectively, it was touching that was barred because, as Martin had once told her, kissing between adults wasn't an African concept. She'd often wondered at his expertise at this alien art.

'Are you impressed with me?'

He laughed. 'You did have a good teacher.' He'd forgotten about Dominic's help. 'But, yes, I am proud of you.'

He took over the controls until they reached his office.

'What time will you be home today?'

'Not late. I'll be back to eat with Mosi.' She wanted to believe him.

She drove alone for the first time through the town centre feeling a new confidence as one of the very few women drivers on the road. She'd known she could drive well enough to pass because the week before her test she'd risked several short trips on her own while Martin had been away on business. Although she'd been told you could get a licence anyway, tales of test examiners taking backhanders – *chai* – her conscience wouldn't allow her to take that route.

This test couldn't have been more different from her first one, three. years earlier, with a faceless official in the middle of Edinburgh's rush-hour. Today driving down acacia-shaded Independence Avenue, past the British Council, the colonial Parliament Building and back around the shimmering blue harbour had been a piece of cake, they'd hardly met any traffic. Now as she neared Kariakoo the road narrowed and she had to negotiate pot-holes and hand-pulled carts piled high with amber mangos and papayas, tomatoes, green and yellow bananas, their 'drivers' hogging the road. There was the occasional battered taxi to contend with too. And the ubiquitous cream single-decker buses whose drivers drove by the rule 'might is right.' Pedestrians, a jostling mass spattered with the vivid colours of women's *kanga* filled the pavements and spilled out onto the road, sidestepping displays of pots and pans spread out in the shade of the balconied pavement. Through her open window the cacophony of voices accompanied the odour of rotting vegetables and diesel fumes. A fly buzzed insistently round her face, attracted by the film of sweat. A queue of carts and cabs built up ahead. Progress was slow.

    Martin had always been beside her latterly when she'd driven through here – giving her directions and grabbing the steering wheel when he feared she would endanger his precious car. She still couldn't work out why he agreed to her learning to drive it in the first place. It was a decent enough car, any car that moved was a trophy, but this red coupé - the only one of its kind in Dar so far as they knew - was wholly impractical: too low to clear the ruts in the road barely any space for Mosi and baggage. As she passed a stationery bus facing the way she'd come, another bus coming towards her abruptly pulled out to overtake a parked vehicle and she realized in panic that both she and the bus were headed for the same narrow space! Couldn't the idiot see her? She glanced in the rear-view mirror: as she thought, there was a solid queue of traffic behind her. She braked and waited for the bus driver to back up. But no, he kept advancing! To her left there was about a foot of space between the car and the crowded pavement. Her heart in her mouth, she veered as far as she dared and closed her eyes as the bus bore steadily down on her. The scrape of metal on metal filled the car.

It was midnight before Martin came back. She'd lain on the bed, racked by anxiety while sweat trickled down her face and body. The bedside fan merely pushed the humid air around the room in waves. What mood would he be in? How would he take it? What were you doing, woman? *He'd* have driven straight at the bus with headlights blazing, leaning on the horn. *He'd* sooner have *died* under the wheels than give a single inch. For him the Red Sea parted. He expected nothing less. He'd say he knew it was a mistake to teach a woman to drive. The histrionics they'd had while he had been teaching her! Shouting and tearing at his hair, her a bag of nerves and completely unable to fathom his instructions. Until the day he couldn't take any more and, without giving her a chance to even take her foot off the accelerator, he'd opened the passenger door and hurled himself out. True, the car was only crawling. He'd ignored her entreaties to get back in the car and stalked off, limping. She'd had to drive back alone, barely able to use the controls for shaking. He'd eventually turned up at home much the worse for drink, obviously very sore. Never referred to leaving her in the lurch. After that, he got Dominic to take over which, she granted, was the turning point. Apart from him being almost as irregular as Martin, reverse parking made *sense* with him, it had boosted her confidence - which now lay in tatters. It was useless lying here crying, it would only make him madder.

He was unusually affectionate that night and she waited till after their lovemaking to confess. Confounding her, he laughed so uproariously that she was afraid he'd wake Mosi. 'You'll have to pay for the repairs, mind you!' He said but she knew he didn't mean it. He was crowing.

All the same, she didn't get the keys even after the damage had been repaired, rather shoddily, she thought. She still had to carry the stuff home from the market on her way home from work and depend on his good will for outings with Mosi to enjoy a glimpse of the sea at Oyster Bay.

A few days later, Martin came home early, almost straight from work. He brought in two bottles of lager and put them in the fridge, saying they'd have them later after Mosi had gone to bed. She couldn't remember the last time Martin and she had spent an evening together.

'I wonder sometimes what you really think of me,' she said when they were sitting side-by-side on the settee. 'You're out so much of the time.'

'I love you, baby, you know that. *Umeniloga!* You've bewitched me! That's what my friends say, they really do. Because I *don't* stay out all night, have to go home to the wife! Things like that. And I won't marry another woman because "Esme wouldn't like it."

'But you're a Christian so you'd have to divorce me before marrying again.' Martin laughed.

'There's more than one way to skin a cat! I've no plans to divorce you, my sweet. I tell you, I'm under your spell. '

'That's what being in love is! What about your child? You're home late so much, Martin, you hardly see anything of her.'

'Nonsense! I spend a lot of time at home with you both. You seem to think children need their father around all the time. Of course, they don't. They need a mother, aunts, grandmothers – lots of women and other children. Men have other things to do – children are women's work. Even in monogamous households the wife isn't alone. Your trouble is you want to live like they do in Scotland these days, one woman two point something children. It's not the African way, *mpenzi*. You have refused to have my relatives to come and live with us. Not even a house-girl! So you get lonely, obviously. It's not my job to hold your hand all the time. If you had company here you wouldn't make a fuss about me going out for the odd beer.'

'But Martin, you didn't tell me this when we planned to come here. I thought it'd be like when we were together in Edinburgh. You shared everything with me there! You cooked, and changed Mosi's nappy and bathed her! I even agreed to calling her 'First' because you were so proud of your first-born.'

'Don't start crying, Esme, please! When I planned to come back here it was with a decent car, not a child and a wife! I'm sorry if you thought it would be like Edinburgh, maybe I did too, but I just can't let my friends think that I've turned into an *Mzungu* and lost all my masculinity, wearing an apron and going in the kitchen. I'd be a laughing stock!

Esme had known somewhere in the back of her mind that this was what it was all about and yes, she could understand what he was saying, but just as Martin didn't want to be a European husband, she hadn't been prepared to be an African wife – not if this was what it involved.

'If you had a co-wife, or at least some of your sisters-in-law with you, you wouldn't depend so much on me. You wouldn't mind me going out for a beer in the evening.'

'Is that all it is, Martin? Having "a beer"? Do you go with other women?'

'Of course I don't! You know you're the love of my life, I would never be unfaithful to you!'

Part Two - Circa 1973
Ch 10: The Ad Agency

Waiting for a bus home from work, despite having stood so often for so many hours in the sweaty press of bodies crowding into the shade of the building, she couldn't ignore the beauty of the panorama before her: the cerulean blue of the horseshoe harbour fringed with the brilliantly flowering flame trees, the cream-painted nineteenth century Lutheran church in the foreground, the cranes of the port on the far side of the bay, barely discernible through the heat haze, like praying mantis.

It infuriated her that people couldn't respect her little bit of space but she told herself such a concept held no meaning here. Her thoughts drifted. She was not particularly looking forward to going home, though, of course, she wanted to be back with Mosi and Alistair - Ali, he was inevitably known as. She hated living in the flats in Ilala now: it was no longer the pristine and tranquil area that they had moved into, one of three blocks of flats. With the addition of nine more blocks, the neighbourhood was now bustling, noisy. A track joining two main roads ran between the buildings and there was a constant stream of traffic.

After twenty minutes a bus hove into sight bringing her back to the present. The crowd surged forward but fell back with a collective groan as the bus crawled straight past their stop, obviously full and leaning alarmingly to one side, passengers hanging out of the open door.

It hadn't been bad there when they'd first moved in and everything was newly-built. Mosi had been able to go to the little nursery school on the estate as soon as she was three. Now six, she had outgrown it and attended the bigger nursery school run by the YWCA in town, travelling in with Martin and herself in the office Combi which came for him every morning. The driver dropped Esme and Mosi off at the school, only a short walk from there to Esme's office. She needed to remind herself how terribly lucky they were to have such a service. Not only that, the driver collected Mosi and took her home at lunch time. Esme couldn't think how they would have managed without such a privilege - which continued even on occasions when Martin was out of town for work. She felt guilty at the thought of it. The driver probably couldn't afford to pay school fees for his older children let alone for kindergarten. Yet how often did she feel sorry for herself? Like now because she had to find her own way home while Martin stayed late at work.

Another bus rounded the corner and pulled into their stop. Yes, it was going to Ilala - at last! She spent the next few minutes battling her way onto the bus – queues were another unknown concept – where she stood squashed together with the majority of passengers like dates in a pack. All were equal here: old, young, black, white, male or female - even when pregnant as she knew too well. They lurched and rolled for quarter of an hour to her stop.

It was a relief to step out into the relative cool as the sun began to drop and a light breeze rustled the coconut palms. She was looking forward to getting home, kicking off her sandals and putting her feet up. She could do without any more incidents with Ali. Since he finally got off all fours aged two-and-a-half, he darted everywhere like a lunatic, his eyes anywhere but where he was headed. If anything he was more of a danger to himself than when he had first learnt to crawl. A few weeks ago coming back from work, as she had turned to mount the last flight of concrete steps up to the flat, her eyes had met Ali's peering over the top step - apparently about to launch himself head first.

'Ali!' she had screamed. Seeing his mother, his face broke into a broad smile of delight as she stumbled towards him catching her shin against one of the sharp edges, her heart pounding,

'Stay there, Ali, *Mama*'s coming!'. She had got to him just before he'd gone over the edge and sat on the top step, clutching him to her. When she carried him into the flat, Esme found

Stella, the heavily pregnant *yaya*, seated on the bench in the children's room, fast asleep. Esme had felt awful about it, but they had to let the *yaya* go, and find a replacement.

The new *yaya*, again some relative of a colleague of Martin's, looked too old to get pregnant but Esme still wasn't too sure she was the right person for the job. She held some strange beliefs about the superiority of white people; it seemed to Esme that having been employed by a series of British families before independence, she had been somehow brainwashed by them. According to her, those were the good old days. Esme's main concern, however, was whether Mama Zawadi was a match for Ali's strength of character but neither would she be too hard on him.

That evening, after Mama Zawadi took her leave, Esme's attempt to sit with her feet up were frustrated by Ali's insistence that they 'Go out, *Mama*!' He tried cajoling and tugging at her hand and when no longer appeased by her pleas of 'In a minute, Ali, *mpenzi*,' he resorted to yelling 'Outside, outside' until she gave in.

At least sitting on the steps of their block as she watched Ali and Mosi and their play-mates sitting at the edge of the car park, on the soft ridge of sand, she could enjoy the balmy evening air.

Suddenly, to her horror, she saw Ali shoot out on all-fours into the path of a reversing car.

She was on her feet in a trice, screaming 'Ali, Ali!' as she ran towards him but was in time only to see him disappear beneath the car wheels. Convinced he'd be horribly crushed, she was crying and shouting hysterically at the driver who mercifully had been driving very slowly and immediately stopped. Then as Esme threw herself onto the ground beside the car she saw Ali crawling out - whole. At the sight of her he began to cry at the top of his lungs and submitted unresistingly to Esme's embraces, but there was no mangled flesh, not even any blood. Her screams had brought out several neighbours, including a woman about Esme's age she had never met before.

'Let me look, I'm a nurse,' she said in English, and to Ali, soothingly: '*Pole, baba*'. Ali succumbed docilely to her calm, authoritative manner as she quickly checked him from head to foot. 'He looks as if he has no injuries,' she said, 'but come inside where I can examine him properly.' She led them into her ground-floor flat where she laid Ali gently on the sofa. He had stopped crying now and was now looking around him in interest at his surroundings. 'No broken bones and no damage at all as far as I can tell,' she said. Esme noticed a slightly lilting accent. 'Look - you can see where a wheel of the car has actually run over his leg.' She pointed to faint red tyre marks on Ali's tan calf. 'But his bones are soft and he is nice and chubby, I think he will be fine but, of course, you need to keep any eye on him.'

She then introduced herself as Mina and over a glass of Fanta they chatted. Mina, a slim, attractive woman in her thirties with light brown complexion and black hair, worked in a private clinic run by the Hindu Mandal but was herself a Muslim. Esme liked her instantly and felt completely at ease with her. Then her husband came back from work. As he extended his hand to Esme and introduced himself as Luka, Esme noticed his big toothy grin and a gold crucifix around his neck. His colouring was similar to Mina's but whereas her hair, pulled back in a bun, was smooth and glossy, his hair had the same wiry texture as Ali's. Lovely - even more mixed up than our family, Esme thought.

That evening, after she had put the children to bed and they were sitting surrounded by crayons and scribbled-on sheets of paper, Esme related the incident of Ali and the car to Martin.

'I feel sick at the thought of how it could have ended. There is simply nowhere safe for the kids to play. They need a garden! I need a garden, I want to be able to do some gardening.'

'Gardening is for peasants,' Martin replied. 'The safety of the children, though, that is a different matter. Do you have to let them out, Esme?' She noted the use of her name, not 'Mama Mosi' or 'Mama Ali' – usually an indicator of his disapproval.

'Are you serious? Can you imagine yourself, as a child, or even now, being cooped up in here twenty-four hours a day or just going out while one of us can hold on to them? You mean let them cry and bang on the door with their fists and keep them in like prisoners? They're children, they have to get out to have fresh air and to exercise and to ... to be children! If you spent more time with them you could take them out but you hardly seem to be here in the flat in the hours of daylight anyway!'

They had argued then, heatedly, ending in Martin slamming the door - the same door he'd advocated keeping shut - as he went 'for some peace.'

When she woke the following morning, she was glad it was a work day. As she showered, leaving the children romping round the bedroom under Martin's eye, she reflected on the realisation that - as long as she kept any concerns about the children at the back of her mind - she was happiest when at work. Although Ali often made a fuss for her benefit as she was leaving, he had got used to her being out during the day.

Entering the first of the four interconnected rooms that comprised the office of East African Advertising Agency, she was surprised to find Mr Carter, the English Managing Director, sitting at the small table that served as the reception desk, the broadsheet *The Standard* spread out before him.

'Morning, Esme,' he said with a resigned smile. 'Tabu won't be in today, she sent someone to tell me, she's lost another of her uncles, I think it was. You'll have to take turns on the switchboard today. Our staff seem to have a very big extended families and a heck of a lot of deaths to mourn.' Esme, smiled back and nodded. Old Carter wasn't at all a bad boss, especially compared to the expatriates in her last job at the British Council.

'I'll take over now if you like,' she said. The phone wasn't exactly ringing off the hook and there were only half a dozen extensions but it wouldn't look too impressive to a prospective client walking in to find the boss on the front desk. Not that many did these days. A call came in at that moment and she answered it as she seated herself at the desk.

'I'll see if Mr Macha is available,' she told the caller, knowing it was highly unlikely that the philandering account executive would be at his desk at eight in the morning. A few moments later, her doubts confirmed, she took a message. She responded to several calls in the next few minutes, most for Kaliwe, the other account executive who had always begun work by the time she arrived. She wouldn't have been surprised if he slept there, except that she knew from their conversations that he was a very conscientious husband and father.

Hassani, the head messenger, arrived then. *'Habari za asubuhi, Mzee.'* Esme said, knowing the title of respect for a senior man never failed to rile him. He couldn't lay claim to the title on the basis of rank, which left seniority in age; no-one knew his actual age but he clearly believed himself to be younger and more virile than the rest of the staff did.

As he took over the switchboard from Esme, Hassani and she exchanged the usual ritual of greetings in Swahili and, as always, the 'news' of the day, home and wife was 'good'. Then they started conversing and he explained that his wife had miscarried. He was now onto his fourth wife, none of the others having obliged him with offspring. Esme couldn't help but feel sorry for him. The staff shared a camaraderie which Carter wasn't part of. It seemed to her to be less to do with his position than his lack of the language. When she had started working there, she had barely spoken Swahili but to her surprise she had found she understood nearly everything that was said. As it had been with French at school, anxiety about making mistakes held her back from speaking it whenever she could be understood in English. Hassani and his team had cured her of that as their knowledge of English was minimal and communicating with them was essential for her job.

Scanning *The Standard* was part of everyone's routine, ostensibly to see how their ads looked, to check up on their sole rival and to generally keep aware of trends and developments in local commerce – alarmingly on the decline lately. It also gave Esme a chance to catch up on such world news as was reported. Martin always read the paper when he was home but she never had the time. She was glad to note today that Nixon had ordered a ceasefire in Vietnam at last. Then her eye was caught by an advert for brand new houses for sale, the first she had ever seen and, even more astonishing, was an accompanying offer of a mortgage. She studied the full-page ad and mulled it over as she typed up the drafted letters and advertising copy in her in-tray; the usual stuff, a few spelling and grammatical errors to be corrected and some rephrasing, just demanding enough to keep her attention but nothing to over-strain the little grey cells. She enjoyed her job.

When Kaliwe next came in with some typing for her to do she pointed out the ad to him. 'What do you think of these houses?'

'What houses?' he asked, with a smile, prepared to be enlightened, taking up his perch on the corner of her desk. Esme had noted that he only sat in the chair opposite her when he had work to discuss. Most of their time together was spent in friendly discussions which she looked increasingly forward to; she and Martin no longer seemed to engage in such activity.

Esme showed Kaliwe the sketches. 'The single-storey houses. Do you think it's a good offer? I really like the look of them.'

Kaliwe was initially baffled as to what was actually on offer; he confirmed that building houses in order to sell them was a completely unknown phenomenon in Tanzania. Esme knew that Kaliwe, like many Dar dwellers, had been struggling for the past two years to build his own house on a small plot of land in one of the haphazard, rapidly expanding suburbs. She had driven past some of these unofficial settlements with Martin and, although the houses for the most part were substantial structures of concrete blocks, Esme couldn't bear the prospect of living without proper access-roads or water and electricity supplies which were all, according to Martin, cobbled together by bungling householders and inept tradesmen.

'It would be impossible for a private enterprise to embark on such a scheme since all the land is owned by the state,' Kaliwe said now. 'I don't actually own my plot of land – the man I paid for it didn't own it either so he didn't have the right to sell it for building on. He's only allowed to cultivate it. But here in Dar, it goes on all the time, the poor peasants who live in the villages around the edges of the town have become rich overnight, selling the tiny plots of land that have been in their family for generations.'

'But it's a good thing, isn't it, if it gives the family a better standard of living?' she asked. Kaliwe liked explaining stuff about local life to her and he never scoffed at her questions.

'Probably some men use the money wisely. Unfortunately, some of them go and blow the lot on alcohol and don't think about the fact that they've got no means of livelihood for the rest of their days. Then when their children start crying with empty bellies they have to go and beg for jobs as security guards with the very people they sold their land to!' Esme knew Kaliwe didn't drink or approve of alcohol.

'Will you employ a guard?' she was teasing him now.

'No, of course not! My house will be tiny and burglars won't be interested in it. Anyway God will look after us.'

She ignored the last remark, she'd had religion rammed down her throat from as far back as she could remember. It was the one area Kaliwe and herself seemed not be in accord over. She looked down at the newspaper spread out on the desk.

'Well, maybe the government is responding to the situation you described. This is organised by the Ministry of Housing.' Esme referred to the small print in the advertisement. 'It says here the houses will remain the property of the National Housing Bank until the mortgage is fully paid off. That must take about twenty years!'

'Better go and talk to your husband about it then.' Kaliwe stood up. 'And I'd better get on with some work.'

At this point Macha came in, his clothes particularly shabby but his broad grin, despite his bloodshot eyes, disarming her, as always.

'Hello, gorgeous.' She pretended not to register the endearment. She persistently treated his flirtatious remarks with feigned disdain but it never failed to lift her on gloomy days. She took a sidelong look at Kaliwe, checking his reaction but he was on his feet, moving towards the door adjoining the studio, his face inscrutable. Macha needed some information from Kaliwe and the two of them went off together. Esme turned back to the advert and found her heart racing. She would have to wait till this evening to talk to Martin and she wasn't confident that he would share her enthusiasm, see this scheme for the unique opportunity it was.

That evening when he arrived home, the kids still up and about, Martin announced he was being sent the following day on business to Arusha in the north of the country. He picked up Ali who hugged his father and gabbled at him. Mosi sitting in her little chair with a picture book on the coffee table in front of her, looked on.

'Why so suddenly?' Esme asked. 'Do you have to go? I don't like being on my own. And I have something I need to talk to you about.' She had hoped to introduce the topic and then give him a day or two to consider it and hopefully come up with a plan for the deposit.

'Of course I have to go! You won't be on your own, anyway, you'll have the children.' This wasn't the start to the evening she'd wanted.

Once the children were in bed she showed the article to Martin. He took the paper from her and she watched his expression as he looked at the artist's sketch and the floor plan of the houses. 'The houses look good. But I'm not prepared to commit myself to such a huge amount of money.'

'But you wouldn't be paying it by yourself – I'd be helping.' Martin still kept hold of the paper, that was promising. She stayed quiet to allow him the chance to read the advert more closely and digest the content.

'Another of the President's ideas, no doubt, financed by more foreign aid, probably a Nordic notion.' Esme kept quiet. 'There are plenty of properties to rent here these days, since the government took over the properties that the owners didn't actually live in.'

'And then kicked them out if they were Asian.' Esme couldn't resist.

'They weren't kicked out, Esme. They were foreign nationals who had lived here for years –

a lot of them were even born here – and yet they refused to become Tanzanian citizens, like you did. Nyerere won't tolerate some people raking in millions while the workers have to pay exorbitant rents to them.'

'Well, this is all part of the same philosophy, then, to provide affordable housing for everyone,' Esme said. This wasn't the conversation she had planned. She still wasn't sure if Martin was coming round to the idea or not.

'Affordable! I'm glad you think it's affordable. The initial payment is a huge amount. I don't have that kind of money lying about, have you?'

'No, I don't but I thought maybe you could borrow it – from work? Think what it would mean for us, Martin, no stairs for the kids to fall down, safe area for them to play. And a little courtyard all to ourselves, doors open letting in the cool air!'

'There's no point in thinking about it - I can't get hold of that amount of money and even if I could, we'd still have to pay it back.'

'The deadline is the end of the month and they'll probably be snapped up before that.' Martin gave her a hard look. 'Esme, just forget about it.'

Ch 11: New House in Dar

They moved after work one Saturday nine months later; Martin had wangled the loan of the office's Combi and driver. Esme felt guilty knowing that after the move he would have to park the Combi at the office and wait for a bus home and hoped Martin really had given him adequate compensation for his willingness and hard work.

Since she and Martin had been together, it was the sixth time they had moved but the first initiated by them rather than events. Esme had no regrets about leaving the flats. She would miss some of the neighbours for a while but there were no real attachments holding her back. The Hungarian woman had moved elsewhere and they had lost touch. Mina the nurse and her husband Luka, who had become good friends, had promised to visit them and as they had a car, went everywhere together and were very sociable, she believed they would.

Their new housing estate was set among coconut palms again: these plantations seemed to cover vast areas around Dar es Salaam. Who owned them? Every now and then a man in a torn T-shirt and shorts of indeterminate colour, a machete on his shoulder, wandered wordlessly into their unfenced back garden. With the aid of a leather belt fastened loosely around his waist and the trunk of the tree, he walked up each of the two trees in their garden to harvest the coconuts.

For the first few days, Esme lived in constant fear of one of the children, or even Martin or herself, being killed by a falling fruit encased in its husk – twice the size and weight of a de-husked coconut - and its mass increased incalculably by the fall of some twenty metres. Luckily, they had a sanctuary within the larger garden – a small walled area which was safe and relatively private, being enclosed by decorative latticed walls taller than Martin.

It was the third time they had moved into a brand new building and not all the houses on the estate were occupied yet, or even completed. However, all those on their little road were finished. Next door on one side, separated by a couple of metres and what promised to be a hedge in a few years time, lived the Mushi family with their eight kids. Both Martin and Esme soon learned to avoid the husband: he would keep them for hours giving them his opinion on the state of the world. The wife apparently taught at a local primary school. She was very pleasant to converse with but every few seconds her voice lashed out in an command or reprimand to any of her children she caught sight of, or who might even have been indoors, and it was a relief when she terminated the conversation to go and keep order more forcefully. Then they would hear the cries for forgiveness of Yohana and Maria, the two older children, accompanied by the sound of prolonged walloping. The kids were only around Mosi's age and had become playmates, never putting a foot wrong as far as Esme could see, but to hear these exchanges you would think they were the worst-behaved children in the country.

On the other side, in the house adjoining Esme's, lived a smartly-dressed, young Ugandan couple. Apparently they were renting from a private landlord. Martin had tried to extract the landlord's identity out of the tenants but they feigned ignorance. Martin concluded that it must be a politician who was above the law which forbade an individual owning more than one residence and profiting from rent while so many urban immigrants were unable to secure adequate housing. The Ugandans could barely speak any Swahili but their English was perfect. However, they spent hardly any time at home and when they did they seemed to have the company of other young Ugandans.

The neighbours beyond next door, she gradually discovered, like Mrs Mushi and herself, had jobs and came home from work to look after the house and children, though all had live-in house-servants who seemingly continued their duties until they went to bed at night. The women of the households met up if they were out in the garden or passing by, but there was no inviting each other in for tea and, once the initial euphoria of the move had lessened, she missed the company she had at work.

One house on the opposite side of the road remained unoccupied for several weeks until Mosi came in from playing one afternoon, full of excitement:

'*Mama*! Guess what! An *Mzungu* mummy has moved into the empty house! They've got a girl and two boys.'

Ulla turned out to be Finnish. Many an hour they were to spend together lamenting their lot: husbands out drinking till all hours, wives at home minding the children. This wasn't what they had signed up to. But what could they do? In due course, they were joined in weekly tea-parties by Jocelyn – the American mother of Mosi's best friend, Jano, at nursery and Marietta, another Finnish woman. These two lived further afield but had occasional access to their husbands' cars. All were married to Tanzanians and wondered what they had got themselves into. The children were all of similar ages and played well together most of the time, although Ali was still very self-willed and was also possessive of Esme so constantly interrupted the women's discussions. The women bemoaned their fate and then got on with it because they could see no alternative.

All their conversations were in English – a second language for all except Esme who they deferred to quite often. It boosted her confidence, as it did at work, to be regarded as knowledgeable on the subject. She realised that her Swahili too was actually a lot better than the other women's. In some ways, as well, her lot was better than theirs: Ulla suspected her husband, a very handsome doctor ten years younger than her, of being a Lothario. Marietta's husband never gave her any money and, as she didn't have a job, always struggled to buy enough food and clothes for the kids. Esme felt disloyal, complaining about Martin, but it was a relief at times to unburden herself. She used to feel she was somehow to blame, that she could have done more to keep Martin's interest in her till she discovered that the others were in exactly the same boat. But then Martin would be loving and attentive for a while and she would feel guilty, especially as Martin seemed not to mind her consorting with the other *Wazungu* wives. This was her – and their - lot having chosen to marry an African man even though, in her case at least, she hadn't been prepared for him to change his behaviour so radically once he set foot back on his own soil.

Of course, her father had warned her: 'Marriage is difficult enough when you're both from the same culture …' And when she had refused to heed his advice, he had wagged a finger at her saying, 'don't say I didn't warn you - you've made your bed, now lie in it!' She had pooh-poohed this notion as she had all his views on society: he regarded all Irish as feckless and drink-swilling (even though he had married an Irish woman who was neither) and men with beards were deemed untrustworthy. As a teenager, she'd been forbidden to associate with the local boys from the council houses – not that they had wanted anything to do with her – because of their inferior class. So how could she possibly have thought back then that he might have been right about cross-cultural marriage? No, she could never go back to Scotland – not just because she couldn't bear her father to have the satisfaction of being in the right - but, much more importantly, because she was quite sure Martin would not let her take the kids and, even if she could spirit them away, she didn't think she could bring herself to separate Ali and Mosi from him. They adored him. The fact that he was hardly ever home before they were in bed didn't seem to diminish their adoration of him. It only increased their yearning: it was true then, 'absence makes the heart grow fonder'. Martin had often walked out in fury following a row, taking a suitcase, saying he would never come back, but she had never threatened it, although she'd been bursting to, because she had no money and she would *never* leave the kids. So even when she was at her most desperate, all she could do was go into the bedroom and sob her heart out. She was trapped and Martin knew it.

Esme read a lot in the long evenings while Martin was out and the children were asleep. In line with Tanzania's socialist policy, books were available to anyone who could read and who lived near enough to a library And luckily for Esme, because so few books had been written and published in Swahili, the vast majority of the library stock was in English. Esme read *The L-Shaped Room* and could relate to so much in it but was shocked by the way the narrator – a woman not much older than herself - had described her fellow-lodger, John, in animalistic terms. Esme could hardly believe that people could think like that in the twentieth century.

Her first encounter with 'negroes' – the polite name for them – had perplexed her rather than anything. It would have been in the early sixties one Sunday morning after church in their little town. Esme's mother had spotted the black man and woman with two small children, standing apart from the mingling groups and had gone up to shake their hands. She called Esme and her brother over and introduced them to Dr Koka and his painfully shy family from Nigeria. Esme had been struck by how diffident even he – a doctor – had seemed. Until then doctors had been placed on high, alongside teachers, as demigods and had behaved like them.

A few years later, visiting Martin on a work-placement in Camden, they had been followed down the street by a group of youths singing the line from the song, 'Black is black'. It had embarrassed and angered her for Martin's sake. He had said nothing, tight-lipped. In Edinburgh it had been more subtle. On the rare occasion they'd been out for a meal, the waiters had studiously ignored them until they had left without being served. It was only when she told her father about her relationship with Martin that she had realised how deeply prejudiced he was. Her mother had only wept and hugged Esme to her.

How she missed her mother at such times. Not that Esme would have told her anything that reflected badly on Martin but she would have known Esme was troubled. Esme well knew that her Ma understood about the pain a husband could inflict – not the physical but the emotional sort.

Ch 12: What's in a Name?

'*Mzungu*!' '*Mzungu*!' Whitie! The all-too-familiar name-calling of the group of children as she passed. It was always the same with kids unless they actually knew her. Then she was transformed into a person with a name – instead of being labelled by the way she looked. She was sick of it. It made her remember how she felt as a child – groups of kids shouting out 'Cattydog, cattydog.' It had been her uniform from the Catholic school that had inspired those shouts. At least she could change into other clothes then and be anonymous. But she couldn't change the colour of her skin.

She'd been using this path for months. But what really made her boil inside was the adults who seemed to find it amusing. Why didn't they tell the brats to shut up? She'd vary her reaction to the taunts, depending on her mood. Sometimes she tried to reason with them: 'My name isn't *Mzungu*. Call me Mama Mosi.' She was aware as she spoke that this was not her own name but, along with every woman who had ever given birth, she was now eternally labelled as the mother of her child.

This injunction only further amused the kids.

'*Nipe hela*, *Mzungu*!' one of them shouted. That infuriated her even more! Asking her for money. An *Mzungu* was automatically assumed to have money to dish out – as indeed most of the expatriates did. If only the kids knew, she was hard pressed to make ends meet at all in this period of shortage and black-marketeering.

Sometimes she really lost her temper and berated them furiously for their lack of manners. Which sent them into paroxysms of laughter. Today she held her head high, clenched her fists and gritted her teeth, feigning to ignore them.

To stop coming this way – just to buy some little thing for the household: some fruit, matches, salt, whatever it was they'd run out of - would be to admit defeat. More than that, she'd be denied what was otherwise a pleasure. It was another world here, so different from the city where she worked, only three or four miles away. It was even a stark contrast to her own suburban housing estate that had been built in the midst of a vast coconut plantation. Here were only a few sandy tracks leading off the main road, bordered with simple square houses – some in concrete blocks with corrugated iron roofs, others older, built from poles plastered with mud and thatched with coconut palms. Away from the children's shouts, it was sleepy and peaceful – the only sounds the sea-breeze rustling the palms, the odd cockerel crow.

By the time she'd reached the little shop – actually a kiosk operated out of one room of the owner's house - the shouts had subsided. The shopkeeper, Mashaka, was his usual affable self. They exchanged the almost ritual greetings - queries about each others' health, home, family and work.

Habari za nyumbani?

Nzuri. Habari za kazi?

Safi. Habari za watoto?

Wazima, Ahsante.

'*Jua kali leo.* The sun's very fierce today,' he said as he measured the rice out in what had once been a kilo margarine tin.

She suppressed a smile. '*Joto sana*,' she agreed. It *was* hot today. It was hot every day - well at least three hundred days of the year. If they were lucky they'd get away with the remaining sixty-five being cloudy enough to reduce it from scorching to steaming – in between the downpours. But, like in England, commenting on the weather was a safe subject, once you'd run out of *habari*s.

She trudged back through the deep sand at the edge of the track, just to enjoy the sensation of burning hot sand spilling over the flip-flops onto her feet. She wasn't even dressed like a *Mzungu* she thought, with a surge of irritation, as she neared the gang of kids and the chorus started up again. Like every other woman in sight she wore a brightly-patterned *kanga* wrapped round her waist, covering her lower half and legs to her ankles. It wasn't as if she went around in a crotch-length skirt and bikini top, as did some of the tourists in town. No wonder they'd started the crackdown on what was considered indecent dress and was very offensive to a lot of people. 'Operation Cover Up' was how the campaign was known on the streets. The trouble was it had got out of hand and citizens wearing perfectly modest outfits - in Esme's view - were being arrested by over-zealous members of the People's Militia because their clothing didn't completely cover their knees. Her thoughts drifted to the next day, Monday, and whether she had anything ironed to wear to work. She'd have to see to that when she got in.

As she passed the back of next-door's garden she waved to her neighbour, Mrs Mushi, who was wielding a heavy hoe above her head, bringing it down into the hard-baked soil. Apart from when she was teaching at the nearby primary school and disciplining her kids, Mama Peter was forever busy in her vegetable garden. No wonder, with eight kids below the age of ten to feed. Even with two salaries she and her husband faced an uphill struggle.

They chatted for a few minutes - Mama Peter wiping her brow with the hem of her *kanga* as she paused for breath. After the usual trading of greetings, the older woman asked: 'Did you hear on the radio this afternoon about those women being kept all weekend in the police cells for wearing indecent clothes?' she asked.

'No – what happened?'

'There was a round-up in town last Saturday after the offices closed at noon – about twenty women were put into a militia van and taken to a police station to be given a telling off. But because all the senior officers had already gone off duty for the weekend, instead of the women being let out later that day, they were kept in all that day, all of Sunday and only released on Monday morning!'

'*Maskini*! Were they all people coming from work or were some of them tourists?'

'No – they never touch the tourists, do they? Well, I have never heard of it happening, have you?'

'No, they always seem to get away with it. Even though they're given guidelines at the airport. They don't care. If a few actually got arrested, word would soon get round and they'd pay a bit more attention to the dress code.'

'*Na kweli*. You are right, Mama Mosi.'

'*Haya*, Mama Peter, I'd better go and make sure I have something decent to wear tomorrow. *Wasalimie nyumbani*.'

Esme went straight to her wardrobe to put out one of her two 'decent' dresses for ironing. Neither of them was there. They must both be still in the dirty washing. That's right,

Mama Zawadi, their housekeeper, had been unwell and hadn't felt up to doing the washing on Friday. It hadn't crossed Esme's mind till now. It was only at times like this that she felt deprived of a washing machine. Most of the time she was aware of how privileged she was to have a housekeeper who did the laborious laundry by hand. But unlike her African neighbours, Esme didn't have her housekeeper living in and on call twenty-four hours a day. Could she really be bothered to wash a dress now and anyway would it be dry by morning now that it was nearly sunset? For once she wished she had a few of those quick drying, non-iron polyester things but she found them intolerably hot and smelly in the heat. She could, as a last resort, cover up with a *kanga*, she thought. But, no, while it felt natural in this neighbourhood, it would feel completely unsuitable in town. A bit like going to the office in England in pair of jog bottoms. She reached a decision: she would wear the dress which she had let down to the last eighth of an inch. It now came half way down her knee. Chances were she wouldn't meet any militia - she hadn't so far. She'd iron the dress after she'd got the supper and the kids were in bed.

Esme went out on the veranda with the tray of dried beans she needed for the meal. There was just enough light from the red-gold sky to be able to pick out those that had weevils in. The air was balmy. She sat with her eyes closed for a minute, enjoying the silky warmth of the gentle breeze on her face and arms. She loosened the *kanga* round her waist and let the air circulate round her legs. It really was the local women who were being targeted by this dress code, she thought, as she scrutinised the beans one by one. Even though it was officially aimed at both locals and tourists, men and women, in reality the tourists got away with - at worst - a stern warning and the local men were unaffected: no self-respecting adult male citizen would be seen outside his back yard in a pair of shorts. They'd had enough of compulsory wearing of shorts during the colonial period or while at school, according to Martin. Full-length, usually well pressed, Western trousers seemed to symbolise their independence just as short skirts and plunging necklines did for the women. Breasts - banished from sight decades ago under the influence of Muslims and Victorian Christians – were now being flaunted by young women who were more influenced by fashions from the West than by religion or tradition.

A mosquito landed on her arm, reminding her of the approaching night. She went back indoors, switching on the lights and put the beans to soak in boiling water while she sorted and washed the rice. It was time the children were back. She'd give them ten more minutes and then she'd have to do the rounds of the neighbours. She wasn't concerned for their safety, she knew they'd be in one or another of their play-mates' homes where they were always welcome, she just wasn't in the mood for all the chatting it would entail. Maybe she was still a *Mzungu* in that respect. She enjoyed her own company at times. Just as well with a husband who enjoyed the company of other men, in some bar, evening after evening. That was what 'normal' men did. Ever since he'd got back from overseas with a foreign wife, he'd been bending over backwards to prove he was still a normal man.

Next morning at the bus stop she surveyed the skirt lengths of other women in the crowd. Most skirts ended just below the knee. A few were decidedly above the knee. She spotted one of her neighbours and went over to join her. Eventually a bus approached. They said hasty farewells and pushed their way into the crowd – now three times as big - surging over the grass verge towards the edge of the road. Once you were in the midst of the scrum there was only one way to go – forward. If you didn't push ahead of you, you'd be pushed aside. It didn't matter who you were or what your condition. Everyone had a single thought only – to get through the bus door. She made it – feeling battered and grimy from the pressing of hot flesh. No hope of a seat of course. Anyway, at least she'd get to work in time. Her colleagues nearly always managed it somehow, even though they came from much further out.

At her stop in the city centre she pushed and squeezed her way out of the bus. She stood for a moment, breathing in the relatively fresh air after the oven-like heat of the bus and the smell of a hundred sweaty bodies. She looked down at her crumpled, cotton dress - ironing that had been a waste of time!

As she rounded the corner onto Independence Avenue, she saw a stream of people running in her direction. As they approached she realised they were all women and she picked out two familiar faces – Shida and Furaha - they worked in the same building as her. One of them waved urgently at Esme and as they neared she called out breathlessly:

'*Mgambo*! The militia are at the top of the street.' Shida cast a quick glance at Esme's hemline and grabbed her arm as she ran, crying: 'Let's go, Esme.' Esme turned with them, anxiety rising in her chest.

'Where are we going?'

'We can get round this way to our building.'

'Are you sure they're not following us? How many were there?' Esme looked over her shoulder without slackening her pace.

'Only one, but it was that short, mad one.' The 'mad militiaman' was legendary for his missionary zeal to stamp out indecency on the streets. It was said he literally measured how far short of the mark women's dresses fell.

'Oh God! Let's hurry up.' Esme was seized by panic. Till now, Furaha hadn't spoken. She was a big woman and was obviously finding the running difficult.

'Esme, why are you running?' she suddenly asked. 'You should not worry. Europeans won't be caught.'

Shida looked quickly at Esme. Esme was searching for a response. Shida answered for her: 'She only looks like an *Mzungu*. Really she is an African.'

'But if the Militiaman sees her they will see a *Mzungu* and they will not catch her.'

'What do you know, my friend?' panted Shida. 'Anyway, we have already arrived – we are safe now.' Shida gave a final glance over her shoulder as she entered the office building. The three of them sat down gratefully on the stairs, panting and wiping the perspiration from their faces. Esme noticed that Shida's tight skirt ended a good four inches above her knees. Furaha's, on the other hand, just brushed the top of hers. After recovering their breath, they exchanged congratulatory remarks on their escape and warned one another to be careful in future. Shida and Furaha went into the freight office on the first floor while Esme dragged her self up to her office on the second floor. It felt like coming home as she went in. Here she wasn't an *Mzungu*; she wasn't Mosi's mother. To her work mates she was 'Esme'.

When they heard what had happened to her that morning she was given tea and sympathy until she was sufficiently recovered to tackle some work. The day passed like any other - a few minor emergencies but no one got stressed and she finished at her usual time, half an hour before the others.

As she stepped out of the building there, directly across the road from her, was the mad militiaman. Till now she'd only seen him at a distance. He was immediately recognisable by his short build and ferocious expression. He was marching straight for her, his eyes fixed on her hemline, and an expression of outrage on his face. As he drew up in front of her, meeting her eyes, she was aware that she was looking down at him. It was not often that she found herself taller than a man but he must be constantly in such a situation. That must antagonise him, she thought, being looked down on by women as well as practically all men. In some rural areas women still had to approach men on their knees and avert their eyes. With an effort she met his manic glare. He held a metre-length ruler in his right hand and thwacked it against his thigh. The veins on his neck stood out with the clenching of his jaw. She really didn't want to have a confrontation with this man. Nor to be taken to a police station cell. She had heard that you were taken into custody for as many hours as the local police thought it needed for you to repent and resolve to mend your wayward ways. She'd seen a cell at her local police station once when bailing out a work colleague: conditions had been very uninviting. She was dimly aware that her heart was pounding and she was trembling but she stood her ground.

He barked at her in Swahili, addressing her as '*Ndugu*' – comrade - clearly not seeing her as a European but as a transgressor of the dress code – didn't she know that it was forbidden to wear short skirts?

By now a small crowd of onlookers had gathered round and was waiting expectantly for some entertainment. Esme was not going to argue the toss as to whether her dress was long enough. She had no desire to have him fumbling round her legs. She admitted it was short and explained about her longer dresses being dirty, addressing him back as *Ndugu*. Her excuse sounded so lame to her own ears that she embellished it with a fictional account of her child being seriously ill, not allowing her time to wash a dress. While she spoke, his face took on a puzzled expression.

'How come you speak Swahili?' he asked, still speaking it himself. He peered at her curiously. His fury seemed to have abated. Esme was on familiar territory now: her fluency in Swahili always fascinated people. She knew she had a far better grasp of the language than most foreigners did – all but a tiny handful of the ex-colonialists having departed the country when land was nationalised and most temporary expatriates not getting to grips with it before they moved on. She explained that she'd lived in the country for many years and had every intention of staying there.

The militiaman looked confused. There was a pause. Then he composed his features into a stern expression and growled:

'Haya, nenda basi. Lakini usirudie tena! Unasikia? Kwaheri, Mzungu.'

She had already started to thank him and assure him she wouldn't repeat the offence when she heard that last word. She hesitated mid-sentence. She met his look. Was there a glint of humour there? She summoned up a weak smile, thanked him.

A cheer went up from the small crowd. The militiaman furiously turned and began berating the crowd, thrashing the air with his ruler. No more the centre of attention, she fled for the bus stop. She felt light-headed with relief but also with anger at being treated like a criminal over a triviality. Did this really contribute to building a positive image for the new nation?

Esme had no recollection of the bus journey home, only coming back to the present as she alighted at her stop. She bought a copy of the evening newspaper from a roadside vendor. As he handed it to her the headline caught her eye:

Minister condemns harassment of citizens, and underneath:

Unauthorised militia swoops to cease immediately.

Beside the article was a photograph of himself and his wife – wearing trousers. They were baggy and not particularly flattering on her ample form but this was a clear signal that trousers were now authorised apparel for women. She stepped into the shade of a kapok tree and read the lead article. The minister had followed up on complaints from the public about the summary arrests in connection with the decent dress campaign. He emphasised that there were established procedures for 'serious and repeated offenders' to be dealt with but that this did not entail public humiliation and detention. Steps would be taken against militia members contravening the guidelines, which were printed underneath. Esme scanned them: ...'Dress length: 'To reach the knee'.

Esme walked on, slowly absorbing the implications. Her dress came half way down her knee – so it was within the guidelines. In that case she couldn't be classed as a 'saboteur' against the nation's efforts to dress decently after all. Why couldn't this have come out yesterday? Thank God what she'd been through wasn't officially sanctioned. But why had the militia been given such a free rein till now? What if she hadn't been an *Mzungu*?

Mosi and Ali were playing outside with their numerous playmates. They ran to meet her, hugging her and laughing but in two minutes they were off again. She wouldn't see them again till the next mealtime.

She decided she'd do something simple for their supper - an omelette would do. She'd have to go and get some more eggs from Mashaka's. She took a shower and put on a clean dress – one of those that came above her knee – and automatically wrapped a *kanga* round her waist before leaving the house.

Strolling along the sandy track - back once more in the easy, tropical pace of life - she appreciated more than usual the space, the breeze, the palm trees outlined against the sky, the tranquillity. She waited for the inevitable cries as she approached the group of kids playing with their home-made cars. Sure enough, one of them spotted her and a voice piped up:

'*Mzungu, Mzungu*!'. The others joined in the chorus.

'*Angalia - Mzungu anacheka*. Look - she's smiling,' they chanted.

Ch 13: Mosi starts school

Although it was five o'clock in the midst of the cool, dry *kiangazi*, the sun was a bright orb half way down the sky and within a quarter of an hour Esme was dripping with sweat. The sandy earth looked innocent enough but was proving resistant to her attempts to break it up with the *jembe*. If truth be told, she admitted, this universally employed hoe was far too heavy for her to raise above her head and swing down with the necessary force. She was also being attacked by large black ants. Her next door neighbour, Mama Peter, had cultivated an impressive area: spinach, maize and beans were already sprouting. Esme's vision of tender young corn on the cob from their own garden was fading fast. Strictly speaking, it wasn't actually their garden but Martin had predicted that, if they didn't claim the virgin land behind their own plot, someone else soon would – only the state, in fact, actually *owned* land but anyone could cultivate an unused patch. She straightened her back, wiped her brow with her *kanga* and resolved to try and wheedle Martin into helping her.

'*Habari*, Mama Mosi. How are the children? Looking forward to *Upe*?' Mama Peter had come out to her vegetable patch and was immediately engaged in picking a bunch of spinach; it was some time since the two of them had met.

'*Nzuri, Mama.*' Esme returned her greeting but was still rummaging round in her brain for the meaning of her neighbour's question.

'Oopay! Universal Primary Education!' she offered by way of explanation.

Esme repeated the word in her head. "oo-pay", upe, Of course, UPE! 'Oh, yes, she replied. 'Seven years worth of free schooling for the children. It's great' With her neighbour's eight kids that'll be a tidy saving, Esme thought to herself.

'Well, make sure you enrol Mosi on the first day. There won't be enough places for all the seven-year-olds this year because there will be a lot of older children whose parents couldn't afford to school them before. They'll take the older ones first.'

'OK, thanks for the advice,' said Esme. 'Mosi's been ready for primary for years but no school will take her till she's seven. She more or less taught herself to read when she was three.'

'In English, of course.' This was somewhat sniffily from Mama Peter.

'But there are so few books in Swahili,' she conceded. English is being phased out as the official language, you know, but Swahili will never completely replace it. It's good Mosi can read English but she'll find it difficult at school, everything will be taught in Swahili.'

'Mosi speaks both languages equally, it won't be a problem. And she can read Swahili very easily because it's phonetic. Ali is another matter, though! He shows only the most fleeting interest in the contents of books and he can barely read a word. And even when I address him in English he responds in Swahili! The kids spend so much time playing outside anyway, once they're showered and fed, they're practically falling asleep on their feet!'

Mama Peter having gathered enough of her greens, was moving towards the house. 'Don't neglect to educate them at home, Mama Mosi! You'll be doing them a disservice by allowing them too much playtime. See you soon.'

I'll do it my way, thanks, thought Esme, resuming her efforts in the *shamba* while reflecting that next-door's kids were never seen out on the estate roads with their peers and, when glimpsed, wore lugubrious expressions. She understood that education was the key to employment and working offspring were insurance for parents against poverty in their declining years, but surely the children's happiness shouldn't be sacrificed? The whole way of looking at children puzzled her. Large families were the norm because of considerable chance of losing some children to illness before they reached adulthood. But half the children she came across seemed to be living with a relative, not their own parents, even though the latter were alive and well. As far as she could tell, such bairns were generally treated by their host families pretty much as their own. Except for that poor orphaned four-year-old who'd been taken in by the woman living in the house on the corner. Mosi and even Ali regularly told Esme that Kati had been beaten. Then they reported that she was tied up to prevent her from running away. She'd consulted Martin as to any recourse open to them.

'Never interfere within a family,' he'd responded. 'There must be a good reason for their behaviour.' Esme was kept awake at night thinking about it.

Some ten days later the lists for enrolment opened and Esme took Mosi to enrol her at the local primary school only to be told that first year was full, to come back again next year. She felt as if she'd been slapped in the face. Despite her neighbour's warning, she had naively believed that there would be sufficient places to absorb the backlog, children of up to ten whose parents hadn't been able to send them to school. Mosi, cried as they walked the thirty minutes back home, keeping to the shade of the mango trees.

They felt salt rubbed into their wounds when Mosi heard that evening from Peter next-door that he had a place, even though he was a couple of months younger than her.

'Nepotism.' Martin had responded bitterly when she told him. It was a tradition that was still very much alive and kicking although supposedly the very antithesis of socialist ideals. In their neighbour's case, being a teacher at the school apparently guaranteed her seven-year-old child a place.

The next day Esme went at lunch time to discuss the matter with the teachers at the nursery school. They agreed that Mosi was stagnating there, the staff could do nothing to challenge her any more. Hedda, a quiet-spoken young German woman whom Mosi adored, suggested that Mosi move to a nursery school which concentrated more on the three Rs. The choices were very limited and after some investigation she and Martin concluded that the best seemed to be one run and predominantly attended by Asians. Unfortunately, its location above a butcher's meant it was invariably enveloped in an aura of ripe meat and flies and was never referred to as anything other than 'Tanganyika Meat' - or more commonly 'Meaty'. It made sense to have both the children there and, though it lacked the warmth of the former kindergarten, they both settled in well and Mosi thrived.

Otherwise life went on as before. One late afternoon, as Esme sauntered home from the bus stop along the coarse red sandy estate roads, greeting neighbours as she passed, she felt a real sense of belonging and contentment. She was part of the advertising agency, she was one of the crowd getting the bus, and at weekends going to the neighbouring Drive In-Cinema on foot, sitting in the small auditorium, braving the mosquitoes. By day, the kids played on the virtually traffic-free estate roads or in each others' houses and gardens. They moved in a pack some ten strong: some a few years older than Mosi down to chubby babies who – when not on an older sister's back - couldn't yet do more than sit firmly on their bottoms with snot dribbling down their faces, cheerfully licking it off. Esme would have to wander round searching for them to call them in for supper, shower and bed. Sometimes Martin came home and ate with them, more often he came after the children had gone to bed. Sometimes after she'd gone to bed. He always wanted to talk, whatever time it was. Not that he always made a lot of sense. She knew now that this was no different from most of the neighbours. And at least Martin wasn't violent.

Mosi was finally enrolled at Oyster Bay Primary School soon after her eighth birthday. It turned out to be a nightmare for Esme but Mosi took it all in her stride. There was no doubt that she was bright and having been to nursery schools for five years, she could do most of Standard One work before she got there. This helped give her confidence and attract less adverse attention from the teachers. That didn't make her an exception from the cruel treatment meted out *en masse* under the banner of discipline: fimbo - the cane. Every few days she'd come back with red welts on her hand. The class had been too slow replying to a question, been too noisy or the teacher had just been in a bad mood. Esme was livid the first time and wanted to go and complain to the Head but Mosi pleaded with her not to. Mosi wanted to blend in as far as possible: difficult enough when some bairns called her an Arab because of her lighter complexion and hair that was less kinky than others. Martin seemed to fail to grasp the issue at all. If she was beaten it was because she deserved it: she should behave herself and she wouldn't get punished. The first time Mosi came back, her face streaked with tears, and showed her swollen hands, Esme, outraged had gone to consult her next-door-neighbour. Mama Peter stoutly defended the school policy of disciplining the children through the only language they understood. Esme should have known this would have been her neighbour's attitude: there had been occasions when they'd distinctly heard the sound of thrashing and a child's voice beseeching, '*Usinipige, Mama!*' Don't beat me! The whole business kept Esme awake at nights but Mosi herself accepted the brutality as part and parcel of school.

Esme felt she was being punished too, by having to iron pleats into Mosi's navy blue uniform skirts made from a coarse cotton fabric known as *jinja*, after the place it was originally manufactured in Uganda. Every time the skirts were washed, the pleats came out. As she did this she reflected on how lucky they were to have electricity – for the iron, for the light - and that she had the time to do it for Mosi. She could imagine dozens of kids living in the surrounding local houses using an iron heated by charcoal, ironing by a kerosene lamp. Or getting up at first light to do it. They'd have to wait for the charcoal stove to be lit and be lucky to get a hot drink or some *uji* down them before leaving for school. And if they were late, there'd be a teacher there waiting to beat them.

Walking back from the bus stop after work one evening another of her neighbours, Deena's mother, had called out to her from her vegetable patch:

'Mama Mosi, come and join in the netball game. We need more players.' Esme shook her head. 'I haven't played netball since I was at school, that's years and years ago.'

'Ah, so you already know how to play it! Good! See you at five o'clock tomorrow, on the field.' She waved her hand in the direction of the area where the older children played football, behind the row of houses where Mama Deena lived.

'I'll see,' Esme said. She was pleased to be asked but nervous that her standard would not be good enough. She hadn't done any exercise other than walking and gardening for years. Full of trepidation, the next day she turned up with Mosi and Ali and a troupe of their friends who played alongside the pitch with the other women's kids. Esme hadn't any shorts, of course, but she'd worn a pair of trousers. That set her apart immediately: everyone else was in their normal clothes with a *kanga* wrapped round their lower half. Far from impeding their progress, their speed and agility left Esme standing. But they played by their own rules – their tactics would not have disgraced rugby players. At the prospect of yet again being charged at by a fourteen stone woman, head and shoulders above her, anticipating the impact on her shoulder, the crunching of bones, the rattling of teeth, the thud through throat, chest, stomach, hips and legs into the ground - Esme decided her opponent was welcome to the ball. She couldn't rid herself of the sense of indignation – this wasn't fair play – they played as if there were no rules. She couldn't take it but who was she to complain? If they were all happy with their own rules, it was her who didn't fit in. She gave up after three evenings. First she invented visitors, then an imaginary stomach complaint and after that Mama Deena and company accepted that she had dropped out for good. All the same, a lot more of the women gave her a cheery wave and exchanged greetings with her after that.

A month after her last netball game, she was driving home, unable to suppress her ear-to-ear grin as she mused on recent events at work. Mr Carter had started slowing down a few months ago. Esme guessed he was in his sixties and knew he had been in Dar for a good number of years. The heat had probably taken its toll. He kept himself very much to himself really but was always pleasant. And then it had got quite busy. She and the rest of the staff never knew whose idea it had been for the Nairobi office to send an assistant general manager but they were unanimous in their verdict: it was a bad move. Certainly the choice of candidate, in the person of Silas Faraker, was a disaster. They mused about the possibility of the Nairobi office having sent him to Dar in order to get rid of him, or to spite him. As he never tired of telling them, he hated everything about Dar: he found the humidity and heat of late January in Dar intolerable after Nairobi. He considered Dar a backwater with its lack of high-rise buildings, its dwindled expatriate community and lack of sophisticated night-spots. As far as Esme was aware, the only venue *Wazungu* frequented was the Yacht Club, at the tip of the Msasani Peninsula. His foul temper, his enormous bulk and complete lack of ability to communicate with the staff made him an object of derision and ridicule. He would bark a command in English at one of the messengers who would just sit there staring blankly ahead for several minutes, while Faraker grew madder and louder. Then the messenger would begin to comply, oh-so-slowly, saying nothing. One day, inevitable cigarette in hand, he held out money to Hassani and barked,

'Get me a carton of Embassy!'

Hassani, as usual, at first didn't respond, although Esme caught the merest flicker of a glance between him and Matias. Silas turned puce in the face and, frothing at the mouth, shouted: 'What are you waiting for? Christmas?' Hassani, Matias and Esme simultaneously burst out laughing. At the end of the month - six weeks after his arrival - Silas was gone. Peace was restored and Kaliwe was appointed assistant manager. Macha was ruffled for a while but he knew deep down that he was too dedicated to the pursuit of pleasure to give enough commitment to the position.

Martin came home early that evening to Esme's glee. It meant he could see the red Mini properly before it got dark. The first thing he said to her as he walked in the door, portfolio in hand, a wary expression on his face was, 'Whose is that car?'

'Mine! At least it is for a year. Then I'll have to give it back to the office.'

'What do you mean?'

'Why don't you sit down and I'll explain. I'll just check the beans.' She went quickly into the kitchen, checked that the level of liquid in the pan was adequate to be left unattended for a while, and joined Martin in the sitting room. There was a cool breeze blowing in through the open patio doors but they'd have to close them in a few minutes before the mosquitoes started invading.

'Remember I told you business at the ad agency has really been picking up lately and you said it was due to all the foreign investment in light industry, manufacturing consumer goods and stuff.'

'Yes, and I still don't see why the parastatal organisations are wasting money on advertising, because there's no competition!'

'Well, anyway, it means more business for us. But, that awful man who was sent down from Nairobi, has gone back. Today the Nairobi office agreed that I should use the car that the company bought for him until it's four years old so they can sell it on the open market. If they get rid of it now, it'll have to go to the State Motor Corporation. You know what their prices are like. I just have to pay for the petrol I use, the office will pay for all the servicing.'

Martin looked non-plussed.

'Why you?'

'Kaliwe already has a car, a bit battered, but it runs. He got a loan from the company to buy it. And none of the others can drive.'

'So, we have a family car again!'

'Well, the only thing is, Martin, I'm the named driver in the insurance and Mr Carter was very insistent that it's only me that's allowed to drive it. But we can go places together now.' Martin harrumphed and got up.

'We'll see,' he said as he left the room.

In the event, it made little difference to how much time they spent together but Esme had less time to dwell on it during the journey to work and back which took a fraction of the time and her energy. There was still the queue of traffic at Selander Bridge, such a bottleneck for all the traffic going from the eastern side of the city into the centre of town. She was able to take basketsful of papaya from the garden to give to her colleagues: the fruit had been literally falling off the trees and rotting because they couldn't keep up with the production. The trees – like banana plants, not real tree, they were soft and fibrous and short-lived – had shot up and started bearing fruit in no time and all the neighbours were the same.

Now she had wheels, she and the kids could visit Marietta's and Jocelyn's. They would also be able take trips to the beach. The problem for Esme was a companion - there was no point in asking Martin. His aversion to the beach had been evident the one occasion he'd felt it would be politic to accept an invitation from his boss and her family for a picnic on the beach. He'd sat the whole time in the shade on a folding chair, wearing his normal knife-edge trousers and shirt, without removing his shoes and socks. a look of utter disdain on his face which he'd tried to disguise with a polite smile from time to time. Back home he'd cursed the sand, the sun and above all the water. Although he'd grown up close to a river, he'd never learned to swim and had not the slightest desire to.

On the next occasion she and her friends met at Jocelyn's, she suggested a trip to the beach on Sunday. 'That's a great offer, thanks, but I think I'll give it a miss.' Esme had expected this from Jocelyn. She had the worst deal of all of them and bore it all with patience and fortitude that verged on martyrdom. Arthur, an urbanised Maasai, treated her like a doormat, coming home at all hours even when he had relatives staying – which was nearly all the time, often three at once, usually men.

They brought a new meaning to country cousins, dressed in their traditional red cloths and sandals, spears on the coffee table, with barely a word of Swahili between them, let alone English. They'd occupy the easy chairs in the living room, watching and appearing to listen to Jocelyn's and her friends' conversation in an unnerving manner, and making comments to one another in Kimaasai. No wonder Jocelyn had a live-in house-girl who slept in the purpose-built servant's quarters attached to the garage. Even so, Jocelyn was always busy organising and serving food to whichever relatives were using their home as a base camp during their trips to Dar. Their people were insatiable travellers, by all accounts, some of them walked the hundreds of miles to and from their homeland in the north. Most of Jocelyn's visitors seemed to be in Dar seeking medical treatment and travelled by bus. No, Jocelyn wouldn't be coming to the beach either.

Still, Esme made a point of taking the kids to the sea every Sunday. Whereas, before she had the car, she had dreaded Martin going out, immaculately dressed as on a work morning, always 'to meet someone,' now she'd be silently egging him on to go. Not that he objected to her expeditions but if he'd been staying at home she would have wanted to make the most of his company. Some weeks she would have the company of Marietta or Ulla, sometimes it was just herself and as many of the neighbouring children as would fit in the car

– she'd leave the choice to Mosi and Ali. They didn't even bother asking any of next-door's cohort because they would never have been allowed out: in any case, they were at church all Sunday morning.

It was a ten mile drive to the nearest of the beach hotels. When she'd first gone to one of them with Ulla, she'd been bowled over by the luxurious surroundings – the swimming pool, the tables with umbrellas, the pool-side bar serving drinks – all theirs for the day for a modest fee – fortunately it was only adults who were charged. Gradually, though, as the economic strictures bit, the hotels became shabbier. Worn fixtures and fabrics went un-replaced. Dar es Salaam had never been a hot tourist destination, but still the number of guests noticeably dwindled till it was beyond Esme's comprehension how the hotels managed to stay functioning at all. The staff hung around with little to do. While the kids splashed happily in the pool, she'd wander down to the beach, drawn to the beauty of it, picture-postcard perfect with palm trees, white sand and the azure blue Indian Ocean rolling in with white crested waves and, apart from the occasional fishing boat near to shore, the scene was deserted. No-one to see or hear her as she gave in to her loneliness.

Ch 14: Letter to Christine

East African Advertising Agency,
Dar es Salaam.
15 October 1975.

Dear Christine,

How <u>are</u> you? Please excuse the typed letter but I'm at work and trying to look busy. I got your letter yesterday and was shocked to hear about you and Alan splitting up. It's so hard to imagine you two NOT together. I know you've had problems but who doesn't? Are you sure this is the only solution? A divorced woman has such a stigma. And that's what life is all about, isn't it? Being married, having kids? I know we had dreams of having an exciting life but I think we knew that's what they were – dreams. Like mine was to travel the world instead of coming to Tanzania on a one-way ticket. It's hard but then, as your mother used to say, "life's no picnic".

How will you cope financially without Alan? And what about the kids? They'll miss him terribly.

I wish you'd think about it again. I often imagine, while I'm lying in bed at night waiting for Martin to come home, packing a bag, leaving it by the door and, when he finally shows up, telling him I've had enough and leaving him staring open-mouthed while I walk out. But that's when the fantasy stops because I've nowhere to go. And, of course, there's no way I'd leave the kids. Instead of that I ask him where he's been till this time and we have an almighty row. Next day we make it up, he promises not to stay out late again and for a day or two he's a model husband. Then the cycle starts all over again.

Martin's best buddy (at the moment) has just split up with his wife. He reckons she was unfaithful to him, which is a heinous offence, naturally, <u>for the wife</u>, and he's sent her packing. She's staying with relatives and the kids are with him. I don't think he ever sees them, though, because he seems to be out with Martin every evening. The house-girl, only a young kid herself, lives with them and the bairns are left with her all the time. Legally the children should be with their mother as they're under seven years of age, poor mites, but the law of the land seldom prevails over the various tribes' traditional law.

Anyway, my own wee ones are fine. Mosi enjoys going to school with her pals and seems to take it in her stride, getting thrashed across the hand. I never got used to it myself and I never wanted it for my own kids. Does it still go on in your schools? Ali goes to a rather basic nursery school near home now. He's not learning a lot but he refused to go into town without Mosi.

Meanwhile, I'm here at work. This is the best part of my day. I really look forward to coming here. Except for what happened to me a few weeks ago. I was on my way to work early for once and I was walking up the stairs to our office on the second floor – (they're the sort with an open well in the middle – you can see all the way up and down). Suddenly, I felt my bag being grabbed off my shoulder. Of course, my heart felt it would leap out of my chest as I hadn't heard or seen anyone. I turned round to catch glimpses of a figure belting down. I yelled at the top of my lungs: "mwizi, mwizi" (thief) but my legs were shaking too much to move. When, eventually I did stagger down I found my bag abandoned just outside the back entrance. Nothing was missing from it. A happy ending, you might think and so indeed did I. But no, that wasn't the end of it because ten minutes later, after I'd told the story over and over again to everyone in the office and had just started to try and do some work, two policemen arrived leading this poor, beaten-up man in hand-cuffs. His face was all bloodied and his eyes puffed up, his clothes torn, he was a pitiful sight. The police said he'd been spotted by passers-by climbing over the wall to the yard beyond our car park. Obviously he'd been meted out a dose of "Instant Justice". They asked if I'd be prepared to identify the man in court as the culprit. Well, I thought damn it, it probably was him: his blue shirt rang a bell alright, but I hadn't actually lost anything and this wee chappie had already been punished enough. So I said, No, I hadn't seen the thief, I couldn't positively identify him. They were not very happy with me and took him away with them anyway. God knows what happened to him after that. The thought of it haunts me at night.

But that aside, I have such fun with my work-mates. Mr. Carter's successor, Mr Bowden, didn't last too long after his wife died, maybe I didn't tell you about that? Well, I'd never met her but apparently she had sclerosis of the liver. A few of us from the office went to the cremation, held at the Hindu temple because it's the only place that does cremations. The notion of it was shocking enough to my colleagues but the reality of it was worse to me as the coffin was put on top of a pile of logs and set fire to in front of us all. A few weeks after that, Mr. Bowden went back to England, not Nairobi where he'd come from to run our branch. He couldn't handle Africa any more, poor old boy. He wasn't an old colonial, there aren't any in Tanzania , he was ex-military and I suppose he had thought a few years living in the lap of luxury in Nairobi would do them nicely but he really wasn't ready for Tanzania.

No-one from the Nairobi office has been near us since. Mr. Bowden had already been training Kaliwe up to succeed him eventually so K. has just been sent a letter appointing him to the post of General Manager, not Managing Director as were the *Wazungu* before him – sorry, I mean Europeans. This seems to be a trend, I must say, there are hardly any Europeans around these days – it's less and less a climate for profitable business as the policy of "Socialism and Familyhood" begins to take hold. Anyway I won't bore you with politics, especially my half-baked version of it.

We've never been really hectic with work, but it's gradually getting more and more relaxed. We aren't making much money, according to Kathleen in Accounts, because there's nothing to sell so what's the point of advertising? But some companies do, like Tuasa Batteries: there's only one local brand of car batteries and nothing's being imported but they advertise regularly!

There's only one other ad agency in the country, and it's here in the capital, run by a local chap called Smith! He did a wonderful ad last week: it featured a line drawing of two Chinese men in their Mao worker's uniforms, beaming and clutching bottles of Coca Cola. The caption read, "Coca Cola the life and soul of any party!" We don't see as many Chinese workers now as TAZARA (the Tanzania-Zambia Railway) is just about finished and which also generates ads! Unfortunately TAZARA doesn't go anywhere near Martin's homeland, it traverses the more westerly side of the country. It would be an experience to travel on it though, it's so big and modern compared to the old German-built railway which goes north and is slower than travelling by bus! TAZARA will really open up the country as well as giving Zambia an outlet for its copper through the port of Dar (this is the main purpose). The trade-off for this was that Tanzania import 5 million pounds worth of Chinese goods such as fancy mugs, thermos flasks and plastic knick-knacks. Unfortunately, cheap though it is, there's a limit to the amount one can absorb in the household. It seems we had to take all the stuff no-one else would buy.

    I feel really sorry for the Chinese workers here to build the railway, though. They're all men, wear uniform and all live together in purpose-built barracks, never mixing with the local populace.

They construct astonishing vegetable plots on waste land beside the roads. It's fascinating to gaze at while you're stuck in traffic! They're laid out in perfect rows, weed-free and bursting with juicy tomatoes, sweet peppers and the like. Rumour has it that they get bumper crops because they fertilise it with their own excrement! I don't think the locals will emulate that particular practice but I have started noticing lots of vegetable plots springing up on odd patches of ground in the suburbs. Especially for a kind of local spinach which grows like wildfire with enough water and can be picked within a few weeks of the seeds being planted. Strange thing is I adore green vegetables now; when I lived in Scotland I wouldn't touch cabbage or Brussel sprouts! Here we eat the leaves of sweet potatoes, cassava, cow peas and even Chinese cabbage lately. Which brings me back to the Chinese gardeners – it's the fact that these foreigners are doing their own dirty work which amazes my workmates and no doubt other locals because the Indians and Europeans who come here always have servants to do it for them. But what's a real source of derision, is that the men are having to do all the menial tasks as well, even the planting and harvesting which is very often "women's work"! But I'm rambling. I was supposed to be telling you about the shortage of work which is a real worry because if I lose my job here we just couldn't manage and I don't think there are many jobs out there these days.

The youngest messenger, Matias, got laid off by Mr. Bowden a while ago because business was so slack and because Matias would be gone forever on an errand. Everyone was horrified but I think he had various side-lines on the go so hopefully he can pursue them because he won't get another job easily and there's no such thing as the dole, or redundancy payment. The receptionist had to go too but luckily she did get another job as she has some typing skills and is quite literate even though her English is a bit rudimentary. So now Mzee Hassani is the receptionist but his eyes are so bad he can hardly read and no-one ever comes into reception anyway so all he does is put phone calls through. The rest of the time he sits staring into space if there's no-one to chat to.

Oh, Javinder, the Accountant, emigrated to Canada. I can't say I'm sorry. He's been replaced by a wee laddie, Karim. Even though there are hardly any Asians left in the country, we still ended up with another Asian accountant because they really seem to specialise in either shop-keeping or accounting. The few Asians left are lucky to have a family business to work in after the 'nationalisation' of so much by the Government. Karim's not bad, he can take a joke even though he's mostly very po-faced and a takes himself terribly seriously. We've had just about every religion in the world in this small office: Javinder was a Sikh, Karim is a Hindu, Pamela, our artist from England, reckons she's a Buddhist, and the rest belong to various sects of Islam or Christianity, not that it makes the slightest difference here. Unlike in Northern Ireland, people tolerate each others' religious beliefs. The situation there is terrible and even for folk in London, not knowing when a bomb is going to go off.

Must get some work done now. Write soon.

Love, **Esme** XXXX

P.S. <u>Please</u> have another go at it with Alan. Write soon.

Ch 15: Shortages

'Mama Yusufu!' Hassani had just returned from delivering letters around the town. Esme looked up from her typewriter. It still rankled slightly that her colleagues wouldn't address her by her given name because she was a married woman and neither did they find it appropriate to use her domestic titles - Mama Mosi or Mama Ali. This must be the British Hooray Henry legacy: the men all addressed by their surname, the women by their surname preceded by their title.

'*Kuna foleni* RTC.' A queue! She was reaching for her bag under the desk and on her feet before Hassani had closed the door behind him.

'What are they selling?' she asked.

'They're unloading sugar now. Some people in the queue thought there might be cooking oil too.'

'Don't you want any yourself?' She was making for the door as he sat down at his desk.

'No, my wife gets everything.' His wife, so far as she knew, was unemployed and would hardly have money for shopping unless he left it for her. He averted his eyes and she guessed the reality was he didn't have any cash to spare. She'd gladly lend him some but quite honestly she felt she should hang on to the little she had till pay-day. You never knew when there could be a consignment of rice or maize meal – anything. And Martin was, of course, too busy doing important work to join the lines of ordinary shoppers. Kaliwe was completely understanding about her need to dash out. He wasn't explicit about who did the shopping in his house – he probably had a myriad of relatives, who had descended on them like everyone else who was employed in town and whom he had to support, on visits that somehow never ended: the ubiquitous extended family. In return, they'd carry out chores for him and his wife.

She only had to cross the road to reach the Regional Trading Company shop. Since the nationalisation of wholesale trade, which had been largely in the hands of the Asian population, distribution of goods moved in mysterious ways. Very little of it got to private shops but so it was with these official outlets. It was aimed at stamping out corruption and exploitation of the masses, fairly sharing out the scarce resources. Highly commendable. So how had it got to this? People used to be able to buy whatever they needed, it all seemed reasonably priced to Esme, even if most of the family income went on essentials. But, since the importation of goods had become strictly controlled to preserve precious foreign currency, shortages had prevailed. At the root of it was Nyerere's vision of African socialism the so-called Famliyhood: *Ujamaa*. According to everyone she talked to, most of the party and government officials who put the policy into practice barely understood it, let alone subscribed to it.

She joined the queue of thirty or so people. There was a militiaman to ensure they kept in a queue, a concept introduced by the military – the word *foleni* derived from 'fall in'. Pity the British hadn't left queuing behind as part of their legacy. It was still a compete nightmare withdrawing money from the bank - like getting on a bus - a rugby scrum for hundreds of people. It would take a whole morning to get near one of the tellers and then to attract manage to give them your withdrawal slip, for scrutiny. Then, after a suitably large pile of other slips had mounted up, a clerk took it behind the scenes where it had to be verified by a second or even third worker. This shopping was a little better organised in that they now they had ration books. If only she could get her hands on enough goods to use up her ration.

A woman came away from the serving hatch of the shop bearing her brown paper bag of two kilos of sugar as well as yellow and blue one-kilo tin of margarine. The margarine had a very unpleasant tendency of coating the inside of your mouth, un-dissolved, but it would offer a change from un-garnished bread. They could fry in it too. She could even bake a cake – if she was lucky enough in the next few days to acquire some wheat flour and milk powder. And eggs. Even the hens in this urban environment were on short rations and barely laid eggs.

Half an hour later she went back to the office clutching her booty. It was going to be awkward on the bus. Perhaps she should phone Martin and ask him if he could pick it up from her. If only she still had the car; it had been wonderful driving it for a year but, having known the luxury of it, it now felt worse than before.

As she entered the office she shared with Kaliwe she saw that he was back from his visits to clients. He looked up from his newspaper and smiled. He didn't smile a lot these days. His wife's health was worsening, it seemed, her mental health. Mental illness was more or less a taboo subject, and it was clear Kaliwe was too embarrassed to discuss it. His hair was receding rapidly, revealing more of his prominent forehead. He didn't chat much any more and when he did he kept bringing in religion. It was as if he was turning to his church, one of the hallelujah persuasion, to escape from the reality of his home life. 'You were lucky, I see.' This was like his former self, taking an interest in the small matters of her life that often no-one else was aware of.

'Yes, it's quite a haul, isn't it?' As she sat behind her desk she saw that he hadn't immediately returned to his perusal of the paper and looked engageable in conversation. 'I don't understand though,' she went on, 'Why there's a shortage of sugar when there are acres and acres of sugar cane in this country and a factory at Kilombero. And why can't we get local-grown rice? It smells and tastes so gorgeous when it's fresh. Or home grown maize flour?' Not that she had yet mastered the technique of cooking *ugali* using the fine, white maize flour without it ending up full of lumps. Kaliwe stood up and wandered over to the window, hands in pockets, an amused expression on his face. Old feelings for him resurfaced briefly before she reminded herself of their futility.

'Believe it or not,' he was saying, 'that coarse yellow meal that is imported from America, is actually better for you!'

'What – *yanga*?'

Kaliwe laughed. 'You are ahead of me! Why is it called that?'

'Because of the colour: it's one of the colours of *Yanga*: Young African Football Cub. Even you must know that everyone in the country supports either them or *Simba*!' Kaliwe shook his head in mock despair and said,

'I was just reading an article about it in the newspaper. The Party wants to reassure the public that there is nothing wrong with this ...*yanga*. It is just a matter of people's digestive systems getting used to it. It is a more yellow type of maize. The reason the meal is so coarse is because the grains have not been husked. It retains more nutritional content.'

'Well, good luck to them in convincing all the folk who've already decided it's poisonous! Hassani and everyone said it wasn't just because it stinks and tastes foul, but because it gives them stomach pains and diarrhoea!'

'Yes, it has affected them adversely because they have relied so heavily on a single staple food since they migrated to this part of the country, especially as it is the only grain you can get in Dar es Salaam. Apart from rice which is considerably more expensive. For most of the populace, it is a choice of *ugali* or hunger. People who have lived in different regions of the country - or even abroad - and have a better income, they are used to a variety of foods such as bread or potatoes or cooking bananas, as well as cassava or millet, so a change in the type of maize meal does not affect them in the same way.'

'That explains why we weren't affected by the yellow stuff in our house. But what I don't understand is why, all of a sudden, local produce is only available on the black market?' Kaliwe frowned disapprovingly.

'That is exploitation of the situation by unscrupulous racketeers. But it is true the state of affairs should not be so bad as it is. The Party and the Government have introduced too many regulations and restrictions and the goons who should implement them are ignorant of their purpose. They just enjoy having power. So the produce from the countryside isn't getting to the markets in town.'

Esme nodded. What was Martin's role in all this? Best not think about that. Instead she asked Kaliwe,

'What about the foodstuff that's imported, like wheat flour? We used to be able to buy that at any local shop. All of a sudden it's become like gold dust.'

'The government has so little foreign currency to spend that it has to limit the amounts it uses on non-essential items. Bread and chapatti are not traditional foods. Yes, town dwellers have come to rely on them for a quick breakfast or midday snack but ..' Kaliwe shrugged and pulled a wry expression, 'these little luxuries have to be sacrificed for the "greater good"! Foreign exchange is needed for farming equipment, fertilizer and the like. And for raw materials for manufacturers.'

'That's a joke! We can hardly even get soap for washing our clothes, let alone for washing our bodies!'

'I know.' Kaliwe laughed mirthlessly. 'Even peasants are suffering, from what I hear people say. It is not something we read about in the newspapers. The back-bone of the country, the millions of crop-producers, cannot get hold of a new bicycle or batteries for their radios or even a new hoe! Of course it is difficult for the government to balance out the needs of every sector and then within each sector, to share out what little foreign currency we have but there is a lot of corruption going on too. *Chai* exchanges hands all the time!' The discussion had left Esme feeling frustrated. She needed a solution to her own situation.

'All my salary's going on food. How do the likes of Hassani manage on what they're paid?' Even to her own ears, her voice sounded whinging.

'Their wives are at home preparing food that takes longer to cook but costs less, like beans and *kisamvu*. Besides having a small *shamba* to grow a bit of cassava and a few cooking bananas.'

'So are we all supposed to go back to subsistence farming? Is that the idea?' Esme thought of her own futile attempts and knew Martin had no intention of getting his hands dirty. Kaliwe sighed. Esme remembered the difficulties he was having at home.

'*Mungu akipenda*. If God wills it. Put your faith in the Lord. He will provide.' Kaliwe's eyes were focussed somewhere in the future and Esme knew the conversation had reached an end even before he went back behind his desk and began shuffling documents.

Next morning was Saturday. Martin was in high humour, sitting with Mosi and Ali at the breakfast table. Neither he nor Esme ate breakfast any more but they insisted the children do. Not that Martin usually had time to become involved, by the time he'd showered, shaved, dressed in immaculately-ironed shirt and slacks and combed his close-cropped, black hair into a perfect cap before offering himself up to the public gaze.

It was becoming increasingly difficult to find something to tempt the bairns on school days, especially when she couldn't get white maize flour to make a palatable porridge. Today, and for the coming week, they had the luxury of margarine on bread washed down with sweet, milky tea.

She watched Martin as he cajoled Mosi into having another half slice of bread. Unable to withstand his persuasion, she was giggling, knowing exactly what he was up to. She'd become a lot thinner in the last two years, since starting school: she agonized so much about doing well and avoiding the beatings. Ali had taken school by storm: he'd been admitted at seven - there was no longer a back-log. It seemed he got away with murder by flashing his smile. Martin to a tee.

Now she joined them at the table to enjoy at cup of tea with the three of them. Martin had come home earlier than usual last evening: they'd gone to bed together. Despite everything, they still wanted and enjoyed each other.

This seemed like a good moment to broach the subject never far from her mind.

'Martin, do you think that things are going to get better soon. It's so difficult to get decent food for the kids, and the price of everything in the market has gone sky-high.'

'Sure, *Mpenzi*.' Martin laughed. 'Our luck has changed for the better. We had that terrible drought in '74 and the farmers were all over the place after the Villagisation campaign. They've settled down again now and they're growing crops.' Martin was ever the optimist.

'Kaliwe reckons the farmers get a better price for their food crops on the black market than selling them to government agencies.'

'It's people sabotaging the system that stops it working!' Martin's smile had evaporated while his voice rose with irritation. The children looked from one parent to another.

'OK, love, don't get upset.' Esme touched his hand. The morning could go one of two ways. Then Martin made a comic expression at the kids and all four of them laughed.

'Anyway.' Martin said draining his teacup, 'the demand for coffee is growing – they can't get enough of it in Europe and America so they're paying a decent price: we have to sell fewer tons of coffee to earn a tractor or a lorry. As long as this so-called oil crisis blows over quickly. The break-up of the East African

Community is probably a good thing, even though the politicians say otherwise. So yes, *Mpenzi*, things will be better, Inshallah.'

Esme sensed that with the conclusion of his economic analysis, he wouldn't tarry much long at the table.

'Martin, any chance you could give me some money towards food every month – just until prices go down?'

'Sweetheart, I'd love to, but by the time they've deducted the mortgage and pension and tax from my salary, there's only just enough to pay for the water and electricity. I can hardly afford a few beers these days.' Esme's allowed her eyes to open wide in surprise but did not give voice to her thoughts. Come on, Martin, if you're not paying for them, who is? He caught enough of her dissent to respond irritably,

'Do what the other women do – start up a small mradi, a money-spinner. You've got plenty of space, electricity, running water – a lot of projects have far less than that to start out with!'

'You mean in all my spare time?' said with heavy sarcasm. 'What kind of *mradi* would you suggest?' Esme could hardly conceal her irritation.

Martin barely paused to think.

'Sell *maandazi*, chapattis or ice lollies.'

'But, Martin, I can't get the ingredients for our own needs let alone all the extra! I don't have the connections. Or relatives I can send to stand in queues, and to help with all the cooking and ….everything!'

What had she expected, for Martin just to smile sweetly and just put his hand in his pocket and pull out a few thousand shillings and promise a similar amount next week when the banks opened? She got up and started clearing the table, not looking at Martin. She clattered the dishes together and withdrew into the kitchen, trying to keep her face expressionless. No point in having another row. To hell with him, he'd be going out anyway . She wished she had the car to go and see Marietta or Jocelyn. Even to have a phone to be able to talk to them. Tears splash into the washing up water. She knew Jocelyn's husband took his role as provider very seriously: not only did he manage to get tins of stuff by the carton-load, he brought buffalo and impala meat home on a regular basis. Mind you with the house full of his relatives that Jocelyn had to cater for, he'd have to provide for them or lose face in a big way. At least Martin didn't bring hordes of people home. And then there was Marietta's husband, the bastard, he was a complete waster! Like that day she'd found Marietta sitting on the step of the veranda, utterly desolate: she had no money and no food in the house to feed the kids – just a cabbage. So what had she, Esme, to complain about? Hen, you have to stop your mithering! You're just going to have to do something about it! She dried her hands and threw the dish towel across the kitchen with all the force she could muster. Then walked out into the back garden. She needed to think.

It was Mama Peter, the mother of Ali's best friend, who came up with the suggestion a few days later when she and Esme discussed the need of a third income in the household. Peter's mother was head of the English department at the teachers' training college. A prestigious position but not paid commensurately, as she was at pains to clarify. They got by in her household because they now grew most of their own food and the rest they bought by the sack load when she or her husband travelled up-country for their jobs or visiting relatives. Esme knew they also brought home charcoal this way and, like most of the other residents on the estate, the house-girl cooked on portable one-pot charcoal *jiko* used outside the kitchen even though, of course, all the houses had electricity.

According to her neighbour, the college had recently been directed by the Ministry of Foreign Affairs to organise English lessons for a group of diplomats who had arrived along with an aid package from the North Korean government. Speaking neither Swahili or English was, not unsurprisingly, proving a hindrance in their diplomatic role. English teaching in the college was geared towards secondary school leavers who had used the language as a medium of learning from the beginning of their school career – unlike Mosi's generation who were being taught in Swahili. Mama Peter saw Esme, a native English language speaker, as a potential solution to her dilemma: Esme could give them private tuition. Esme was stunned. Where would she begin? Just because she spoke English didn't mean she could teach it. At first Tanzanians had found her difficult to understand in English but she had managed to tone down her Scottish accent over the years and they still said she was correct in sounding the letter 'r' so they could hear it in words like 'word'. They failed to understand how it became 'wuuhd' from the mouths of English people!

Mama Peter offered to lend her an English Language text book and, even better, she would put her in touch with two English volunteers, two VSO's who were soon going back home after having taught for two years at the college: they might have books they could let her have too.

Frances and Tom came round on their motor bikes the following Saturday afternoon. This caused a minor stir amongst the juvenile population – motor bikes, even light ones such as these, were an enormous novelty. Furthermore, they were ridden by *Wazungu* but to cap it all one of them was a woman! Judging by the small crowd of children gathered around the parked bikes and the number of teenaged boys who casually sauntered by, Mosi and Ali's reputation must have shot up the ratings.

Esme felt a stab of apprehension when she saw them dismounting in front of the house: these were the first Brits ever to have visited her at home and the first she'd spoken to since leaving the British Council. She soon found though, despite their posh English vowels that the couple were informal and affable. They were apparently used to an even less salubrious lifestyle than Esme and were so thrilled by the prospect of tea with milk that Esme also brought in a few slices of bread and margarine which they devoured steadily, suspending conversation till the plate was empty. They did look half-starved now that she thought about it. Mosi and Ali were fascinated by their every move, but most particularly by their determined consuming of the bread: the children were to imitate the volunteers' earnest expressions over many a meal, ending up in helpless mirth.

The couple gave her several books of different levels but warned her that the Koreans might not yet be up to even the first level. 'How on earth will I start then?' Esme could feel panic rising in her chest at the vision of blank faces before her.

'You can start with naming objects in the room. Using the indefinite or definite article as appropriate, of course.' This was Tom. He was a little full of himself, she saw now. The terms rang a distant bell from her school French classes but her face must have reflected the blankness of her mind.

'You know – the floor, a door. That sort of thing.'

'And you can use pictures.' The rest of the advice went over Esme's head.

Tom and Frances called in again a couple of days before their departure at the end of the month with another book. Unfortunately, the margarine was finished but they took it well. Aye, she thought, her mouth watering, they'll be anticipating the thick layers of butter they'll be slathering on their bread once they get back home.

Frances also brought a couple of dresses and asked Esme if she'd like them. It had been a while since Esme had been given any hand-me-downs – not since she was expecting Ali. Then the half dozen maternity dresses from Martin's English colleague's wife had been in pristine condition: these were, well to be honest, dirty! She accepted the dresses graciously and inspected them properly after the volunteers left: actually, they were of a good quality and stylish. She soaked them overnight in bucket of soapy water. Two new dresses would boost her wardrobe considerably.

A couple of days later, after Mama Zawadi had given the dresses a through drubbing in the wash and Esme ironed them carefully, they turned out to be a bit worn if you looked closely but otherwise quite passable. The main thing was the length came down just below the knee and though it was a bit tight across the bust the skirts were wide. A year ago even she wouldn't have been able to get into these – Martin complained about her loss of curves but she preferred her more svelte outline. She twirled in front of the mirror, the vermilion with tiny white dots went well with her colouring. She had a faint tan these days, years of weathering - or was it leathering? - had replaced her earlier pallor and her face had lost that pudgy look. She reckoned she had improved with age. Even though she knew the proposal of marriage from a stranger in the street, a young Asian, was entirely prompted by the prospect of a European passport, in the back of her mind was the notion that he couldn't envisage being espoused to someone who wasn't attractive in some way. And now she was going to be an English teacher!

Mama Peter arranged everything. She bargained valiantly on Esme's behalf: there would be no more than four students (not eight as they'd wanted), they would come twice a week for an hour (and not every day, including weekends) and they would pay twice what they had originally offered – a week's fees would make a sizeable difference to Esme's food budget. She would just have time to get home, say hello to the kids – once she'd tracked them down - and clean herself up a bit after the rigours of the bus journey. Once the lesson was over, she'd just have time to get the supper on the cooker so it would be ready for the kids by the time they'd showered, around seven.

Somewhere at the back of her mind she had a vision of herself as a figure of authority, if not exactly feared by her students, certainly held in some awe. Her experience of Oriental people was limited to occasional Chinese restaurants in Scotland where the waiters tended to be deferential and smilingly silent. She knew they were reputed to be inscrutable but assumed this to be something of a cliché. The students themselves must be quite anxious about their first lesson. She'd do her best to put them at their ease. All the same her breathing became laboured each time the prospect loomed in front of her. She barely slept the night before the first scheduled lesson.

Even so, in the event, on the first afternoon they caught her on the hop by arriving a few minutes ahead of time: she had long-since adapted to 'Swahili time' which gave you a good fifteen minutes' grace and, her bowels having turned to water, she emerged from the loo to find them inside the front door, jabbering away, each making off in a separate direction.

'Oh, you're here already!' She spoke loudly to draw their attention to her and gestured towards the living room. Two of them followed the direction of her hand. She made for the long dining table which she had earlier pulled away from the wall, where her books and pens lay ready. The students proceeded to ignore her: one studied the meagre contents of the low bookcase, the other went out of the patio door.

'Would you like to sit down here?' she said, loudly again. Smiles and more chattering. 'Shall we start the lesson?' No reaction. She realised that she could still only see two of them. Where were the other two? She tracked them down – exploring the bedrooms, one in the spare room where she had the ironing board and her mother's old hand sewing machine, the other in Martin's and her bedroom. She was fuming.

She adopted her strictest school mistress tone, normally reserved for the children's worst transgressions. She thought words of one syllable were called for her and this time she got her message across. In another five minutes she had rounded them all up and got them seated at the table, all beaming expectantly at her. She had forgotten entirely what she'd planned. In any case, she had not been prepared for such an apparent complete lack of English. Somehow she muddled through but by the time they left she was utterly exhausted and dispirited.

Next day she consulted Mama Peter. 'You have to show them who's boss right from the first moment! Make sure the door is locked before they arrive tomorrow and stand behind it – even if you have to wait for half an hour, it doesn't matter! Then you open the door and point them to where you want them. Block the way to the rest of the house! Put a barricade up if necessary. Send the kids round to me before hand I'll keep them here till the lesson is finished. And make sure you start and stop exactly on time: none of this Swahili time. You'll see they'll start asking questions at the end of the hour, trying to extend it. Have you got your objectives clear for yourself for tomorrow?'

'My what?' Esme knew now that the whole venture was doomed.

'I suspected not. Let me check at home, I might have some notes you can use.'

Esme sat on Mama Peter's doorstep and closed her eyes, offering her face to the warmth of the evening sun. It was so pleasant at this time of year. Like a Scottish summer without the midges. A light breeze teased her skin. Yes, the Koreans were a handful alright but she'd sort them out.

Ch 16: Hedda Next Door

> C/o East African Advertising Agency,
>
> Dar es Salaam.

Dear Christine,

It's so long since I heard from you I thought I should just drop you a quick line and ask you what's wrong? I guess it's been really hard for you since the divorce. The kids must miss their father terribly and you must find it ever so lonely. I can understand why you might not feel like writing but you know you can say anything to me. I don't expect you to always write an entertaining letter. I just need to hear from you.

We're all alright. Mosi's coping with school, she's such a stoic. Ali starts in September – there may be trouble ahead! Martin is his same old self, no better no worse I suppose.

Work isn't busy at the moment, when has it ever been? I'm getting a bit bored by it now. Reading the papers can only take so long though there have been a lot of interesting articles lately about the UN Decade for Women. I was wondering if the sex discrimination laws have made any difference to your life? It must be well over a year now since they came in. In theory, here the constitution gives women equal status with men in most things but "tradition" is another thing altogether. It's interesting how men, who can afford it, don't worry about breaking with tradition when they drive cars instead of walking, or drink cold bottled beer instead of warm, porridge-like local brew. But when it comes to women going out together for a drink while their husbands stay in with the children, "Good God no! That's not our tradition! We'd be a laughing stock! People would say my wife is a prostitute!" which was Martin's reaction when I was stupid enough to suggest to him going out for a drink with Marietta and Jocelyn. It didn't matter, as it turned out, because their husbands reacted in exactly the same way!

Obviously there are much more serious examples of inequalities here, about pay and education and the fact that rural women do everything: looking after the children, cooking, fetching water and firewood, as well as doing most of the agricultural work. All with either a baby in their belly or on their back or – more likely – both. Well, it's tradition, so that's all right.

It was exactly the same the way we felt put upon in Scotland but thought "this is how it is". My Mother, as well as looking after us bairns and doing all the cooking and the cleaning, had to work till all hours and in all weather on the farm with my Dad, yet he was always the one described as The Farmer and she was his just "the farmer's wife". Never mind the fact that it had been her father's land and – only because she had no brothers – it was then <u>her</u> land.

Enough of my rantings! Write and tell me what's going on over there these days. Has anything changed at all? I suppose the news has been taken over for months by the Queen's silver jubilee. I'm sure you were out waving your flag!

Meanwhile, I have to go out and look for something to cook tonight. Please write soon, even just a few words.

Esme XXXXX

While she was dispiritedly surveying the scant contents of the forlorn, privately-owned supermarket for anything edible, Esme bumped into Hedda, the German volunteer who had been Mosi's teacher at the nursery school where she had been so happy. Mosi had adored her teacher and Esme had been very drawn to her, though their acquaintance had been fleeting. She was soft-spoken and gentle; a tiny, dark-haired woman (the looks Esme so coveted), now heavily pregnant. Esme had always felt overwhelmed with gratitude when talking to Hedda and now, embarrassingly, found her eyes fill with tears of emotion. Fortunately, Hedda seemed far from assured herself away from her own arena – faltering over her English and blushing. But the conversation between them flowed. Hedda was aghast when she heard what Mosi had to endure at her present school.

'The thing is, though,' Esme said, 'Mosi just shrugs when I get upset about the state of her hands and tells me, "It's alright really. We're used to it. It's the same for everybody."'

Esme knew that being accepted, belonging, was of paramount importance to Mosi and it seemed that Hedda understood without judging; she neither condemned Esme as an over-anxious parent nor the education system for archaic practices.

'I've actually started some teaching myself'.' Esme regaled Hedda with an account of the Koreans and their first lesson, enjoying it in the telling far more than in the experiencing. 'Aye,' she concluded, 'it turns out that they're actually as enthusiastic about learning English as they were about investigating our house but it's still an uphill struggle for me, with no training.'

Hedda gave Esme some encouragement and suggested a few techniques that worked with Hedda's own new pupils whose knowledge of English was rudimentary. The irony of using the same *modus operandi* on these grown men as on kindergarten children was not lost on the two women.

Hedda told Esme that, with her baby due imminently, they were desperate to move from the second floor flat she and her husband Karl, also a volunteer, rented in a tenement block. The building had been constructed by, was owned by and occupied by Asian families who, superficially, were friendly but who hadn't embraced the German couple in any way. However, Hedda's chief lament was the lack of garden and the long, steep flights of stairs. She and Karl had looked in vain for rentable accommodation within their meagre budget. As they conversed, a recent chance encounter between Esme and her Ugandan neighbours replayed in her memory.

'The couple who live next door are going back to Uganda in a few weeks. I know they're renting but I've no idea who owns the house. Come and see *our* house and if you like it, you could talk to our neighbours.'

A couple of months later Hedda and family were Esme's next door neighbours. They became close friends: Ali and Mosi were always welcome there. Mosi, in particular, was besotted with the tiny baby, Zenia. Ali loved their new puppy whom he had named Spotty by announcing to him the first time they'd met: 'You're spotty!'. Esme's cat, Pipi, befriended them all next door, including Spotty. Karl was open and friendly towards Esme. He was a well-built man, with roaring red hair; he smiled and laughed a lot. He reminded her of how Martin had behaved early in their acquaintance. It brought home to her how seldom she saw that in him any more. At first she found it difficult to reciprocate to Karl's approach: she was still uncomfortable and unskilled with *Wazungu* men. She simply lacked the practice – either before she'd left Scotland and certainly since. Tanzanian men were different - apart from her work-mates who it had taken years to get to know properly. Generally they either flirted with you - normally, if they weren't a friend of your husband's or, if they were, respected you like their mother, even addressing you as such: *mama yangu*. Yet gradually she formed an uncomplicated, affable relationship with Karl.

She was envious of Hedda to discover that once Karl returned from work, he shared all the household chores - a pattern they had adopted prior to Zenia's birth and had now expanded to incorporate her care. The couple – defying Tanzanian norm - employed no-one to help in the house.

In discussion, Hedda gently challenged Esme's acceptance of her lot, such as, on one occasion, Martin bringing home friends without prior warning and Esme complying with his assumption that she would provide a meal for them. Esme regretted having complained about it to Hedda, forgetting for a moment that she wasn't one of her old friends she was used to swapping grievances with. Sensing Esme's wish to back-pedal, Hedda was at pains to make it clear that her remarks were in no way personal - Martin seemed a good person. Nevertheless, these observations made Esme uncomfortable in a way she couldn't put her finger on. She explained that plans evolved spontaneously and - without a phone - it was impossible for warnings to be given. Anyway, guests didn't need inviting, hospitality wasn't even a concept, there was no word for stranger – or at least it could only be translated by the same word – *mgeni* - as for a visitor, a guest. The word for welcome: *Karibu*, was one of the first words foreigners were told; it also meant 'near': *Karibu* mgeni. 'Come near, stranger, welcome guest!'

Esme laughed. 'At least it's not like in the old days, I only have to give Martin's guests a meal.'

'What do you mean?' Hedda asked.

'In the old days, travellers used to stop at the nearest village before nightfall, maybe having walked all day. So they'd be given food and drink, a bed for the night and the services of his hosts daughter or wife for the night!'

Hedda blushed and tried to laugh. It was clearly her turn to feel uncomfortable.

'Martin wouldn't dream of offering my services, don't worry!'

Opportunely, at that moment Karl, who had been holding Zenia in his arms so she could watch the comings and goings of the local children, summoned Hedda to breast-feed the hungry baby. As the two women parted to go about their respective duties, Esme realised she'd been neglecting her old friends Jocelyn, Marietta and Ulla since Hedda moved in next door. She resolved to get together with them again soon. They understood her situation.

Over the weeks, through conversation, Esme learned that Hedda and Karl adhered to a Marxist philosophy, despite both having been employed by Christian organisations. Esme had grown up with the notion that communism smacked of something unsavoury. Wasn't that what the cold war was all about? And Vietnam – which had got out of hand. The regimentation of Chinese and Korean men in Tanzania had done nothing to endear her to the philosophy.

The Korean students presented her with a glossy, coffee-table book full of colour photographs of smiling adults and children dressed in pastel colours, posed amongst pristine modern buildings and streets. It was so unreal it was comic. She showed it triumphantly to Karl and Hedda. It wasn't the ideal society they envisaged and they were in complete agreement that no-one would ever manage to tame Tanzania to such an extent. Rather, their vision chimed well with President Nyerere's experiment with 'African socialism'. Echoing 'comrade' or 'brother' as a form of address, he had introduced the term '*ndugu*'. It had been a seldom-used Swahili word for a distant family member but had really caught on now in everyday conversation, and even though many people used it initially with much mirth and derision, it was amazing how rapidly they had replaced the traditional terms: *Bwana* 'mister' had acquired overtones of 'Sir' since the colonial period and for women *Bibi* and *Binti,* roughly the equivalent of Mrs and Miss. The term *ndugu* did away with all these distinctions. But, of course, Socialism aimed to have equality in more than terms of address: the jokes that circulated maintained that now there was equality in poverty. This was far from reality but the slashing of salaries of public employees was a step in the direction of diminishing the gap between the incomes of the majority of the population, *wakulima,* the peasant farmers and the urban elite. Unfortunately, whether out of ignorance, scepticism or impatience of the realisation of this ideal, stung by collectivisation and shortages, the peasants were flocking into town seeking their fortune.

Hedda and Karl had mastered enough Swahili to communicate on a day-to-day basis; this alone would have set them apart from the other *Wazungu* with whom Esme had crossed paths. Karl, comfortable with himself, had become fluent while Hedda's fear of making mistakes - like Esme at the beginning - had held her back. Nevertheless, ultimately their plan was to take Zenia home and bring her up in Germany. Their aim was not, as was Esme's, to make their home in Tanzania. She warned herself not to get too attached to them but she couldn't help herself.

Esme and Hedda, often with Karl, would spend many intervals in the early evenings cooling down on the steps in front of one or other of the front doors, squinting against the rays of the sinking sun through the fingers of the coconut palms, drinking in the evening jasmine, chatting until the fruit bats wheeling overhead and the whine of mosquitoes heralded home-time for the children and, inevitably, for Esme too.

Martin remained aloof. Esme sensed an unvoiced hostility towards them which baffled her: he was usually at ease with foreigners, after all this was *his* country. Anyway, he was around so rarely during the hours of daylight that he barely saw them. However, one Saturday morning, Martin - spruced up as usual - was just about to set off 'to see someone' when there was a '*Hodi!*' at the door. As Martin opened it Esme, clearing away the breakfast things, glimpsed Karl beaming cordially on the doorstep.

'I come to invite you all to a small birthday celebration for my thirtieth birthday this afternoon!' Nothing in his open manner or cheerful voice could have been construed as provocative but to Martin it was a red flag to a bull.

'My wife and children will not be coming to your house this afternoon or any other time. And I do not want you speaking to her again.' Karl's expression was one of bewilderment.

'But I invite you all, Baba Mosi! It is with my wife and child also. What do you think we do?'

'I am not discussing it any further.' Martin replied through clenched teeth and he closed the door in Karl's face. Esme was shocked into silence. Few things riled Martin and she had rarely seen him so incandescent. Why?

'Martin, what's got into you? It's a tea party! You were so rude to Karl and they've been such good friends to me.'

'So I hear! I've heard all about how much time you spend with your carrot-headed neighbour!'

'Martin are you crazy? Hedda is there all the time! And the child.'

'You wouldn't be the first pair to find a way round a few little inconveniences like that!' Esme somehow kept her anger out of her voice:

'I've never heard such nonsense in my life!' and she kept the rest of her thoughts to herself. You're not going to sop me seeing the! You're not here half the time anyway!

Martin glared at her, she could see his mind working as he decided on his next move. What had got into him? He hadn't been drinking this morning, though he did still smell of it from the previous night. Thank God the kids had already gone round to play at Mercy's. Maybe he *was* actually worried about losing her.

'Martin, hen, I'm not interested in Karl that way. I'm not having an affair and I'm not even thinking about having one. So please just put your mind at rest.' Her day-dreams about Kaliwe didn't count because he didn't appeal to her any more, and anyway she knew neither of them would ever have translated fantasy into reality. Anyway what was the good in antagonising Martin. She didn't want a fight.

'Stay at home then, hen. Her tone was conciliatory.' See for yourself that nothing goes on. If I wasn't on my own so much I wouldn't spend as much time with them next-door.'

Martin checked his watch. 'I have to go and meet somebody. He sounded as if he'd already lost interest.

She spent the Saturday morning as usual, catching up on chores. The radio played Congolese and Tanzanian 'jazz' in the background. It didn't much resemble jazz in her opinion but she supposed the term derived from the use of the same instruments as in a jazz line-up. To her it was far more rhythmical it compelled you to dance. How long had it been since she been out to dance? As she sorted out the kids room, she cast her mind back to the era when the only time Martin would be out in the evening, was when they went together. It had been almost weekly in Kisasa, at the social club, it had been so easy to walk there and pop back to check on the sleeping Mosi. But the point was, back then Martin had enjoyed her company and hadn't been ashamed to show it. These days they went no-where together and she barely left the house in the evenings.

Rarely, she went to the local kiosks after dark, when she was really stuck for something. Taking the children with her was a real nuisance as they had to get dressed for outdoors instead of for bed and there was always a risk of mozzie bites. Once or twice, to simplify matters, she left them with Hedda and Karl but she knew it probably disrupted their evening, getting Zenia to bed, and so tried to avoid it. Once the kids were asleep and she'd finished the chores, she could read uninterrupted. She told herself she was lucky to have the time, the space, the books and the electric light to be able to enjoy reading.

All the same, part of her envied the inhabitants of the village behind the estate, glimpsed on these walks to the kiosk. The place was a hive of activity, people sitting outside their small darkened mud houses, dimly viewed by the glow of kerosene lamps, mostly tiny local-made ones emitting barely more than a candle-glow but hundreds of them twinkling in the dark evoked a yearning in her. Voices and laughter filled the air, folk milled about. But the price they'd pay for this was malaria. Martin reckoned traditionally most people didn't associate being exposed to mosquito bites with the fever, blaming instead a curse. But maybe they just preferred to take their chances than be enclosed in a windowless hut for the entire evening as they would be during the night. Martin said that in the countryside people sleep outside when it's hot but here in town there are too many tribes mixed together, too much unemployment, too much petty theft and the risk of violent attack.

Anyway, she wouldn't be going out that evening but she had the birthday party to look forward to. She was definitely going to that, whatever Martin said.

Ch 17: The Wake

'Whatever's wrong, hen?' Mosi burst in the front door, leaving it wide open behind her. Esme knew her daughter's wild tears and sobs must be due to more than the sort of trivial incidents that sent Ali in paroxysms of grief and anger.

'Alma's dead!'

'Alma! Fortuna's wee sister? When? Was she ill?'

'Yesterday she was playing with us and last night they took her to hospital and now she's dead!'

Esme did her best to console Mosi. They talked for a while about illness and death and why it happened. Not that Esme had any answers, nor did she pretend to. After a while Mosi said she had to go back to be with Mercy. Esme thought it best to let her.

She went to tell Mama Yohana, next door, and to ask her if they could go together to offer condolences. The whole business of death and bereavement was so imbued in tradition, it was a minefield she was afraid to tread in without a guide.

'We should give them some time to organise everything, we'll go a bit later on. I'll call for you.' Mama Yohana said, every inch a school teacher. She looked at the hem of

Esme's dress, apparently falling short of the dictates of modesty.

'Would you like to borrow a pair of *kanga*?'

Esme suppressed a surge of irritation. 'No thanks, it's fine. I have some.' Mama Yohana didn't wear *kanga* to work but the minute she got home she wrapped one round her lower half. Esme tended to keep one to hand to don when she ventured into the world beyond the estate.

She knew the custom was for friends, neighbours and colleagues to go in person to offer condolences to the bereaved family but somehow the occasion had never presented itself before: all the deaths that had affected her acquaintances seemed to have occurred in their ancestral homes, not in Dar. But a comment of Martin's had stuck in her memory: in Scotland they'd once seen a group of suited and hatted mourners disembarking from a funeral cortege. 'In Tanzania,' he had said 'A funeral is not seen as an opportunity to show off our finery. We show our respect to the bereaved by wearing our oldest and shabbiest clothes.'

Later that day, as the two women walked along the red murram road, Mama Yohana kept up an incessant stream of prattle about her children's behaviour, progress at school, the problems with her *shamba* …..

An un-seasonal shower earlier in the afternoon had laid the dust. The coarse, red earth crunched noisily underfoot. In the weeks since Esme had last been this way, some of the gardens had flourished spectacularly: a shrub she didn't recognise, creamy lily-like flowers dripping from its branches, red hibiscus trumpets, sprays of yellow and orange she didn't know the name of, shocking pink oleander, and bougainvillea in every hue imaginable from apricot through tangerine to mulberry. Pity so few flowers were perfumed: the smell of damp earth prevailed.

The front door stood ajar. On the steps lay an assortment of sandals and shoes. Esme followed Mama Yohana's example and stepped out of her own sandals and into the small hallway, a replica of her own. Thin voices raised in a dirge greeted them. They entered the darkened living room, it was wall to wall with people seated on the floor. There was no furniture, just people. As her eyes grew accustomed to the gloom, Esme realised that, actually, they were all women, their heads draped in *kanga*. The pungent mixture of perfume, *udi* and body odours was overpowering. Mama Yohana was picking her way between the seated bodies to the furthest end of the room. Esme saw that Alma's mother sat there, supported by the wall, her face haggard and tear-stained. When she reached Mama Alma, her neighbour dropped to her hunkers and took her hand, murmuring words of condolences. Esme heard the word *Mungu* several times and remembered that Mosi had said Alma and Mercy's family were regular church-goers. So much so that Mosi had been pleading to go with Mercy to communion classes starting next month, despite neither Esme nor Martin ever having encouraged religious practice of any kind.

Esme wondered what she would say. What do you say to a woman who has just lost her child, her baby, a beautiful, bright wee girl with an infectious giggle? Esme could barely speak beyond whispering '*Pole*', tears trickled down her face. Mama Alma burst into fresh sobs, clinging onto Esme's hands.

'*Ahsante*. Thank you for coming, Mama Mosi.' She managed between convulsions of weeping.

Following Mama Yohana, Esme squeezed herself into the tight space on the floor, created by several women bottom-shuffling aside. She seated herself on the palm-frond mat with her legs folded to one side. She felt ashamed for worrying about getting the protocol right instead of focussing on what had brought them all there in the first place.

The tune they were singing sounded vaguely familiar. Then It dawned on Esme that it was hymns they were singing, and some of the women had hymn books. Others joined in lustily without the aid of the written words.

She seemed to be the only one who hadn't a clue.

It was stifling. Sweat was running down from her armpits and her forehead under the extra layer of *kanga*. Her buttocks and legs began to ache, then go numb, she longed to stretch them out her legs in front like some of the women but there wasn't room. Sitting crossed-legged, she knew, was utterly taboo. The singing came to an end. Only the sound of soft crying and the buzz of a rogue fly. A woman called out softly,

'*Arubaini na sita.*' Forty-six. The whisper of tissue-thin pages followed as those with hymn books flicked through searching for the right page. The singing resumed. Another woman came in, gingerly picked her way through avoiding hands and feet, and crouched before Mama Alma who again began to shake with emotion. A couple of women quietly left.

And so it went on. Each newcomer brought on a fresh bout of crying. It was heart-rending. But no-one was embarrassed. Surely this was more normal than having to 'bottle it all up, keep a stiff upper lip, take it well, be strong.' Esme concluded that relatives would be taking care of the other children to allow their mother her time for grieving.

Eventually, Mama Yohana stood up and looked down at Esme.

'*Twende*' she mouthed.

Esme struggled to her feet, pins and needles invading the whole of her legs, and staggered after Mama Yohana out into the painfully bright sunlight.

They walked in silence for a few minutes, her neighbour uncharacteristically subdued. A thought suddenly struck Esme.

'Why were there only women? Where were the men?'

'Oh they don't sit together, the men are outside. You'll see tomorrow.'

'We're coming again tomorrow?'

'Of course! There will be people there all night. The burial will be tomorrow, leaving here at eleven.'

Esme thought she should go. She knew it would be OK at work, everyone else had had time off for funerals. She asked Martin to phone. She went with Mama Yohana and, this time, she kept a sharp look-out for the men. How had she missed them before, they were sitting on chairs in the garden, in the leafy shade, drinking beer. They were talking in normal voices, not whispers. A young woman was bringing out refills, beads of condensation forming on the ice cold amber bottles on the tray, beads of sweat stood out on the woman's brow.

Even though Esme knew what to expect, the claustrophobic intensity of the dimmed room, the restrained whispers of the women and the mournful hymn-singing, overwhelmed her momentarily. Go on Esme, she told herself, don't be so pathetic. She resumed her place on the floor.

Before long, a woman made her way over to the bereaved mother who was collapsed, exhausted, against the wall. Several women helped her to her feet. They supported her through and out of the room. A terrible cry rang out. One by one the women got to their feet and filed out. Esme followed, towards the source of wailing and keening as the womenfolk filed past the tiny coffin, open to reveal the child's appealing, dimpled face in repose. Esme could not hold back her tears.

Eventually she found herself in the back seat of a car with three other women somehow wedged in beside her. The rest of the day passed in a blur. The lengthy church service, the standing round the grave in the blistering sun - when she was glad of the *kanga* draped over her head, partially shading her face. Mama Alma had to be held up throughout the interment of her youngest child. This was why most families had so many children, losing one or two was often seen as inevitable, though no easier to bear. The notion of losing Mosi or Ali was too awful to dwell on.

Back at the house, they resumed their positions on the mats. Esme thought of the men outside, free to stretch and move, to drink, to converse, to help pass the time. She could see that having so many women showing solidarity must be a comfort to Alma's mother but, surely, she needed to talk. In fact that was what started to happen. The singing lapsed, respectful chatting began among the mourners and more women shuffled nearer to the grieving woman. A low hum of voices filled the room and occasionally a smile was exchanged.

Esme noticed after a while that there were fewer women in the room: Mama Yohana had disappeared. Maybe Esme could go home now. She felt exposed as she got to her feet and traversed the room, dropping to her hunkers to murmur good-bye to the chief mourner.

'*Pole sana, Mama.* I …, I don't know what to say.'

'What can anyone say. Thank you for coming.' Alma's mother attempted a watery smile. 'But why don't you wait and eat with us?'

It hadn't occurred to Esme that there would be food. How on earth would they feed this crowd?

'Em, I have to go and cook for my husband. Thank you.' No-one could argue with that but how embarrassing to reveal that Martin wouldn't be here. He'd shown no interest in any of the neighbours.

Outside, she peered round the side of the house. A canopy of palm-thatch had been constructed under which half a dozen women, mostly neighbours Esme recognised, were busy with charcoal braziers, massive aluminium trays and cooking pans: sorting rice, hacking up huge chunks of meat, peeling onions, painstakingly slicing tomatoes.

Esme's face burned. No-one had asked her. She would always be an *Mzungu*. Why don't you go and offer to help then? she asked herself. She couldn't answer the question.

As she walked back she wondered what it was she really wanted. She did want to be accepted by the other women but what if it meant waiting hand and foot on men? Did she wait hand and foot on Martin? When he was around, of course. Maybe she did. Why couldn't he be more like Karl? Why couldn't she be more like Hedda? And what was all that guff in the newspapers about women and men being equal?

Her own rain cloud followed Esme round for weeks, although the real weather was like a perfect summer in Scotland. The glorious sun-lit days were cooled by a playful zephyr which she thought had disappeared with childhood. Hedda and Karl's time in Tanzania was almost up. What would she do for *real* friendship? Hedda had, in her gentle way, contested Esme's socialising almost exclusively with women whose lives were similar to her own: that of an *Mzungu* married to a *Mwafrika*.

'But they understand what it's like, Hedda!'

'That is my point, precisely, Esme! It seems to me that you all complain to each other about the *problems* which are the same for each and every one of you and it helps you to put up with your situation. That means you never do anything to change it! I don't say it is *wrong* that you see only these people, but I see that you are not happy. I *hear* from you that you are not happy and that your *friends* are not happy. I don't say you should not be friends with them, I only say it is good to meet different *sorts* of people who have different *kinds* of experiences.'

Esme didn't disagree with Hedda but where would she meet these people? People who spoke a language she understood? Her Tanzanian neighbours and women she met at her work-place accepted as normal that their husbands were out in the evenings and never lifted a finger in the house – that's how it had always been and always would be, as far as they were concerned. Esme thought secretly that Martin actually compared well with a lot of them.

In the meantime, life went on. Since the Koreans had left, Esme had acquired two

Hungarian students. The couple had moved into the estate amidst the usual frenzy from the neighbourhood kids at the appearance of *Wazungu*. Esme had deliberately strolled past their house several times until she'd had the opportunity to meet them. With their first conversation, Esme had spotted their potential as students and perhaps, over time, friends.

During the ensuing lessons it became apparent that, as folk went, they were perfectly pleasant just somewhat lacklustre. Ferenc was a mechanic whose remit was to maintain the fleet of double-length articulated 'Ikarus' buses - a nine-day wonder on the streets of Dar - contrasting starkly with the over-worked, battered, old vehicles which had till now comprised the city council's service. Such an opportunity – to work abroad on an expatriate salary - had been beyond the couple's wildest dreams before Hungary joined the donor group vying for influence in the newly-emergent socialist state of Tanzania. Boriska had given up her lab work to accompany her husband and, it laboriously emerged, she was finding it very difficult to adjust to being a dependent wife.

'In my country, we all works – womans and mans.'

'Er, one woman, all *women*. One man, all *men*,' interjected Esme and not for the first time.

'Why here I no allowed work?'

'It's complicated,' said Esme making what she hoped was a sympathetic expression. She didn't relish trying to convey her own understanding of the government's rationale for denying work permits to accompanying wives of expatriates. It had never occurred to her to be up in arms about it like Boriska. The rules seemed logical – the government was protecting the rights of its own people to work: employers had to make a sound case for recruiting expatriates *before* bring them into the country by detailing the specialised skills demanded by the post. Esme herself, years earlier, had become a Tanzanian citizen and had the corner of her British passport cut off to render it unusable: dual citizenship was not acceptable – if you were in, it had to be with both feet. She sighed deeply and reached for her *English for Foreigners,* its red cloth back looking sadly faded.

After several hours of tortuous conversations with Ferenc and Boriska, Esme could only conclude that their motivation for travelling half way round the world was purely lucrative. However, as students, they were bliss compared to the Koreans.

The day Esme had been dreading arrived: the Krolls were leaving after six years in the country. Esme had known them for five of those but, although it had only been for the last two that they'd lived next door, during that period the family had become part of her daily life.

At a quarter to six in the evening she went out and sat on her front doorstep to wait for them. She knew that they'd be packed and ready well before the car came for them at six – they had retained their German-ness in that regard. Sure enough, Hedda came out at ten to and Esme squeezed through the gap in the hibiscus hedge to join her just as the Combi from Karl's workplace arrived to collect them.

Hedda handed Esme a book.

'Here Esme, this is for you.'

'But you've given me loads of things already!'

'Ach, just things we don't need! This is a bit special. Karl didn't finish reading it yet but I insisted we have to leave it for you. We will get it in German when we are back.'

Esme took the dog-eared paper-back and read the title. '*The Female Eunuch.* Weird title!'

'Write to tell me what you think of it when you have finished reading it. I found it very interesting, but the English, it was difficult for me sometimes. Karl and me, we didn't agree about everything but it makes you think a lot.' She thanked Hedda, seeing that her eyes were glistening.

'And now I must say good bye. Take care, Esme. Keep in touch.' She embraced Esme.

'Bye, Hedda.' Esme could hardly get the words out through her constricted throat as she hugged Hedda tightly. Esme had been determined not to cry but the tears splashed down her cheeks. It was all she could do to keep back the wail rising in her throat.

Karl, toddler Zenia in one arm, approached smiling sympathetically to embrace Esme with his free arm. The gaggle of neighbourhood kids, never to miss such an occasion as the departure of the *Wazungu*, tittered at this salacious spectacle.

'Esme, if ever you are travelling back to the UK, come via Frankfurt and visit us. All of you, the kids, Martin. We will be happy to see you.'

'Och, aye. Fat chance of that!' Esme managed a laugh through her tears.

She watched as the van was loaded and drove off, the Kroll's waving till it turned the corner. Esme was conscious of every pair of eyes on her – Ali's and Mosi's and every last brat's.

'Kids go and play, will you. I'm going for a rest.'

Inside, she threw herself on the bed and cried for quarter of an hour or more. It wasn't just for the Krolls, it was everything. Everything was so ... so pointless.

Eventually she sat up aware that she would need to get the children in. She picked the book off the bed and flicked through the pages. It looked heavy-going. She stopped at a section in bold black print about being 'the toy of man' written in 1792. She flicked further on. The words 'vibrator', 'bitch', 'vagina' leapt off the pages. She might have to keep this out of Martin's sight. Actually, she'd better disguise the cover – the kids might ask awkward questions about the shocking picture on the front depicting the skin of a woman's torso suspended from a pole.

She shoved the book to the back of her underwear shelf, buried deep beneath her faded, dingy old pants.

Ch18: After the Krolls

In the weeks that followed the Krolls' departure, an emptiness inhabited her chest, she was imbued with a sense of loss. Martin had noticed her low mood and had been caring and attentive towards her. It had lasted two days.

Sometimes she meandered around the estate in the late afternoon, the hour she would have shared with Hedda and Karl, the air filled with a fragrant warmth. Maybe she would exchange the odd word with other neighbours but they were busy with their vegetable plots, their cooking and their kids and that's all they ever seemed to talk about. She pined for the wide-ranging debates and the laughter. She hadn't realised how much laughter had become part of her life, until now, when it was absent.

There were days when she felt as though she would burst with the pressure inside. It happened at work sometimes. But it was mostly at home that the feeling overwhelmed her: in her breasts, her chest, her throat. Did she ache for another person's caress? No, that wasn't it. It was more that there was nothing around her, the air was so thin and empty that there was nothing to keep the energy inside her from bursting out. She wandered about the house and garden in a daze, trying to focus on the chores or on reading a library book. She couldn't understand herself. It wasn't just that she was sad or depressed or lonely though, at times, she felt all of those. And then one evening, watching the crimson sunset throw the palms into silhouette, it dawned on her: she was bored; bored out of her skull; bored out of her skin; bored to tears - tears which now ran down her face.

'I can't stand this another day!' Even as she addressed the coconut tree, she knew she had no choice. She kicked the ridged trunk, stubbing her bare toe excruciatingly and drawing blood. At least now she had something tangible to cry about.

That evening, the kids in bed, a couple of months after the Krolls' departure, she rummaged through her underwear and retrieved the book. At the back of her mind was the nagging awareness that she'd been putting it off for fear there would be no going back. The picture on the front made her shudder. She fashioned a sheet of foolscap paper into a jacket and sellotaped it to the inside cover.

Over the next few weeks she spent every spare minute reading. She was instantly gripped by the arguments about learned gender roles, about intellectual sexual equality and about the functioning of the female body - much of it a revelation to her - a mere mother of two. It was unlike anything she'd ever read previously: novels apart from those boring literature texts in her one year at uni. It stretched her brain and frequently she needed the dictionary . Some words - mostly to do with sex, like 'fellatio' and 'cunnilingus' – she didn't find there.

Most nights, Martin still out, she read in bed until her eyes began to close and her head to nod. One night she heard the front door open while she was still reading. Hastily she shut the book and pushed it under her pillow.

Next morning, going back to take a fresh handkerchief from the wardrobe shelf, Martin found the book on the floor at her bedside.

'What's this?' He looked uncomprehendingly at the plain white cover.

'Oh just a book from Hedda. I didn't want the kids asking me to explain the picture on the front. I wouldn't know how to.'

Esme maintained a casual tone though her heart was thudding. She kept Martin in her sight through the mirror propped up on the crudely-constructed plywood dressing table. Failing to remove the paper intact, he ripped it off to reveal the provocative illustration.

'Nasty! Doesn't look like your usual taste for romantic slush.'

Actually, thought Esme, not half as nasty as some of the grizzly murders depicted on Martin's reading material – in the days when he stayed in long enough to read.

'No, ..'

There was a double-honk at the front of the house.

'*Baba, gari imefika!*' sang Mosi's voice down the hallway.

Martin handed the book to Esme. 'I've got to go – look after it properly then if you don't want the children to see it. See you later.'

'Good bye to you too, darling,' Esme muttered to his departing back, her throat still tight with anxiety, now mixed with relief and ... anger! He hadn't even bothered to ask what the book was about! Not that she would have had the slightest idea how to respond.

In the following days, her head was in a whirl: she couldn't make sense of all of it – men were being blamed, for sure, but she was left feeling it was also her own failing for not being 'liberated' though she had never thought of herself as being un-liberated but the more she thought about it, the more she began to feel resentment. She was no longer sure what she was anymore. The ideas in the book were too much to take in. Ideas churned round in her head, she began to question everything to do with her relationship with Martin. One evening he came home earlier than usual. She was weary and had showered, planning an early night. Martin seemed in high good humour as he teetered slightly into the bedroom.

'How's my own little wifey?' he hugged her and nuzzled her neck.

'I'm OK – just tired. It's been a long day. Then Ali got into a fight and came home covered in blood. He's alright though. And Mosi found a dead kitten and was distraught! And now I'm wondering to what I owe the honour of your company at this early hour.'

'I just wanted to be with my honey!'. His warmth and smell were beginning to have their effect on her. She nestled into his embrace. 'What is there to eat?' he asked, between little kisses on her forehead. She unfailingly put his name in the pot every evening but his share usually ended up in the fridge before she went to bed.

'The fish-seller came round today so we got some kingfish.'

'That'll do nicely! I'll have a shower while you heat it up.'

She felt a flash of annoyance. But did she want an argument? She sighed and wriggled free of his arms. She sat on the bed to get the full benefit of the floor fan and wiped the sweat off her face with a *kanga* .

'Martin, love, I'm really tired and I'm ready for bed. Couldn't you heat it up yourself? Please?'

Martin stood stock still, his shirt half pulled out of his trousers.

'It's not much to ask, Mama Mosi. What's the matter with you? She searched for an answer. What was the matter with her? Did she want to provoke Martin? Why couldn't he come home and eat with them when the food was hot in the first place?

'OK, don't answer then!' Martin turned and in a few minutes she heard the shower. She didn't know what to do so she did nothing. She continued to sit there, listening as Martin came out of the bathroom. She strained, holding her breath, for sounds of his movements, waiting for the clatter of saucepans or the soft pad of his flip-flops approaching down the hallway. Nothing. What was he doing? Had his anger diminished or was he now in a seething rage? Maybe she should go and heat up the food. They could still have a cosy evening together. No, she wouldn't give in now. She was aching with holding herself in wait.

She awoke in the night, shivering, having lain down where she had been sitting at the end of the bed and had been in the full blast of the fan for hours. She crawled into bed and pulled the sheet over her. There was no sign of Martin.

When she next met up with Jocelyn, Marietta and Ulla she showed them the book, minus its white mask.

'This will give you something to think about! You have to read it.'

Marietta, the successful secretary at the Finnish Embassy, picked it up and glanced briefly at the front and the blurb on the back cover. She snorted and shook her head.

'Feminism! Women's Lib! No, thanks!. I'm surprised at you, Esme. You'll be burning your bra next!'

'What are you talking about, Marietta?'

'Haven't you heard about these women in America and Europe – feminists – who march and burn their bras? There are so many jokes about them in the newspapers we get at the embassy.'

'No. This book is the first I've heard about feminism and it's not a joke, what women have to deal with.'

Marietta raised her eyebrows exaggeratedly and turned down the corners of her mouth before passing the book on to Ulla, saying, 'Here, Ulla, maybe this is what you need.'

Ulla giving a grunt, without even bothering to put out her hand for the book and said in a flat voice, 'I don't read any more. It wouldn't be my kind of thing anyway.'

Jocelyn, ever sensitive to the feelings of others and equally wary lest emotions surfaced, hurriedly intervened: 'Wow, hot stuff, Esme.

Anyone for more tea? How about you kids, anyone for more juice? Hey, you guys, stop fighting!' And she had escaped, busying herself with domestic duties.

Esme had one last attempt to keep the issue afloat: 'Some women wouldn't put up with the way our husbands carry on. If you change your mind let me know.'

Marietta wasn't finished yet: 'We can use men for our own purposes! Why worry about all this equality?' She laughed and stretched out her long, tanned legs. 'By the way, Esme, I have a new English student for you. A new attaché, Markku, he's gorgeous. Can you take him on – I mean, give him English lessons?' she giggled coyly at the *double entendre*.

And so the conversation had quickly turned to every-day matters. Esme and Marietta, after some negotiation, arranged for Markku to call round one evening before dark, Esme was adamant she didn't want to give the neighbours - or Martin - cause for suspicion. Before she left, Esme resignedly collected her book from where it lay, abandoned.

In the back of the Beetle, Ali and Mosi were quiet, content with their afternoon's playing and ample supplies of fruit juice and home-made maandazi, giving Esme the chance to reflect on the exchanges with her friends. Their complete lack of understanding or interest in the book hurt. Marietta was practically a lost cause these days. She had changed: she seemed to consider herself practically a diplomat, mixing almost solely with the embassy staff and apparently having the money to support her new lifestyle. Her kids wore a sad expression lately. Esme gathered that Marietta was forever out in the evenings, leaving the children with her new *yaya*. Esme pondered the unpleasant feeling she'd become aware of: disapproval, resentment even, but also envy. Maybe Marietta was right: she didn't need liberating. She didn't seem to care that she must appear a tart to some people. Her husband didn't seem to cramp her style at all. She was financially independent of him and physically she might well be his match. In fact, she spoke of him almost with contempt. Esme knew that Marietta went out a lot with her colleagues of both sexes from the embassy apparently oblivious to how it was construed but if Esme was truthful she was unsure whether her behaviour was really wayward or was this just what modern Western women did? Christine back in Scotland certainly didn't – she was stuck at home with the kids.

Ulla, on the other hand, was near the end of her tether with her husband's philandering. When Esme had first met her Ulla had considered herself extraordinarily lucky as a plain, thirty-five year old teacher at home in Finland, to meet and marry the dark, dashing doctor – newly qualified in her home town.

They had three children in quick succession. Nothing would now separate her from her kids and she felt trapped to endure whatever treatment their father dished out.

Esme sighed. She did so miss the Krolls. Another student would help to get through that lonely period between work and the kids coming in from playing.

Ch 19: The Women's Group

C/o East African Advertising Assoc,
Dar es Salaam.

20th September, 1978.

Dear Christine,

I've just read this mind-boggling book 'The Female Eunuch'- have you heard of it? Have you read it yet? You must! There's so much in it about women, sex, the relationships between women and men I can't begin to explain it but it's unsettled me so much I don't know what to with myself any more. Neither does Martin, it seems. He's just keeping out of my way. It means, as well, that the kids see even less of him than they used to.

Now I understand so much more of what you said in your letters – God, it's so frustrating not being able to talk face to face or even on the phone! I appreciate now why you couldn't go on living with Alan and why you felt it important to change your bank account into your name rather than his, and I can relate to the bank teller's reaction (brainwashed like the rest of us!) but, most significantly, I fully comprehend your utter frustration with this response.

Your classes sound so exciting and it's fantastic that people in Scotland are beginning to be converted to Marxism. I know barely anything about it myself but Hedda and Karl were ardent communists and, if Karl's behaviour is anything to go by, the sooner all men are converted the better! There are all sorts of references to it in that book, as well. Before I read it, I was utterly amazed to hear about the reaction of men-folk in Leith to you girls going out to the pub! I thought it was only here that it would happen. Even now, I can relate to your poor friend because, of course, Martin's response would be exactly the same if I were to say I was going out for the evening with my pals. But at least the men in the pub aren't hostile even though all the jokes about leaving your husbands in their pinnies must be exasperating. I bet you always have a witty comeback for them though!

Meanwhile life here goes on just the same. Ali started school a couple of weeks ago. Mosi was lucky (even though she had to wait for a year to get a place) because for her first three years her class had desks to sit at. Not so Ali! Numbers have reached astronomical proportions because of the policy of free primary schooling for all seven year olds. They couldn't hold the flood back. Ali and his class mates have to take newspapers to sit on. Woe betide any kid who forgets – not only will they have to endure the ignominy of a soiled appearance but will have to put out their hands for a thrashing as well.

    Kaliwe has just presented me with some gripping stuff he wants typing pronto so I'll have to sign off.˙ Write soon. Take care.

    Love,

    Esme XXXX

That afternoon she arrived home from work a good fifteen minutes earlier than usual: for once, Selander Bridge hadn't been clogged up with traffic coming out of town.

    Normally Mama Zawadi would be poised for departure, waiting to don her *baibui* the moment Esme entered the front door, tying the satiny, black outer-garment under her chin as she gave a summary of the children's doings. During this exchange, through Esme's mind, inevitably would flitter the notion of a black widow which had first occurred to her all those years ago when she confused the words *baibui* and *buibui* meaning 'spider'. Then Mama Zawadi would be gone. Esme perfectly appreciated the fact that the other woman had a life of her own to get back to.

Today, however, Mama Zawadi was still scurrying round with piles of clean, dry clothes. It struck Esme how little she actually knew about her house-keeper's life, the two of them really had no time to talk, they simply changed shifts.

'Just leave the clothes, Mama Zawadi, and get away a bit early. Will there be anyone home when you get there?'

'My man might be back. He doesn't have a regular time to come home.'

'Men usually don't, do they,' replied Esme and, as an afterthought: 'Does he drink?'

'Oh No! He's a devout Muslim.' Mama Zawadi began the enrobing process while she spoke. 'My former husband used to drink, although he was a practicing Muslim, and I swore I'd never live with a drunkard again.'

'What happened between you?' Esme had never liked to bring the subject up herself but she had often wondered. 'Did you leave him?'

'No, I'd have stuck it out even though it was a nightmare, living with him.' The older woman's voice had dropped in pitch and volume and her eyes were staring into the distant past. 'He used to beat me – all the time - but I couldn't leave my children behind. No, he threw me out. First he brought home another wife, which he's not supposed to do according to Islam without his first wife's permission. Then he accused me of seeing another man. It was rot! One of the men in our neighbourhood used to like me and joked with me a lot but l never let him come near me. It was all just an excuse for my husband to get rid of me. His new wife had refused to share the home with me.'

Esme searched for appropriate words. Mama Zawadi sniffed and busied herself with arranging the folds of her *baibui*.

'How could you bear it? Where's your daughter, Zawadi, now? And your other children?'

Mama Zawadi shrugged.

'It was God's will. The children are with their father, of course. And their step-mother. I heard that they used to cry all the time for me when I left first but they're all right now. Zawadi's fifteen. She's going to be married soon. If her husband agrees, I might be able to visit her then. We keep in touch through my sister.'

'And this man you're with now, you didn't want to have children with him?'

'I did want to! That's why I agreed to live with him. As well as because it was very difficult after my husband sent me away. I came to Dar to stay with a cousin but she had no room for me so, as soon as I got a job, I had to rent a room on my own. No-one respects you, a woman on your own, so after getting together with Saidi, I decided to move in with him. But God didn't will that I have any more children. Luckily, he had children already, they're grown up now, so he wasn't that bothered. Otherwise, he'd also probably have got rid of me!'

'Yes, but if he'd had no children already and you had, it could hardly have been your fault!'

'Not at all, Mama Mosi!' she laughed at the *Mzungu's* naivety. 'It's always the woman's fault. Just the same as if she can only have girls.'

By this time, she had her *baibui* secured on her head, falling to just short of her ankles, her dress concealed, apart from an alluring 'V' to waist-level. Grasping the door handle, she bade Esme good-bye and was gone.

What would Germaine Greer have to say about Mama Zawadi's experience, wondered Esme, as she unpacked her shopping bag. So much for the author's theory that, faced with the threat of domestic violence, all you had to do was look unimpressed. It wasn't the first time Esme had heard of such monstrous behaviour but having an experience related to her at first hand had shaken Esme. It put Ulla's situation into perspective.

The response of her friends to her offer to lend them her book had altered Esme's feelings towards the other three; it was as if, when they had met on the two subsequent occasions, there had been a thick, opaque mosquito net separating her from her friends. She sighed as she resumed her evening routine, trying to forget about the book. Nevertheless, different aspects of it churned around in her mind. That was the trouble with her life: it didn't keep her brain occupied; too much space for thoughts to spring unbidden into her head – about how hum-drum her existence was and where it was all leading; Mosi and Ali would grow up and hopefully be successful adults and probably go off and leave her doing exactly the same thing. With a pang of guilt, she mentally promised her mother she would answer her letter next day.

That night in bed, a long-forgotten incident surfaced in her consciousness: a few years ago, a Canadian woman had joined one of their gatherings at Jocelyn's. Jocelyn had presumably invited Lynne in the belief that, being another *Mzungu* married to a Tanzanian, she would be glad of their company.

'So you guys do this regularly? Like a tea-party?' She had said 'pardy', of course. She had appeared open and friendly, in that slightly irritating North American way, but Esme had felt she was assessing them rather than participating.

'I guess this serves as an informal support network.' At the time, Esme had judged Lynne, from her haphazard array of garments and thick horn-rimmed spectacle frames, to be an eccentric. With her choice of conversation and phrasing – about the 'intimidating posturing' of President Amin from the other side of the Ugandan border - Lynne had come across to Esme as high-minded and erudite. At the time, Esme sensed she wasn't alone in feeling slightly intimidated by her, particularly when they became aware that she was a lecturer at the university. Jocelyn then threw into the conversation the fact that Lynne had a PhD. Lynne had not joined them again.

Now, looking back, Esme felt embarrassed at the memory and at the realization that the *Mzungu* wives club could have had nothing to offer her. As she lay awake in the dark, Martin's side of the bed empty, Esme reasoned that, if anyone could, Lynne could help her understand what was going on in that book and resolved to contact her.

Breakfast next morning was the usual scramble. Inwardly, Esme seethed, watching Martin sip his tea on the patio, aloof from the havoc in the living room, enjoying the crispness of the early morning air. He had an amazing ability to appear bright-eyed and fresh at break of day, regardless of the hour at which he'd doddered in the previous night. At the sound of a vehicle pulling up outside Martin re-entered the house; Esme couldn't help but notice how the v-neck and reveres of his smart, new short-sleeved Kaunda suit, in a subtle eau-de-nil, enhanced his oval face. More so than the round, collarless neckline of the Nyerere suits, now less popular – not that the President himself was in any way passé, indeed he was rallying the country behind him with Amin's antics at the border.

Some mornings, if the kids were ready when his driver arrived for him, Martin would give them a lift to school - a mixed blessing because Ali would have time to become filthy playing football before he got into class - but Martin wouldn't wait. He *couldn't* wait, she corrected herself. He had to be there at 7.30 on the dot: as head of department he had to set a good example. This was one of those occasion.

'Bye, Ali, Mosi. Bye Esme.' No kisses. Just gone.

In the few minutes' lull between the children's departure and her own, she composed a note to Lynne. No point in beating about the bush – she outlined her idea and asked Lynne to phone her at work. She would get the post box number from the directory at work and give the letter to Hassani to post with the office mail.

A few weeks later they met, at Lynne's suggestion, at the only Chinese restaurant in Dar, probably in the country. It felt very decadent, profligate even, to lunch out in this posh restaurant on the ground floor of this new seven-storey structure - the tallest in Tanzania. The meal, however, was a disappointment: the restaurant was more of a canteen and the food was nothing like the Chinese food she remembered from Edinburgh; in fact it was not much like food of any kind. In the event it was unimportant. Esme showed Lynne the book. She was full of enthusiasm, fascinated, as Esme had been, by the cover and the blurb.

'This feels like forbidden fruit!' she said. 'You know, of all the shortages we've endured for the past years, what I miss most of all is not the sugar, or the cooking oil or even the toilet paper, but books! OK there never was much of a selection but at least you could go into a couple of stationers and handle half a dozen or so paper-backs. And with no-one getting permission to travel outside the country now for conferences, it's dire!'

Esme was immensely grateful for Lynne's response to the book that now felt like her responsibility.

'Yes, I know,' she replied, 'Books are like gold-dust now. My friend at home posted me a book last Christmas and I never got it. Mind you, my mother's parcel of games for the kids didn't arrive either.'

Lynne wasn't listening, she was flicking through the pages, already engrossed.

A week later Lynne phoned her again.

'Hey, Esme, I found the book sensational! OK, a lot of it is boloney, as I'm sure you thought too, but I admire her guts in putting it out there! And like you said, she does propound some arguments that warrant closer consideration. I'd like to pass it on to my social anthropologist friend – Sirkka, if that's OK with you?'

What, Esme wondered, was a social anthropologist? She wanted to read Esme's book?

A few weeks later, Esme heard from Lynne again: Sirkka had passed the book onto Josefina, a Tanzanian Economics lecturer, who in turn passed it onto a colleague in her department, Ambani. Eventually the five women met in Sirkka's university quarters, a small self-contained house. Esme was bemused at the realisation that Sirrka lived alone and had come alone to Tanzania from Finland. It wasn't as if she was a frumpy blue-stocking - an old maid – she was an attractive woman. In fact, Esme gathered that she had a male colleague who stayed with her regularly. How did the university authorities view that?

The other women were as animated as Lynne about what they had read. Sirkka asserted that the book was overdue and the real achievement was to have got it published in the first place. Its huge success was proof of how much it was needed. Esme was on fire. They began to meet monthly to discuss other books that they were able to acquire via expatriate colleagues travelling abroad.

Esme could hardly believe that such radical thinking had started as long ago as 1963 – five years before Esme had left Scotland - with Betty Friedan's book, *The Feminine Mystique* and that she had been so completely unaware of it until now. None of the TV programmes or women's magazines that she had seen in Scotland had featured it, and certainly not her mother's *Woman's Weekly*. Frieden had identified 'The Problem that had no Name'. Now, with hindsight, she recognised that it was the very problem that had beset her after Hedda and Kurt had left. No, that wasn't quite it. It had been the conversations with them that had begun stirring up the slimy discontent which had been amassing - barely disturbed - for years. God, she couldn't remember when she hadn't been dimly aware of the slime - even when they were kids and her Dad had taken her brother everywhere with him leaving her to help her mother. But she had ignored it, not knowing what else to do.

The group increased in number to seven. After the first few meetings the women agreed to introduce some structure to the meetings, taking turns to present a summary and hypotheses on the selected reading at the outset of the session. Esme had neither demurred not concurred but inwardly vowed she would not be taking on such a task. She couldn't possibly do it.

Esme ducked out each month, the others were so enthusiastic about volunteering that she thought she might get away with it indefinitely. One day before the meeting, however, Lynne discretely suggested that it must be Esme's turn to present. Their next reading was a slim volume, *Wages for Housework*. Esme nodded, feeling the panic spreading through her chest. Lynne suggested they meet up when Esme had drafted her summary and they go through it together, prior to her presentation.

'You can't give up now, Esme! You're the founder member of the group and you have great ideas. You're just not confident in communicating them.' Esme's anxieties were mollified, to a degree.

Even after Lynne had given her pointers and polished it up, Esme agonised over the presentation in the days leading up to the meeting, her digestive system in crisis. She delivered the synopsis in a cold sweat, trembling like one in the grips of malaria. When she had finished, Lynne beamed her thanks, and the others nodded encouragingly. Or politely.

Relief blocked out for her the beginning of the debate that followed – she was limp, thankful she was no longer in the limelight - but soon she was drawn in. Ambani and Josefina were both married, Ambani even had two children. Because of their very different experiences from Western women, they had difficulties with the very concept of a 'housewife'. They found it hard to understand why the latter shouldn't have careers as well as families, something educated Tanzanian women took for granted: surely that was the whole point of education, even to primary level?

On her way back to her domestic responsibilities, Esme allowed herself to feel pleased with her effort. And she acknowledged, that having prepared the presentation, her grasp of the topic gave her the confidence to participate in the discussion. The issues for women were different in the western world. At least these days married women in the UK were *allowed* to continue working after marriage, unlike in 1942 when Esme's Aunt Marjorie had to get a dispensation from the Education Board to continue her employment as a teacher. She checked her watch aware that her own 'housegirl', a mature woman who could barely read or write, whose dependency on the meagre wages Esme paid her, rendered it difficult for her to refuse to work three hours overtime once a month so Esme could go to her meetings at the university.

Over the months, the group went on to read academic papers written locally. They had to rely on photocopies, often smudged and faded: like everything else – ink for photocopying was always in short supply. Esme was astonished at how much research about the gender gap had already been carried out - mostly by indigenous scholars - comparing wages of women factory workers to men's, the number of girls in school compared to boys, the type and amount of work carried out by rural women compared to their men-folk.

It took Esme some weeks to fully absorb the reality around 'housework' in most of sub-Saharan Africa. Most houses were so small and simple there was no housework as such but the maintenance of the actual structure might well be women's work, daubing the walls with mud and dung.

The term 'housewife' in the Tanzanian context was virtually irrelevant because although women did bear and raise children, laboriously prepare and cook food, walk miles to fetch water and firewood, they weren't stuck at home – they were also left with the bulk of the agricultural work – growing both food and cash crops. It was, however, the men who took care of marketing the agricultural produce and the proceeds were theirs. Childcare, as a concept, barely existed either: within hours of being born, babies were carried on their mothers' backs while the mothers resumed the planting, weeding and harvesting. Back at the homestead, children too old to be carried, too young to farm, had to fend for themselves and each other, perhaps with an infirm relative or neighbour close by.

Esme lapped up all this learning. The problem for her was the language used, English yes, her mother tongue which was not the case for Sirkka, Ambani and Josefina, but academic English. Although, eventually, she felt she understood such phrases as 'there is a need for theoretical clarity in the analysis' and 'housework is work incompatible with the possibility of human self-actualisation,' she doubted if they'd ever trip off her tongue. At the same time, she was aware of what a privileged position she had come to occupy. She must write and tell Hedda.

The Hill - as the university was known - soon became a familiar sight to Esme, one that was very easy on the eye. From a distance of several miles the new, white, tower blocks were prominent on the sky-line. Nestling among them, attractive, white, staff bungalows were dotted around on the series of hills. The Hill, cooled by pleasant breezes, had no need of air-conditioning. However, for the students, with only the beleaguered bus service to connect them with the town six miles away and only leg power to take them up hill and down dale between lecture theatres and halls of residence on campus, it was hard work. And then, of course, there was the water problem. She remembered that the water supply had struggled to reach their flat on the second floor in Ilala so how could it be expected to climb six floors of the buildings, having already struggled up the hill?

The success of the group had led to several requests from women faculty members to join. As it grew, so the group was becoming more formal. From now on they could no longer be accommodated in people's living rooms in comfy chairs but needed the space of a seminar room. It was initially daunting to Esme but on a day-to-day basis she felt more alive than she had done in years.

Then Lynne conveyed worrying news: the Dean had got wind of their meetings on faculty premises without permission to do so. The group had no official status and was banned from meeting. The women were furious. Ambani voiced the general concern of the women:

'I know what their problem is! They're all men and they feel threatened! Till now we have been united with our male counterparts in our fight against neo-colonialism and capitalism, in alliance with the proletariat and the peasants. Now we have seen that within those groups of people the world over, there is another struggle to be joined: one half of them is being exploited by the other half! We female academics have joined another battle. The authorities are afraid. And so they should be!'

A heated discussion followed. Esme could only look from one speaker to another in awe.

'What we have to do is make ourselves into some grandiose-sounding study group. We just think of an impressive title.'

'Red tape abounds here as it does in the whole government bureaucracy. There is a long-winded procedure to set up a society. We've been allowed one last meeting.'

'What would happen if we carried on meeting anyway?'

'We'd lose our jobs, that's what!'

'Oh yes, this is serious!'

'But we're not going to give up, are we?'

'Of course not. We need to give ourselves a proper name. Set of aims and a constitution.'

As the discussion continued it became clear to all that there was a lot they could actually do to give themselves a genuine reason for existence in official eyes but they would need money.

'The Scandinavian countries are looking for initiatives by women to fund. We should put in a proposal.'

Over the next few weeks, small groups worked on different aspects of a draft proposal. It was to be a research project – issues concerning the majority of Tanzanian women – but this was not just ivory tower stuff, research for its own sake, it was to look for ways of taking the findings of the research to the people it was about, to their benefit.

The process of being involved with this development of the group was exhilarating but, after a meeting, Esme would have to rush back to relieve Mama Zawadi. To Esme, the irony was that the opportunity for educated women, like those in the group, to pursue a career - or a passion - at the same time as maintaining a household and bringing up children was entirely due to the fact that other women, who had barely any schooling, did their domestic work for them. Esme wondered if she was taking advantage of her house-girl, exploiting her. But wasn't she, Esme, also being exploited? She'd have to go home and start cooking for the family. Family? It didn't feel like a family, it was her and the kids and a fella who came and went as he pleased. Should she really be putting up with Martin? What were her options? What about her friends and her acquaintances - whose model was best? She was just one of millions of women, married with kids – what was it all about? Why get married? Why have kids? Why not? Why anything?

Ch 20: The Journalists

'Food's ready, Esme, Tara.' Pete opened the door of the office and peered round it. His open smile met Esme's as she looked up.

'Thank you.' said Esme, pushing back her dining chair gingerly to avoid scraping it on the floor, and getting to her feet. This was her third day in the job and this call to lunch, at least, was a familiar routine. But *everything* was so different from anything she had experienced before.

'Be right with you, honey.' Tara addressed Pete without taking her eyes off the capitals appearing on the paper in front of her. Unlike Pete, she could touch-type. She ripped the telex tape from the puncher and threaded it in. Esme was still fascinated by this machine - she hadn't even known of their existence before this. A one-armed-bandit leapt to mind each time she walked through the office door and was confronted by it. She dawdled, reluctant to leave just when the action was starting. Tara keyed in the distant telex number but – as usual – the lines out of Tanzania were busy and she had to retry.

'Don't wait for me, Esme. I'll need to make sure this goes through.' Again Tara spoke without shifting her gaze, flicking her, long, thick black hair back over her shoulder. She was so pretty, so beautifully yet appropriately dressed, in Heidi skirts and sleeveless, silk blouses in rich hues. Esme, wished she was the one staying back to send the report but Tara and Pete didn't seem to think of giving her only the menial aspects of the work. Esme would also prefer them both there for lunch: she found it so hard to converse with men. No, it wasn't all men. It was *Wazungu* men. She'd not found it difficult to relate to Tanzanian men once she and Martin had cemented their relationship. She walked gingerly the length of the parquet-floored corridor from the appropriated bedroom and, conscious of her sun-bleached, shapeless cotton dress and dumpy, freckled flesh, went into the spacious sitting room which opened into the dining area and kitchen beyond.

Pete, a plate laden with food and a fork in each hand, pushed the heavy armchairs with his thigh on their oiled castors over the polished wood floor into a triangle. She found it irksome, eating in an armchair, having to juggle with plate and fork - knives weren't even offered - trying to avoid dropping food on her clothes, worse still on their expensively upholstered furniture. It wasn't as if they didn't have a dining table - there was one a few yards away.

'Here you go, Esme!' With a generous, boyish smile he handed her a plate. 'Take a seat, don't be shy!'

She attempted to smile back while thanking him, sinking into the armchair and taking the proffered plate. He took one of the other two and began eating with gusto. The food smelled delectable. She couldn't tell what it was other than that it had a lot of chopped, uncooked vegetables and mayonnaise which Pete had apparently made himself - she wasn't sure if that was out of preference or necessity. Her employers had a supply of commodities she'd either never seen in her life or hadn't seen since she left Scotland where they had rarely eaten salad and then it had been with a bottle of salad cream. For some reason, salad was regarded with great suspicion by Tanzanians, Martin included.

Mmmh, it tasted absolutely gorgeous! She would say so, when they'd finished. She didn't want to look too keen, to let on that she wasn't used to this standard of food.

Pete was very good-looking: tanned, blue-eyes and blonde hair. In his plaid cotton shirt she could see him wearing a ten-gallon hat, on the back of a horse. If she were Tara she wouldn't be leaving him alone with another woman for a minute. But, let's face it, there's no way Tara was going to see her as a threat. All the same, she hoped Tara wouldn't be long, it was so difficult making conversation with Wazungu men. But he chatted away undeterred between mouthfuls, even through them, and seemed happy with her monosyllabic replies. She was struggling to work out the rules of this new world. To know where the demarcations lay between private and public, employer and employee, men's and women's roles.

Despite that, it had raised her self-esteem to realise that she'd impressed Tara and Pete with her skills although they knew very little of her background. They hadn't asked for a CV and the interview had been a chat over a cup of coffee in these very armchairs. She guessed that was to make sure they could work alongside her in such close quarters and that they'd previously grilled Pamela – a friend of theirs as it had turned out - who must have said something about her personality as well as her ability to type accurately in English and speak Swahili fluently.

Evangelina, the *yaya,* trudged in from the garden and exchanged greetings with Esme and Pete. Shruti, her employers' three year old daughter, misleadingly blonde and angelic in appearance, ran in two minutes later.

'Hi, Esme! Hi Pete!' Whatever happened to 'Daddy' or 'Pops' or whatever. And didn't the child know to address grown-ups as 'Auntie'? The woman and child went to join Bernadi in the dining area, adjoining the kitchen. Esme heard Hamedi, the gardener's voice, as he came in the kitchen door and any minute they'd be joined by Shruti's playmate from next door and the whole lot would sit chatting round the table for half an hour or so. By Esme's standards, Pete and Tara were obviously very well-off but they were incredibly generous with it.

Tara joined them mid-way through their lunch and after Esme had finished hers and tried to show an appropriate degree of gratitude she returned to the office. It was a relief to have the small room to herself, three was definitely a crowd in here, with the two filing cabinets. Tara had given up her desk along with the portable typewriter to Esme for the hours she was there and it worked out OK as one the other of her employers were often on the telex or the phone and coped with the spare chair and the corner of a desk, a spiral bound notebook always in the hand. One or other or both often went off to do an interview or whatever else it was they did; and Pete and Tara seemed to work there many hours after Esme had gone.

She heard the crunch of their brand new Toyota in the drive as her employers left. They were going to the airport to cover the arrival of some British diplomat. Whenever they headed off to a reception at the Kilimanjaro Hotel or to interview a visiting foreign President, she felt like Cinderella as she stayed behind to do the filing. But she would have to get used to it. They were planning a couple of weeks away soon and she would be here on her own. They were training her up to hold the fort in their absence: to take phone calls, though all their clients would be informed in advance of their absence. She wouldn't be filing reports to the BBC and *The Guardian* and all the other media like they did but she'd have to be extra vigilant in scanning the two daily newspapers and the Catholic weekly as Tara and Pete would be relying on her to spot any significant articles in the English as well as the Swahili papers. At the moment, she was anxious that she'd dismiss an article as unimportant so kept asking whichever of her bosses was around while at the same time feeling guilty for disturbing them all the time.

On the whole, she was quite enjoying being challenged in a semi-intellectual way but her brain was tired at the end of the day from unaccustomed use. She was familiar with scanning the newspapers from the advertising agency – but this had to be more thorough. For the time Tara and Pete were away there would be no news reports going from Tanzania to the outside world. Luka had said that there wasn't much going on these days so their reports wouldn't be missed. All the same, she wished she could fill in for them. They were going to phone her, just to check nothing exciting like a coup or an assassination had occurred - the sort of event Western media thrived on.

As she drove the quarter of a mile home, she reflected on the irony of it – now that she worked practically on her own doorstop, she had a car – even if it was a beat up old Beetle.

All those years when she had several miles to travel to work, she had to fight for the privilege of a place on a bus. Not only was she earning more now, there were all kinds of perks with the job – the lunches, for a start. But she felt – what was it? Lonely. She missed all the jokes and teasing with the others. Bernadi was OK but he clearly wanted to stay within what he perceived as his own boundaries and stay within the company of Hamedi and Evangelina. She missed Kaliwe, though less than she had expected, as well as Macha and the others but she knew that, now the children were less demanding, she had outgrown that way of work – squandering time in chatting and not being really stretched any more. Yes, she was in a good place now.

Dar es Salaam,

30 January 1980

Dear Christine

I'm sitting on a bench in the relative cool of an acacia in full bloom. The abundant flowers suggest its popular name - the flame tree. It gives off a faint tang of pepper. If I close my eyes and concentrate, I can feel the slightest of breezes on my cheek. Otherwise, it's perfectly still. And very humid. I'm outside Eddie's car repair workshop - again. He's muttering to himself and shaking his head.

Yesterday – Saturday – Mama Yohana from next door asked me if I wanted to go to buy some fresh rice from a village near here. Fresh rice is delicious and has a wonderful fragrance, so different from the stale old stuff we get in the shops. My neighbour is a primary school teacher, and a very strict one apparently, but it so happens that she has relatives farming in nearby. She was draped in beautiful red and yellow *kanga* to impress and, what with her being a well-made woman anyway, and having her youngest on her lap and another on the way, not to mention the bundles and baskets stuffed in every nook and cranny round her, it was quite a feat installing her in the front seat of the Beetle. We packed the rest of her brood into the back seat: Yohana, Juma, Mahmud, and the twins Salma and Safia, ranging from two years to six, perfectly behaved with a wary eye on their mother. (No room for Mosi and Ali so I prevailed upon Martin to stay at home with them since it was in a good cause.)

The pity was we hadn't quite got to the sandy track and were still on the tarmac when the car went up in smoke. I may not have mentioned the previous occasions, but this is the third time this has happened. No-one told us that Beetles have this propensity for spontaneous combustion, for self-immolation. Unless it has something to do with its state of decrepitude. I think it's related to the engine being air-cooled rather than water-cooled, as are normal cars, which may account for the engine being in the boot. Which meant that yesterday I didn't see the smoke till the fire had well and truly got going. Or at least, I didn't recognise it as smoke. When I glimpsed it in my rear view mirror, I thought it was a particularly dusty and dirty patch of road (I use the term 'road' loosely, of course). Then the acrid fumes reached me. Only, at first, I assumed we were in the vicinity of a bonfire of old tyres – which happens more often than you might imagine. Then the car began juddering and emitting splutters.

I was out of the car like a shot, yelling, 'Moto, moto, tokeni!' trying to get everyone out. Mama Yohana was firmly wedged in, struggling to extricate herself and the baby. The car's only a two-door so I had to drag the five kids out from the back-seat through the driver's door while they were screaming '*Mama, Mama*!' and crying and waggling their hands from the wrists and straining away from me trying to get to their mother. Eventually she popped out like a cork, by which time I'd managed to haul the children, screaming blue murder, into the bush at the side of the road.

I burnt my hand opening the engine cover and great flames leapt out at me. I was crying and sweating and shaking and shouting 'Help me, help me!' to Jamila who was trying to tie her baby on her back to free up her arms. I started scrabbling with my bare hands, trying to scoop up sand from among the grass and flinging it into the engine. The tongues of flame devoured it and licked higher. Then my saviour, my knight in shining armour, emerged through the black smoke. Actually, a grizzled farmer about a head shorter than me, making his way jauntily back from his field, his jembe (a hoe-cum-spade) on his shoulder. He waved me away, doused the fire with spade-fulls of sand in thirty seconds, commiserated with us, shook my hand and disappeared over the horizon. Obviously all in a day's work.

You'll find this hard to believe, but I actually drove the car home. This morning Eddie came and towed it here. And he doesn't look too happy right now.

~ ~ ~

Esme hadn't really meant to tell Tara about the Women's Group, she'd

had a feeling that Tara would want to get involved in it and, sure enough, she did. In fact, the expatriate world being such a very small one, it turned out that Diane Simpson, one of the two new expatriate group members, knew Tara and she'd not only told Tara about the group but also that Esme was a member.

'How come you didn't tell me, Esme?' Tara sounded quite indignant although her face wore a fixed smile. 'I had no idea you were engaged in such an interesting project. The group sounds fascinating!'

'Yes, it is. I didn't think you'd have time for it, you're so busy already.'

'Oh, but this is an opportunity to influence a really crucial area of development. And I hear your funding application has been approved!'

'How did you hear that?'

'Diane gave me Lynne's phone number and she thinks it'll be fine for me to join – apparently your constitution allows for a third of the membership to consist of non-citizens. So I'm coming to your next meeting and if the group okays it, I'm in! Say, I could give you a lift, save your gas.'

Of course, they went together to The Hill, in Tara's swanky car. Esme, always anxious before the meetings, found herself short of breath, her heart thumping in her chest. She had just begun to feel a bit more confident and now Tara would be listening to her every word and questioning her on it. Tara, of course, was her usual equable self, oozing self-confidence.

They found a note pinned to Lynne's office door telling them the room number where they'd find the group. With the funding secured, they could now meet openly and use the seminar rooms. However, securing a free room for the meeting had been another issue as Tara and Esme learned from the others, the majority of whom were faculty members. They'd been assured by the bursar that there were no free rooms and had only found one by trooping around several buildings prior to the meeting. It was becoming clear to the group, from a number of events, that the university administration was deliberately being obstructive.

Tara's membership was approved. Her credentials were good: she had a sound academic background and was known from her articles and broadcasts for her leftist leanings. She was well-versed in Marxist theory and fitted right into the group. Even though she'd just joined, she had no qualms about expressing her opinion, which she seemed to have on every issue discussed. Esme was torn between admiration and resentment.

The main issue for the group was implementing their plans: they'd envisaged dividing the main group – now consisting of twenty members – into a number of sub-groups, yet to be defined. Not surprisingly, Tara got support for her suggestion to work with the media; others were to be more academic and research oriented. Apart from the advantages of working and even living near to Tara – the practical nature of the media cluster was clearly Esme's best bet. They arranged to meet up in two weeks time with the other two women - local journalists to pool their ideas as to the nature of their first project.

As luck would have it, the day Esme brought home the carton of goodies, shipped in from Kenya by Tara and Pete with their own much larger order, Ali and his pals were outside the house investigating a 'snake's den'. Only two snakes had been found in all the years they'd lived here – one on a bush outside the front door and one clinging to the wall behind the book-case in the children's room – so she hoped this one was more imagination than reality.

'*Mama*, what's in the box?' asked Ali, never one to miss a trick.

'Nothing important.' She planned to stash things away and bring them out in dribs and drabs at appropriate moments.

But it was too late. Ali called out to Mosi, 'Come and see what *Mama*'s brought home!' and they and all their friends were suddenly crowding into the kitchen.

'*Jemani, vipi! Nendeni kukcheza!* Go off and play!' and she stood with her back to the carton on the kitchen table, her arms folded defensively. She switched to English which only her own children understood. 'I'm not opening this box while all your friends are here. Maybe later.'

Seven pairs of eyes were trained on her face questioningly. She was tired and could do without this. And Mama Zawadi was in the kitchen doorway, waiting to bid her goodbye.

'Haya, twendeni! OK, let's go!' Mosi propelled the bunch of children out of the front door, turning back to tell her mother, 'Ali and me will come back in a minute.'

Esme couldn't begrudge them the excitement – it was like Christmas, or at least like Christmas when she'd been a small child, not like Mosi and Ali's Christmases, poor kids. Their faces reflected the wonder of the such exotic items as processed cheese triangles, a jar of Marmite which was the one item Esme was fairly sure to have all to herself, a bottle of clear, golden cooking oil, bars of Lux, an enormous tin of dried milk and even a large bar of chocolate which Esme put in the freezer: they would have one square each at weekends.

Inspired by the familiar tastes of spreads and knowing how soon they would be gone, the next weekend she bought a kilo of shelled groundnuts and set about making peanut butter. She'd seen Pete make it in the blender – you needed a bit of cooking oil to get it going. First she 'roasted' the nuts in a dry frying pan over the electric ring, thanking her lucky stars it still worked and they had electricity. She couldn't have faced this on a charcoal stove like many of her neighbours. Then she put the nuts into the big wooden mortar, with a few drops of oil, and began pounding with the heavy pestle. Hours later she had a concoction slightly resembling crunchy peanut butter. Delightedly she spread it on slices of bread – itself a prized commodity and presented it to the children when they next came in complaining of hunger. Ali took a suspicious bite and immediately spat it out onto the floor. Mosi having held back, politely shook her head and said 'No, thank you, *Mama*. Please can I have some empty bread.'

Esme was frustrated and disappointed but could hardly blame the children. 'Esme,' she muttered to herself, 'will you never learn that this isn't bloody Scotland? The kids don't miss your kind of Christmas or peanut butter because they've never had it, and surely there are more important things to worry about.'

She continued to muse while she did her chores. One of the worries was the invasion by Amin. Ordinary people like herself didn't really know what was going on since the announcement under the emblazoned headlines AMIN INVADES TANZANIA – but even Pete and Tara couldn't find out a great deal more. But one morning when she went to work – they'd obviously been busy in the office for many hours, apparently after a phone call from a contact in the president's office. Tara looked haggard but happy – Pete the phone to his ear was pacing back and forth within the limits of the phone cord, a mug of coffee in his free hand. He crashed the receiver onto its cradle and whooped with joy,

'We can go with them! Tara, we're going next week. Esme, Tara and I are going with the Tanzanian army to kick Amin's troops out of Tanzania!'

The next week was an absolute whirlwind of activity. Esme's first thought had been that she'd be expected to cover the news from Dar – a thought that both thrilled and terrified her – but it turned out that her bosses had rookie freelance journalist friends in the States who had been waiting on tenterhooks for such an opportunity.

The two weeks they were away the whole country was holding its breath, waiting for the outcome. There were, of course, Tanzanian journalists also accompanying the troops but press releases were very guarded. Meanwhile Esme, Janine and Burt poised to file reports from Dar es Salaam, were valiantly trying to find any news to relay to the outside world but had to be content with mostly bland official statements. Was it that the Dar-based politicians didn't want to say what was going on or didn't actually didn't know? Phone connections between Bukoba, on the Tanzanian side of border with Uganda, and Dar weren't totally reliable at the best of times and with the economic shortages, spare parts for repairing aspect of the country's infrastructure, including communication systems, were often hard to come by.

It was only when it was all over that they were given the news: that the Tanzanian army had succeeded in not only pushing Amin and his invading army out of the north west of the country but had pursued it all the way to Entebbe, the capital of Uganda, and defeated the invaders so thoroughly that Amin had fled.

Ch 21: Decision Time

Martin came home early, really early. Esme was still cooking. She was frying kidney beans, which although soaked overnight, were chewy. And no amount of onions, tomatoes and spices would disguise the musty flavour. It would be the third time that week they were eating these ancient dried beans as their evening meal. Martin insisted on the children having two cooked meals a day even though he was never the one to cook them. Anyway there wasn't much else they could have. The treats from Kenya hadn't lasted long.

'Hello, Sweetheart.' He came into the kitchen, put an arm round her shoulder and kissed her on the lips. Esme overcame her surprise sufficiently to return the kiss. His breath smelled of beer, but faintly. He hadn't had too much.

'What's up, Martin?' She remained stiff, noting the kikapu, the ubiquitous palm-leaf basket, that he'd deposited on the kitchen floor with a clanking sound. It contained half a dozen bottles of Kilimanjaro lager. 'Are you expecting company?'

'No, Esme, keep your hair on!' He removed his arms. 'I've got some news for you – we've something to celebrate.' As he spoke he was taking the bottles from the basket. Four went into the fridge, the remaining two he put on the kitchen table beside Esme, took the opener from the shelf and removed the metal caps. His finger prints remained in the condensation on the amber glass. What was this about? He reached for two glasses from the shelf.

'I see you haven't forgotten your way around the kitchen then?' Esme aimed for a teasing tone – she wouldn't have risked such a remark normally.

'Careful!' Martin tapped her nose and she pulled back, irritated. He filled the glasses, fastidiously tilting each one and sliding the liquid in to minimise the froth.

'Leave the cooking and come and have a drink,' he said nodding towards the remaining glass and bottle.

'OK, I won't be long, just got to put this on to simmer now.'

She joined Martin on the settee in the living room. He put his arm round her again. This was so unfamiliar as to be almost erotic. But she wasn't going to be seduced into behaving as if everything was normal between them, to overlook all the absences and indifference just because it suited him.

'Esme, I'm getting promoted. I'll be in charge of the government finances for a whole district!'

'Oh, well done! Which district?'

'I'm coming to that. Morogoro District.'

Alarm bells rang in her head. 'Morogoro! That's hundreds of miles away! In the middle of the country. There's no sea. That's what they call it, isn't it: *'mji kasoro bahari'* – the town without a sea.'

'Don't melodramatic, Esme. There are hundreds of towns in Tanzania, in the world for that matter, that aren't beside the sea. Anyway, Morogoro has mountains.'

'Well, whatever it has, I can't move. Not now. I'm in the middle of typing the book for Tara and Pete, and we're starting up a lot of activities in the women's study group.'

Martin put his glass down on the coffee table with unnecessary force.

'You'll find another job, no problem with your English, and there's bound to be a branch of the Women's Union there.'

The Women's Union, in the opinion of her study group, was a club for the wives of politicians, officially linked to the political party and totally ineffectual. She decided this wasn't the time to disillusion him.

'I don't want another job, Martin. I like the job I have and there are so many advantages to it. And what about this house? It's our own house, you expect us to abandon this? And what about the kids, they're really settled at school? No. Martin, say no for once.' Then remembering, she added 'And I've got my English students!'

Esme realised she was shaking with emotion. She needed breathing space or she felt she would leap at Martin and start flailing him with her fists. She looked out through the patio doors. She could see the bats beginning to swirl round in the pinkening sky. She realised the screen doors had been left open and got up to close them before too any more mosquitoes got in. She felt tempted to walk out into the garden and keep on walking.

Eventually she asked, 'When do you have to go?'

'The end of the month. The house will be ready for us then too.'

'The end of the month! Martin, I can't possibly be ready to move then – it's only two weeks away. I have to give a month's notice at work, anyway. But apart from that, I can't let them down, I've got to finish typing the book. And the kids can't leave school in the middle of term.' She was aware of the shrillness again.

'Esme, you're over-reacting.'

She sat down again and took a deep breath.

'You'll have to go ahead and get things sorted for the kids and me. Then I'll have time to pack up the house and everything.'

Martin, paused in the process of replenishing his glass, and glanced up sharply at her.

'So you're saying you won't move till the end of term? And when is that?'

'In about six weeks' time.'

At this moment, the outside door burst open and Ali came charging in as if the bats of hell were after him.

'*Mama*, I'm hungry!' Then seeing Martin, his eyebrows shot up,

'Hi, *Baba*! What you doing at home?'

Mosi peered round the open door and smiled with delight on seeing her father.

'*Shikamoo, Baba.*''

'*Marahaba*, Mosi.' Martin beamed at his daughter, at fifteen showing promise of becoming a striking young woman; she and Esme had already begun to battle about coming back from friends' at a reasonable hour in the evening. Ali just smiled at Martin who grumped at his son for his lack of respect. Esme seized the moment to recruit support:

'Kids, we're going to move to Morogoro! *Baba*'s got a promotion.'

'Morogoro! That's in the middle of nowhere!' Ali's face had darkened. Mosi's looked stricken. 'Dad, it's not a good time for me to move! My exams are at the end of the year, they're very important!'

Esme was gratified. Maybe between them they could get him to back down.

'Well, I've got an important position at work. I'll be in charge of a District!

'Will you get lots of money?'

'No, Ali, in Tanzania important men don't always get lots of money. This is a poor country.'

'I don't want to move.' Ali was adamant.

'Why do we have to move?' Mosi asked. Martin's patience was clearly wearing out as he replied,

'I would have thought it was obvious! Your father has been given a responsible job and it necessitates the family moving!' Martin got up. 'Your mother will explain it. I've got to go and meet someone.'

Esme felt an almost overwhelming desire to grab Martin around the throat and squeeze. Instead, she gripped her glass with both hands and drew in deep breaths to try and stop the thudding in her chest.

Next day she told Tara of Martin's plans. Esme was never quite sure of her position with Tara: they were two English-speaking women of about the same age who worked in close proximity but there was a gulf of education and wealth between them. At times, however, this gulf seemed to narrow while they shared concerns about children or women's issues. At any rate, Esme felt more at ease with her than with Pete.

'Oh, Esme, that's awful!' Tara said. ' What are you going to do? Morogoro! We don't want to lose you, of course, either here or in the women's group, but you have to do what you feel is right.'

'I don't know what is right! That's the trouble.'

Martin did not resume his normal habits the day after his announcement. He helped the children with their homework. When he looked at Mosi's Swahili exercise book Esme was gratified to hear him admire her neat writing and the fact that she nearly always got ten out of ten. When he opened Ali's dog-eared *daftari* Esme braced herself for a tirade. Instead, she could almost here the effort he made to keep his rebukes unsaid. Mildly he said, 'Ali, can you try and write more carefully in future? And listen to what the teacher says, then you might not get so many crosses!'

'Yes, *Baba*,' Ali said and he probably meant it, so pleased he was to have his father take an interest.

Towards herself, Esme could tell he was ambivalent – impatient for Esme to see sense yet wary lest he scare her off completely.

The truth was his old magic wasn't working on her any more. She had been disappointed times beyond counting. To protect herself from constant hurt, she'd grown a layer between her innermost feelings and him.

But the children needed him – how happy they were now with him.

The end of the month approached. Martin was to take up his post on the first of the following month. The tension fairly crackled. Esme still hadn't given Martin a time when she and the kids would move. Martin decided he would come back after a month and they could sort things out then. He left in the department Land Rover at dawn. The children were still in bed. Esme felt wretched after he had left, alone without her support and taking only the basics for survival. But it was only temporary, wasn't it? No, she couldn't think that far ahead.

By evening Martin's absence was palpable. It was one thing for him to be out, knowing he could be back any time, quite another knowing he wouldn't be back at all. But he had been on safari lots of times. She'd get used to it, like she had then.

There were lots of compensations, of course. Knowing that it was only her and the kids eating, she didn't always have to cook a proper meal as long as she filled the kids up with something: drop scones and pancakes were favourites, depending on whether she had sour milk or not, and the rest of the ingredients. There was a more relaxed atmosphere in the evenings, the door securely locked, no expectation of it opening at any moment – or not. No anxiety about what mood Martin would be in when he did deign to put in an appearance.

He wrote to her that he missed them. He even posted her a photo of the house. It was big, it was old and dilapidated and it looked isolated. It gave her the horrors.

He phoned her at work.

'Have you decided yet?'

'I haven't finished typing the book yet, Martin. Tara and Pete still haven't finished writing it. There are four more chapters planned but it shouldn't take more than a few weeks. They haven't got a precise deadline but the publishers are putting a lot of pressure on them.'

A month later, Martin came back for the weekend. He'd had to come by bus because the office vehicle was grounded due to lack of spares. The bus had broken down and he'd had a dreadful journey. It had taken three hours longer than it should have. This time his patience had worn thin and when she wouldn't - couldn't - give him a definite date for him to arrange the removal, he pointed out that there was nothing to stop his taking Mosi and Ali to live with him. They parted on bad terms.

She didn't sleep well at nights despite the knowledge that she wasn't going to be woken up by Martin coming in at whatever hour he chose. She would wake to the empty bed and the noises of the night, lying awake for hours, wracked by guilt and misgivings.

But by day there was so much going on. Besides work where she was under pressure to keep pace with typing the book, she met up with the other members of the drama group, often twice a week, to work on the script for the plays. The first series – probably going to be four - were on pregnancy among adolescents, depicting different situations young women found themselves in. She worked with Halima and Sirkka from the study group and two women broadcasters from the national radio station who impressed Esme with their commitment and enthusiasm. They hoped to broadcast these plays after they'd been performed in local communities. They were finding ways of incorporating statistics which indicated the number of teenage girls who had to leave primary school – most never made it to secondary school, no-where near the ten percent of boys who did. Esme helped with interviews with teachers, parents and even a sugar daddy. These girls were being victimised, preyed upon by older men. When they got pregnant they were kicked out of school, often by their families too. The babies were often the ones who suffered most. Esme couldn't possibly leave in the middle of this. Martin couldn't see it.

After a couple of months he started to put heavy pressure on her. The kids missed him constantly, asking when he would be back. They wanted to go and see him.

One day Mosi said, '*Mama*, perhaps we should all go and live with *Baba* after all.'

'No!' Ali was vehement: 'I want to stay with my friends.'

'You'll make other friends, Ali.' Esme tried to convey a confidence she didn't feel.

'I want *Baba* to come back and live here.' Ali was angry now. Esme knew this situation wasn't good for them.

'We'll go and visit him. Next time he phones, we'll arrange something. I understand what you mean, Mosi. And, Ali I know how you're feeling too! We need to go and see your father – he misses us too. And we can see what it's like there. We might like it!'

Ali shot her a dark look but said nothing before he went to his room. Mosi came and leaned her head on Esme's shoulder, they were the same height now.

The visit made her feel worse. It was worse even than she imagined – the kids absolutely hated the house, its location, what they saw of the school. And Esme could imagine no prospects of work for her: there were only a few government offices and no businesses that might need her English.

Back at home, she was wracked in turn with indecision, remorse, defiance. She began to feel unwell, nauseous and light-headed. Her joints ached, she felt weak. Paracetamol did nothing for it. Two days after they came back from Morogoro, she came home from work and went straight to bed, but couldn't sleep. She decided it must be malaria. She started a course of chloraquine. A week later she felt worse. She felt as if her limbs were shackled, there was a ringing in her ears and an immense heaviness in her head and bones. At night, although she felt she was never fully asleep, her mind was filled with fiends and terrifying situations from which there was no escape.

It was in the middle of the night, lying awake after a nightmare, that a thought occurred to her and sent a shock through her body: when did she last have her period? When was she last with Martin? God, no wonder she feels so nauseated! Her head whirled, there was no time to lose. The next day was Saturday – Pete and Tara weren't expecting her but the Family Planning Clinic would be open.

It was busy, as usual, but it wasn't crammed with patients and she knew from experience the clinic was a model of efficiency and courtesy. As far as she knew, she was the only *Mzungu* to use this clinic and the staff always remembered her and, she suspected, discretely manipulated the queue to give her preferential treatment. It wasn't long before she was called to the sister's room. Esme liked her kindly, professional manner.

As Esme began to explain her concerns, her eyes brimmed with tears. Sister Humba listened carefully to Esme and then examined her.

'Mrs Yusufu,' she said in a gentle tone, 'I can't detect a pregnancy. I don't think you have malaria and you haven't had it confirmed by a blood test. Are you worried about something?' Esme nodded and tears spilled down her face. She wiped them quickly with the back of her hand. She must stop this, she was making a fool of herself but more tears defied her while she tried to summarise her situation.

'I think I know someone who can help you. Please wait here.'

Esme sat in the small room in stupor of exhaustion. She wondered where the nurse was going but it seemed to have little to do with herself. In what seemed like a few minutes, she was back.

'OK, Mrs Yusufu, please come with me.'

Sister Humba led her through the hospital grounds a short distance to a small, single story building. A notice near the door announced 'Psychiatric Unit'. Esme stopped, panic-stricken.

'Why are you bringing me here?' she felt betrayed and alarmed.

'Don't worry! Nothing's going to happen to you. There's a very nice doctor who has agreed to see you. I promise you he will help you.'

The sister put her arm through Esme's in a companionable way and led her through the double doors. Esme felt she could trust her and hadn't strength to resist.

The doctor was an elderly *Mzungu*. He introduced himself, saying he was from Switzerland and was a consultant psychiatrist. As he shook her hand and met her eyes, she felt safe, with a little prompting, it all came pouring out, about the strain of living with Martin, the strain of living without him, the children's unhappiness, her work, the plays. 'And I don't know what to do,' she finished, by now sobbing uncontrollably.

The doctor listened intently. 'No wonder you're not feeling well. You're being torn in different directions by everyone's need of you. But in the end you've got to decide what it is you need. Do you have a friend you can talk to? You've been bottling this all up. You need to talk to a friend and work out what's best for you.'

'You don't think I'm mad then?'

'No, Esme, you're just completely worn out with anxiety.'

'So I don't have malaria either – I'm not actually ill at all?'

'Oh, yes you're ill, all right. But the cause is what's running round in your mind, not parasites in your blood stream. Your body has become exhausted as a result. I can give you something to help it recover but you have to sort out what's troubling you.'

His gentle concern was balm to her. He understood her anguish. Why couldn't Martin understand?

He gave her an injection of vitamin B complex and some in tablet form to take home, as well as – best of all - something to help her sleep.

As she drove home, she decided she would go to see Jocelyn. It had been weeks since she'd seen her. Jocelyn hardly ever left the house once she got home from work. How did she cope? She put up with Arthur and all his extended family with never a complaint. Ali was already home from school, she had to wait for Mosi. She knew Mosi would want to come with them to see Jocelyn's kids.

It was a relief to find Jocelyn on her own: for once there were none of her husband's semi-clad, country cousins ensconced on the settee staring at her with undisguised curiosity.

'Have you people had any lunch, Esme?' Jocelyn's American twang had not diminished in all the years away from home and she was as welcoming as ever.

She put a bowl of stew and another of rice, along with some plates and spoons, on the dining table.

'Help yourselves to buffalo stew. We have an unending supply from Arthur's hunting!

Maybe it was just the way Esme felt but it seemed to be the toughest, most unappetizing meat she had ever eaten. Ali, the fussy eater, devoured every morsel and asked for more. Mosi, arranged the lumps of meat around the rim of the plate and sent an appealing look to Esme who shrugged her assent.

Meanwhile Jocelyn, having eaten earlier but was incapable of sitting down and relaxing, kept up a running commentary and fussed with glasses of water and salt and offering second helpings.

When eventually they had eaten what they could, while the house-girl cleared the table, the children went to join their peers outside and the two women sat down to talk. Esme began to tell Jocelyn about her morning and before long everything she'd been worrying about came pouring out. She couldn't stop herself crying.

'Hey, Esme I didn't realise Martin's government quarters were ready for you and all. Gosh you've been hanging on here while he's on his own! I think you're feeling tremendous pressure to join him but now you're committed to this stuff with the women's group and your employers. Difficult! I guess what you're feeling is guilt!'

'Yes, I'm feeling guilty. But what about all the evenings I've been at home on my own before he moved. Never knowing what Martin's up to or when he'll be home.'

'But, Esme, you know what men are like. He's a normal, full-blooded man. You wouldn't want him to be a nancy-man, at home with an apron on.' Jocelyn seemed to find this thought hilarious.

To give Jocelyn her due, she provided Esme with the refuge she needed, and before they left, had plied them all with tea and maandazi. However, Esme was no further forward in her decision. But, that night despite it all, after taking the tablets, she slept soundly until the sun was well up the following morning.

During breakfast, a car pulled up outside. Esme saw through the window that it was Pete. That would set the neighbours' tongues wagging.

She opened the door to him, and she saw that his kids were in the car.

'Hi, Esme. Here's a letter for you. We picked up the mail from town last evening after a dinner there but we thought it was too late to come round then.' She was touched by his taking the trouble.

He handed her a well-filled, airmail envelope. She recognised the handwriting. It was from Christine.

Christine was replying to her letter of about a month earlier – she'd written back relatively quickly. If only Christine was here! Esme pressed the letter to her chest and she felt her eyes smarting.

It took a while before she could see clearly enough to read the letter. It didn't have the answer she was looking for.

'You're the only one who can decide what's right for you,' Christine had written. She opened the patio doors and surveyed the garden already shimmering in the heat.

She had a lot to do, she'd better get started.

Part Three
Ch 22: Morogoro

The balcony off the living room of their flat commanded a supreme view of the Tanga-to-Dar railway line. Directly in front of their flat, the line was spanned by a footbridge. A constant stream of pedestrians and cyclist filed over the bridge in both directions. The trains, Martin informed her, only passed once a day. No wonder no-one she knew ever travelled by rail. To the right of the bridge, in the middle of a sun-burnt field, lay a primary school, deserted as it was Sunday, but promising to be full of raucous children the next day. On the other side of the bridge, a jumble of small habitations stretched in the distance. The faint blue profile of the Uluguru mountains tinged the horizon.

Martin was trying hard. She had just resigned herself to moving to Dodoma when he had been abruptly transferred to Morogoro. Having sung the praises of the first place, he then had to say how much better the latter was. Going by its location, only a hundred and twenty miles from Dar, and at two thousand feet high, slightly cooler than the coast – and certainly than the central plain – she thought it probably was a lesser evil. Only time would tell.

'Let's go for walk, I'll show you around,' Martin said now. She couldn't remember the last time they'd been for a walk. He pointed out amenities to her as if he had invented them – the market, the bus depot, the bank. All closed, of course. She was dismayed at the general ugliness. Everything was relatively modern, compared to Dar, but already shabby. Pavements, where they existed at all, were crumbling. Off the main street, they walked at the side of the road on the tracks worn bare in the scrubby grass verge revealing red earth, hard-packed by hundreds of feet. But little sign of those feet today. When vehicles did pass, lurching along narrow, pot-holed roads, they showered Esme and Martin with dust. The houses were unremittingly small with corrugated iron roofs. Not a single gracious building. The only trees they passed emitted a nauseating smell from their dirty-white blossom.

And the place was practically deserted.

'Why is no-body about?' she asked Martin.

'It's Sunday. Most people are Christian here. We're inland. Not so much of an Arabic influence as in Dar. And this is just a small town, don't forget.'

How could she? The Sunday afternoon hiatus deepened: from childhood this had dampened her spirits no matter where she was, who she was with or what she was doing.

To the north, south, and west rose the mountains, hazy, offering some solace with their greenery and occasional rocky outcrops. To the east the still brown land stretched away flatly as far as the eye could see. A hundred miles from the Indian Ocean.

No wonder people in Dar referred to this place as *mji kasoro bahari,* 'town without a sea'. Esme felt land-locked. Down here in the town no cooling sea breeze disturbed the air, laden with unshed rain. She remembered, that one of the carrots dangled in front of her by Martin was the cool, mountain air. She wiped her brow with a handkerchief: it came away tinged with rusty-red.

'I thought it was supposed to be higher here - that it would be cooler,' she said

'At the regional headquarters it is a lot cooler but you didn't want to live there remember? You said it would be too isolated. I did tell you it was a warmer down in the town but you insisted, even though I had a big staff house and garden up there.'

That mausoleum! She knew he was right, of course. She couldn't logically explain why she had felt such an aversion to the small enclave of offices and staff houses dating back to the colonial era when they had visited Martin for the weekend. Well the town was a dump but at least it had more life than that hamlet surrounding the administrative base.

Back at the flat, Martin's ebullient mood seemed not to have been dented by Esme's lack of enthusiasm for her new home. He took Ali and Mosi out on the balcony and joked with them about the passers by below. Esme couldn't bring herself to unpack. She joined them. It was a novelty for all of them to be together. Martin was evidently overjoyed to have his family with him, to be a complete man again. He had promised her over and over that he would not resume his old habits of going out drinking if she joined him. But that first evening he told them he had to go out and see someone, it wouldn't take more than a few minutes. Mosi, Ali and herself spent the evening unpacking and forlornly looking out at the mountains.

She had made a mistake.

'I've found a job for you, *mpenzi*.' Martin's first words when he arrived home from work the following day.

'What?' said Esme, hearing how ungracious she must sound. 'I've probably already got a job, Martin. Thank you.'

'This is a real cushy number. The manager of the outfit that repairs the regional vehicles heard my European wife has come to live here...'

Aye, along the rest of Morogoro , thought Esme.

'….and they need a lady to do their typing. In good English of course.'

'Sounds exciting!' said Esme with a roll of her eyes. 'I can't wait.'

'Yes, doesn't it.' Martin, oblivious to her sarcasm, was beaming,

'I'm already well-known in Morogoro, you know. And that will be a nice little job for you. You'll have plenty of time to do other things.'

Like what? Hang around here waiting, for you to come home? She was still sore about the night before.

'The manager of the water project would like you to go and see them tomorrow afternoon.'

'OK, Martin, it will be interesting to meet these people and find out more. But I've got a job interview at the university in the morning, don't forget.'

'I don't suppose that will amount to much. They probably just want to have an *Mzungu* working for them.'

'Well, the head of the division went to the trouble of phoning in response to my ad and he said he had a vacancy for an Office Management Secretary.'

'I still can't believe you actually advertised yourself in a national newspaper!'

Martin had brought this up every time the issue of work came up and sometimes when it hadn't. Esme forbore to reply. She had already explained but had stopped short of apologising for not consulting him prior to placing the ad via Kaliwe - who had also been slightly incredulous. She couldn't see the problem: job vacancies were advertised so why not jobs wanted? The proof was in the pudding: she would taste that when she went to meet the sole respondent to her advert: the Head of the Division of Forestry at the University of Agriculture the only other university in the country besides the one in Dar es Salaam. He had sounded alright on the phone, speaking in good English with the sing-song accent denoting his northern roots. Martin shared some of the common resentment against this successful tribe but she had no axe to grind.

The following day, meeting Dr Mushi in the flesh, she had felt a guarded respect for him. He was no older than Martin and seemed very professional. The job combined a number of strands: allocating work to three typists, monitoring the budget, keeping the head's appointments diary, cataloguing staff publications. It sounded challenging but not daunting. He explained that he had kept this vacancy open for a couple of months waiting for the right person and he was keen for her to start the following Monday. Remembering that the flat actually had the rare luxury of a phone already installed, she promised to phone him.

He felt it perfectly acceptable that she would need to discuss it with her husband before making a decision. In actual fact, she wanted to see what the other offer, the one Martin had spoken about, entailed.

She was pleased she still had the Beetle. Both the uni and the water project lay a couple of miles outside the town – in opposite directions. Each road seemed to lead towards the mountains which, however, tantalisingly retreated from her as she approached. The manager of the water project was a florid, overweight Dutchman who spoke in jovial, if somewhat improvised, English.

'Ach, Mrs Yusufu, this is not a difficult job for a lady. You just type us a few letters every afternoon and most days you have lots of time to chat and read magazines. The boys are a nice, friendly crowd, they are happy when a girl is with us!'

Even though they were offering as much money for the half-time job as the university was for a full-time one, she had no hesitation in deciding. Martin was at first incredulous and then annoyed. He wasn't attractive when he was annoyed: his eyes bulged and he blustered.

'For heaven's sake, Mama Mosi, why would you want to go and work with a bunch of scruffy students and lecturers? What's the point when you could get more money for less work? I would have thought you'd enjoy working with other *Wazungu* – you all think the same way.'

Shut up, Martin! What do you know? She was furious but kept her retort unspoken. There was a point beyond which she knew it was unhelpful to push him. Instead she looked out of the back window, through the washing strung up on the kitchen balcony, to where the mountains were closest and where the university lay on the lower slopes.

'The job with Pete and Tara in Dar was very interesting, Martin. It had nothing to do with them being *Wazungu*. I need something to get my teeth into. Besides, there are still quite a few expatriates at the uni.' Martin rubbed his chin and was quiet for a minute.

'And I won't be looking at the clock and the door, waiting for you to come home so much if I have an interesting job,' she added.

Martin harrumphed. 'Suit yourself then, but don't come crying to me when it gets too much for you! '

He got up, stretched and started towards to door. 'I have to go out now.'

She started work the following Monday, the same day that Mosi started her Secondary School. Ali had joined the primary school across the way the previous week, having been befriended by one of the boys in the flats he went cheerfully. For Mosi it was an ordeal and Esme felt really sorry seeing her anxious eyes over the breakfast table. Mosi hadn't managed more than a mouthful. The margarine from Pete and Tara had run out and the dry bread was hard to swallow.

The head's charm, she discovered, could as easily be turned off as on. He kept her waiting in the general office for twenty minutes that first morning while she introduced herself to the three typists, two women and a man, all younger than herself. She observed them, chatting in the local language, Kiluguru, and laughing and wondered if she was the source of their amusement. When Dr. Mushi did summon her, it was via the internal telephone. He remained seated and extended his hand across his huge desk.

'Good morning, Mrs Yusufu,' no effusive smiles today. He outlined her duties till her head spun and handed her a ledger book a couple of feet wide. It would be her responsibility to complete its innumerable columns. By the time he dismissed her she felt utterly miserable and was convinced she had made another mistake. Not that she would get any sympathy from Martin.

Matters didn't improve a great deal over the following weeks. She felt very grand in her spacious office adjoining the general office on the opposite side to Dr Mushi's but she also felt very isolated. She met faculty members by degrees – a very mixed bunch. About half were Scandinavian expatriates. Gradually the original staff were being replaced by locals as they came up through the ranks. Two of the young Tanzania PhD holders who occupied offices across the corridor were friendly and popped in to chat frequently. But before long she realised their conversation was peppered with innuendo and suspected they had ulterior motives.

The most positive aspect of the job was the location of the university - on the lower slopes of the mountains. She took advantage of the special bus that picked up staff from town and laboured uphill to where the single story buildings spread over the small plateau. Along the driveway, the bus passed the faculty of veterinary science on its way to those of agriculture and forestry. Further off, scattered on the lower slopes of the foothills, were the staff houses. Above, the green mountains beckoned. The sight of small dwellings perched on precipitous slopes, occasional patches of remaining forest interspersed with rocky outcrops, fascinated her and taunted her daily.

One of her duties was to enter every expenditure under the appropriate budget head in the ledger and compare it with Accounts Departments records. At first the clerks in accounts had resented what they saw as her checking up on them but gradually through sheer perseverance, by turning up every few days with a cheerful grin, Esme wore down their truculence and they would exchange at first pleasantries and, eventually, chats and jokes. If they hadn't seen her for more than a week, they would greet her with cries of 'where were you?'

Every time she walked from the Forestry building through the grounds to the Administration block she glimpsed the mountains between the trees, above the Agricultural Extension and Forestry lab buildings, looking almost close enough to touch. She was gazing at them one day, clutching her ledger to her, when Dr Aartisahri, the longest standing member of the forestry faculty, happened along.

'Morning, Mrs Yusufu. Thinking of going off for the day?'

'Och, I'd love to! It looks so tempting but I suppose it's impractical to think of attempting it. I'm not exactly used to mountain-climbing.'

'Oh, you don't need to be. There's a road going up close to the top of the tallest mountain round here. The government built a radio mast up there and there's an old hotel, Morningside. It's a wonderful walk.'

Esme decided there and then to take the family at the weekend. Martin, of course, didn't acquiesce to her suggestion.

'Esme, you must be mad! I'm not against a walk – I took you round the town, remember? But up mountains ….! Forget it!'

'It doesn't matter. I'll take the kids.' It did matter but she knew that if she let Martin's non-participation cramp her style she would do nothing at all. Mosi looked dubious:

'*Mama*, they look very high. Are you sure?'

'I've been told by one of the lecturers, a road goes all the way up and it's a great walk! Ali, you're interested in wild-life – there will be all sorts up there!'

'Snakes, probably!' Martin interjected. Esme suppressed a surge of irritation – he was trying to put them off but Ali perked up at this.

'Alright, Ma,' he said.

They set off on Sunday morning about ten. The sun was already high in the sky, but the crumbling tarmac road that ran out of town, was flanked by large German and British-built houses shaded by massive ancient mango trees whose dark foliage formed a high canopy over the road.

Gradually the houses and trees stopped. The tarmac gave way altogether to a track in the red earth, cut into the rock and embedded with large rough stones. Between the occasional stumpy tree, scattered boulders and brown scrubby grass they got a glimpse of the town spreading out below.

'This is more like it!' Esme said. 'Come on kids, you're lagging behind!'

Mosi and Ali said nothing for a while. Esme knew they were beginning to flag already as indeed was she. This would have been unaccustomed exercise on the flat but they were now struggling up a steep gradient and there was no respite from the sun's fierce rays, though Esme had tied a cotton scarf around her head.

They continued in silence for a while.

'Ma, how much further? It's hot!' Ali said at last.

'I don't think it can be much further,' Esme tried to sound confident.

'*Mama*, I'm tired.' Mosi mopped her brow with her sodden handkerchief.

Esme decided it was time to play her trump card.

'As a special treat, we'll have lunch at the hotel at the top!'

'Lunch! At the hotel!' Ali was impressed – this was almost unprecedented. 'I'll race you there!' and he set off.

'What's it like, the hotel?' Mosi asked.

'I really don't know, but you can see it from the University, it must have a lovely view.'

They soon caught Ali up and the three of them plodded on in silence. Walking was difficult on the rough terrain, quite apart from the steep incline, with sharp pieces of rock protruding and stones becoming dislodged.

They stopped at the sound of voices approaching and Esme realised they were coming from behind them. Round the bend appeared a middle-aged man pushing a bicycle, a young woman with a baby tied on her back and an elderly woman, chatting and laughing. Esme and the children watched them approach in disbelief: they progressed with the ease and agility of people walking on the flat.

'*Habari, Mama,*' the man greeted her. '*Mnaenda Morningside?*'

Esme confirmed in Swahili that they were heading for Morningside.

'Do you know what time they serve food until?' she added.

'Food!' the man looked mystified for several seconds then as the penny dropped, he laughed 'No, there's no food! The hotel has been closed for many years. Many, many years!'

The two women joined in the laughter. Esme would have gone crimson had she not already been like a beetroot and the sun. She reminded herself that they weren't laughing at her, it was their way of dealing with the embarrassment.

'Ok, thank you.' She said, forcing a smile, and turned back towards the children while the three villagers resumed their sprightly ascent.

'You said there was a hotel, Ma! You said you were going to buy us lunch!' Ali was practically spitting with anger.

'Where are those people going?' Mosi's eyes were on the track up which the trio had departed.

'They must live up there. People do. I'm sorry kids, I made a mistake. It'll be easy going down.'

'I'm never going anywhere with you again!' Ali shouted and he started off at a trot downhill, disappearing round the next bend. Mosi, her most tragic expression on her face, said with feeling, 'Don't ever ask me to go for a walk again, *Mama*.'

Another mistake, Esme thought as she had one last glance up the mountain at the unattainable dwellings and *shamba*. She braced her legs against the precipitous downward slope, stumbling and turning her ankles. When they eventually reached the outskirts of the town, hot, dusty and exhausted, she bought them all bottles of Fanta but it did little to mollify the kids.

Back at the flat she looked regretfully at the mountains and promised herself she'd get up there one day.

Ch 23: Settling In

By the time a couple of months had passed, she found that she was missing work by the time she got back home and had begun to look forward to going back the next morning. For one thing, she was closer to those alluring, moody mountains with their patches of glowing light, mysterious shade, velvety green and steely grey, ever-changing with the sun and the clouds. For another, she had once again become part of a community, bigger and more diverse than at the advertising agency and, although not as interesting as working with Tara and Pete, she had a certain status in the department and beyond. She had mastered the work - the accounts were straightforward enough - and the boss and she had a tacit agreement to restrict contact with one another to what was strictly necessary.

As she went about the campus exchanging greetings and pleasantries with staff from other departments, she was aware of her minor celebrity status as the only European woman working at the university. The number of European males - the expatriate lecturers - was gradually being replaced by local lecturers as they qualified, as no doubt was happening in academic institutions all over the country.

While at her desk, like many others, her office door giving onto the corridor remained open to allow the air to circulate, and she often absently observed people passing by. She couldn't help noticing how much younger the local department members were than their expatriate counterparts; would their lack of life experience matter in the long run? Dr Humba and Dr Salim (oh, how they loved to hear their titles – no first names were used here!) were sorely lacking in women to add to their conquests since female lecturers and students in Forestry were non-existent and there were very few female students in the other departments. She knew from her study group in Dar the reason for so few women at the university - in the villages it was girls and women who did the bulk of the farm work and, more often than not, they weren't sent even to primary school. She attempted a serious debate about it with Dr Salim as he perched in his familiar way on the corner of her desk, reminiscent of Kaliwe.

'Why is it, do you think,' she asked, 'that when ninety-five percent of the population are peasant farmers, and it's *women* who do most of the work on the *shamba*, women are so under-represented here?'

'Women are good at simple tasks but their main responsibility is the bearing and rearing of children. That is why you don't see any here – except in admin, of course,' he nodded in her direction and smiled smugly.

'That's complete nonsense! Dar university is teeming with women. Not fifty per cent yet but it's perfectly normal to see female students and lecturers, even heads of departments!'

'Well this is a tough old occupation. You need to be strong as well as brilliant! A woman wouldn't know where to begin.' And he laughed heartily and got up.

'It's exactly the same in Europe! You won't find any women foresters!' he flung this at her as he left the room. The infuriating thing was that she suspected the pompous nitwit was probably right.

What she missed here was the company of like-minded women, someone she could feel at ease and share confidences with. It had become easier with Pili, Fatuma and May, the clerks in the head's office as the weeks had gone by; while the head was out of the building she'd make the effort to go and sit with them. Even though they were all smiles and friendly remarks, she always wondered what they said behind *her* back. On one occasion, in May's absence, Pili derided May's new dress and, on another, Pili herself came in for some back-stabbing from May and Fatuma about her flirtatious behaviour with a lecturer. The irony was, Esme reflected, that she was being just as hypocritical - mentally.

Back at the flat, there were the kids but they were rapidly turning into teenagers: Mosi, a little belatedly and in her own temperate way; Ali with gusto though he was still only in his thirteenth year. They had made their own friends and were often out till supper time - curfew time. After that they were in their rooms, ostensibly doing homework but mostly, it seemed to her, listening to the radio and chatting: Esme was glad they seemed to enjoy each other's company, unlike herself and her own brother who had very much led their own lives.

She tried to befriend her neighbours but there was scant opportunity; people didn't hang about outside the flats like they had in other places: it was just an ugly concrete yard giving access to the garages under the building. The flat dwellers were mostly professionals - occasionally they met on the stairs and along with the usual greetings would be the usual, *'Karibu nyumbani*, welcome to our home, come and see us.' She would reciprocate with *'Karibu kwetu.'* She could never tell whether these customary welcomes were heartfelt or merely rhetorical.

Early one evening she felt at such a loose end that she decided to make the effort to get closer to her neighbour in the flat opposite. Esme knew from their frequent but brief exchanges that she was a teacher in one of the nearby primary schools – luckily not Ali's. The door was answered by a girl a couple of years younger than Mosi.

'Is Mama Jasper in?' Esme asked. The girl nodded and shyly whispered *'Karibu'*, and while Esme sat in one of the wooden armchairs, the girl disappeared. Esme sat waiting for five minutes before Mama Jasper appeared, wearing just a *kanga* , her arms and shoulders beaded with water.

'Mama Ali, *Karibu, Karibu*!' Mama Jasper beamed, '*Nimefurahi sana, Karibu*!' apparently delighted. 'Excuse me,' she indicated her state of dress, 'I was just having a shower.' She looked as if she'd literally stepped straight out of the shower and put the *kanga* on without drying herself. '*Nakuja*, I'm coming,' she said in the customary, contrary way and went into the kitchen. She came back with a small tray on which lay an unopened bottle of cola and a glass which she set on a small table in front of Esme. Esme hated cola. Her neighbour ceremoniously opened the bottle in front of her. This custom – carried out without exception by anyone opening a bottle for her - never failed to amuse her; according to Martin it was to re-assure a guest that no poison had been surreptitiously added. What of all the drums of homemade maize and millet beer, the gourds of palm-wine – so easily interfered with?

Mama Jasper (Esme would never know her given name) sat on the edge of the chair opposite. They exchanged the usual questions – how the kids were – Jasper was the eldest of three small boys – how work was, how their husbands were - and gave the customary answers: everything was fine. After a few minutes Esme's neighbour stood up and excused herself saying again, '*Nakuja*, I'm coming,' as she left the room.

And there Esme sat. She could hear muted voices and the sounds of pots and pans n the kitchen but Mama Jasper did not reappear as the minutes ticked by as Esme sipped the noxious brew and looked around. She was always surprised at how little care and cash professional people spared on their homes compared to their personal attire. The room contained the barest of wooden furniture, a few hand-embroidered doilies but nothing else in the way of ornamentation.

Twenty minutes later Mama Jasper brought in a plate of fried sweet bananas, with a fork alongside and placed it on the table beside Esme.

'*Karibu*, Mama Ali.'

Food of any type was the last thing she was expecting: dusk and the universal meal time was rapidly approaching. However she felt afraid to cause offence by refusing and instead feebly protested, 'Oh really, there was no need to go to any trouble!'

'*Asubutu*! Not at all!' was the laughing reply. Esme tried to join in the laughter. Alone again, she began eating the sticky bananas.

They were tasty as a snack but this quantity was daunting. She wondered if it would be more diplomatic to leave some, to show that they had been very generous or to finish every scrap to show how delicious they were. In the end she reached saturation point half way through and thought she'd be sick if she had another mouthful. The problem then was how to take her leave in the absence of her host. Ten minutes later, frustration overcame her fear of causing offence and she got to her feet and called out in the direction of the curtained doorway to the inner part of the house.

'*Ahsante,* Mama *Jasper. Nakwenda sasa.* I'm off now.'

Mama Jasper came bustling through.

'Why are you in such a hurry! Stay and rest a bit longer!'

'Thank you but I've got things to do at home.' And after several assurances that the other was welcome to visit any time, Esme made her escape.

She told Martin about it next time she saw him, when she got in from work next day. He was reading the newspaper in the living room, having already eaten and showered, bare-chested to take advantage of the cool current of air passing between the windows at either end of the room. He was wearing a coarse cotton *kikoi* from the waist down. It always put Esme in mind of a table cloth with its large white and blue squares. Esme sat down next to him on the settee, unfastened her leather sandals and kicked them off. She put her feet up on a small wooden stool. The flat was cool compared to the stuffy town. Martin folded the newspaper with an air of resignation not lost on Esme. This was practically the only time of day they talked.

He shrugged.

'She was just giving you the chance to rest.'

'But she knows I hadn't come tramping from some village in the hinterland! She's an educated woman.'

'Exactly, she works all day and has things to do when she comes home.'

'But so do I! I just went to chat, to be neighbourly. I don't understand why she couldn't spare a few minutes to sit with me.'

Martin shrugged again.

'She was treating you with respect, as a guest. Just accept things as they are, Esme.'

Esme had never felt lonelier.

'Just like I have to accept that you convinced me to move from Dar under false pretences. As soon as we arrived you resumed your old habits. Or are you going to prove me wrong and stay in this evening?'

'Esme, every time we have a conversation does it have to be a confrontation? I have someone to see today, as it happens. There are plenty of evenings when I stay in.'

Esme stared at him in exaggerated amazement. Though she was quite sure he could see her out of the corner of his eye, he kept his gaze ahead of him as he got to his feet.

'Don't start again, Esme.'

He left the room. Esme just sat. she had no interest in the discarded newspaper. She had another long, empty evening in front of her. No, she corrected herself: she had her kids. Mosi and herself often chatted while they prepared the evening meal together. She regularly tried to involve Ali but it was like pulling teeth. After making sure the louvers were fully open – his room smelled none too fresh, she would go and sit on his bed where he was sprawled amongst a jumble of rumpled sheets, exercise books, and clothes of a dubious state of cleanliness.

'Cooking is women's work, Ma!' he would say. 'And I've got homework to do.'

'Well you could have done your homework before you went out to see your pals. *And,* just because women usually cook doesn't mean men can't, you know,' she would answer. 'It's a pity you never saw your father doing it when we lived in Scotland, when we first knew each other. I didn't think he would stop doing it the minute we arrived back in his own territory.'

'Oh, Ma. Turn the record off, will you. You're always saying that. I'll help clear up after.'

And she would smile and give up. She knew it meant he would take his own plate and very little else to the kitchen. But at least it was something. More than her father had ever done. She didn't want to make an enemy of Ali, after all.

More in a desperate attempt for company than for the money, Esme put up a small advertisement on the notice board in the admin block for English tuition. It resulted in one student, the wife of one of the Finnish forestry lecturers. Kerttu, like her husband, was about twenty years older than Esme, slim, elegant and charming. In their first session, seated at the circular dining table, Esme found that, as her husband had said, Kerttu spoke English quite well. She wanted to practice holding conversation, to increase her fluency and confidence. When Esme broached the topic of family – a topic which had worked well with most of her students – Kerttu had bristled.

'I do not want to talk about anything personal,' she said, intent on arranging her notebook and pencil in precise symmetry, her hands shaking. Her face showed no emotion. 'Sorry, I do not want to be impolite but I cannot talk about such things.'

After that Esme made sure she confined their discussions to impersonal themes: politics, the economy, history – not difficult with Kerttu so well informed. She had been a top flight secretary in Finland and could probably have done Esme's job with her eyes closed.

In one of their lessons Kerttu had asked her

'Why you may work, and I may not?'

Esme decided to overlook the syntax.

'I'm allowed to work because I'm a Tanzanian citizen. I gave up my British citizenship partly for that reason.'

'You gave up your *birth* citizenship! Do you not feel terrible?' Kerttu's expression was of horror.

'Not really,' Esme replied. 'I can go back to Britain to live and work at any time because, as I was born there, I have the Right of Abode – it's printed in my passport.'

'Really?' Kerttu smiled with relief. 'Do you think you will go back?'

A good question, Esme thought.

'I've always planned to stay in Tanzania for the rest of my life and I'm proud to be a citizen. People treat me in a special way when they know - I think they're pleased that I've chosen to join in with them. Of course, most people I meet don't know about my nationality, but they're tickled pink, I mean, they're delighted when I speak Swahili fluently and obviously know quite a lot about how to, well, act, be respectful to elders and things like that.'

'You have never been back to Britain in all the time you have lived here – you told me fourteen years?'

'Not yet. We couldn't afford it before and nowadays, of course, you have to apply for a permit for any foreign exchange and you need a cast iron reason for it – that's a colloquial expression, by the way.'

'What means, sorry, what does it mean: "cast iron reason"?'

'A strong reason, in the eyes of the Bank of Tanzania as to what is essential travel.'

'You mean like for education?'

'Yes, that sort of thing. Maybe a very important conference – it depends, if they decide it will be beneficial to the nation it could be approved.'

Kerttu shook her head.

'It's terrible.'

Esme shrugged.

'Not when you think that less than five percent of the population would be in a position to fly abroad and it's the other ninety-five percent who are toiling away to earn the foreign exchange by growing crops for export.'

By the time Esme had explained the unfamiliar vocabulary and Kerttu had grasped its implications they had both had enough of the economics of socialism.

'You miss your family very much?' Kerttu asked.

Esme was taken aback for a moment by the question from someone who had declared personal matters off-limits. Esme looked out of the window, reflecting on how she would answer. She always sat in this position for the lessons, and indeed for her meals, with the view of the mountains in between the washing. If she half-closed her eyes, deliberately unfocussing her vision, she could be looking at the Moffats with White Coomb shrouded in cloud as she had so often while trudging round the farm.

'I never got on very well with my father. We get on best when we're far apart. I do miss some of the others. Especially my mother and my friend Christine.'

'Why they don't come to visit you? They could have a beautiful holiday at the beach or go to the game parks for the animals?'

'It's very expensive for a holiday. As for my father, he served in the army in Egypt for five years during the Second World War and, as he never tired of telling us, that was five years too long in Africa. He won't come and, of course, he won't let my mother come either. They never even go south of the border!'

'What about your friend, the one you told me she writes to you?'

'Christine! No chance! She'll never be able to afford it.'

'Don't you find it very lonely?'

Esme could feel a wave of self pity rising up her chest. She'd be blubbing next!

'Och, I don't have time to be lonely, I have my work and the kids and looking after this place.' She glanced at her watch and saw with relief that they had only a few minutes left and they needed to spend that discussing Kerttu's homework.

Esme came to look forward to their twice-weekly lessons when Kerttu began to smile and even share a joke. In between meetings, Esme looked for interesting articles in the local press and in the copies of *Time* and *Newsweek* that were occasionally passed on to her by the expatriate lecturers. Then, a few weeks after the start of the sessions, Kerttu's husband told Esme at work one day that Kerttu was unwell and wouldn't be coming any more. A couple of weeks after that he told her she had gone back to Finland. Esme was not entirely surprised, but it was a real blow. She would miss Kerttu's visits.

P O Box 922

Morogoro

Tanzania

3 March 1982

Dear Christine

As you can see from the address, I'm here, in Morogoro, though not in a post box, I hasten to add. However, the post box is my very own. Unlike, in Dar es Salaam where the only way to obtain your own box was to inherit it, I was able to rent one (for pea-nuts) straight away here. Does that mean the good citizens of Morogoro don't have any friends, don't write letters or is it just a one-eyed town? I hear you ask. I suspect all three.

Why Morogoro when I said we were moving to Dodoma?

Well, a lot has happened: I was just coming round to the idea of moving to Dodoma (very reluctantly, I can assure you, when Martin suddenly got <u>another</u> transfer, to come here. As it happens, this place is much nearer to Dar and has plenty of water, being surrounded by mountains. I have to say, after a couple of months, it's started to grow on me.

There have been lots of changes to get used to. Mostly I miss the Women's Study Group and my old friends of the 'white wives club' but I had really started to grow away from them already. I still haven't found anyone or anything that I can get my teeth into, as it were. Work is OK but not as interesting as it was with the journalist. Our daily life is so-so. Martin – he's much the same as always, of course - had taken on this 'housegirl' known as Mama Tatu, via the usual method - a relative of a colleague. She works hard but never exactly as I'd do it myself, of course. This makes me feel guilty because she does all our dirty work – washing our clothes and dishes and cleaning the house - as well as shopping in the market every day and cooking it for our lunch. It must sound like heaven to you but for some reason that I can't put my finger on, I can't seem to like her.

Anyhow, I work near enough to come home for lunch on the staff bus, but I have to eat on my own with Mama Tatu, a strange situation, because Martin and the kids have to wait for meals, the kids have bits of fruit, not nearly enough I suspect. At the university, we have an hour's lunch break but Martin's workplace and the schools still follow the traditional way of working straight through from 7.30 in the morning to 2.30, probably because it's too far for a lot of people to go home for lunch and even where there are cafes and food kiosks, most people can't afford them.

It's a great help of course, Mama Tatu doing our shopping but I do enjoy going to the market on Saturdays and sometimes on Sunday mornings.

It's full of the freshest of fruit and vegetables that have been carried down from the mountains that very morning – in baskets on people's heads! Carrots, lettuces, capsicums, aubergines, spring onions, tomatoes, bananas, papaws, mangos, all kinds of pulses. How the villagers manage to cultivate anything on those slopes is beyond me! And a few women bring down pots they've made from the local terracotta clay, their natural colour. They're still used in some households for cooking and as water coolers – as they were in Mabalo. No prices are displayed in the market, the seller weighs up the customer, so to speak, and sets the price accordingly, then you bargain if you think it's a rip off. They're getting to know me now – just as I'm getting to know them and who to patronise and who to avoid. They even greet me by name, well one of my names: Mama Yusufu.

Getting to know the neighbours is harder! We see them coming and going from our balcony and occasionally wave to them. All the women seem to be well-educated (I mean beyond primary school) and are in salaried employment – one is a doctor at the local hospital, a few are nurses and teachers. But I've got to know the mother of one of Ali's friends – by the strangest of coincidences she was the midwife who delivered Ali at the maternity hospital in Dar! We get on quite well have a cup of tea together, maybe because she's Kenyan, married to a Tanzanian, an incomer like me.

My other "friend" is one of the three women agricultural students who's taken a shine to me. Dina, as mad as a hatter, she really doesn't care what anyone thinks of her. She turns up at my office at any time and perches on my desk, swinging her legs, chatting and trying to get me to go for a stroll round the campus which I admit I do sometimes. Then I won't see her for a week or two. I invited her back to the flat for a meal one day. She ate like she'd been starved – she's as thin as a rake. She won Mosi and Ali over with her charm and wit but Martin – who only spent two minutes in her company before he went out – was very snooty about her and said girls like her were very cheap. From what she tells me, she does seem to exchange services for goods but only if she likes the fella, I mean she's a bit of a 'good time gal.' And though I admire her free spirit, she's not exactly striking a blow for women's equality.

You won't be at all surprised to hear that Martin – despite all the promises – has barely changed his ways. I know you'll say "I told you so" but in the end I felt the kids and I had to move to be with him.. Anyhow, I think he's getting better lately, there's hope yet.

Ali came in at that point and the letter lay around for a week or so until she hastily signed it and sent it off.

Admin workers like herself, as well as Tanzanian lecturers, worked throughout the year with a meagre annual leave allowance. It was dull during the long break at the end of the academic year without the students and most of the expatriate staff, in what was summer in Europe. It was the cool season in Tanzania and in Morogoro it was cooler than Dar; in lots of ways it was like summer in Scotland - often cloudy.

It couldn't last, of course, and in early October the temperature and humidity, though still reasonable compared to Dar, had already increased. It was a relief to be surrounded by that buzz of activity again when the students and the rest of the academic staff reappeared.

Amongst the passers-by, through her open office door, she began to notice some oddly dressed young *Wazungu* who seemed to be based at the far the corridor. Their odd attire was out of place among the semi-formality of the Tanzanian lecturers and students who, like Martin, favoured dark trousers with razor creases and light coloured short-sleeved shirts, and the expatriates who tended towards the more casual but always well-ironed - khaki shirts and trousers. The newcomers dressed in crumpled shorts and T-shirts – apart from the woman who wore brightly coloured swirling skirts or neatly fitting trousers. By degrees Esme ascertained that there were three men and one woman, often in each others' company, laughing and chatting away in voluble French which was always, frustratingly, just beyond her understanding – her A-Level French had long rusted in the far recesses of her brain. Above all, Esme envied them their air of confidence and their camaraderie.

A couple of weeks into the term, she spotted a garish, hand-written poster on the main students' notice board:

French lessons – FREE! Every level, everyone welcomed.
Every Monday 4.30-5.30 lecture room 4.

A thrill ran through her. She barely noticed the superfluous 'd'. Four-thirty was the time she finished work. Was it just intended for students? She scrutinised the wording again - she supposed she could go. This poster had to be the work of those enigmatic newcomers. She could re-learn her French *and* get to meet them too.

Over the evening meal, seated round the dining table, she told the kids she'd be starting French classes. Ali looked uncomprehendingly at her, a spoon-full of rice stopped mid-way between plate and mouth.

'You're going to go to classes that you don't *have* to go to! Why?'

'I love speaking different languages. Don't you enjoy being fluent in two languages?'

Ali shrugged. Mosi put her spoon down on the plate and looked at her mother.

'Does that mean you're going to be back late?'

'Just a bit late, and it's just one day a week! In Dar I used to be out a lot at meetings and stuff and you didn't mind.'

'I did mind but I couldn't very well stop you. *Baba*'s never at home either.' Esme noticed then that Mosi's face had become longer, thinner and her expression, as now, was often tinged with melancholy. Esme wanted to hug her, reassure her and make her smile but at the same time felt a surge of annoyance.

'Well it's because your father is out socialising till all hours that I need to see people.'

And, by the way, she thought, you two are rarely in before meal-time anyway.

'You won't mind then, if you're not here, if some of my friends from school come round, will you?'

'No, that will be fine. You always have friends round at the weekend.' She didn't add that at least, that way, she knew where they were and who they were with.

'Even boys,' Mosi added, casually starting to clear the table. Aha, thought Esme. Mosi never talked about boys but Esme knew they were bound to be of great interest to her by now. And vice-versa, no doubt. Mosi had the shape of a woman already, and besides her large brown eyes, light brown complexion and black hair, when she smiled her face lit up.

'As long as they're well-behaved like the girls are, I don't see why it would be a problem.'

'What will *Baba* say though? I bet he'll kick up a fuss.'

'I'll talk to him. How about you all talk about your assignments sometime, call it a homework club? He'll be alright about it.'

'A homework club!' Mosi laughed. 'OK, Ma, *safi*!' Esme gathered from the use of the currently popular expression that her suggestion had met with approval.

They cleared away the rest of the supper things together. Ali had, as usual, sneaked off while the two of them were talking, today even leaving his plate with his uneaten greens. Esme hesitated for a moment before adding his plate to the pile. She could have insisted on him coming back and doing his share but this evening she preferred to savour this moment with Mosi. Though the subject was dropped, there was the hint of a smile in Mosi's eyes.

Before she went to her room to do her homework, she gave Esme a peck on the cheek.

'I hope you enjoy your French tomorrow,' she said.

Esme felt her eyes moisten and her heart gladden.

Ch 24: French Lessons

'How was the famous French lesson then?' Ali asked. Esme sat on the side of his bed where he slumped over a dog-eared exercise book, chewing the stump of a pencil. Esme automatically turned down the volume of the tinny radio belting out Tanzanian pop music from the bed-side table.

'Well, thank you for asking, Ali. It was really quite good. There was a great turnout – I suppose about fifty students. It was a terrible squash.'

'So, what did you learn?' Ali sounded just like his father. He put his exercise book aside with the air of one glad of the diversion.

'What did I learn? Good question, young man! I learnt the names of the two French people: Paul, Jean-Pierre and Solange.' she practiced her French accent on the names although conscious that it would be quite lost on Ali. 'I've seen the woman with them at the university but she wasn't at the class. I'd quite like to meet her too.'

'So, do they speak English,' asked Ali.

' Well, they'd have to wouldn't they? Their English isn't that wonderful, actually. Even I had a bit of a struggle to understand them and you can tell they're new to the game.'

'Ma, teaching is serious – it's not a game.'

'You're quite right, Ali, I shouldn't trivialise it. I think you may have put your finger on the problem, in fact. The French boys seem to regard it as all a bit of a lark and the Tanzanian students were totally phased by their casual attitude. You guys are not used to such informality from teachers and lecturers.'

Ali looked uncomprehendingly at her. 'So are you going again?'

'Yes, next week. But it seems I was the only one there who had done any French before so I'll be in a class of my own! The rest will be in two groups – just because of the numbers, they're all absolute beginners.'

'On your own! It sounds worser and worser!

'Worse, Ali, not *worser*. No, I'll learn much more on my own.'

'Do they charge the same as you do. When you teach English?'

'No, they said it's free – just their contribution to the community.'

'Free! They must be stupid!' Ali shook his head in disbelief. 'Who's going to be your teacher – John, Paul, George or Ringo?'

Esme laughed.

'Very witty! I don't know yet. They're going to decide among themselves. I'll let you know. What's your homework? What subject?' She turned her head to try and read his exercise book and resisted the temptation to comment on his scrawling, indecipherable hand-writing: it was bad enough that the kids had so few text books that they had to rely so heavily on notes copied from the board.

'History. We have to learn about Biafra. But it's not even a country so I don't see why we have to know about it!'

'It was a country for a very short time. I remember when it declared itself an independent state because it was the day Mosi was due – only she was late.'

'What, the thirtieth of May nineteen sixty seven? Ali traced his notes with a grubby finger.

'Yes. And then Tanzania recognised it after we got here – not you of course, me and Dad and Mosi, the next year. So there was a lot about it in the newspapers – the Biafrans were delighted to be recognised by at least one country. Poor things, that was one of the better things that happened to them.'

Esme told Ali of the terrible atrocities and the short lived political independence of the country that had stuck in her mind, somehow entangled with her memories of coming to terms with the changes in her own life.

The Frenchmen usually gave her a cheery wave and nod as they passed her door and stopped to exchange a few words when they occasionally met outside her office. When Solange was with them, she looked friendly but said little. They seemed a very tight-knit group and a bit out on a limb: too unconventional for the Tanzanian staff and too young and footloose for the Scandinavians who were in their thirties and older, almost all with families in tow. Esme felt slightly responsible for them, being something of an oddity herself and having got here before them – not to mention being more familiar with the country. Not that they gave the impression of needing support – they exuded confidence.

The next Monday, Jean-Pierre came into her office while she was in the middle of totting up the month's expenditure in the ledger.

It was the first time Esme had really been face to face with him. He was tall and sinewy as he stood in front of her and very tanned, weather-beaten even.

'May I?' he asked as he nodded towards the wooden armchair in front of her desk.

'Of course,' she said, hoping the boss wouldn't choose this moment to walk in.

Jean-Pierre's mousy, sun-bleached hair looked as if he'd cut it himself without a mirror and his nose and smile were slightly crooked. The sum of the parts, however, was strangely attractive – perhaps because of his large brown eyes which were now trained on her with an intensity which disquieted her. She was still useless at talking to *Wazungu* men.

'*Ça va?* Esme.' Then he said something in rapid French.

'*Ça va bien*. Sorry. My French is very rusty!' Esme felt her face burn.

'*Désolé!*' He looked unabashed. 'I ask if you are well and if we 'ave our next lesson today?' His accent was very strong.

'Yes, I'm looking forward to it. Are you to be my ... teacher?' She judged that he was younger than her but not enough for her to feel maternal towards him.

'*Ton professeur à ton service*,' he said and bowed deeply.

Esme noticed he didn't use the formal 'you'. She didn't feel they knew each other well enough to be using the familiar form. It was all very disconcerting.

'Because it will be two of us only, I suggest that we use our office. We do not want to be in a large lecture room?'

'Your office? Down the corridor?' Esme asked, nodding in that direction. She couldn't recall ever having occasion to venture down to that end.

'Yes, zuh last on zuh left, before zuh outside door. Zuh mirror-image of this room in fact!' He beamed at the discovery of such a serendipitous coincidence. Esme noticed that rather than his eyes narrowing when he smiled, they appeared to grow rounder giving him a slightly manic appearance.

'OK. Same time - half past four?' she said. For a moment Jean-Pierre looked uncomprehending.

'Ah, yes, fourr-sirty.'

Esme nodded. She was beginning to see a way of paying for her French lessons.

At the end of the afternoon, she waited in her room pretending to finish something off while the other staff nearby locked their doors and said their goodbyes. She feared it would attract a lot of comment if they knew she was staying behind to see one of the French men. She knew this suspicion of any un-chaperoned social contact between a man and woman was completely out of date in Europe but it was still as strong here as it had been back in Kirkcudbrightshire.

The session went well enough despite - or because of – Jean-Pierre being completely unprepared. She was embarrassed by her poor French accent and her lack of vocabulary but Jean-Pierre beamed with pleasure each time she repeated a sentence correctly. They agreed to meet again the same time the following week.

The Thursday that week was a holiday. Esme woke as Independence Day morning dawned with a feeling of expectation which she couldn't identify. Perhaps it was just the holiday association of the date, the ninth of December, which in Dar in the early days had meant the trade fair full of exotic exhibits and free samples. That had all changed with socialism, of course, and the trade fairs had become smaller and confined to local industries showcasing their meagre products – none of which were widely available in shops - and a few exhibits from communist countries. Esme had stopped making the effort to go a few years ago and she didn't expect that Morogoro would host anything like that. However, this year it was to be Morogoro's turn for a visit and public address by President Nyerere.

Esme and the kids sat round the table at breakfast. It was a leisurely start for the kids even though they wouldn't be free till later in the day: they had to attend the celebrations in school uniform with their class-mates and sing and chant patriotically.

Martin sat on the settee with a mug of tea in one hand, rifling through a batch of papers on the coffee table in front of him.

'Martin, can we go together to the stadium?' Esme asked. 'I've never been in it before and, well, it would be a chance for us to go together.' For a change, she added in her head.

'Sorry, I have to work this morning. I'm meeting someone shortly.' He looked at his watch.

'What, are you going out to the office? It'll be closed, won't it.'

'No, I'm meeting him at Mama Perina's.' Martin shuffled the papers together and put them in his attaché case.

'A bar?'

'A hotel.'

Esme snorted derisively. She passed the dilapidated colonial-built residential house occasionally. Its reputation was less than salubrious.

So Esme went on her own to the stadium. Had it been the distance involved in Dar she would hardly have bothered but this was so close to the flat that they could hear the roaring spectators at the weekly football matches. One of the pluses of living in this wee town, she reflected.

Despite her scepticism – aware as she was of the obligatory participation on the part of the school pupils, the Militia and other participating groups - she felt buoyed up by the wave of emotion generated by the music from a brass band, choirs, mass display: marching, singing, callisthenics – doubtless inspired by the communist block but the lack of precision made it apparent it was made up of human beings, not the brain-washed robots as depicted in photographs she recalled from the book given her by the North Korean students. What really gave the celebrations their own identity was the *ngoma* performance – the drums accompanying the rhythmic, cavorting and chanting of the semi-naked dancers.

She had been able to identify Ali and Mosi in their respective class groups simply by the colour of their complexions: it was more tricky for Mosi, being barely lighter than her class-mates, but Ali stood out a mile with his fair complexion and hair glinting blonde in the sunlight. She was glad that, although it was her colouring he had inherited, it was the self-assurance from Martin that allowed him to carry it with such aplomb.

It was now second nature to make eye contact with the numerous strangers who greeted her courteously as she scanned the faces of the crowd of spectators around her for a familiar one, This obligatory meeting of the eyes both heartened and wearied her – she supposed it was because she hadn't grown up with it but everyone round her did it and the fact that she was an *Mzungu* was neither here nor there. But she encountered few familiar faces, no-one she could exchange a few words with.

Then as it was all over; a number of people began to congregate in the middle of the field around the visiting band – perhaps examining their instruments. A colourful figure stood out amongst the assemblage. With a shock, she recognised the outlandish figure of Paul, one of the French horticulturists. What on earth was he wearing? It appeared to be baggy, pink dungarees with an oversize scarlet T-shirt. Had he no sense of dress at all? He was really odd. Seen from such a distance, his earnest, engaging expression was indiscernible and she was struck by his ungainly, unselfconscious posture – hands in pockets, head thrust forward as he wandered amongst the musicians. He had stopped to talk, first one hand gesturing, then the other, almost as if conducting the band! Perhaps she could talk to him. No she didn't want to. What would she talk about? He was very odd. Very tanned though and his blonde hair caught the sun-light. Then it seemed everyone had descended from the stand and was on the pitch, taking a short cut out of the stadium. She could no longer pick out Paul's form. She wondered whether to follow the crowd and try and bump into him. But she immediately rejected the notion as absurd. She left the stadium via the back way, as she had entered it and was at home, just as Ali and Mosi were arriving.

The next day Esme looked out for Paul passing her office door. Sure enough he ambled along mid-morning, and stopped in the doorway. She couldn't make up her mind if he was good looking or not: he was certainly startling in appearance with his shoulder-length blonde hair and high cheekbones; his irises were pale grey in the centre, ringed by a darker grey.

'Bonjour, Esme! Ça va?'

'Bonjour. Did you enjoy the event yesterday?'

Paul's eyebrows shot up and disappeared into his tousled locks which fell all around his face, ears and neck.

'You saw me? You were there? Why did you not cry out to me? We could 'ave been together.' He walked up to her desk and swung his over-stuffed leather satchel from his shoulder onto her desk, scattering her papers. His expression was so tragic, Esme had to laugh.

'You were too far away. It was easy for me to spot you at distance.'

'Why I didn't see you?'

They chatted for a few more minutes. Conversation came very easily to her with him. He had an almost childlike earnestness. He was, in fact she reflected, not much more than a child – maybe early twenties? They were interrupted by a grim-faced Dr Salim – quite unlike his usual leering self. He looked Paul up and down contemptuously, seemingly noting the Frenchman's casual, slightly grubby jeans, yellow T-shirt hanging down to mid-thigh level and his open leather sandals, caked with the soil of the horticultural unit. The lecturer nodded tersely at Paul who smiled back obliviously greeting him with a cheery but unacknowledged 'Good Morning'. With a blank expression Dr Salim handed Esme a slip of paper.

'Mrs Yusufu, could you get out a copy of this publication for me,' he said and, in a heavily sarcastic tone added, '*If* you have time, of course, but I do need it rather urgently.' and remained standing by Esme's desk.

As Paul turned towards the door he gave Esme a concerned look. Esme grimaced in Dr Salim's direction and shook her head. Paul winked as he went on his way. Esme felt full of light-headed happiness for the rest of the morning.

For the first few weeks whenever she intended to say something in French she found it was a Swahili word or phrase on the tip of her tongue but gradually this lessened in frequency. And then she noticed that sometimes the voice in her head spoke French - a phrase she'd learned at one of the lessons which she hadn't thought about since or a long-forgotten word that sprang to mind to describe a feeling or person she'd met. Just as with Swahili, certain French expressions captured an essence which English could not. Her favourite phrase was one she couldn't help applying to herself though Jean-Pierre had used it to describe his young female colleague, Solange. Esme had barely exchanged two words with her because she, like Esme, was *'coinçée dans la peau'* - stuck in her skin. Esme liked the look of Solange : although her smile was shy, it was warm. Esme felt a desire to befriend the younger woman – she looked not much older than Mosi, for heaven's sake, but she didn't know how to approach her beyond saying 'hello'.

    She hadn't seen Paul, the fair-haired one, again to talk to since that day he'd come into her office although he had lingered at the door several times; when he saw she was with someone, he had given a hesitant wave and carried on, casting a wistful look in her direction. Or had she imagined that? On the one occasion she was alone as he passed he had been deep in conversation with Solange, gesticulating in that engaging manner he had. The two hadn't even glanced her way.

    After the third of her individual French lessons, Jean-Pierre said, as he always did, with his lop-sided grin, *'Bienvenu chez nous.'* She was unsure if it was a direct translation of the Swahili rather than a typical French phrase.

    'Thanks, but I have to get home,' she replied automatically in English: her brain too tired to translate into French after an hour of it. But five minutes later, as she stood waiting for the bus outside the admin block, she felt her heart heavy at the prospect of going home. Why did she '*have* to get home'? Martin wouldn't be there, the kids would be fine for another hour or so, they wouldn't even notice her gone. She knew Martin wouldn't approve but – if he found out she was late home - she would say she had been visiting Solange. He would find it even harder to comprehend than herself that Solange lived together platonically with two male colleagues, but no matter. Before she could change her mind, she turned her back on the bus stop and climbed the slope to the staff houses.

As she waited, she wondered who would open the door. It was Paul, scruffier than ever in crumpled, frayed shorts and vest.

'Esme! *Bon soir! Karibu!* How surprising! I mean, it's a good surprise!' He beamed. She tried to construct a sentence in French but all the words that came to her tongue were Swahili. Paul must think her an idiot, standing saying nothing. He ushered her in and blustered in English,

'I hope it's alright, Jean-Pierre invited me to come after the lesson but I said I couldn't only then I realised I've forgotten my key and I'll be locked out so I wondered if I could wait here till the later bus?' She was out of breath and Paul took a few moments to catch on to what she was saying.

'Of, course!' He grinned and waved her into the small sitting room with an exaggerated gesture. '*Jean-Pierre!*, he bellowed towards the inner house, '*Come! Esme is here!*'

Jean-Pierre thundered down the stairs wearing only shorts so brief she wondered if it was his underwear. He too looked delighted. Esme, blushing and sweating, explained once again.

'You should forget your key more often zen!' he said. There followed a rapid exchange between the two men resulting in the three of them going out to the back garden now bathed in the evening sun,

'Sorry, we have no wine to offer you, but would you like a glass of cold beer?'

Solange joined them. She seemed very young and vulnerable beneath her crisp manner and brittle laugh. Esme realised she was, like herself lacking in the confidence the men possessed in abundance. She could only be in her early twenties, like Paul. Jean-Pierre might be a few years older but still nowhere near her own age. God, life was passing her by! The four of them sat and watched the sunset while Paul and Jean-Pierre plied her with questions about Morogoro and how she came to be there, with enormous interest, all the time checking their English with her.

'You will correct our mistakes, Esme?' Paul asked in what she now recognised as his habitually earnest way, as if the tiniest of details was vital to his welfare – as if whatever pearls of wisdom she uttered were of the utmost value.

'It's difficult to correct *all* your mistakes. I mean, your English is very good you don't make *big* mistakes.'

'We make a lot of little ones, isn't it?'

'A few.' Esme tried to shrug and screw up her face to dismiss them as unimportant.

'What we really need,' Solange said, in her light voice, 'is someone to correct what we write in official correspondence. Maybe we could show you what we 'ave written first before we type it?'

Esme was incredulous to learn that they had no secretarial support in the office and no help with the housework at home – they wouldn't contemplate having anyone to do their menial tasks. Their only gripe was sharing a house, there was no escape from one-another. At the same time they understood that the university had a shortage of staff accommodation. They were not as Esme had assumed, long-term friends, having been recruited separately as volunteers to their horticultural project and had only met once before coming to Tanzania.

She had lost track of the time until the mosquitoes began to bite and Jean-Pierre suggested moving indoors. It was only then that she realized the gloaming had crept up on them. She looked at her watch: nearly seven. 'Oh, I must go home! The kids will be back by now and wondering where I am.'

'You go by bus now?

'Yes, I think there will be a bus – I don't know the times in the evening.'

Another unintelligible discussion between the two men ensued after which Paul turned back to Esme and beamed:

'I take you 'ome by car.'

The car was unlike anything Esme had ever seen, let alone ridden in: a banana yellow miniature version of a four wheel drive which Paul drove as if he was in a safari rally. As a result she was bounced almost through the roof every time he hit a pot hole, a not infrequent occurrence.

'Where do you want to drop off?' he asked as they drove through the main street, past the market.

'Just up there on the left,' she replied. 'You can turn the car here,' she indicated a side road. 'I live in the block of flats through there.' She cringed at the vision of him driving right up to the flats: although she could count on Martin not being in, she could equally count on the neighbours peering out and speculating about her being driven home by a male *Mzungu*.

And kissed three times on the cheek – an unknown phenomenon for the locals.

'Where have you been?' Martin was sitting on the settee opposite the door, his expression unreadable but the tone of his voice was menacing.

I went with Solange to her place after my French lesson. She invited me.' Her heart pounded but she knew she'd done no wrong, apart from lying.

'Just like that! Did you let us know you'd be so late? The children have been worried sick about you.' His controlled features and the stillness of his body told her he was coldly angry with her.

'The offices were closed so I couldn't phone. Martin, when do you ever phone to tell us you'll be late?'

'That's different and you know it. It's not usual for you to be late.'

She was shaking with emotion: a tumult of anger, fear and the lingering excitement of the evening. She put her bag down on the dining table, realising she'd have to start cooking immediately. The rhythmical beat of Morogoro All Stars floated down the corridor. Not the sound of teenagers worried sick.

Mosi pulled back the gauze curtain screening the hallway from the living room.

'*Mama*! You're late! I wanted you to help me with my essay! I didn't know where you were.'

'You see!' Martin said, his face impassive but his tone baleful. He got up and walked towards the door. He didn't turn his head as he said: 'I'll see you later.'

'What time?' Esme spoke to his retreating back – deliberately disregarding the fact that *he never* said what time he would be back.

'Don't wait up for me. I'll be late.' He closed the door, none too softly. Esme could feel Mosi's eyes on her as Mosi remained stock-still, the curtain still in her hand but Esme didn't trust herself to meet her daughter's eyes. They were stinging with angry tears. Her throat hurt with stifled sobs. She swallowed hard.

'Right. I'll be with you in a minute, Mosi. I'll go and see what I can cobble together for a meal later and put something on the cooker while you make a start on your essay – list some points.'

Mosi had followed her into the kitchen and was standing with her arms folded an injured expression on her face.

'I've done that while I was waiting for you.'

'For God's sake. I'm home now!' Esme banged a saucepan onto the draining board. 'And you'd better get used to me being late because this could be the first time of many!'

'You didn't say that to Dad!'

Esme spun round to face Mosi an angry response forming in her mouth but caught it before it escaped to wreak havoc. Esme's fight was not with her daughter.

'No you're right. But I will. Mosi, I don't like scenes any more than you do. You don't really mind me seeing friends once a week or so do you? But OK, you didn't know I was going to be late.' She put her arms around Mosi, taller than her by an inch now. Mosi softened her stance enough to put her head on Esme's shoulder and a limp arm on her mother's back. Esme knew the girl hadn't fully forgiven her yet: she held onto grudges, just like her father.

Esme rummaged in the bottom of the store cupboard and took out a couple of arrowroots. 'Give me a hand with these first, sweetheart,' Esme passed the fine-haired, irregular root vegetables to Mosi.

'There are some *kunde* left over from lunch time and a bit of beef stew and rice but we need to leave some of that for your father, *in case* he decides to eat when he gets back.' Esme's tone was scathing.

In response Mosi gave Esme a disapproving glare which Esme ignored. Well, Esme reflected, from Mosi's perspective, Martin's night-time habits would be considered perfectly normal by society at large and it was Esme's behaviour that was anomalous. She had often spoken to the kids about her complete rejection of such an attitude but action spoke louder than words. However, this wasn't the time for discussion: Esme would need to bide her time but not too much of it. Mosi was fast turning into a young woman.

She half-filled a plastic basin with water from the kitchen tap and handed Mosi a small sharp knife from the drawer.

'Tell me what this essay's about while we peel these, then we'll go and tackle it.' A sudden thought occurred to her, she hadn't seen or heard Ali since her return to the flat.

'Is Ali doing his homework? He's very quiet. What did he say about me being a bit late home?' she emphasised the word 'bit'.

Mosi tsked her disapproval. 'He wasn't bothered. He said you'd be home in your own good time!'

Esme tried to not to crow but felt a warm glow in her chest.

'And was he right?' she looked sidelong at Mosi.

'Yeah, but next time tell us you'll be late!'

The weekend came and with it the wistful awareness that Esme wouldn't see any of the

French people. At least at work she could hope that they'd saunter past the office, stop and peer round the open door; seeing her, they'd come in and exchange a few words. It never failed to leave her with a flush of pleasure.

The weekends were a chance to catch up on the household chores that either Mama Sele hadn't done properly or Esme couldn't expect her to do in the first place. Quite often on Saturday or Sunday she would go into town. Sometimes she bumped into people she knew: neighbours, fellow workers or students from the university but otherwise there was very little to do in town beyond the necessities – the shops were pretty bare; occasionally the kids needed some item of clothing and she'd go to buy the material and take it to a tailor. There were hundreds of tailors up and down the country and Morogoro seemed to have its fair share of them - working away with their treadle machines in any shade they could get, often in shop doorways. The prices they charged were so low that they must have needed to work all the hours that God sent to keep body and soul together. But the quality of the work often didn't warrant charging more and there would always be someone cheaper round the corner. Through trial and error, amongst the hundreds of male tailors, she found a young woman whose work was neat and accurate and Mosi was comfortable being measured by her rather than the men.

Otherwise weekends were her only opportunity to write letters to her parents and to Christine since she wouldn't have dared to carry out her personal correspondence under the nose of the Head.

So she kept herself busy but all the time she was looking forward to being back in the office where she could keep her eye on the door for the French people. She missed them at weekends.

Ch 25: Morogoro with the French

'Hodi!'

Esme looked up from her typewriter to see Jean-Pierre in the doorway.

'Karibu,' she replied, smiling. They were always welcome, these French people.

'Habari za kazi?' How is work? They amazed her the way they had picked up everyday-Swahili in such a short space of time. Most expatriates didn't learn as much in four years as they had in four months.

'Nzuri.'

'I change to English now – or maybe French?' he said with his crooked smile.

'Er, not French, thank you!' Esme shook her head and pulled a face of mock horror. All the time she had French visitors in the office she was aware of the possibility of the Head coming in.

'Would you be so kind to check this letter to the vice-chancellor.' Jean-Pierre asked, handing her a sheet of squared mathematical paper covered in spiky green writing. 'It could 'ave some spelling or grammar mistakes?'

Inwardly, Esme smiled at the word 'could'.

Over the next few weeks, it became a regular occurrence – either Jean-Pierre, Paul or

Solange would bring a draft of a letter. They seemed to speak English much better than they wrote it. Sometimes she wished they'd just explain what they wanted to say and let her compose it, it was so tricky getting the balance right: it had to be intelligible but she feared offending them by re-writing whole swathes. It was always a compromise.

Solange, initially very reticent, began to warm towards Esme. Esme always a supporter of the under-dog, lost her own inhibitions in the face of Solange's insecurity. Solange also began dropping into Esme's office, initially with one of the boys, then on her own. On one such occasion she asked Esme to join them for dinner later in the week. At first Esme felt panic-stricken: not since that disastrous occasion when Esme had turned up at Pamela's in her nightdress had she been invited to someone's house for a meal: she was still a novice in *Mzungu* protocol. It was different with Tanzanians - you turned up unannounced and you hung around while they caught a chicken, killed it, plucked it, disembowelled it, hacked it to pieces, put it in a pot and cooked it. As a child, her family had never invited people for dinner nor were her parents ever invited out. Occasionally they had family over for Sunday dinner at two in the afternoon but that was hardly the same thing.

She decided to confront her fears head on.

'Solange, I hope you don't mind me asking, but is it formal, I mean what should I wear?'

Solange laughed. 'No, it's just us, it's not formal at all. Just we, by oursels. Nothing to worry about.'

At the meal, it was just Solange, Paul and herself and it was indeed completely informal: Solange was as always neatly and attractively dressed in a short-sleeved broderie anglaise blouse and cotton print skirt in hues through scarlet to purple. Paul was attired in crumpled but fresh-smelling dungarees and T-shirt: he looked freshly showered, his damp tresses falling into his eyes. He ate with gusto. Sitting opposite him, she had every opportunity to take in his enthusiastic gesticulations and his earnest expressions as he explained about his work.

The food was delectably different from anything she'd had before.

'What is this made of she asked as the flavours of the unappealing- looking grey mush that was the starter ricocheted round her mouth, bouncing off her palate.

'It is, *bien*, zuh aubergine cooked in the oven, smashed up wiz olive oil and garlic – quite a lot of garlic, actually,' said Paul, happily placing a slice of bread directly onto the table, 'With a *soupçant* of lime juice'.

'Everything is from the market – except the oil, of course. We get a few delicacies from the embassy in Dar sometimes,' Solange added, looking uncomfortable.

Esme reflected that since Martin couldn't abide garlic in food they never used it. Aubergines, or eggplants, as she knew them, were off the menu at home: along with salads, sweet peppers and a myriad of mountain-grown fresh produce: to Martin and the kids it was '*Wazungu* food'. Neither had it been typical fare for the farming community of Dumfriesshire. So up until now she had done no more than admire the aubergines' glossy purple plumpness in the market.

'We try to convince the indigenous population to eat these as well as to grow them for the market but they just laugh!' said Solange. 'It is understandable that to change to eat raw food: lettuce, tomatoes and those things, it would be a big change for them but even they will not consider to cook aubergines and carrots!'

'What do they eat?' Esme asked.

'What zeir ancestors have eaten for all time,' replied Paul, waving his hand to indicate the past millennia and knocking over his glass of water.

'Beans wiz maize-meal made into *ugali,* or wild leaves with *ugali.*

Sometimes, for a special occasion, zey buy rice from zuh market, and of course for very special occasions zey kill a chicken. And eat it with *ugali*.'

It sounded much the same as Esme had encountered elsewhere, except that more rice was eaten on the coast where it thrived, and the higher the income the more beef or goat could be purchased. She thought about telling the others this but somehow the words didn't come.

Paul brought in the main course: this consisted of instantly-recognizable ingredients: beef and vegetables but in a sauce of such delightful flavour and consistency that Esme could not begin to imagine how it was made.

'Who is the chef?' asked Esme.

Paul and Solange laughed.

'It was me today,' said Paul 'But it depends. Whoever is in zuh mood. We fight for the kitchen sometimes, we all love cooking. When Jean-Pierre is here he insists. He likes to er…carry out trials, you say? Like we do at the horticulture unit. Sometimes it is very successful.' He added with a suppressed smirk.

One day, a few weeks later, Paul asked her if she would like to join them for a picnic at the weekend, up in the mountains. She was beset by misgivings: how would she explain it to her family. Should she ask if she could bring the kids? But really, they were such townies and could see nothing in the bush to attract them. Besides this was a grown up thing – it was her, Esme, they had invited not Mama Mosi or Mama Ali. And certainly not Mrs Yusufu. They had never met Martin, of course, and knew barely anything about him. They all tended to act as if he didn't exist. She blocked from her mind the avenue towards which this notion led.

The French didn't know exactly where she lived or much about her situation at home: she hadn't volunteered the information and they hadn't asked. She guessed that they guessed correctly how things were. All the same, they should know where she lived and meet Mosi and Ali: though, if that did happen, it would really hit home to her friends how much older she was than them.

On Sunday afternoon she was about to leave for the picnic when she became aware of a gentle tapping on the door. She opened it to find a lanky youth dressed in well worn shirt and trousers and wearing flip-flops. Something in his face looked familiar.

'*Habari gani?*' They exchanged greetings and she hesitated in the doorway, unsure of whether she ought to invite him in or not.

'I'm Sulemani, young brother of *Baba* Mosi,' he informed her diffidently in Swahili.

It was news to her that Martin had a young brother but she discerned a familiarity about those enormous, luxuriantly fringed eyes in his gaunt face.

'You've forgotten me,' he said. I was much younger when you saw me last, when you came to Mabalo. I've just come from Mabalo. Have I found *Baba* Mosi in?' he asked. Whenever Martin' s relatives turned up he was never in.

'He's not in,' Esme replied. 'You're his young brother...?'

'Yes, his mother and mine are sisters.'

Well, she conceded to herself, that might well be the case, she couldn't keep track of Martin's relatives and in their book, yes, that would make him a younger brother. Damn, damn, damn: she'd couldn't possibly turn him away. and she couldn't leave him alone.

'*Karibu,*' she said aloud opening the door fully and standing back to allow him through. He sat down in an easy chair and she sat on the settee opposite.

'*Habari ya safari?*' How was the trip?' she asked.

'Fine. I came by ship. The engine broke down and we were marooned for a day. The food and water ran out. Then the engine was repaired and we arrived in Dar es Salaam this morning. I walked to Kariakoo from the harbour and got a bus.'

'*Eh, pole sana!* You must be must exhausted!'

She knew propriety forbade that she ask him if he was hungry or that he would say if he was but she thought it a fair bet that he was broke and hadn't had a square meal for several days. She went to make some tea and cut some slices of bread. She had nothing to spread on them but she didn't suppose that would bother him: bread was probably a luxury at the best of times and right now he'd most likely be grateful for raw cassava.

She gave him the tea. What was she supposed to do now? Paul and Solange would be waiting but she couldn't leave this boy here on his own. Apart from it being the height of bad manners, she didn't actually *know* if he was an in-law or, indeed, if he was trustworthy.

She stood at the window and stared at the velvety emerald of the mountains. She looked haplessly at the black telephone on the hall table: it was only because it had already been installed when they moved in to the flat that they had such a luxury. Not that they could afford to phone many people and certainly not Scotland. But the French had not been lucky or influential enough to succeed in their application to get a phone installed in their house: the waiting list never seemed to get any shorter.

She resumed her seat in the living room. Sulemani had taken a newspaper from the pile on the shelf beneath the coffee-table and was engrossed in it.

'How are Mama and *Baba* Martin?' she asked, 'And his brothers and sisters and their children?'

Sulemani looked up briefly and replied 'They are all fine,' before resuming his reading. She sat looking at the top of his short-cropped, tightly-curled black hair, reflecting on how neat it appeared despite the rigours of his journey on the high seas while hair like hers became tousled in the slightest breeze.

She made several attempts at conversation with Sulemani. At each he answered politely and then carried on devouring the contents of the paper. She felt the heat of annoyance rising up her body but at same time she knew that was being childish. It was, apparently, normal behaviour: she'd encountered it before when people came and were waiting for Martin or the kids to get ready to go out with them. So that was it, he was waiting for Martin to come home, for the real householder. Well, he would have a long wait!

The clock on the bookcase ticked. Tears stung her eyes. Paul and Solange would be wondering what had happened to her but they would go without her anyway. She got to her feet. Two could play at this game, she thought bitterly.

'*Nakuja*. I'm coming.' she said. Weird language she reflected: it really means 'I'm going'. She went into the bedroom, closed the door threw herself on the bed and sobbed.

Sulemani stayed two weeks. Martin took him out with him a few times in the afternoon but sent him back to the flat in the early evening. Mostly he hung around, listening to the radio. She knew it was taboo to ask a visitor how long they were planning on staying but she asked Martin. He had merely shrugged and said, 'He's just come for a bit of a holiday, a change of scene.'

At least Sulemani got on well with Ali and Mosi, they chatted and laughed together on the veranda after school but the kids had their own friends and he was, Esme guessed, a bit of a country bumpkin to them. Esme felt sorry for him but he seemed unable to open up to her at all so while he was always impeccably polite they never had what amounted to a conversation. She was relieved when he left for home.

A few weeks later, she managed to screw up enough courage to invite the French trio for a meal one Saturday evening, as she said, to make up for her non-appearance for the picnic – not that they had shown anything other than the utmost concern for her. She needed the whole day to prepare it – unlike them, she couldn't toss off a gourmet meal after a day's work. She had primed the kids – Ali especially – to be on their best behaviour. This was a new venture for all of them. She didn't know what to do about Martin. She didn't think it wise to keep him totally in the dark in case he found out about it - she could hardly swear the kids to secrecy. After much agonising, she decided to try and bluff her way out of the predicament. Two days before the visit was due, as she was bringing in clothes from the line Martin, came into the kitchen for a glass of cold water before setting off on his usual evening jaunt.

'Martin, I'd like to invite some friends from the university round on Saturday evening. Those French people who've been running the French classes.' She didn't see the need to explain that the classes had long since folded. 'Would you be able to stay in and meet them?' She hoped she didn't sound as if she considered his absence a disaster but, equally, as if she was desperately hoping he'd agree. What if *did* say yes?

He seemed to be considering his reply as he tipped his head back and downed the last of the water. He placed the misted glass on the draining board and met Esme's eyes. For a second she was carried back to a period when such a look would have melted her bones but almost immediately she guessed what his answer would be.

'You didn't mention this before. What's brought this on? No, at such short notice, I won't be able to stay in for the meal. But I'll welcome them to the flat before I go out.'

'That could be tricky. It will be a bit too early to invite them for dinner before the time you usually leave.' She glanced at her wrist watch. Five o'clock. A loud thumping in her chest echoed in her ears.

'Tell me what time they're coming and I'll come back to be here.' Martin said testily. 'I presume that since they are *Wazungu* they will be punctual?'

'I was thinking seven o'clock.' He would come back when he'd already had a few to drink and there'd be no knowing what he'd say. She couldn't bear to think about it. 'Yes, I'm sure they'll be punctual.'

On the Saturday morning she awoke at five, just before the muezzins' calls, and had to endure the dissonance of all the three chants simultaneously. She wondered how many homes like theirs lay in the intersection of the three concentric circles of individually melodious sound. Lying there she became aware of her mind and body: she was - as her mother would have said – a bag of nerves. The only guests Esme had ever catered for till now were the odd relatives or buddies of Martin – aye 'odd' being the operative word. They'd arrive, of course, uninvited and unannounced: it meant they took pot luck. Now she remembered that the goat-meat needed to be defrosted and, since sleep had eluded her, she pushed back the top sheet and slid out of bed, careful to avoid disturbing Martin. She would have her shower later, she decided as she draped a *kanga* round her body, towel-like below her armpits.

As she made herself a cup of tea, she reflected on her plans to cook *pilau* containing bite-size chunks of goat-meat. Martin, of course, didn't like the spicy flavour of the rice so they didn't have it on high days and holidays like the rest of the population. She would have to cook some goat stew and plain rice for him. Rather than use the ready-made spices from the market, she would roast and grind her own with the pestle and mortar: the flavour was much more vibrant when fresh. Even though Mosi had promised to help her peel the cardamom seeds, as well as to peel and slice the onions, potatoes, garlic and tomatoes, Esme knew she would be busy for the rest of the day.

To her huge relief the evening passed without major incident. The aroma of the spices greeting the guests on arrival had elicited exclamations of delight, setting off Mosi and Ali - still behind the partitioning curtain in the hallway - into uncontrollable giggles much to the amusement of the French. However, when the kids bashfully took their seats round the table, they were awed into silence. All three guests tried to draw them out; Solange, in particular, recounting the exploits of her young brother, Mosi's age, only to be rewarded with monosyllabic replies. But Mosi and Ali's open faces made it clear that their lack of conversation was due to shyness rather than surliness.

Best of all Martin never did show up. Jean-Pierre had asked,

'Where is your husband? Is he not joining us?'

'Oh, sorry,' Esme replied, feeling herself blush, 'he had to go to see someone – a relative. A sick relative. He doesn't really eat in the evenings, well maybe later he might have something when he gets in.'

The three of them looked bewildered and murmured that it was a pity, they would have liked to meet him. She couldn't be sure, but she though the look Paul had given her seemed to be full of concern.

Soon after that occasion they suggested the kids join them for a trip into the mountains. She wasn't at all sure how it would work or that she wanted to have the kids enter her own private life. But she asked them anyway:

Ali's response was to contort his face in mock horror:

'What out in the bush amongst the peasants?'

Esme disliked this commonly-used translation of *wakulima* which meant agriculturalists. No doubt it originated from the colonialists but accurately reflected the superior attitude of waged employees,

'Farmers, Ali, please!' she corrected him, feeling a mixture of relief and regret.

'No, thanks, Ma,' replied Mosi with a sardonic smile. 'We'll leave you to your country bumpkins.'

Meals with the French became a regular occurrence. Mostly it was with Solange and Paul but sometimes Jean-Pierre issued the invitation and he did the cooking; as Paul had said, it was often experimental with quite varying results. In Esme's view, he fancied himself as a cordon bleu chef. The other two were the essence of tact and, even when the food was verging on unpalatable, not a word or look passed between them to suggest that they found the food anything other than perfect. Esme was impressed at the absence of two-facedness that she had assumed was human nature, till now.

Few bus trips operated in the evening and the Beetle had been grounded for weeks for lack of spare parts. Her old red Raleigh bicycle that she had brought from Scotland was still going strong, despite the punishment it had endured at the hands of the kids and their friends in Dar. At least once a week, she would cycle the couple of miles to the campus after lunch at home: although only a couple of miles, it was uphill most of the way but, of course, the homeward run, after dinner, was exhilarating in the cool of the gloaming, her hair whipping back, the sharp collisions with insects against her face, neck and bare arms.

As the weeks went by, increasingly, it was after seven o'clock, nightfall, by the time the meal was over. As the French didn't like her riding home in the dark, undiluted by any street lights, one of them would drive her home after dinner, helping her lift the heavy bicycle onto and off the back of the pick up. She still had to carry the bike up to the second floor flat, often after a glass or two of wine. She then had to negotiate the bike through the living room, the kitchen and out onto the balcony lifting aside the day's washing. But this was a small price to pay for such a privilege.

Her life was transformed: she flourished on the banter and laughter. As a result of the cycling, walking in the mountains and her constant state of animation, she had lost the weight she had put on in her first few months of vegetating in Morogoro. When she surveyed herself in the mirror, the eyes that were reflected back at her sparkled with *joie de vivre*. Solange had cut her hair and given her a bottle of conditioner which had tamed the frizz to exuberant curls. She found herself wondering if Paul found her attractive then tried to banish any such thoughts from her head.

Then there were occasions when she went on excursions with the French. She felt more alive than she had since the period of women's group meetings and the plays. She missed that still, it had given a meaning to her life. She had yet to tell Paul, Solange and Jean-Pierre about it. She loved the fact they accepted her at face value – they knew nothing about her past life yet she felt confident that they would be interested in whatever she had to tell them.

She would see Paul and Solange most days on campus apart from the days when they went to the villages when they would be too late back for her to see them. Her relationship with each was very different. Solange talked a bit about her parents and brother at home, about her relationship with colleagues in the university and the students. But Esme was unprepared for the arrival one evening for dinner of Devin, one of the third year students. Solange never spoke to Esme about Devin but from then on he began to come regularly to eat. Jean-Pierre, in the meantime was apparently becoming more involved with life beyond the university and ate with the group less and less. That left the four of them. Esme knew this would not look good to the Tanzanians on campus - were they to find out. Or Martin.

Meanwhile, at the flat, life went on as before: in contrast, it seemed monotonous, irksome even. The kids had their friends – more and more they came home only just in time for the dusk curfew which, since she returned home at least once a week after dark herself, was becoming increasingly difficult to enforce.

One weekend, having concocted some excuse at home, she travelled with Paul, Solange and Devin to some villages in the mountains, further afield, places of whose existence Esme had had no previous inkling. Although it was in their time off, Solange and Paul showed them some experimental plots they had established together with local people in co-ordination as part of an outreach programme from the university. The French duo confidently perceived no barriers of language, culture, education and life-style which Esme herself felt self-conscious about . She admired their commitment and zeal to revolutionise rural horticulture to include new, more-marketable and more-nutritious vegetables. When Paul explained it to her it all made sense but she had a strong feeling that Devin, though he was quite circumspect in his comments, wasn't convinced that a trio of young French people together with a bunch of suit-wearing Tanzanian academics, were going to be able to convince the small-holders to totally abandon centuries-old practices. They might go along with the experiments so long as it attracted attention and investment but once the *Wazungu* went back to *Ulaya*, who could tell?

Paul and Solange's view seemed to be that so far there had been scarcely any real attempt to involve the locals in improved farming techniques; instead, modern production methods had simply been practiced on large scale resulting in two parallel systems. Esme was fascinated by the topic.

One Sunday afternoon as pre-arranged she cycled up to their house for a drive into the mountains. Solange wasn't there – Paul grinned as he told her that she had left early in the morning with Devin who had spent the night with her. Jean-Pierre, as it seemed was increasingly the case, was staying with a group of local dancers in one of the mountain villages.

'So it means it's just the two of us,' Paul beamed. Her stomach did a flip. What would that imply to the Tanzanian staff members who lived in the adjacent houses, seeing them driving off together? They were already casting sideways glances at her whenever they passed her chatting to the French men and who, she knew from Dina, were already gossiping about her: apparently they assumed that everyone was like them: only interested in the people who happened to be of the opposite sex for one reason.

They had an enchanted day: they drove up the rutted track to Morningside, passing the village where snotty-nosed toddlers and children of all ages waved and shouted *Wazungu*, beyond the abandoned hotel, as far as vehicles were permitted. Leaving the pick-up, they continued on foot into the dark coolness of the forest. The trees were different species from those she knew from back home but the mysterious dimness was so reminiscent of her excursions as a teenager to the Merrick Kells that she was filled with delight: those were the times, escaping from the dreariness of the farm, that she had appreciated the countryside, nature. She experienced the same thrill now, and more.

Later, after Paul had dropped her off in town and she was walking along the sandy footpath that led to the flats from the main road, the sun a flaming red ball sinking behind the trees beyond the railway track, her mind in turmoil, she decided she would write to Christine later that evening; she had so much to tell her she wouldn't know where to begin.

Ch 26: Branching Out

Morogoro, 12th July 1984

Dear Christine,

What's up? I've had no letter from you for ages. I hope things are OK with you. Or has a letter from you got lost in the post, like before? The time I heard from you was in March when you told me about the miners' strike (which did get a lot of coverage in our national daily, by the way, sympathies here being with the miners, naturally.)

If you <u>haven't</u> written, you'll be surprised to hear from me but the truth is I've nothing better to do this weekend because the French have gone to Dar and left me behind! It does prove, if proof were needed, how much I do rely on them. Their company makes me feel like I'm really living. Without them, I'd go mad like I very nearly did that time in Dar, because I have no choice but to hang on here with my kids – pair of monkeys that they are at times.

But the kids are the reason I'm here at all and, on the whole, I'm happy that they're well and in good spirits and they don't give me too much grief. Ali and Martin are at daggers drawn most of the time. Ali idolises Martin but he's had a mind of his own since the day he was born. These days he is disagreeing openly with his father on an exponential scale. And, while Martin's not as robust as he was (how would he be with his lifestyle?), Ali, who's now fourteen, has shot up and filled out in the last few months and the two of them are now about the same height. And to boot, Ali has passed the national exam for secondary school which so few kids do and this has boosted his confidence even further. Not only is he as big as his father, he's as fit as a lop, thanks to the school's keep-fit regime. Not that they have a gym or any sports equipment but all the school grounds are entirely maintained by the bairns - they cut the grass with long-handled slashers. After school he plays football and with the non-existence of TV to lure him indoors, he's out and about all day. It actually makes quite interesting watching in itself - the ongoing drama between Ali his Dad - and it takes the attention away from myself.

So what about myself? I'm learning a lot lately about Morogoro and, in particular, about the inhabitants. According to Paul, two tribes are local to the area - with no love lost between them - one from the plains (about whom, I confess, I know nothing) and the other - the Waluguru from the Uluguru mountains who, incidentally, speak Kiluguru. (That's the way it works : Wa- for the people, U-for the place, Ki- for the country: for English, Waingereza, Uingereza, Kiingereza, it's the same for French and German, Portuguese etc. On the other hand, Scotland - because it didn't maraud round these parts - is virtually unknown and is variously referred to as Uskoti, Uskochi and Skotilandi! Mostly it's equated with England – or London - highly vexing. But I digress. Most of the people working in the services in town and at the regional headquarters and the university are the same motley mix of tribes as we found in Dar. Most of them seem to look down on the mountain folk as 'backward' because they haven't embraced 'civilisation', preferring to live in the mountains, mostly without piped water, electricity, phones, medical care or much in the way of schools. And because the terrain makes it too difficult to reach (I can personally testify to that) and organise these folk, there they stay in splendid isolation. A bit like myself, here in the flat before I met the French!

Work is the same – the challenge has gone out of it now that I've learned the ropes. I'm looking out for something else at the university but none of the support staff ever leave to create a vacancy, in contrast to the shifting population of the academic staff. The clerks etc all seem to be settled locally and having secured a steady job are hanging on to it. There too, if it wasn't for the French I'd be climbing the walls...

Out onto the page poured an account of how her friendship with the trio had blossomed over the past months; notions she hadn't been prepared for, emotions she hadn't voiced even in the privacy of her head, were deposited onto the paper and sealed in the envelope. Martin must never read this.

The French were staying on in Dar till Tuesday to celebrate *le quatorze juillet* at the embassy with the entire French population of Tanzania, actually a mere handful, most French expatriates presumably favouring their former African colonies to Tanzania with its German and British legacies.

To relieve her sense of abandonment, instead of going home for lunch on the Monday, she went to look for Dina at the halls of residence; she hadn't seen her for many weeks. Students were draped about languidly in whatever shade was available. A low murmur of chatter drifted around. Though it was the cool season and deliciously refreshing in the mornings and evenings, the noon sun was still to be avoided by all but the proverbial mad dogs and Englishmen. Aye, and this mad Scottish lassie, she thought, as curious eyes followed her.

Dina was sitting on a bench, her long bare legs stretched out in front of her surrounded, as usual, by a group of optimistic male students. Esme could never be sure how much of Dina's come-hither behaviour was merely flirtatious and how much was in earnest: perhaps that was her attraction. At any rate, she used her body to serve her purposes: to her it was an asset as much as her intelligence and education and she'd be a fool to waste it.

'Esme, *kisura*, I was coming to find you later,' she called out, catching sight of Esme. She slid from her perch and came towards Esme, pulling her by the hand to sit on some steps in the shade of a building, away from the listening ears. After the usual lengthy greetings and excuses she went on to say,

'I have become friends with the wife of one of the Finnish lecturers. She is from Thailand and has been doing some work with women. She will leave in a few months and she wants to hand over her work to someone to continue it. I told her about your work with the women's group in Dar – you are the ideal person with your experience. She would like to meet you.' This was delivered with a triumphant flourish, both hands proffering this award.

Esme was lost for words.

'Well, are you not pleased! Or are you too busy with your French friends these days?' Dina studied her nails with a mock-injured air.

'How do you know about them? Is that why you haven't been around lately?'

'I have been busy, *rafiki yangu*. The students like to gossip, you know, and the lecturers too, the Tanzanian ones. They know I am your friend so they tell me what you are up to. You are actually causing quite a scandal.'

'God, you mean I'm under surveillance all the time! But, listen, Dina, tell me more about this Thai woman. What work is she doing? It's not that I'm not interested – I was just so taken by surprise.'

As Dina explained it, Jaidee's work involved some new-fangled prototypes of braziers for burning charcoal more efficiently. During power cuts when kerosene was in short supply, Esme had occasionally resorted to the using the one-pot charcoal burner made of scrap metal, sold in every market place in the land. But Esme had not readily taken to the bending and squatting required for culinary activities on this portable stove.

'But Dina, you've been to our place, I don't use a *jiko*, we use electricity.'

'Yes, but you're a woman! Women cook, women talk to women. Jaidee has been working with some of the male lecturers on some of the technical stuff but they don't know anything about cooking and they won't go near a kitchen! Does *your* husband?'

'You must be joking! OK. I get the point. But what about Tanzanian women – can't Jaidee hand-over to one of them?'

'For example? Do you know of anyone in Morogoro who has shown any interest at all in women's work, who is able to communicate in English as well as Swahili?'

Dina was waving her arms about like a demented windmill and glaring at Esme.

'In Dar yes, but not in Morogoro. What about you, Dina? You could do it.'

Dina laughed. 'Me! I am only interested in one woman's issues – my own. No, you are the only one.'

'Give me time to think about it, Dina. I'll have to get back to work now. Can you come over to my office tomorrow?'

'Alright, but I am expecting a "yes" from you.'

It was always going to be yes, Esme reflected some weeks later. She had been drawn in irrevocably: she had met Jaidee who, she told Esme, was from a well-off family and was a graduate in Art History. She had been bored without work in Morogoro and having seen what she thought were wasteful charcoal stoves made of metal – known in the plural as 'majiko', had brought an example of a pottery one back from Thailand which she had seen used in the rural areas. Her houseboy had found her a potter from one of the villages and helped Jaidee to commission some copies. She showed one to Esme: it was rather like a large, rough flowerpot with a pottery grate on supports a couple of inches from the bottom and an air-hole situated below the level of the grate. Jaidee explained that the potter had made the stove using the methods local potters had been using for traditional cooking and water pots for millennia.

'You can see such pots in the market, ' Jaidee, a tiny, fine-boned woman with a mass of black hair told Esme. 'I wanted to work with the university to develop this project in the countryside but, as a foreigner, I couldn't get a work permit or any funds. So I've just done it voluntarily. The university, has given me some help but they are all men and they're all scientists so, of course, have difficulty understanding what I want. And they *claim* that they don't have time to visit women in villages.'

So she had enlisted the help of a German lecturer working in the Outreach department whose role was to work with small-holders, which was the vast majority of the population. He had given a few stoves to local officials for their wives to try at home.

'So, you mean, a man gave the stoves to men? Sounds like the blind leading the blind!' Esme said.

'Exactly!' said Jaidee. 'Without you, this whole project will be stillborn.'

Esme told Paul, Jean-Pierre and Solange about it over a meal.

'I feel completely out of my depth in this. I mean, I know nothing about pottery, or cooking on charcoal, or about rural life. It would be interesting to work *alongside* Jaidee. Since I speak Swahili and, I suppose you could say, I have some experience of interviewing women for the plays in Dar, maybe we could have made a go of it. She's going to take me to meet this German lecturer, Gerhard. The potter who makes the stoves works at his place and he's involved somehow.'

All three of her friends began to talk excitedly at once. She laughed, looking from one to the other. Eventually, they spoke in turn – they were full of enthusiasm for her involvement and offered her all kinds of support.

'You know,' said Solange, 'We are already doing extension work so you can come with us like before and talk to the women about cooking and so on.'

'I've met Jaidee a few times, she's really nice,' said Paul, 'But Gerhard, well, he's a bit ... how can I say? He's a bit *special*. I've spoken with him a few times. If you like I can come with you,'

'OK, thanks, both of you,' said Esme. 'How do you mean, Paul, "special"?'

'He is in reality very *sympa*, yes sympathetic deep inside, but his outside is quite difficult.' Paul would say no more. None of them, Esme had noticed, ever spoke ill of anyone; this was the nearest to it she had heard from any of them. She wasn't looking forward to this meeting.

Jean-Pierre looked at her intently. 'I can sense that this is very important to you. Follow your 'eart, Esme. Let me know if I can assist if you wiz something but probably you won't see me so much.'

Esme had already noticed he was absent more often than not when she came to the house.

'I 'ave this passion for dancing.' he went on, 'Not western dancing, African dancing.'

The son of a French colonial administrator, he had been born in Africa and had travelled widely on the continent. Since adulthood, in every country he visited, he had sought out local dancers.

'And now I 'ave been invited to join a group of *ngoma* in a village in the mountains. It means I will 'ave to practice every weekend and when they're 'ired for a celebration I will be performing also!'

Esme was stuck for a reply. It was so unexpected. '*Ngoma*? Great!' she said feebly.

Jean-Pierre beamed. ' Yes, *ngoma* is the drums but it, as well, is the name given to the 'ole phenomenon,' he demonstrated with his hands an entity the width of the dining table,

'The other instruments, the singing and the dancing. ''Ave you never seen the *ngoma* round here it?'

'Yes, I've seen it, heard it a few times, just passing by.' She recalled Sunday afternoons in the flat when she had heard the drums and singing and then seen a troupe of male dancers, mostly in shorts and bare-chested, along the track in front of their flat, across the bridge and off into the jumble of houses beyond, followed by an assortment of haphazardly attired men, women dressed in *kanga* and flip-flops, and barefoot children. Martin had dismissed them as *Waluguru* down from the mountains to celebrate one of their women getting married to someone educated for a change. She had been enthralled by the rhythm, the unfamiliar sounds. She had once been to the village museum in Dar to a dance performance from a tribe in central Tanzania and she was familiar with the homogenised versions choreographed for political rallies but she knew each tribe had its own distinctive music and dance.

'You must be the only *Mzungu* doing it!'

'Yes, I know!' His eyes shone out his bliss.

She went to look for the pots in the market. It struck her how vibrant it was, unlike those markets in Dar that seemed to cater very much to European tastes. The traders here seemed more laid-back than their city counterparts. The produce in Dar was generally less fresh because, she now realised, much of it had travelled from the Uluguru mountains. Further back in the market, where daylight struggled in, were found mounds of evil-smelling dried fish and dried pulses, maize flour and older rice - the staples. Here she found a few simple, ochre pots: unvarnished, cool and satisfying to the touch. She loved their round smoothness, the earthy smell, the dark smoke swirls. They were unembellished save for a silver-grey line around the rim.

Soon after, one afternoon after work, as agreed, Paul called into Esme's office, his leather satchel stuffed to bursting on his shoulder. As they walked the few hundred yards uphill towards Gerhard's house, she wondered how many unseen eyes were following their progress. She tossed back her hair and kept her chin raised. Let them look.

Paul indicated a bougainvillea-covered bungalow set among mature trees. While waiting for their '*hodi*' to be answered, Esme drank in the heavily-scented jasmine air. She glanced around the dim veranda for the source and saw the vine clad with tiny white flowers rampaging up the house's wooden supports among the dancing dust motes in a stream of sunlight. She looked back towards the door to find Paul's gaze on her. His smile, as their eyes collided, sent a painful jolt through her chest.

'Hello?' They both turned to find a young European woman standing in the doorway, a tear-stained child attached to her skirt. She called out to her husband who lumbered to the door. Tall and bulky, he was wearing crumpled khaki shorts and grubby shirt. His once blonde tresses were straggling round his ears and neck and plastered sideways over his bald pate.

He merely grunted in response to Paul's introductions.

'Ve go *hier,*' he intoned, leading them round to the back of the bungalow, to a wide veranda. His wire spectacles slid down his nose and he tilted his head back to see out of them: too gone-to-seed to pass himself off as the hip rocker, he was affecting the absent-minded professor.

A middle-aged African woman, clad from head to foot in *kanga* sat immobile on the edge of the veranda, apparently waiting for them.

'She is the potter who make the stoves. She do it here because Jaidee haf not enough space at her house.' Against the wall lay the tools of her trade: a mud-stained plastic bucket, some polythene sheeting, a large wooden pestle and mortar – the type used to pound grain. No sign of a potter's wheel.

'It iss very crude, zeir messod,' said Gerhard.

Esme and Paul greeted the woman and, since Gerhard had made no attempt to introduce anyone, Esme did so and offered an explanation as to who they were and why they were there. The potter responded quietly and hesitantly saying she was called Shaida and lived in a nearby village; she pointed to some local houses on the hillside behind the university, built from the same red earth that they stood on.

'So,' said Gerhard, ignoring Shaida, 'You intend to take over wiz zis project?' he fixed Esme with his unblinking stare. He would possibly have been quite good-looking once, before he went to seed. 'You haf experience wiz extension vurk?'

While Esme searched her mind for an apt response, Paul answered:

'Esme has lived in Tanzania sixteen years, and is fluent in Swahili. She's done a lot of work with women in the past. She has been out with us to the villages and, of course, she has excellent administrative skills and,' he raised one eyebrow in Esme's direction, 'her English is perfect.'

Esme burned with both embarrassment and gratification. Paul was laying it on with a trowel.

'So you vill haf to learn also to make the stoves. And to ask the women who use them if they are good.'

In reverse order, Esme thought. No point in making more stoves if they're no good. Anyway, I'm not a potter, what is he on about?

Gerhard explained to Paul, disregarding Esme, he had delivered five stoves about three months ago to households identified by the chairman of the village.

'Yes, I'd like to meet the women of those households,' Esme looked up at Gerhard.

'Then you vill haf to ride on the back of my motor bike!' Gerhard grinned gleefully as if waiting for this moment. Again, there was a pause. Both men were waiting for a response. She had never been on a motor bike in her life.

'Fine', she said with what she hoped was complete unconcern. It was agreed that they would go on Saturday morning.

They took their leave from Gerhard and as they trudged further uphill towards Paul's place, he smiled approvingly at her.

'You are lucky!' he said. 'I would love to go on a motorbike into the countryside.'

He was always so *optimistic*. He made her reflect on all that had just happened.

'Yes,' she replied. 'I am lucky. But it's all a bit daunting, you know, it seems I'm getting into something a bit much for me. With Jaidee leaving and just Gerhard to deal with!'

He stopped walking and put an arm across her shoulder. His touch sent a tingle through her but she reminded herself the gesture meant nothing: he often laid a hand on Solange which was what had confused her initially. It was just her straight-laced Catholic upbringing reinforced by Victorian British and Muslim Tanzanian morals that made casual physical contact between the sexes taboo.

'Don't worry. I will help you,' Paul was saying. 'We can write down everything that has been done so far so that we can analyse it and assess what the next steps should be and what resources we will need!'

Esme noticed the 'we'. They would be in this together.

'It hadn't occurred to me that we'd need to write it down. I suppose I hadn't thought that far ahead – to looking for resources. I can't really take this all in yet.'

'Well let's see how you get on this Saturday. I'm getting really excited.'

And, at that moment, so was she.

Ch 27: New Ventures

During the next day Esme mulled over the question of how much of the stove business she should divulge to Martin. After all, there was nothing *wrong* with what she was doing. She braced herself to tell him when she got in from work. He was, as usual at this time of day, emerging from the bathroom wearing a towel, having had a nap and a shower after his long shift at work.

'Martin, can I tell you about something?'

He sat on the bed resignedly. As she sat opposite him on the stool, she narrated the visit to Jaidee, omitting Dina's role in view of his disapproval of their friendship, and told him about the meeting with Gerhard Schift and Paul.

'How does this Paul fellow fit in?' Martin asked.

'He's a kind of mediator between Dr Schift and other people.' She was rather pleased with her improvisation. In fact, she couldn't quite envisage what other people these might be.

'Up to now, Jaidee has been the one talking to different people. What do you think, Martin, about me getting into some kind of promotion of these stoves, as a means to stave off deforestation?'

'Do you know anything about deforestation?' Martin was not being exactly encouraging.

'Well, no. Apart from the fact that it's a huge problem in the mountains. Do *you* know much about it?'

'No, but I'm not the one getting involved.' He picked up his watch. 'Sorry, I have somebody to meet.'

Esme got to her feet. 'So that's all you have to say?'

'Well, if you think you can sort out the problem, good luck to you.' He went opened the wardrobe door and began rummaging around in it. She left him to it, not knowing if she had got the reaction she had expected – she didn't know what she had expected. She felt a mixture of disappointment and relief. There had been no chance to tell him about the motor cycle but she decided that he'd given his tacit approval to whatever she needed to do.

On Saturday she rode her bicycle up to the university campus, arriving at Gerhard's a few minutes after ten.

'I was thinking you were not coming,' was Gerhard's greeting. She felt her irritation rising, but was too anxious about the forthcoming ride to respond. She deeply mistrusted motor bikes since the time in Dar es Salaam when she'd accepted a lift the short distance between the bus stop and home and touched her calf against the exhaust pipe. The resultant burn had taken weeks to heal.

And now, having climbed on the back she could see nowhere to cling to other than Gerhard's bulk. Her proximity to his armpits revealed that he did not use deodorant. To her relief they immediately headed away from the main campus where curious eyes would follow her. Instead they followed a track that led round the lower slopes of the mountains. The path was shaded by a mix of coastal coconut palms and the massive avocado trees that thrived in the higher, cooler climes. At the sound of the engine, bare-bottomed toddlers, accompanied by older children in well-worn garb, emerged from the undergrowth of banana, sugar cane and cassava.

After about ten minutes, Gerhard stopped the machine.

'We go here first.' He nodded towards a square Swahili-style house with a corrugated iron roof, bigger than any of its neighbours. Esme dismounted stiffly. She had worn trousers to maintain her decency on the bike but now felt uncomfortable waiting on the shallow veranda as the woman of the house emerged clad in *kanga* . How could Esme not have thought of wearing one herself?

'*Jambo, Mama?*' boomed Gerhard. '*Jiko mzuri?*'

His Swahili was worse than his English: 'stove good', indeed!

Esme greeted the woman and introduced herself. She explained that as Jaidee was soon leaving, Esme had come in her stead to get the stove-users' opinions.

'*Ehee, ndiyo, jiko ni nzuri sana.* The stove is very good. Here it is,' the woman enthused. She squatted down and extricated the stove from a corner of the veranda, beneath an assortment of clutter - Esme caught sight of a palm-leaf basket with a broken handle, a child's punctured ball - before the woman whisked them behind her back and pulled out the stove.

'*Ni nzuri vipi?*' Esme asked. It seemed appropriate to try and get a bit more information, especially as there were no ashes or bits of charcoal in the bottom.

'*Linapika vizuri sana.* It cooks very well,' replied the woman eagerly.

'And does it use less charcoal?' Oh dear, that was a leading question, she reflected.

'*Ndiyo.* Very little. It's very good.'

'*Ahsante, Mama.*'

Gerhard had heard what he wanted and was ready to move on. Esme followed him on foot to the second house, only a few doors down the sandy path.

'*Hodi!*' Gerhard bellowed, even though a women was seated on a mat under the eaves of the thatched roof, legs outstretched in front of her, plaiting dried palm fronds into a strip for making yet another mat. Esme never ceased to be impressed by the apparent ease with which women sat with their back's unsupported yet perfectly upright, no sagging backbone or rounded shoulders. She could only surmise that carrying buckets of water and bundles of tree branches on their heads from an early age super-strengthened their muscles.

'Karibuni, Karibuni!' The middle-aged woman got to her feet in one swift movement and unfolded wooden chairs for them before she disappeared inside the house, saying *'Nakuja.'* Esme would have followed her inside but felt she could hardly inflict Gerhard on the inhabitants.

When the householder emerged several minutes later, she had the stove in her hands.

'Here it is!' she said with a flourish as if triumphant at having found it.

'How does it cook?' Esme asked. Gerhard seemed more interested at this point in the contents of his nostril.

'Nzuri sana,' enthused the woman. Standard reply, thought Esme.

'What about charcoal?'

'Yes, it uses charcoal,' the woman looked unsure of herself.

'Does it use a lot or a little?'

'Oh, very little! Yes, it's very good.'

It was the same at the next two houses. Esme noticed in one of them the stove was full of cobwebs. At the fifth house, when no-one responded to their hodi they found the children playing at the back of the house; they said their mother had gone to fetch water and she didn't use the stove. They saw the ubiquitous metal version apparently in regular use but no sign of the pottery one. At last, thought Esme. an honest answer. Gerhard, however, was delighted with the afternoon's findings.

'We can tell Jaidee, the women are very happy with the stoves.'

Esme described to Paul everything that had happened. She had collected her cycle from Gerhard's and instead of heading downhill towards town, had continued up the hill to Paul's house: she was so close, she couldn't resist. She had never just dropped in since that first day when she'd claimed to be locked out. Paul was on his own and, after his initial surprise, seemed delighted to see her.

They sat, sipping fresh lime-juice, on a mat under the *mkungu* tree, its wide glossy leaves forming an umbrella.

'What was your conclusion then?' asked Paul.

'I don't think any of the women were actually using the stoves,' replied Esme.

'What did Gerhard think?'

'Oh, he was convinced the women were genuine in their praise.' 'But you think that they don't like the stoves even though they say they do? That they were telling lies?' Paul delicately brushed a tiny iridescent green insect from Esme's arm, barely touching either. Esme was aware of how near his fingers had been to her skin. His eyes met hers briefly. The conversation barely faltered.

'I suppose, in English, we'd call them "white lies"; I don't think the women regarded them as lies at all.' Esme replied, considering the women's behaviour. 'I think they just said what they thought we wanted to hear. Maybe afraid to offend us? But I don't fully understand why.'

'Per'aps we do not need to understand it. It is not the most important thing.' Paul said, smiling. 'That which matters is to know what they really think, and you think they don't like the stoves?'

'I don't know if they haven't actually tried them. And if they haven't tried them, I don't know why that is either.' Esme traced the outline of a stove on the misted glass, then looked up and met Paul's glance again.

'It's about observation, is it not? If I compare it to 'orticulture trials, I will look objectively at the plants, at 'ow well they are thriving, and this is what you 'ave done in a few minutes. I think you need to spend more time with the women, see what it is they normally do.'

'Well, yes, but isn't it also about them feeling we're on their side and that it's not going to get them into some kind of trouble, giving their real opinion?'

Paul laughed as he said, 'You are already developing expertise.'

Esme searched his face, unsure whether this was sarcasm, but seeing her expression he touched her hand lightly and said,

'I mean it genuinely. I am a scientist and I think sometimes I mess up when I am discuss with the villagers about their cultivation methods, especially the Tanzanian ones. I grew up in a French village and - you can imagine - zere are - there are - many similarities but mostly I find 'uge differences in the cultures. You 'ave already got used to local people.'

'Well, a bit, I suppose. Apart from the academics, a lot of town folk I work with aren't so different from those in the countryside because most of them still have their parents and their extended family in their home village. I find Tanzanians measure success not so much by how many goods and chattels they possess but by how many relatives they can support and there's a great deal of to-ing and fro-ing.'

'*Comment?*' he made an exaggeratedly bewildered expression.

'Coming and going.' She smiled amusedly at him.

Paul pressed her to stay for a lunch of bread, cheese and fruit while they carried on talking. They agreed Esme needed to find out more about everyday rural women's experiences, away from Gerhard. She would accompany Paul and Solange the following week. So much the better that it was the same villages she had visited a few weeks ago. Tanzanians seemed to have a great ability for remembering faces – they paid attention to the people they met, even passed on the road. She felt confident that the villagers would remember her and be flattered that she was paying them a return visit.

Lunch over, she felt she ought to go home and see the kids. Tears blurred her vision as she rode down the hill. It was becoming more and more difficult to tear herself away from Paul and, she reflected with a sudden clutch of her stomach, he seemed equally reluctant for them to be parted.

She'd had to invent a death in Martin's family to be allowed by the Dean to take a day's leave in the middle of term time. Rather than join them at the university, her friends had picked her up from home and, for fear of being spotted passing through town in the cab of the pick up, she'd covered her head and shielded her face with a *kanga* . Her friends thought her cloak and dagger tactics over-done till Esme related to them, as they lurched up the track to Mgeta, examples of the Dean's sarcastic comments and possessive manner and why she was sure he would vehemently oppose her efforts to branch out into this kind of activity while working for him.

'It's such a feather in his cap to have an *Mzungu* as his secretary.' As she had intended, this metaphor led the focus of attention away from herself to the English expression and comparable French ones, until the first village appeared silhouetted against the skyline.

They passed several women carrying huge bundles of firewood balanced on their heads. Sometimes they were only girls of ten or eleven, the collection as big as themselves. Really, she, Esme, didn't know what the meaning of hardship was. But to live up here in the crisp air, nothing but birdsong and goats bleating to disturb the calm, the world down below shimmering in the sunlight, that had to be worth something.

*

'Esme! I haven't a single shirt ironed! What am I supposed to wear to work?' Martin was shouting through the door of the bathroom.

Esme, under the weak dribble of the shower, had suds in her hair all over her body. She wasn't sure how long she'd been there, laboriously working the 'Gardenia' soap up into a thin lather: in her thoughts she had been in the mountains under a trickling waterfall surrounded by cool rocks and ferns, the hands sliding over her skin weren't her own...

Damn, she thought, I completely forgot his ironing.

'Sorry, Martin, I'll do you one now.' She hurriedly rinsed off the soap and emerged from the bathroom with a towel around her.

One look at his face told her Martin was really furious. She hadn't seen him at all the day before because she had left early while he was still asleep.

She had gone with Paul, Thierry, Solange, Devin, to visit a tarn up in the mountains. She had rationalised that it had been an opportunity to spend some time in the kind of environment the villagers lived in though, in fact, they had barely encountered any one but themselves: it had been the most wonderful, carefree day. She had got home in time to have a late supper with Ali and Mosi but Martin, of course, had gone out. She hadn't even thought about the ironing. Even Ali ironed his own school uniform now and, though Mosi was perfectly capable of doing more, Esme resisted the temptation to load her with domestic duties that would vie for time with her studies, as was the case for most school-girls.

'It's not the only thing you're neglecting either, the ironing. The place is a mess, you're obviously much more interested in running around the countryside with those French friends of yours than looking after your family!'

Esme felt light-headed. She hadn't seen him this worked up for a long time. Had somebody said something to him?

'Martin, I'll iron a shirt for you now.' She reached out to take the shirt from his hand. He softened his stance.

'Thanks.' He seemed more hurt than angry. She didn't want him making it difficult for her to carry on with her outings, with 'the project', as they'd started calling it.

'Sorry, I've been a bit negligent,' she said. ' I've been so busy lately with the stove stuff,'

She hurried out carrying the shirt and a few minutes later lay it, hastily-ironed, on the bed. Martin pulled her to him and embraced her. She felt suffocated.

'Martin,' she forced a laugh, 'you haven't got time for this.'

'No, not now, but later I will.' Guiltily, she registered the sinking of her heart.

She was busy that day with the-end-of-the-month reconciliation of her own record expenditure and the official version in the Accounts Department. A new clerk had started and she was certain he had erroneously entered several items against Forestry's budget code. She had to use all her wiles and accumulated good will to get the senior clerk to check it and, eventually he spotted the source of the discrepancy. It meant she had barely time to dwell on what had happened that morning or indeed the previous day. She kept an eye out for Paul and company but, although they had said nothing about being off campus that day, she saw nothing of them.

During her numerous walks between Forestry and Admin blocks that day, her eyes, as always, were drawn towards the bluish haze backdrop of the forested peaks. And each time she would be reminded of the villages and the women. She understood the university's concern about deforestation but looking at those peaks now and remembering walking yesterday in the tingly, damp shade with the pungency of rot and mould filling her nostrils, it was hard to comprehend. If she lived there, if she had to gather firewood to cook on every day, she would no doubt have a different understanding? Had the university scientists asked the women? She doubted it. But *she* could try and ask them about it. It seemed such an obvious need now. She would talk to Paul about it.

It was during one of these trips that she saw Kerttu coming towards her. She looked much healthier than when she had been to Esme's for her last English conversation, what - a year ago? The Finish woman smiled as she approached and greeted Esme warmly. They chatted for a few minutes then Kerttu said, 'I've been hearing quite a lot about you lately.' Her voice was strong and confident and reminded Esme of her strength of personality before she was overcome by depression.

'Oh? What have you heard?' Esme asked, irritation rising, moving the large ledger from under her arm to the front of her body, encircling it with her arms.

'That you go off in the woods with that young French man after your work instead of going home to your husband and children. Maarti of course doesn't care – he just told me what his Tanzanian colleagues are gossiping about and that they are making it a big scandal.'

Esme's face flushed. 'Honestly! They've just got horrible minds!' her voice was shaking. 'Sometimes I visit my French friends, Solange and the others, and a couple of times Paul and I have taken the path through the woods round the edge of the campus.' Kerttu nodded her understanding but Esme wasn't finished - she was boiling:

'Just because Tanzanians think modernity is everything – tarmac roads are preferable to country paths and they won't take a single step more than they absolutely have to - they can't understand it was nothing more than that: a walk in the woods! And because *they* get up to all sorts behind their wives' backs!' As she spoke she was aware of a pestering apprehension at the back of her mind: how likely was Martin to get wind of this tittle-tattle?

Over the next few days she became more conscious and suspicious of the sideways looks, the smirks and the innuendo from Dr Athumani and Dr Sawete such as, 'You've been doing a lot of overtime lately, Mrs Yusufu'. She was fuming inwardly but to them she behaved as though she was quite unaware of this undercurrent.

The idea, the women explained, was to follow a circular route gathering most of the wood on the second half of it. She tried to take in the sharp scents and sights of her surroundings of scattered trees on the mountainside – she guessed this was the 'Miombo woodland' described in the Faculty documentation - but was distracted by the sheer hard slog of the climb. By the time they started on the descent, she was seriously out of breath and sweating profusely. It was only ten o'clock but the sun was high and the sparse woodland afforded scant shade. At the top of their arc, they were still about a fifteen minute walk away from the denser forest reserve on the crest of the mountain, where the public was prohibited.

'Do you ever go in there?' Esme asked, pointing upwards.

'Not usually. Only if we can't get enough firewood down here – maybe when we fire pots.' Esme noted that with interest, though not sure as yet of its significance.

The uphill hike had taken its toll. Her companions, however, were not even breathing heavily. Her efforts at balancing just one branch of dead wood on her head caused hilarity but she was determined, if not to succeed, then at least to fail with a good grace. Mariamu had made a coil out of a rolled up *kanga* which she fitted on Esme's head. This in itself had caused considerable glee among the group of six women, ranging in age from about fifteen to fifty. She tried not to feel sensitive at being the butt of the joke; they talked about her in Swahili even though she had demonstrated that she spoke and understood it. Or was the reason they used Swahili rather than *Kiluguru,* their everyday language, in order not to exclude her? Esme noticed they used it a great deal normally and she understood not one word. Anyway, they had brought her with them and were apparently enjoying themselves.

'*Mzungu hawezi kubeba kuni kichwani!* The white woman can't carry firewood on her head!' was a frequent remark, accompanied by giggles.

'*Jemani, ninajaribu!* Hey, folks, I'm trying!' she would say, with determined jollity, as the bloody wood fell off, followed by the *kanga* coil.

In the end, she abandoned any attempt at carrying wood, concentrating instead on picking her way through the maze of low tree branches, brambly bushes, rocks, spiky grasses and – for all she knew – snakes and scorpions.

'Do you ever see any snakes?' she asked.

'Oh yes, sometimes.' Mariamu, known as Mama Lusi, answered. She was the appointed guide – it was her husband Chales, an employee in the horticulture unit, who had arranged this expedition for Esme, starting out from his village - nothing more than a tiny hamlet really - called Songea.

'Do you ever get bitten?'

'*We* haven't but Mama Edina did a few years ago,' said the eldest of the group. Turning to look behind her at her companions, she asked,

'Do you remember?'

This question generated great animation – they talked for several minutes in *Kiluguru*.

Mariamu, turned to look at Esme – they were descending the hill now on a narrow footpath which obliged the women to walk in single file. 'They're saying that her relatives took her to the *mganga* but the snake's poison was too strong and she died.'

'That's terrible!' said Esme. 'But it's such a long walk down to the hospital in town I suppose they couldn't get there in time.'

'Oh these days a lot of people do walk down when they're sick – or even get carried – but others don't want *Mzungu* medicine.'

By this time the women had gathered a sizeable bundle each, tied up either in a rag of a *kanga* or a length of sisal twine. Some of the branches reached six feet long and were as thick as her arm. None of the women was hefty - the Waluguru people tended to be small framed. Esme couldn't imagine where in their bodies such strength resided.

Esme asked them if they hated collecting firewood.

They laughed. '*Hata!* Not at all,' said the eldest-looking woman. 'It's just one of the things we have to do. We go together a couple of times a week and we get to chat together.'

'Other days we have to go to weed or plant in the *shamba*. That *is* hard work. This is a nice change.' This was from one of the younger women. She had a baby suckling at her breast, slung in a *kanga* . As Esme watched it, the child's eyes closed and its mother put down her bundle of wood for a few moments while she raised her arm and swivelled the sleeping infant round to rest in the small of her back. One of her companions helped her replace her collection and she continued down the hill, to all appearances unencumbered by any load whatsoever.

'What will the women be doing for the rest of the day?' Esme asked Mariamu after the other women had dispersed to their own homes - mud and wattle constructions with thatched roofs - all within a few yards of one another on a wide irregular shelf on the mountain.

'We'll cook some *ugali* and beans for the midday meal, and have a bit of a rest. Then we'll get some water from the spring to wash the cooking utensils and cook the evening meal,' Mariamu said as she gingerly lifted her load of branches from her head and deposited it on the ground. Esme lifted it up a few inches with one hand.

'*Jemani!* That's so heavy! That must weigh as much as a twenty litre bucket of water!'

'Yes, they're about the same, replied Mariamu. And of course Esme had seen such buckets carried regularly by women. She shook her head in admiration. Mariamu just laughed.

'*Tumezoea.* We're used to it.'

'Will you have to cut that wood up into smaller pieces?' Esme asked.

'Some, yes, but it won't take long.'

'Will your husband help you?'

Again Mariamu laughed. 'Of course not, it's women's work!' She adjusted her *kanga* and it occurred to Esme she was ready to move on to her next chore but was too polite to say so.

'Just one last question, Mama Lusi, are there any potters here in the village?'

'Hmm.' Mariamu straightened up, wiped her brow with the corner of her *kanga* and thought for a moment. 'A lot of the older women know how to make pots but it's not often I see them doing it. There's not much demand for pots these days.'

'I see, thanks.' Esme was sure this information would prove useful at some point in the future but in what way she couldn't tell now.

'You're welcome to eat with us,' Mariamu added.

'Oh, thanks, but Paul will be coming to collect me and we have to go somewhere.'

'Is Paul your *ndugu,* your relative?' Mariamu asked, looking puzzled.

'No,' Esme said, 'We're not related but we're working together on a project.'

'Doesn't your husband mind you going around alone with him?'

Esme felt her face go hot. 'No,' she said emphatically, forcing a smile, 'He knows it's just work.' She felt a surge of irritation but it was tinged with anxiety. Why couldn't people just mind their own business?

'I'll just sit here and write some notes.' She nodded towards the shade of a fried egg tree - so named by Paul and the others because of the shape and size of the marvellous seeds which dangled from its branches. She had plenty to write - and to think about. How was what the women did – picking up dead branches from the ground – contributing in any way to deforestation? It wasn't as if they were going around cutting down trees. No, actually, she reflected, it was the men who made and sold charcoal down on the plain who did that. So stoves that used less *charcoal* were needed, for sure. But Mariamu and her friends used *firewood* and here on the mountain, at least, they seemed not to mind collecting it - to quite enjoy it even. She was going to have to talk this through with Paul to try and make sense of it all.

The next week she started her apprenticeship with Shaida, making stoves. A few weeks after their visit to the village with the stoves, Gerhard had found her sitting watching Shaida's work and, in his booming voice, repeated 'You vill haf to learn to make the stoves yourself, not chust to watch!".

Esme wasn't yet persuaded of this: she knew nothing at all about pottery except that it was an expertise that took a lot of skill and it seemed to her ridiculous that she should be expected to learn to make them when Shaida already knew. In any case, as she had said to Paul, wasn't it putting the cart before the horse? Why learn to make the stoves if they weren't going to be of any use to anyone?

Paul had argued that it was another line of enquiry - maybe she could find out more about the problems by being involved at the very start of the process. And Shaida would be a great source of information once she and Esme became better acquainted.

There were days when she was unable to slip away safely from the Faculty, when the Dean was around sticking his head around the door or summoning her in with petty queries. But as often as she could she walked the short distance to the Schifts' house. Shaida's movements were slow, deliberate and a stove took several days to make; Esme learnt that she wrapped the part-completed pottery in polythene before she left for home each afternoon.

One day after an absence of several days Esme found three fired stoves. The terracotta surfaces were tinged with grey swirls and black patches. As she admired them, she noticed many hairline cracks.

'You have, 'em, burned these?' Esme asked Shaida. She didn't know if that was the right terminology.

'Yes, I've burned them,' Shaida said nodding.

'Where did you do it?' Esme looked around.

'I took them home. When we fired the pots, we did the stoves.'

'You carried them home? How? On your head?'

'Yes.'

'That must have been hard work, they're heavy!'

Shaida shrugged.

'They're really good,' Esme smiled. She loved the rough feel of the transformed clay.' She didn't know what to say about the small cracks. 'You had made quite a lot of stoves ready for firing. Are they still at home?'

'Yes but they're broken. They broke in the fire.'

'Oh, dear. What a waste of your work!'

Esme was at a loss. These three stoves represented weeks of Shaida's work. Was this the best production method? Was this the best producer?

'Shaida, why do you think they broke?' Again the potter shrugged. 'I don't know, perhaps the fire was too hot.'

Esme tried to probe this further but she reluctantly became convinced that Shaida's reticence wasn't due to her being resentful about Esme's prying questions about their cooking habits and use of fuel, or even that she was shy: she was just not very bright.

Esme made a plan with Shaida to visit her village; Shaida waited till Esme finished at the office and led her up a steep path to a ramshackle hamlet outside the university campus. Shaida's extended family, many women and children, welcomed her to sit on a mat in front of one of the huts. It looked very poor and ill-kept compared to Songea, from where she had collected firewood, and other small villages Esme had visited with her friends. Although Shaida's relatives were not unfriendly, they showed no curiosity about Esme and were not forthcoming in any way. When Esme questioned her own judgement, she remembered the day collecting firewood, the witty banter of the women, particularly Mariamu's telling remarks. The contrast in her exchanges with the two groups persuaded Esme reluctantly that the problem lay with poor Shaida.

She could see no point in discussing it with Jaidee who would be gone in a few days and was no longer involved. Esme shuddered at the thought of initiating any discussion with Gerhard – if ever he found her with Shaida he would hector her to start making the stoves herself. When she tried to convey to Paul that Shaida was not the right person for the job, he was very resistant to the idea of letting her go. It caused their first disagreement.

'I think that maybe it is that you are not communicating in a good way with her. I have found her to be quite OK,' he said, with hands outspread; to Esme his gesture clearly said 'give me strength'.

'So did I, at first. But you haven't spent any time with her. I'm telling you Paul, I can't work with Shaida.'

Esme went home that evening and cried. She felt very alone.

The next day Paul came to see her in the office and offered an olive branch.

'If you don't mind, I will make a time to go myself and talk with Shaida. I mean you and me we will be there together. Tomorrow is good?'

They arranged to meet at lunchtime – Esme gladly forfeiting her lunch. As he asked Shaida to explain the way she made the stoves and what the pitfalls and potential improvements could be, Esme could see his cheerful, patient manner wearing thin. He was met with incomprehension and monosyllabic answers at best until, she saw, he conceded defeat and said to them both, '*Tutaoanana baadaye*, I'll see you later,' and continued on up the hill home.

Later that day, he admitted to Esme that she had been right but for the time being they had no choice but to manage as best they could with Shaida.

'But I do understand it is difficult for you,' he added as he lightly touched her hand and looked at her in his earnest way. Somehow, that made it all right.

Paul dropped by her office the next Friday morning. 'Esme, have you heard the rumour, that President Nyerere, he will resign?'

'No! Surely not! I can't imagine Tanzania without him. He's been the leader since, well, before independence.'

'And that makes ...,' Paul's eyes looked towards the ceiling as he did the subtraction, 'Twenty-three years!'

Esme felt tears filling her eyes and felt stupid. 'I know he must be exhausted but, all the same, I can't think of him resigning. Still, it's a consolation to think he may be one of the first African presidents to retire of his own free will – and live to enjoy his retirement!'

Paul looked sympathetically at her for a few moments, then said,

'Esme, tomorrow evening we go to dance in the town – will you join us?'

She was dumbstruck for a moment. She had never heard of any dancing that went on in Morogoro. In the early days in Dar she and Martin had gone a couple of times to out-door 'nightclubs' - as she recalled taken by her brother-in-law Dominic – but she had never been to dance in Morogoro.

'Dancing? Where?'

'Devin knows of somewhere that the students go, near the market. Do you want to meet us at the dancing place?' He hovered in front of her desk, obviously not intending to stay.

She played it out in her head: walking into a crowded dance hall, alone, looking for them, everyone's head turned to look at this unaccompanied white woman; students who knew her and maybe members of staff, people who knew Martin, knew she was married to Martin.

'I don't think I could....'

'But it won't be the same without you!' His voice and face were so tragic she almost laughed. He sat down heavily, clutching his bursting satchel. He fingered a lock of his unruly hair, a habit he had when unhappy.

'Esme, I have to go now, the others are waiting for me to go to the village.'

Oh, to hell with it, she *would* go to the dance!

'Could you maybe drive round to our place and just stop in the car park? I'll run down when I see you. Would you mind?' God, she hated to be such a ninny.

The clouds lifted from Paul's face as he rose to his feet and headed for the door. His hand on the door-jamb, he paused, his eager expression restored. '*Bien*, we will pick you up about nine o'clock? *A demain!*'

She nodded, a hollow anxiety already filling her chest.

She would never in a million years have thought she'd enter this place: she must have passed it hundreds of times, on the end of a row of shops which gave on to the bus stand and market place. Its dingy windows and peeling exterior hadn't warranted a second glance from her but if she had looked in she'd have seen a dreary bar, draped with barflies. It abounded with barmaids in tight dresses revealing large amounts of breast and clinging to their ample bellies and bottoms. Martin had said it was her bottom that had attracted him to her in the first place – she had never been sure how to take that. Now she determinedly banished Martin from her thoughts.

Devin had brought two of his fellow students – smartly-dressed, intelligent young men like himself – perfectly likeable. Thierry had put in a rare appearance – he spent most of his time with his *ngoma* troupe these days. He and Paul were in their baggy t-shirts and jeans. Solange looked wonderful in a well-fitting, well-pressed sleeveless blouse and pair of dark trousers. Esme was wearing one of her work-day cotton skirts and tops. The whole group of them stood out like sore thumbs in the seedy gloom. Sodas were bought and swigged from the bottles. Then they were dancing: apart from one customer worse for wear pushing a waitress round the floor – it was just them. The music from a tinny speaker was familiar western pop from the radio. Most of the time she had no idea what or who it was but occasionally she had picked up names from Mosi and Ali: Michael Jackson's 'Thriller', Madonna's …… The group faced into a circle, each dancing to their own rhythm and steps, Esme acutely self-conscious about her lack of practice and expertise. Paul seemed oblivious to her gaucheness – each time their eyes met he raised his eyebrows or smiled conspiratorially; he was radiant.

After an hour or so, a slow Jim Reeves came on. The dancers faltered in their steps, trying to adjust to the tempo then one by one shrugged and sauntered over to the chairs. As Esme turned to leave the floor, Paul caught her hand and pulled her towards him, holding her around the waist. She felt as though the breath had been knocked out of her as she put her hands on his shoulders. He looked down at her, still smiling. The already dim lights fell further. Three or four other couples shuffled around the dance area in the centre of the terrazzo floor. The closeness of Paul burned into her, buzzing filled her head as she let it sink onto his chest. Of their own accord her hands inched around his neck, her body pressed into his.

The moment the music stopped, Paul moved gently back, dropping his hands. She felt as though doused with cold water as the lights brightened, the tempo quickened and Paul began to dance solo. She forced her body to follow suit. feeling cold where his body had been against hers at the same time burning with shame as it dawned on her he had not returned the pressure but had disengaged from her embrace as fast as he could.

Next time a slow number came on, Paul asked her if she would like another soda and went to the bar. She sat down, smiling weakly, beside Solange who - Esme thought - gave her a strange look. She was glad conversation was impossible with the blaring music. Paul handed her drink to her and stood drinking his some distance off. Soon after that, Esme found herself following the group out to the pick-up and they dropped her off, at her request, a few hundred yards from the flats. She couldn't distinguish Paul's voice amongst the chorus wishing her good night.

Her main dread was that Martin would be home waiting for her, keen to follow up on his amorous advances of that morning. She crept into the flat, sandals in hand: all was quiet, their bed was empty, She tiptoed across the hall and peeped in on Ali and Mosi: both were peaceful. She breathed a sigh of relief, she had not been missed but she swore to herself she would never do anything as rash and irresponsible again. If Martin had been home ... It didn't bear thinking about.

All night she tossed and turned in anguish at her misguidedness, her stupidity, her mortification! How could she have got it so wrong with Paul? She recalled his looks, his touches. Of course, touching between men and women wasn't significant with the French in the way it was between folk from her part of the world, and in Tanzania - apart from a handshake - touching was simply taboo. With the French, kissing on the cheek was normal but with Thierry and Solange it was a ritual, a warm greeting - three quick kisses with cheeks brushing - but with Paul it was always four kisses with fervour and his lips always made contact with her cheeks. At the thought, her cheeks burned afresh with shame. She had obviously misread his body language. She wished she would never have to see him again.

Ch 28: Small Beginnings

'How is it going with the pots?' asked Solange, helping herself to more salad. Esme put down her knife and fork and leaned her elbow on the table resting her chin in her hand.

'Oh, the stoves? Actually, you were right. If I could find out how the women make pots round here, I might be able to find out what's wrong with the stoves. I need to see real potters at work and watch when they actually do the firing.'

'When will you find time to do these things?' Paul asked. 'You must have time to spend with your family and some time with us, he looked round at Solange and Devin who nodded and murmured agreement.

Paul was behaving as if nothing had happened. When Solange had asked her to join them the following day she had begun to invent an excuse. The thought of facing Paul was agonising but so too was the notion that they would no longer be friends. Solange, it seemed, sensed her hesitance and gently pressed her to come. In the end she had been unable to resist the chance to be near him again.

But she was glad, whatever happened, not to lose their friendship. In a strange way, this felt like her family too. They accepted her so completely as she was and were protective of her, like now. She smiled and shrugged and resumed eating. Paul reached for a chunk of bread and began to vigorously wipe his plate. Between mouthfuls, he continued:

'I think we have to forget what Gerhard says about you making the stoves and just see if there is any justification in going on with this project. Can you find three families who can test those new stoves for some weeks? We must try and get some evidence and then we can make a case for some financial support.'

'But how is that going to help? I still won't have time even if we have the money. We would have to employ someone else.'

'Why would it have to be someone else?' Devin asked. He ate sparingly and had already finished his meal and was leaning back against his chair. The three of them looked enquiringly at Esme.

'You mean *me*?' She pointed at herself, flushing to the roots of her hair.

'Yes, Esme, you.'

'Me?'

'Yes, you would be a full-time project worker.'

'My full time job?'

'Yes.'

'Or maybe you love working for your Dr Mushi so much you couldn't bear to leave him?' Solange said teasingly, getting to her feet and beginning to clear the table. Devin joined her.

Esme stood to help but Solange waved her towards the sofa.

'Leave the vessels. Me and Devin will do everything. You two talk.' The two of them finished clearing the table, carrying the dishes into the adjacent kitchen. A dreadful realisation had dawned on Esme and as soon as the kitchen door closed behind the others she asked Paul,

'Who else would be employed? Not Gerhard?' Paul sat beside her with a notepad and pencil in his hand.

'No-o ...' Paul sounded unsure. 'His position would be honourable.'

He twirled the pencil round between his fingers.

'I think you mean honorary. What position?' Esme's heart was thumping now.

'OK, honorary. I think he has to be the director or something. He is known to the university, I mean, you are too but ….'

'I know what you mean, I'm an underling.'

'An un-der-ling.' Paul savoured it. 'Nice word.' Esme's emotions were clattering round inside her. It was difficult to conceptualise this version of the future.

'And you? What would your position be?'

'An honourable adviser,' Paul beamed. Esme laughed despite her horror at the thought of an official involvement with Gerhard.

'So just us three?'

'Well you must be something more than just a worker – a manager! So, Madame Manager, you must choose your staff.'

'Well, whatever Gerhard says, I will not be the one making the stoves! There has to be a potter. Paul, I can't work with Shaida, I've told you. Please understand, it's not for want of trying.'

Paul touched her hand lightly. 'No, I do understand now. You must choose the right person to work in your project.'

'Well, honourable adviser, I hope you'll respect my judgement more in future. That really hurt me you know.' He leaned towards her and rested his forehead against hers.

'Sorry, Esme.'

She didn't know who made the first move but the next thing they were kissing and clinging on to each other. Her head buzzed as if filled with a myriad of insects and her heart soared.

'That other night,' he began, 'I didn't realise that you had tender feelings towards me – I was not prepared for something like that. But now...'

A voice somewhere in her head reminded her of her vow made all those years ago when she had been attracted to one of her Finnish students, Markku, flirting over his English books: she would never be unfaithful to Martin. But now the welling up of bliss swamped the voice and took over her mind and body as Paul held both her hands in his.

'I just don't know how it can be, I mean for us, you are married,' he kept hold of her hands but moved slightly back. 'And you know that I will not always stay in Tanzania, just for another year and a 'alf maybe.'

She lifted her shoulders, and turned down the corners of her mouth. 'I really don't know what will happen, I just know how I feel at the …'

A metallic crash and laughter from the kitchen made them move apart just as the adjoining door opened.

'You two carry on, just do not pay attention to us,' Solange said as she put a pile of files on the table. Devin moved quietly about the room, seemingly looking for something.

Somehow Esme managed to continue discussing practicalities about the project while Paul jotted down notes. He knew of several international aid organisations based in Dar es Salaam; some of his compatriots talked of them when he met them at the French embassy. He believed this was exactly the sort of small project that was currently in favour. Esme told him of her experiences with the women's group in Dar when looking for funding. Of course, she added, she had not been directly involved in submitting the proposal: it would be a new experience for them both.

'You must write the main part of the proposal, you say the "text"?' Paul said.

Esme felt a rush of panic. She would have to get help again from Ingrid, the new Norwegian agriculture lecturer. She had helped Esme to write a short report for Gerhard of her first trip to the village when she had gone with Paul and the others. Ingrid had read Esme's first draft and politely suggested that she organise it by topics – location, type of fuel, cooking method etc. It had never occurred to Esme to write it other than in chronological order, beginning with their time of arrival and their invitation to drink tea in their first house call. Esme blushed at the memory of her naïve initial efforts and was immensely grateful to Ingrid for saving her embarrassment in front of Paul.

Now she suddenly became aware of the passing of time and looked at her watch. 'I should be going now.'

As they walked towards the front door, Paul said,

'It will mean we must spend a lot of time together before we get the funding.' He gave her his earnest look. She loved the darker ring around his grey-blue irises, the thick dark lashes in such contrast to his flaxen hair.

'I don't mind that, but can *you* afford the time, Paul?'

'I will make the time. Can you come on Sunday? The others are going somewhere, they told me they won't be here. Come at two.'

As always, they exchanged four kisses on the cheeks but the intensity of these electrified her.

'Will you be at work tomorrow?' she asked.

'No, we will go to the village and stay one night so I will just be home late on Saturday.'

'Ok, then I'll see you on Sunday.' she answered, her chest in danger of bursting open, her head dizzy.

'Until then.' He waved as she mounted her bike and watched her as she rode to the corner. The rush of air cooled her burning cheeks as she free-wheeled down the hill to the darkening town, singing and laughing to herself.

With two days to get through before seeing Paul again, Esme didn't know how she was going to survive. She couldn't sit down and read or relax in any way; she found herself cleaning out cupboards and corners she had no interest in. She then felt the need to show the kids how much they mattered to her and on Friday evening decided to cook one of their favourite meals.

'Mosi, *mpenzi*, could you help me with the coconut?' Esme stood in the doorway of her daughter's bedroom where Mosi lay on her bed, her head propped in her elbow, reading from the page of an exercise book filled with her neat hand-writing. Mosi lifted her eyes from the page to look at her mother but remained inert.

'Sorry, sweetheart, I know you're studying,' Esme added, feeling guilty now.

'Why can't you learn to do it yourself, *Mama*?' Mosi said but she put the exercise book aside and slowly pushed herself into a sitting position with her legs over the side of the bed where she remained sitting looking questioningly at Esme. This was a ritual they followed every time Esme asked her to perform this particular task.

'You can't teach an old dog new tricks, Mosi. I keep telling you! Mind you I have learned plenty of others but, for some reason, this defeats me. You're so good at it.' She added with a false smile, fluttering her eyelashes.

'God, Ma, stop, you look retarded!'

'Thanks, Mosi. You say the nicest things!'

'Ma will you go and make noise somewhere else, please!' Ali's voice came from his bedroom next door. Esme stuck her head round the door. As usual, he was sitting on his bed, propped against the wall doing his homework, the radio crackling out some indistinguishable western pop music.

'You two sure know how to make a person welcome!' said Esme. 'You won't be complaining when I make a noise calling you for your meal, I suppose!'

'Course not,' replied Ali, not bothering to look up.

Mosi, meanwhile, had got to her feet and came and put an arm across Esme's shoulder: they were the same height now, their eyes level.

'Come on, *Mama*, lead me to your coconut.'

In the kitchen, Esme, as always, stood admiring Mosi's skill. She held the coconut in the palm of her left hand over the sink and with a heavy metal rod about a foot in length delivered a sharp, firm blow to the centre of the nut. The coconut fell into two neat halves in her palm, the milk dripping into the sink.

'Well done!' said Esme.

'Nothing to it,' Mosi said keeping her face expressionless but Esme knew she was enjoying having her efforts appreciated.

'Pass me the mbuzi, Ma, please,' she said putting the two halves onto a metal tray.

Esme took the folded wooden implement, inexplicably bearing the same name as a goat, from the bottom of the pantry and unwrapped the rag from around the serrated blade fixed into one end before carefully handing it to her daughter. While Esme began peeling cassava, she couldn't help but keep glancing at Mosi's deft movements as she opened the mbuzi and set it on the floor. Seated sideways on it, only a couple of inches off the floor, she set to, the serrated blade scraping away the inside of the first half of the nut. It wasn't very often these days that the two of them were on their own.

'We're making headway with the stove project, Mosi. We'll be writing a proposal for funding next.'

'What does that mean?'

While they worked, Esme explained as best she could their plans and hopes. She mentioned all the players, Solange, Gerhard, Shaida, and Paul - guiltily omitting her feelings towards him which, she inwardly reflected with a leap of her heart, he now seemed to return.

'It all sounds like a lot of extra work to me,' was Mosi's verdict. She now had a metal colander full of the moist, finely-grated coconut flesh and proceeded to immerse it in a pan of water and squeeze handfuls of it. She strained out the last bits through the colander and repeated the process until she had a thick white liquid. She discarded the now useless gratings in the rubbish bucket under the sink and rinsed her hands.

'Yes, you're right, Mosi, it is a lot of extra work but it's so interesting and, I hope, worthwhile! It's like when I was in the women's group in Dar, I'm learning so much.'

Mosi shrugged and shook her head. Her facial expression showed her incomprehension but her voice was affectionate.

'As long as it makes you happy, Ma. I've got to finish my revision for the test tomorrow.'

'What subject?' Esme asked.

'Swahili. We have to learn this poem by Shabaan Robert and answer questions on it.'

'I see. Tell me about Shabaan Robert. I mean, I've heard the name, there's a school in Dar called after him.'

'Well, he was the most important promoter of like, modern Swahili literature, probably ever. Lived beginning of this century. His poetry was supposed to have promoted Swahili as a language for the whole country. Different from traditional stuff. OK?'

She escaped to her room before Esme could enquire further about it. Esme called after her 'This won't take long, I'll give you a shout when it's ready.' She hummed to herself, realising with a start it was a piece of choral music by Palestrina that she'd heard at Paul's. As she simmered the cassava in the coconut sauce, tidied up the kitchen and stirred the beef stew she pondered the fact that something else he had introduced her to was a range of music which was unlike anything she'd heard before. She remembered the last time she had been with him: 'France is a country of many possibilities,' he had said one day as they sliced up vegetables for a ratatouille in his kitchen. 'I think you would like it and your French is quite tolerable these days.' It was a day-dream she dared not dwell on. With an effort, she pulled her thoughts back to the present before summoning the kids for their supper together.

She lay awake for hours on Saturday night, half listening for Martin coming in. She had been feigning sleep more and more frequently lately. Mostly he let her be but sometimes he caressed her and whispered in her ear, 'Are you asleep, *mpenzi*?' on a wave of beery breath which once would have eroticized her but these days repelled her.

That night she heard his footsteps coming up the hallway, as she always did, since he refuted the notion of taking his shoes off at the front door 'like a peasant'. She prayed ardently that he would leave her alone as she listened, trying to remain inert and control her breathing, while he came into the room, removed his shoes, his clothes, went to the bathroom and, a few minutes later, came back into the bedroom. She felt the slight vibration of the mosquito net as he lifted it, then a twitch of the top sheet as he raised it and slid into the bed beside her. She could feel his breath on her bare back and forced herself to remain still, keep her own breathing regular. After several minutes, she felt him turning and within seconds he seemed to be asleep. Relief seeped through her but still sleep evaded her: guilt vied with the feeling engendered at the thought of Paul's proximity, his eyes on her, his touch and the awareness of his caring for her. Or had she misunderstood his intention, was she simply reading into his demeanour what she wanted? What did she want anyway? Surely not to risk her reputation or betray Martin. And worse, Esme reminded herself, he could throw her out and keep the children. She knew of so many women in that situation. Esme knew she was being a complete fool but she didn't seem able to help herself.

Next morning she was shaking so much the she could hardly cycle straight. She gave up and dismounted on the last uphill stretch leading to Paul's house even though it was already two o'clock. Paul knew she had been re-programmed into generally following Swahili time and, in any case, she was incapable of hurrying up those last few yards. As she tried to lean her bike against the wall by the back door, it fell over with a clatter. Picking it up and setting it straight, she half expected Paul to appear, beaming. Or would he be looking serious and soulful?

She called out 'Hello?' tentatively as she entered the kitchen and again as she entered the living room. No reply. She stood uncertainly for a few minutes then called again.

'Oh ca va, Esme. J'arrive!' Paul's voice rang down the hallway. He arrived a few minutes later looking bright and alert. They exchanged the four kisses as always when away from the office.

'Sorry, I didn't hear you come. I was reading a very interesting book.'

'Oh.' Esme could think of nothing to say. It didn't sound as though he shared her state of anxious anticipation.

I will tell you about it later,' he continued, pushing his hair back from his eyes.

'So!' he clapped his hands together enthusiastically. 'Let's cook on our stove!' 'I have some firewood from around the garden and some I brought from the horticulture unit.' Esme wiped the sweat off her brow with a large cotton handkerchief.

'Great.' she said.

'You want some water?' he asked her as he took a jug out of the fridge.

'Yes please,' she replied, taking the glass he filled. They both drank deeply.

'You see,' Paul said, 'I have been thinking about this since we last met.' So have I, Esme thought.

They carried the foodstuff and pans out to the garden under the shade of the acacia trees, Esme wondering how many of the neighbours' eyes were on them.

'What we do, you see, we compare the performance of the two cooking devices: the traditional way, which is three stones, of course, and our portable pottery stove.'

'So, should we divide the firewood into two piles and see which gets used up first? Something like that?'

'Exactly!' beamed Paul.

They lit the kindling in the compact stove with some difficulty. Feeding the fire through the small, arched opening in the bottom was fiddly but in due course, the pan of potatoes resting on the three supports on the rim of the stove came to the boil. Meanwhile they arranged the three stones Paul had brought from his last trip into the countryside in a triangle, representing the traditional 'stove' used in every household in the countryside. On this they rested a frying pan over an open fire on which they fried some sliced onions and minced beef.

Esme admired Paul's concentration, the curve of his back, the way his hair fell over his eyes. His hands were quick and strong with the fire: for a second she wondered what they would be like touching her body and immediately broke into a fresh sweat, her face burning though she was not close enough to the fire. He seemed unaware of her, so absorbed was he in his task.

'We did a lot of camping as kids. It's good to make fire again,' he said, happily adjusting the kindling.

As they ate their improvised meal they could see at a glance that the pottery stove had used much less firewood and now, while the embers of the fire were fading and darkening, the stove glowed red within, boiling the water for tea as rapidly as on an electric ring.

'Of course, Esme, this is not a scientific experiment but it gives us an indication that the stove is really, comment-on-dit, efficient.'

'Yes, it's enough to make me think it's right to try and promote it,' Esme replied, realising with a surge of pleasure that there was every reason for them to continue their work together.

Tea finished, lamentations over about the scarcity of coffee since the boiler at the one and only coffee processing plant had exploded, the conversation dried up. Esme became aware of the silence between them.

'Shall we take these in?' Paul asked presently, nodding towards the plates and cutlery.

In the kitchen he turned and gently drew her into his arms. Her heart thudded so loudly she was sure he would feel it.

'I am all smoky and sweaty,' he said. 'Shall we 'ave a shower? I get you a towel.' He led her down the narrow hallway to the bathroom and as he was turning to go back they found themselves face to face with only centimetres between them. He put a hand lightly on her shoulder.

'Shall we maybe shower together?'

She pulled him after her into the bathroom by way of answer, heart thudding. They undressed keeping their eyes on each others faces until they both stood under the stream of water soaping one-another. She had so longed for his touch that a few minutes later when they lay on the bed she was shaking with desire and they climaxed together noisily. Afterwards, lying alongside him, stroking his body, he stroking hers, she could hardly believe this was really happening. Somewhere at the back of her mind she knew there was an outside world but she blotted it out.

As they lay still naked, hands entwined, cooling off under the ceiling fan, they heard Thierry's voice at the door calling 'Hodi!' They exchanged looks and stayed as they were, giggling quietly as they heard him walk around to the back door where his footsteps told them he had found Esme's bike. They could almost hear the cogs of his brain whirring before his retreating footsteps told them he had given up.

'Well, the cat is now out of the sack!' Paul said. 'But I don't mind, do you?'

'No-o,' Esme replied dubiously. 'It's OK for Thierry to know.' But, she thought, I suppose all the neighbours, our workmates, will draw the same conclusions.

Every time she heard the name Regan after that it reminded her of that day. As they drank tea afterwards in the sitting room, only their bare toes touching, they listened to the World Service commentary on his landslide victory at the polls - Ronald Regan had been re-elected for a second Presidential term.

Esme was glad she still had the small portable typewriter that since acquiring from Pete and Tara she had only used for letters to Christine. At the side table beneath the window in the bedroom, Esme tried now to compose something about the work she had done so far, X-ing out and restarting dozens of times until tears of frustration filled her eyes and she hurled the crumpled sheets across the room - or tried to: they fell a few feet from her desk and she had to retrieve them before Ali or Mosi caught her red-handed, behaving in the way she scolded them for.

She knew she would have to get help but she couldn't bear to expose her inadequacy to Paul: he was so much more knowledgeable than she was anyway and she felt her dignity demanded that she didn't involve him in this.

So once again she approached Ingrid. They stayed behind after work a few days. Mostly Ingrid understood easily what Esme was trying to explain and this time she had less difficulty abandoning her letter-style for a formal, third-person account and to categorise most aspects of the work. Ingrid helped Esme express her concerns about the trials conducted by Jaidee and Gerhard, only being dragged in at the tail end and how they needed to conduct properly organised trials. For Esme it was a revelation, putting her muddled thoughts into official-sounding prose. She felt very confident showing it to Paul.

They hadn't been alone together since that Sunday – in fact they had barely seen one another since some friends from Dar had been to stay with Paul the following weekend. So it was two weeks later when they managed to go for a walk together in the mountains. It was to be a chance to catch up on the project planning and to relax. Paul's words had been 'We need to spend some time together,' delivered without any hint of his intent. She hoped it was more than the project that he had in mind but she sensed that he was as ambivalent as she was about the sanity of deepening their relationship.

On the drive up they passed close to Songea, the hamlet she had been to, collecting firewood . Children heard their pick-up labouring in four-wheel-drive in first gear up the incline and as they rounded the corner before the village they saw a line of kids in ragged attire silhouetted against the skyline on the cliff above the road. They waved and jumped up and down excitedly, calling '*Wazungu, Wazungu!*' much as pop fans might shout out the names of their idols.

Mariamu came out just in time to waylay them. Paul brought the pick up to a halt on the relatively level stretch of ground upon which the settlement was built.

'*Karibu*ni! Welcome!'

'Oh, dear, she thinks we're coming to visit them.' It was the natural assumption: without phones and with life so unpredictable, people were accustomed to ad hoc visits. Esme's heart dropped: what if Paul accepted the invitation? She would have no time alone with him.

'*Karibu*ni, tule. Come, let's eat.'

While Esme kept a fixed inane smile on her face, Paul did the talking through the open window on the side nearest Mariamu:

'Thanks, but we need to keep going and we've brought some food with us.'

This sounded lame to Esme since the road didn't go anywhere other than access for those who had official business with the radio mast or the forest.

'Ah, you're going for a walk,' she nodded knowingly. She had apparently already come across the weird ways of *Wazungu*, going for a walk with no purpose other than the walk itself.

They left the pickup at the point where the track petered out into a trail of rocks and clay and continued on foot. From the droplets still clinging to the leaves and blades of grass, Esme saw that it had rained here that morning even though down in the town it had been stuffy and rainless. As they emerged from the coolness of a natural cleft between two steep sides of mountains, she felt the heat of the sun on her skin again. She let the splendour of it all sweep over her – the rust of the earth, the emerald and straw-yellow of the sparse grass, the racing puffs of clouds in the vast sky. She stood and closed her eyes, absorbing the atmosphere of quietness, far off sounds of cock-crow, the occasional bleat of a goat, the solitariness. Her body felt exerted from the climb, the lightest of breezes played on her skin. She drank in the mountain smells of earth, plants crushed beneath their feet, distant wood smoke wafting on the breeze. She had the sense of being between two worlds. She wasn't sure how long she had stood like that when she felt Paul's eyes on her. She opened her own eyes and met his smile.

'Time to sit down and eat and look at what you have written?'

After they had eaten, Esme sat motionless, waiting for Paul's reaction to her introduction to the project proposal. It was only four pages but she believed it had been honed and polished until every word counted. As he finished reading and put the pages down on the picnic mat, he looked at her and said:

'This is really good! I am astonished! You have told everything that I know and even some things I was not knowing.' She blushed and her eyes filled with tears. She busied herself re-arranging the few packages wrapped in tea-towels. She wondered how much he would have praised her had he known that she had only put it into a coherent form with the help of Ingrid. But for now she was more than gratified.

As they continued to discuss the potential needs to start the project, they lay back on the mat. The sunlight filtered gently through the leaves, making the temperature at this altitude pleasantly warm. Like a glorious summer's day at home, Esme thought.

'When I read your preamble, I thought about the book I read before I came to

Tanzania.' Paul reached out and caressed her hand as he lay with his eyes closed and explained about Schumacher's Small is Beautiful and his philosophy of 'enoughness'; how the author had written it in response to the energy crises in the seventies and trends such as globalisation. Esme was fascinated. It seemed to her that the government here was embracing the notion that 'big is best' - establishing state farms and huge factories - quite the opposite approach and not always successful: like the coffee plant that had blown up.

Esme drew closer to Paul. Although they talked languidly, her heart was racing. They were well above the village here but they weren't so far that she felt safe from a chance passer-by, after all, as Esme knew, the women sometimes wandered quite far in search of firewood.

She voiced none of this but Paul may as well have read her thoughts. After a moment's lapse in the conversation he squeezed her hand and, turning towards her, asked, 'Shall we maybe take a little stroll into the forest?'

They glanced around them to make sure they weren't being observed and darted into the gloom. There beneath the high canopy of the trees with only Paul's tee-shirt and some trampled down ferns between them and the forest floor they made love in whispers, stifled groans and giggles.

When they emerged, blinking in the sunlight, Esme had no room in her head for the doubts that tried to creep in; her whole being was just too full of bliss.

For a moment they linked fingers as they strolled back towards the car but Esme knew there were eyes everywhere and regretfully loosened her grip. It was time to go back to their lives down below: Paul to prepare for his lectures next day and Esme back to the kids and Martin's absence.

Ch 29: The Launch

Esme turned the heavy key in the lock and pushed open the door to her new office. The simple wooden table and straight-backed chair came into view in the stream of sunlight that entered as the door swung in. This cell of a room wasn't much, admittedly, but it was all the space the Saint Martha's Centre could spare – and it was a base from which to work. In any case, this room was only a stop-gap and, more to the point, she wouldn't be spending much time in any room: she was no longer a pen-pusher but an 'outreach' worker. This was one of the many terms she had become familiar with as she learned that what she had been doing informally, almost spontaneously, was a recognised role in the growing industry of Rural Development. A year after her first tentative forays into stove-making, she now had a fully-funded project for the next three years.

For once, this year, 1985, Esme had wished she could work on the first of January but it was a holy day at the Training Centre and she'd had to wait till eight o'clock on the morning of the second of the month to start working officially: so far the sole employee of the project. She swung her canvas bag off her shoulder and sat at the table. She would start with a list of what she needed: a few bits to furnish the office would be a good place to begin. And she'd need a ledger to keep a record of expenditure - entirely her responsibility.

She peered out the door through the dazzling sunlight into the Centre's simple garden surrounded by small buildings. Banana plants, scarlet canna, yellow and white oleander grew around an attempt at a northern European lawn, testimony to the origins of the missionaries who had established the Centre for the edification of pastors' wives, the women who had often not kept pace with their husbands in the desired social graces.

Esme sucked the end of her pencil. The downside, of course, was that not only would she be amongst the good ladies of the church but her boss was now officially Dr Gerhard Schift, the honorary Director. But ironically, that was one of the advantages of being based here on the opposite side of town from the university. For once Gerhard, a staunch Christian, had been useful. The Agricultural Outreach Department where he worked had initially been delighted to host the project to continue the work started by Jaidee but only if was led by one of their staff members, despite the fact none of the all-male staff had been even remotely interested in the stoves until funding was involved. Esme's involvement had been ruled out by the department since she had no academic qualifications and therefore could not be considered for employment by the university. Esme had been mortified, Paul had been devastated and Gerhard, to Esme's amazement, had been incensed. She smiled as she remembered him purple in the face, taking it as a personal affront.

'Ve vill show dem!' he had ranted. And then he had come up with his brainwave, and had approached this church-run Centre where training was given to the pastors' wives in the activities deemed by the good missionaries to be useful to pass on to their flocks – sewing, tye-dying, baking, hymn-singing and, now, stove-making! He had brought Esme and Paul to St Martha's, along a muddy track, in the buffer zone between the town proper and the countryside. It was surrounded by modest vegetable plots interspersed with newly sprung-up villas and more established small permanent dwellings. It was away from the hustle and bustle, leafy and tranquil.

To Esme, more important than having the pastors' wives as trainees, was that they had a base from which to reach out to the local communities, without the bureaucracy of the university. But how would she cope with the religious ethos of the place?

She shook her head to bring herself back to the task in hand. She made three shopping lists: one of things she hoped to get in town, one for Dar es Salaam and the other of items that would need ordering from abroad, for which a small budget had been allocated. The whole point of the project was to start something that could be replicated locally once the funding was over, three years' worth at the moment, so any imported materials had to be justifiable.

She gazed out into the garden for inspiration. It was great, she reflected, to be away from the sideways looks, the smirks and the innuendo from the Tanzania lecturers in reference to her and Paul but the other side of the coin was that now the chances of seeing Paul through the open door were non-existent. For a moment she couldn't help but wonder what he was doing. Although the university students were on vacation, the staff were supposed to be working. He was probably checking out his irrigation systems or something.

'Come on now, Esme, you can't waste time day-dreaming,' she chided herself. She was going to be talking to herself a lot at this rate until the Christmas break at the Centre was over and the new intake of trainees arrived. And until she had an assistant, of course.

As Esme checked her list, the room darkened. She looked up to see the ample figure of the Centre's Principal silhouetted in the doorway.

'Hodi, Mama Yusufu!'

'Ah, Mama Nisha, *Karibu*! Come in!' Esme got to her feet and extended her hand.

They exchanged greetings – particularly long ones since it was the start of a new year and Mama Nisha repeatedly brought God into the conversation. As they stood talking, Esme mentally added to her list a chair for visitors.

'Sorry I wasn't here to welcome you to St Martha's on your first day, Mama Yusufu. I have relatives staying with me for the holy period.'

Esme remembered that most of the staff lived on the site.

'That's quite alright, but please call me Esme.'

'Don't you want to be called by your married name, Mama Yusufu?'

'I prefer to be informal,' replied Esme. And don't bring my kids into this either, she thought.

'Esme! Lovely name. Alright, Dada Esme, if you prefer it. Come now, I'll show you around.'

The newly titled 'Sister' Esme followed meekly in the wake of her host as she showed her the series of bungalows which included the trainees' dining room, the five dormitories which each slept six, the homes of the sewing instructor, the deputy principal and the farm-manager all set in neat gardens with vibrant flowering bougainvillea and hibiscus bushes interspersed with spindly purple herbaceous plants.

'Who looks after the gardens?' Esme asked.

'We have one young man who comes in to help with maintaining the grounds and the farm, but the trainees do most of it.'

Esme learned that the next group of trainees would be arriving in a week's time and she had been allocated two hours a week to teach them to make stoves. Her head went into a spin. So soon! What would she teach them? Their proposal had been to train them in a completely different type of stove, one developed in other countries, which would not require pottery skills but would utilise the much more common skill of mud-plastering. Esme felt panic-stricken; she still had so much to learn about this herself.

To Mama Nisha she said, 'It's going to take a bit of time to sort everything out. Two weeks will be too soon. I'm hoping to recruit an assistant.'

'And you'll succeed with God's help!' was the response.

'Mmm,' said Esme. After some discussion she succeeded in delaying the start of the training but Mama Nisha was quite clear that the new trainee intake should be able to add stove-making to their certificates after three months. She had already promised it to the Bishop.

Esme managed to make her escape eventually and drive into town. She was much nearer to town here than at the university, but that had been served by a staff bus. She wondered how she would have coped had she not, at last, been able to get the old Beetle back on the road. As she drove the five minute journey over the rutted track, as always she met the eyes of all the folk she crossed paths with, whether on foot or driving, until she turned onto the main road. It took another five minutes to the Centre of town and the market place. She had an idea, well Paul had originally had it, that if she could find good pots in the market and then trace their maker, she might find a new potter she could work with.

Outside the covered market, in the sun, the dust and exhaust fumes, women squatted selling chapatti, soup and little piles of onions or tomatoes. Inside, beyond the luscious mounds of gleaming fruit and vegetables, beyond the pungent smells of rotting fruit and dried fish, she found the household items. Nestled among the coconut graters, floor mats, shopping baskets and the ubiquitous portable metal stoves – *majiko* – that they were aiming to replace in due course, a few pots were to be found. She exchanged pleasantries with the stall-holders - as in every market, all men - as she examined the pots. The orange colour of the clay was in all cases nearly obliterated by dark patches from the firing. Essentially, only two designs existed: the cooking pot and the water pot, each example being identical to the others. No wonder Shaida had found it so laborious to make stoves – she had never come across pottery other than these two items. To Esme it was apparent that the whole success of the project depended on her getting potters to make something entirely new: convincing people to adopt them for their own use was only phase two.

'Why are there no pots for sale?' she asked one stallholder. 'I used to see them in the market.'

'You can still find some,' he said indicating vaguely the area behind him. 'But most women prefer to use these.' He indicated the towers of *sufuria*, the handle-less aluminium pans that came in about twenty sizes, nesting within one another like Russian dolls. Light, unbreakable and easy to store, she wasn't surprised really, she already had the impression that most of the townsfolk used them.

'Don't even the women in villages use them?' she asked, her hopes beginning to dip.

'Oh, probably they do but if they need one they can either make one themselves or, if they're not a potter, they ask their mother or one of their sisters to make them one.'

'You mean ... Is it only women who make the pots?' she asked, wanting to confirm her belief.

The stall-holder looked at her aghast as he replied: 'Of course it's only women! Do men cook or fetch water? No, so they don't make the pots for it either.' He shook his head at such a ludicrous notion.

Almost on the point of giving up, in the furthest corner of the market, Esme came across a portly, elderly man with a ready smile and thick cataracts on his eyes. He wore a white, embroidered Muslim cap more commonly found on the coast; he also stocked a supply of them on his stall. More to the point, he also had pots on display, which were bright terracotta with barely a blemish, decorated artistically with silvery-grey lines.

She greeted the old man and picked up a pot to examine it. It was a thing of beauty. She could smell its earthiness but as far as she could tell from its warm, firm feel, it was well-fired.

'These are all sound,' said the old man, tapping sharply against one with a knuckle, making it ring. 'You won't find any better in the whole market.'

'Yes, they are good,' agreed Esme. 'Do you know the potter who made them?'

The old man seemed to enjoy some private joke, chortling to himself before he replied.

'Yes, I know her. Do you want to place an order?'

'I might. I have something to show her that I'd like her to try and make for me. Can you tell me how I can meet her?'

'No. I'll do better than that. I'll take you to her house!' he said.

'You know where she lives! Is it far?' Esme was thinking of the road up the mountain and her poor car.

'Hata! Not at all! It's very near. Two minutes by car.' He assumed, of course, that as an *Mzungu* she had a car. Again the stall holder chuckled. 'She's my daughter so, she lives in my home!' he was still enjoying the joke.

They arranged to meet at his stall at the same time the next day and he would take her to the potter.

Esme felt the encounter and her conversation with the old man was propitious. She wasn't quite sure what to expect but she knew she could do nothing without a good potter. She spent the rest of the day buying a few minor items and settling into her new premises.

Next morning, Esme went to the stall as agreed. As soon as the stall-holder saw her, he smiled and called out to his neighbour to mind his wares in his absence. She would have liked to accompany him on foot, if only to prove that at least this *Mzungu* was capable of walking but because she had the heavy stove to take with her – Jaidee's prototype - they had to go by car. It was clear from her passenger's fumbling with the door-handle and the way he sat on the edge of his seat, clutching the dashboard, that this was a novel experience for him.

His home was in an area new to her: although it joined on seamlessly with the town, it appeared to have grown spontaneously, without official sanction as they drove on rutted tracks - though scattered amongst the mud-plastered houses were more substantial block-built ones.

The old man ushered Esme into the enclosed backyard of his home and there he introduced her to his daughter, Tausi. After opening a folding wooden chair for her, he excused himself to go back to his stall. The potter was a pleasant-looking woman of about thirty years old, Esme judged. Around her were a number of pots in various stages of completion.

They chatted for a while about Tausi's method of working and the need to let the pots partially dry before she could smooth the outside with a pebble dipped in water. Esme learned that the silvery lines decorating the pots, if applied before firing, were permanent but faint so in order to attract buyers Tausi traced over them afterwards. As Esme examined a finished pot she saw that the silvery-grey paste, derived from grinding little chunks of rock, came off on her hands. Esme examined a piece of rock and, with a start, recognized that it was graphite.

'Do they use this in pencils?' she asked.

'Yes,' answered Tausi. 'I heard that the colonialists took it from the mountains in the old days, but what they really were after was the wood for making the railway.'

Aha, thought Esme, that would mean it was they who were responsible for the deforestation, not the villagers!

'Did your family used to live in the mountains?' Esme asked.

'Yes, my parents did. But they moved to the town with their parents when they were children.'

'So you speak the local language, Kiluguru?'

Tausi laughed and said something incomprehensible to Esme.

'Obviously you do!' she said.

All the while they talked Tausi was moulding pots; to start with she formed the kneaded clay into coils and built up the sides of the pot on the base of an upturned wooden mortar, normally used for pounding maize and suchlike. She used it as a sort of reverse wheel: the pot stayed still while she moved backwards around it. As the mortar stood on the ground and reached to only just above her knees, Tausi was bent over for long periods of time, but her movements were fluid and apparently effortless. To mould it into shape she applied a worn maize cob, frequently dipped in water, on one side of the wall of the pot, her free hand against the other side. Then she made finer adjustments with the aid of an old mango stone. Esme was struck by how swift and deft her hands were, so unlike poor Shaida's.

Satisfied that she had found a competent potter, and that she had allowed a seemly period of time to elapse before getting down to the purpose of her visit, Esme showed Tausi the stove she'd brought.

'Would you be able to copy this?' she asked, and explained its use.

Tausi was clearly astonished at the notion of a stove made of clay rather than metal but if she thought Esme was mad, she hid it well and was plainly glad to have such a commission. They agreed that since the stove would need a lot of clay and time, Esme should allow a week before going back to see its progress.

The week passed quickly enough – there seemed to be no end to the preparations - but Esme felt that the project hadn't properly got under way. At home, things were the same as always – she could still have been at the university for all the difference it made to the family. Paul constantly appeared unbidden in her thoughts and with an effort, often with a smile, she pushed them away.

When she went back to see Tausi's progress with the stove on the appointed day her heart was beating fast. She braced herself for disappointment whilst, at the same time, hoping desperately for a perfect replica of the sample. What she found was something in between. Esme could see immediately that Tausi had skimped on the thickness of the walls, and the pot-rests were exaggerated but otherwise its proportions were good.

On this occasion a younger woman was seated on a stool in the corner of the yard beside the kitchen carefully slicing fat handfuls of dark-green pumpkin leaves into a pan for the midday meal. She greeted Esme in an open and friendly way and said she was Karima, Tausi's younger sister. Esme settled down beside Tausi and patiently tried to point out the subtle but essential differences between the original stove and the copy. Tausi had trouble understanding Esme's faltering explanations as she struggled with the unfamiliar vocabulary. Unexpectedly, Karima spoke up, her manner a delicate balance between customary deference towards her older sister and an apparent desire to help.

'What I think she means, Dada,' Karima said to her sister, is to make the wall thicker from the inside of the bowl so that you don't change the shape on the outside.' She looked at Esme and asked 'Is that right?'

'Yes, that's exactly what I was trying to say!' Esme said. This procedure continued for a while: Karima re-interpreting with apparent ease and, a touch of humour, Esme's instructions and Tausi following them with near-perfect results. Esme was delighted and was drawn to the young woman's cheerful demeanour and youthful enthusiasm. Just as the thought occurred to Esme, the question came unplanned out of her mouth: 'Are you a potter too?'

Karima hesitated. 'Well, yes. I learned to make pots as a girl growing up and now, while I'm looking for a job, I make some to earn a bit of money. But there's not much demand for pots these days.'

Esme knew then she had found a second member of staff for the project. Karima was incredulous at first then overjoyed. She would start the following Monday.

The two women soon established their roles: Esme was the elder by some twenty years which, according to traditional norms, automatically gave her higher status and Karima either addressed her as Dada - big sister – or Dada Esme. Of the two of them, Karima spoke better Swahili, naturally, but barely knew any English. She had good literacy skills but depended on Esme to interpret the stove literature that she had requested from an organisation in England that specialised in the spread of 'intermediate technology'. Esme of course held the purse strings for the project and had a vision of what the project was aiming to achieve. Karima very quickly cottoned on to this vision. With her knowledge of the local way of life she had a great deal to contribute, quite apart from her pottery skills, which turned out, if anything, to be even better than Tausi's.

One morning, a couple of months after Karima had joined the project, she and Esme were sharing tea brewed on one of the stoves that they were testing, and eating maandazi Karima had bought on her way to work. They relaxed in the meagre shade offered by the lee of one of the staff houses on the patch of land that they had been allocated between the vegetable garden and an area containing half a dozen goats, a cow and some chickens which was euphemistically referred to as The Farm. Esme's eye was caught by the headline in the piece of greasy newspaper in which the buns had been wrapped:

'Mandela refuses freedom'.

The struggle against apartheid in South Africa had always been featured prominently in Tanzania's reporting of world news but, as she picked up the tattered fragment, Esme realised with a jolt that she had been so engrossed in the project that she hadn't read a newspaper for several weeks.

'We are so lucky in Tanzania, aren't we?', she said to Karima. 'I suppose you won't even remember a time before independence?'

Karima laughed: 'I'm only twenty, independence was the year before I was born! We learned about it in history lessons, of course.'

'Tanzania has always been peaceful - unlike most of its next-door neighbours. Can you name the countries that surround Tanzania?'

Karima laughed again: 'Let's see, Kenya, Uganda, Congo, Zaire,' she counted them on her fingers, 'Rwanda, Burundi, Zambia, Malawi, Mozambique.'

'Eh, that's ...' Esme's response was interrupted by a male voice calling 'Hodi!' It took Esme a moment to register that it was Paul's voice, by which time he had come into view. Her heart clutched at the sight of his dear, smiling face, enthusiasm shining from his eyes: it seemed so long since she had seen him – though it had only been a week. No longer able to pop into one-another's offices, they saw each other only by arrangement, and such times were all the more precious for it.

For a moment she thought it was her he had come to see, forgetting that having been so deeply involved in the early stages of the project - the proposal, the meetings with the donors, the negotiations with the university - giving her encouragement and self-belief, it was only natural he should want to keep in touch. And she was glad he did.

'Jemani, vipi mambo?' his greeting demonstrated that his Swahili was, if anything, more colloquial than his English. Karima was obviously impressed by him: Esme noted with irritation that she gave him a coy sideways glance and giggled. Paul seemed unaware and looked meaningfully at Esme. Both knew it was not the time and place for the kisses on the cheeks. In English he said,

'I asked someone tending the garden where I could find Esme and he said "Ah, *Mama* Majiko" and then he showed me the way.'

Esme laughed, Madam Stoves was yet another epitaph to add to the list.

'I 'ope you don't mind that I come without I telephone first because I know someone 'as to come from the Principal's office for you.'

'Of course, I don't mind. You're welcome any time.' It was, as always, a delight to see him. By now Karima was looking curiously at them. Paul dropped to his hunkers and began examining the four plastic buckets full of clay.

'Where do you get this from?' he asked switching to Swahili again.

'Karima showed me where she and her sister get clay. She's very skilled at identifying suitable pockets. The ground all looks much the same to me, red earth.'

Esme could now lead them to the spot as it was marked by a dodoki tree that was notable by any standards with its dried dangling fruit – that turned out to be what they looked like: loofahs. On these expeditions to the foothills Esme made an effort to dig up the clay to fill up the buckets, wielding the heavy hoe above her head, but both she and Karima knew it was the younger woman who did the lion's share. It was such a joy for Esme to be out in the fresh air in such beautiful countryside, never mind that the sun was beating down on them and they were dripping with sweat. Nothing to break the silence but bird song and the thudding of the jembe against the compacted earth.

'But I'm learning,' she added hastily, taking a pinch of moist clay and manipulating it. 'I can feel the different sand content now. Too much is not suitable. And we have started building a kiln, she pointed towards a circular brick and mud construction about four feet in diameter. She and Karima had laboured for many days, moving loads of hand-made bricks delivered by the local brick-yard in a wheelbarrow to their patch of land, mixing mud with their bare feet – a strangely repulsive yet addictive sensation – and painstakingly building the circular wall. 'It has to reach shoulder height,' she said demonstrating by standing next to it that it only came to the top of her thigh.

'Jemani, safi!' Paul said as they strolled over towards it. 'That is quite something!' Esme noted that he had switched to English. 'How do you know how to make such a ... a contraption?'

'We're copying and adapting it from a diagram in one of the books I got from England.'

She had a sense, then, of belonging to a wider community that, she now realised, Paul was not part of.

'You are learning a lot, aren't you?' There was admiration in his voice and face. 'I am wondering if you can come this evening. I will be alone.'

Esme felt a tumult of emotions. She should be leaping at the chance to spend time alone with Paul but it suddenly seemed so, well sort of calculated.

'I'm, I'm not sure.' She replied. 'What time were you thinking?' Obviously, she would need to go home and sort out food for the kids and make an excuse for going out again.

'Whatever time you come it doesn't matter. When you like.' He was looking earnest, she could sense he wanted to take hold of her.

'No, I don't think really I could make it today. Sorry, can we make it the weekend.'

Paul looked taken aback. 'Well, if you are sure, Ok.' That was the trouble, she wasn't sure. She could easily envision the two of them in a passionate frenzy but something about it wasn't right.

'Let's make it the weekend, Paul,' she said this time with more conviction. Becoming aware of Karima standing uneasily beside the kiln, she said 'Gosh, we must get on with some work!' and summoned up a little laugh to break the tension.

'*Karibu* tena, Paul. Welcome any time,' she said, extending her hand. He squeezed her hand and tickled the palm with his little finger. She flushed to the roots of her hair, as she snatched her hand away hoping Karima hadn't seen this: it was a sign she had taught Paul, having learned it from Martin. It meant 'I fancy you'.

'Come on Saturday then, Esme. I'll be waiting.'

Ch 30: Meeting with Gerhard

A couple of weeks after Paul's visit to the Project, Esme knocked on Gerhard's office door.

'Come!'

She pushed open the door to be greeted by a musty, male smell she immediately associated with her father. Gerhard's long, bulky back was bent over the desk opposite the door. She tried to focus her thoughts on the purpose of the meeting: to present her third monthly report.

'Good morning, Gerhard.'

Turning only his head, he peered briefly over his glasses.

'I chust finish marking this terrible essay.' She stood for a few moments, her chest tight, her stomach churning, waiting for an invitation to sit down and, when none came, surveyed the possibilities. The two wooden upright chairs were piled with books and loose sheaves of papers. The low armchair behind the door held only a pile of files. Resignedly, she pushed aside the accumulation on the top of the nearby cabinet, making room first for her own load of files and then the pile from the chair. She took her report from her bag and skimmed over it yet again. The real problem, she thought, was not knowing exactly what *form* the criticism would take. She felt very alone: Paul and she had agreed on the broad sweep of strategy, leaving the implementation to her, but as her experience and knowledge had grown and he had been able to fully concentrate on his own work, a narrow gulf had opened up between them. Karima, invaluable though she was, depended on Esme for direction. And now she was to face Gerhard's scrutiny.

Overhead the fan creaked rhythmically. It kept time with her thudding heart. The papers on his desk rustled in their attempt to escape from the random objects weighing them down. Had she got at her fingertips every possible detail Gerhard might demand? The report in her hand shook. She was back in the classroom waiting for the tyrant teacher to bring the ruler down on her knuckles.

Gerhard muttered indecipherably as his red Bic cut swathes through the lines of handwriting before him. Suddenly he threw down his pen and spun his chair round, its loud shriek causing her to start. He settled himself comfortably, hands clasped over his stomach, resting one ankle on the other knee, and frowned down his nose at her sunk into the chair opposite him.

'So. How is the progress?'

She began to read off the points from her prompt sheet.

'Karima and I have made good headway in the design modification, after a lot of experimenting, and we've tried out various sources of clay. I think at last we have found a suitable one ...'

'How many haf you made this month?'

'How many stoves? It's here somewhere...' she said. Damn! How could she have been so stupid! She'd known it would be the first thing he'd ask. She remembered that she'd recorded all the results from different models separately – the total held no significance for the work yet it seemed the only piece of information that was of the slightest interest to Gerhard.

'In total twenty-one.'

'I ask, how many haf YOU made?

'What, me personally?' She was dumbfounded.

'Yah. That is what I said.'

'But, Dr. Schift, I didn't think that was my job. I suggest the various designs to Karima and it's her job to actually make them. She's far more skilled than I am, and much quicker - obviously. Then, when we try them out - cooking on them - I keep a record – look I've got the tables here. We've narrowed it down to two types now – they're very encouraging.' His piggy eyes stared at her over his spectacles.

'I repeat my question. I make it clear from the beginning that YOU should learn to make them. You can't even tell me how many you haf made!'

The heat of Esme's anger spread from the pit of her stomach till her face was burning and before she knew what she was going to say she was shouting,

'Why don't you come and see for yourself? Why won't you listen? I'm sick of coming here month after month listening to you!' She was on her feet looking down at him with no idea what was coming next. 'If you want to know how many I've made, come and count them. I've got better things to do than waste my time on meaningless numbers just because it's the only thing you can understand!' She heard her own voice, faintly registering that she would be heard the length of the corridor. She pushed her report and pen into her bag and carried on, not waiting for Gerhard to respond:

'If you came to see what we're doing, you *might begin* to appreciate it.' There was more. At the end of the tirade, she gathered up the files, picked up her bag, and opened the door.

'I am not coming back here again. Ever!'

Gerhard had said nothing. She could see his stunned expression as, still shaking, she hurtled in the pick-up back towards St

Martha's. She replayed her words over and over in her mind. Had she gone too far? How would she explain to Paul and the funders? How would she justify her action? It could mean the end of the Project. Her job.

Back at the Project office, she took the files out of the car and discovered in slowly dawning disbelief that these were *his* files. That could only mean that her own were still in his office. Scheise!

    She wanted to tell Paul about it immediately. Apart from anything else, she needed him to collect her files; nothing could induce her to go back to Gerhard Schift's office. But, more than that, she desperately wanted to share with someone the awful encounter with that man, to seek advice. Luckily, it was only two days until they had planned for her to visit him.

As she drove to the university, after two tortuous days, she remembered the last time they had been together, the Saturday after he had been to the Project. It had been different. They had made love but she had felt a strange detachment, almost as if she were watching them. The knowledge that in a few months he would be packing up to go home seemed more and more significant somehow. There was no logic to the notion, she told herself, but it felt as if he was abandoning her, abandoning the project. She was going to have to learn to manage on her own – soon – but at the moment she was sure Paul was still solidly behind her.

After exchanging the usual kisses, before she had even sat down, she poured out her account of the meeting as it had unfolded. She finished with an assertion that surprised herself, 'But I'm not sorry. He is completely impossible to work with!'

Paul was at first shocked and then he laughed uproariously.

'I wish I had been there! To see his face.' He sat on the bed and gently pulled her down beside him.

'But what am I going to do?'

'You don't need Gerhard any more, do you?'

'No, I don't *need* him but he *is* the nominal head of the Project. I can't just *sack* him! What about the funders, well Ilse mainly?'

'It is you she knows. She has never even met Gerhard, he is just a name on the proposal and, yes, it helped a lot to have a senior academic supporting our application but it is not, I think, any more necessary.' Paul put an arm around her shoulder and started to undo the buttons on her shirt. 'I like this strong Esme.'

She felt a surge of irritation, and pushed his hand away. 'Paul wait. This is *important*. What should I do next, should I just leave things as they are?'

'Yes, wait and see what 'e does next.'

Esme sat forward on the edge of the bed. 'No, I'm going to phone Ilse and explain it.'

'Yes, you explain everything as you have explained it to me – she will understand, for sure.'

Esme felt somewhat mollified and responded gratefully to Paul's embraces and kisses, relishing his special fresh smell, but when he slipped his hand inside her shirt, she pulled back.

'No, Paul, I don't think I'm in the mood for that today. I've got so much on my mind.'

'Well, I can take your mind off those things – anyway you are doing really well, why do you worry?' Nevertheless, he dropped his hand to her lap. She took hold of his hand in both of hers and studied the long sunburned fingers, still with bits of soil trapped beneath his nails.

'Actually, it's more than that. It's not just about now, not being in the mood. I want us to keep on seeing each other, but not in that way,' She looked meaningfully at the bed.

'What are you saying, Esme? That you don't want us to make love any more?' His shoulders slumped, he looked almost pleadingly at her.

'Yes, that's what I mean. It's time to end it.'

'Is this because of your 'usband?' Paul sounded alarmed.

'Martin? No, it's nothing to do with him. I see so little of him, he just uses our flat as a service station. No, it's about us. I ... I just can't see where it's going.'

'What has changed? It was always going to be like this, was it not? You staying with your husband and children, and me going home to continue with my studies?' he shrugged and made a moue, looking so stereotypically French that she couldn't suppress a smile.

'It's me that's changed, isn't it?' She squeezed his hand. 'I've so much to thank you for, for all the support you've given me – inspiring me to get involved with the stoves and everything. I don't feel that all there is for me is to hang on here, waiting for the kids to grow up, I've got so much to *do*, and even though I worry sometimes, I *enjoy* it.'

'That's wonderful; you know I'm very happy for you,' Paul stroked her cheek as he spoke, 'but we can still, you know, have fun at the same time, can't we?'

'Of course, I want us still to be friends. But not that kind of fun ... it just doesn't feel right. I have to get prepared for you going away.' It didn't sound convincing to her own ears, she didn't fully understand it herself.

'I think we have to start being "just good friends" from now.'

As it turned out, Ilse, her programme officer, was hardly bothered about this unknown German doctor from the university. Esme had recently submitted a brief progress report which had given Ilse all the information she needed to reassure her that the proposal was being adhered to so far.

'Fine, Esme, I'll put a note on the file. I cannot see that it makes a difference.'

Esme sighed a huge sigh of relief. Paul had been right as he had been about so many things.

Ch 31: Christmas

She could already feel the heat of the sun through the cotton curtains before she pulled them back. Six pips rang out from the radio followed by the announcer:

'Six o'clock, Friday, the twenty-fourth of December.' She went from the living room into the kitchen and made herself some tea. It was hard to remember those early Christmases in Tanzania - they were just a blur of disappointed expectations – so now she had learned not to have those expectations. But not how to fill the void they left. The thought of Christmas always made her spirits sink.

One Christmas day that stood out from the rest had been in Dar when her Hungarian student and his friends had taken her and the kids to the beach. She had really enjoyed that. It was so different that the lack of the usual Christmas trappings didn't matter in the least. In fact the issue for her was not that she didn't have holly or a tree or wintry weather, it was the complete absence of anything other than the utter sameness, the same as every other day.

As she turned she glimpsed Mosi entering the bathroom. Mosi waved limply in her mother's direction. Esme cursed herself for not using the toilet as soon as she had got up since Mosi would be in there for half an hour, oblivious to all entreaties. What was it about teenage girls? It wasn't as if Mosi's cohort were dictated to by magazines or television programmes, neither of which existed, rather they were treated exactly the same as the boys at school and given no leeway whatsoever. Officially, anyway. Esme began to make the tea and put out the bread for anyone who wanted it. Breakfast was not a family occasion.

'Morning, Mama Mosi,' Martin made a slight detour by coming to the kitchen door rather than crossing the living room towards the balcony for his ritual taking-of-the-air. Nevertheless, there was no kiss today either, she noted with a pang. It had been a while since she had even registered this but it was hard to remember the last time he had demonstrated any affection unless as a prelude to a sexual advance.

'Morning, Martin. Everything OK?' and on impulse she went up and offered him a kiss which he accepted, showing only a flicker of surprise.

'Yes, everything is fine. I got a letter yesterday informing me that I will be made head of our division, for the whole of the country. It's a very big promotion.' She hesitated a moment, absorbing not only the news itself but the fact that he hadn't made it his business to tell her till today.

'Oh, congratulations! That's good, isn't it?' Then, as the realisation struck her, Esme's heart went into overdrive. 'You won't have to move from Morogoro, will you?'

'Well, I will, of course. All divisional heads are based in Dodoma.'

'Dodoma!'

Martin hitched up his trousers and fingered his belt. 'Not till after Christmas, in the New Year. Plenty of time of talk about it and make arrangements.' He went out onto the balcony. Esme was shaken thinking of the implications for her and the kids – they would have to move all over again. Mosi and Ali hadn't long really settled into their new schools, made friends. And now she had the project.

As usual she was busy during the day, one Karima and she had planned to spend at St Martha's. Christmas Day loomed over her though, as she went about her work, she saw no tinsel or holly, heard no jingling music; no doubt the Centre would be ringing with hymns from midnight onward. She wished Christmas just didn't exist, that the White Fathers and the Jesuits and the whole lot of bloody missionaries had never set foot in Tanzania, or the continent of Africa for that matter. No-one would have been the worse for it. Of course, Martin would have been called Abdallah or Tumaini or something and she never would have met him because he wouldn't have been educated in English and ended up in Edinburgh. And Mosi and Ali wouldn't have been born; she could never wish for that.

When Karima left she wished her a 'Krismasi Njema' even though the younger woman was a Muslim; Esme had always been wished 'Idd Mubarak' – a Blessed Eid – it worked both ways.

Since the Project and the Centre rested on Saturdays - unlike government workplaces - and Monday would be a work day for the nation as usual, it felt no different from any other Friday as she tidied up at the end of the day. So why did she have this fluttering in her stomach, as she walked to the bus stand? This anticipation. Of what? Of Santa coming? Don't be silly, Esme, there are no chimneys and no snow for his sled!

She made a mental list for the market of what she would cook for Christmas Day dinner. It would be a special meal: she would pretend that the skinny little chicken was a plumptious turkey, they would have roast potatoes, carrots and cauliflower. She would make gravy from the chicken juices and thicken it with grated *maghimbi*, having learned from Dina that it had good thickening properties. What about dessert? A fruit salad, of course. But the kids didn't regard that as a treat – unlike her they'd grown up with mangos, papaya, pineapple, passion fruit, pomegranate. In fact the only fruit Ali really liked were tamarind seeds that

Wazungu considered the inedible part of the fruit.

She decided to look for something for the kids before getting the heavy stuff from the market. As pay-day in November had approached she had asked Martin what he thought they should give Mosi and Ali for Christmas.

'Clothes, surely,' he had replied. 'Isn't that what children get? Same as at Eid and Easter?'

'I know that's what happens in most families but, as I said last Christmas and the Christmas before and every Christmas since we've been together, as far as I'm concerned it's parents' *duty* to dress their children so, to me, clothes aren't really proper presents. I can understand it in poor households, that's different.'

'Well, if you feel rich enough to give them toys as well, I'll leave that to you.' Martin had said. During the course of the conversation he'd got up from the settee and made his way across the living room to the outside door of the flat and by this time he had his hand on the door-handle.

'Ali really needs a new bike. That one he's using is falling apart – not surprising as it used to be mine before Mosi's, and Mosi would love some little gold earrings.'

'That's your department, Mama Mosi,' he'd said glancing at his wrist-watch. 'Sorry, must go now, got to see someone.'

'Ok, then, how about you forking out for the clothes?',

'No problem, I'll do that. Leave it to me.'

And that had been the last she had heard of it.

She had looked at the bikes and the gold earrings and realised they were beyond her budget without Martin going halves with her. She had found some pretty but fake gold earrings for Mosi which she would probably only wear a few times and for poor Ali she could find nothing except a rather sad looking football. Martin was right in that there was no tradition of present-giving or indeed providing youngsters with play-things and, when you thought about it, when had it stopped kids playing? All they needed was the space and other kids – neither of which were in short supply – and the freedom which kids had here. The problem was, Mosi and Ali didn't fit in exactly, they had been brought up with *her* expectations of Christmas.

Now at this eleventh hour, she wandered round the couple of dozen tiny shops – mostly open to the street and barely wider and deeper than an arm-span: the two stationers stocking yellowing *madaftari* for school kids, several drapers' shops festooned with pre-cut lengths of *kanga* and *vitenge*, these days locally-made and less vibrant than in former years, and white vikoi for men to drape round their waist – something she had never seen Martin wear. Should she buy something for Martin, she wondered. She rummaged round in her memory for any present she could recall him buying for her in Christmases gone by and came up with a blank. Leaving Christmas to her apparently included buying her own present.

She perused the few bales of fabric on the shelves stacked behind the counter. She supposed she could buy a dress length for Mosi, surely her mother could get *that* right. She would give Mosi the money to take it to a tailor with her own dress design. The choice really wasn't difficult, it was easy to dismiss the gauzy stuff, the large floral print more suited to an English country cottage armchair, the lurid purple and green stripes which instantly brought back the memory of a pair of pedal-pushers she had once made herself – absolutely *not* Mosi's style – and felt moderately smug coming away with her newspaper parcel of a pleasant dark rose cotton with discreet burgundy dots. She imagined how subtly it would set off Mosi's dark slimness.

She had almost given up with Ali when she bumped into Gadin, or Gadini, as his mates on Jobless Corner called him, the tearaway son of a shopkeeper. He had wild curly hair, uncharacteristic of his Indian community, and a mischievous glint in his eye. Nominally he worked with his parents in their general store, but he was a lot easier to find wandering the streets. He knew and befriended everyone.

They chatted a few minutes, Esme making a mental note that, much as she liked Gadin, she fervently hoped that Ali would not follow a similar path.

'So you on your way home?' asked Gadin.

'Yes, but I can't find anything for my son for a Christmas present.'

Gadin rummaged around in the back pocket of his grubby green trousers and produced a cassette, the type used for home-recording.

'Madonna's latest, he said with a salacious leer, 'including Like a Virgin.'

Esme shrugged. 'Who's she?'

'You don't know Madonna? Don't worry, Ali will. She's one hot chick!' his animated expression faded as he caught himself and added, 'Oh, *samahani*, *Mama*.'

Esme raised her eyes to heaven, 'Don't worry. I know how you boys go on. How much for the tape?' He named a price that was double what she'd just spent on Mosi and after some haggling she brought it down to the same amount – she felt it a fair deal all round.

With a sigh of relief she crossed the bridge over the narrow fast-flowing stream, turned left after the chemists and followed the footpath over waste-ground - in all a five-minute walk to their flats. Martin had already gone out when she got back. She unpacked – hiding the presents, chatted with the kids and stood her three Christmas cards on the bookcase – from her parents, her brother and good old Christine – and got on with the usual evening chores.

It was in the small hours that she heard the front door and saw Martin's silhouette in the bedroom doorway. As he got into bed, with all the tact she could muster, she said: 'Martin, please could you stay in tomorrow and spend some time with us. It is Christmas after all.'

'Of course I will, *mpenzi*.' He lay down and was instantly asleep.

He went out at eleven promising to be back for lunch at one. At two-thirty, she put the meal on the table.

'Mosi, Ali,' she called up the hallway to them, each in their own room, Ali listening to his tape, Mosi doodling in an old *daftari* designing her dress. They liked their presents. She hung onto that thought.

They ate in near silence. Mosi tried hard.

'The potatoes are really nice, *Mama*. Aren't they, Ali?'

Ali shovelling food into his mouth, nodded vigorously. 'Chicken's lovely too. Can I have some more? No point in keeping any for Dad, he won't be back for ages. Anyway, he said he'd be here so serve him right if he did want some.'

She realised that Ali was bracing himself for her usual defence of Martin and when none came, the three of them were silent. Esme didn't trust her voice but placed the second leg of the chicken – normally reserved for Martin - onto Ali's plate. She had reached a decision.

Mosi's anxious eyes hardly left Esme during the rest of the meal. Ali, she could see, was feigning nonchalance and she thanked him inwardly for it. She found she was sweating despite *The Standard* fan whirring at full speed beside the table. Fanning herself with one of the palm-leaf table mats helped to contain her agitation and she managed to remain seated at the table until the kids had finished eating. Neither of them ventured to comment on her unfinished meal.

'Please clear the table, kids. I'm going for a lie down.' Her voice sounded unfamiliar to her own ears.

It was some two hours later that Ali tapped on her bedroom door. She had stopped sobbing but she could barely see through her swollen eyes.

'You can come in,' she called.

'Ali! I thought it was Mosi,' her voice croaked.

'Mosi said I should leave you alone, but I was worried, Ma. We could hear you!' He sat on the edge of the bed and she reached for his hand.

'Sorry, hen.'

Mosi came to the doorway. 'Are you alright, *Mama*?' she asked.

'Come in, sweetheart. Yes, I'm alright. Now.' she indicated the stool beside the bed for Mosi to sit on. 'Bring it near, will you?'

She sat herself upright and taking Mosi's hand in her free one she looked from one of her offspring to the other.

'I've made the second hardest decision of my life.' She paused as the feelings of betrayal, anger and trepidation for the future pushed against her barrier of composure. 'Your father has been given a new job, a promotion, but it's in Dodoma. He's going to move there in the New Year.' She paused, looking for the words that would soften the reality. 'I can't move this time. I mean, I'm going to stay here. I want you both to stay, not to have to move schools again.' Even as she said it she knew

Martin was almost certain to exercise his legal right to keep 'his' children.

'Well, *I*, certainly don't want to move to Dodoma!' Mosi was emphatic. '*Baba* won't go if we all refuse.'

'Don't be stupid!' Ali seemed to have grasped the implications quicker than his sister: his face was working to hide his feelings. 'Dad will have to go where he's sent. And we'll just have to go too. We tried staying in Dar when he got moved to Morogoro and look what happened - we ended up following him here anyway. So what do you mean, Ma?'

Esme screwed up her courage. 'I mean, I've made a decision to separate from your father. I'm going to stay here, with the project.'

'But, *Mama*, we have to stay together!' Mosi looked and sounded stricken. 'I have to be with you both! Anyway, *Baba* won't agree.'

'We'll have to work out just how we can all see each other lots. It's only a couple of hundred miles away, it's not the other side of the world, or even the other side of the country.'

Ali was pale. 'You mean you'd leave Dad to stay with the project?' his voice was trembling. 'Or have you got a *boyfriend*?'

Esme's heart skipped a beat. She was glad now that Paul was no longer part of her life.

'No, Ali, I haven't got a boyfriend and it's not that I would put the project before the family. It's just not ... easy to explain. Your Dad and me, we ... it's very complicated...'

Ali didn't wait to hear any more and before Esme could read his face, he got up and left the room. His bedroom door slammed and reverberated throughout the flat.

Part Four

Ch 32: Moving On (January 1986)

Esme was driving through the gate of St Martha's, having dropped Karima off at home on their way back from the village, when Mama Nisha flung open the screen door of the office and yelled 'Simu! Dada Esme, simu!'

A year ago Esme had put the project on the waiting list for their own phone line, or even an extension from the Centre's phone, but it was quite possible that the project would expire before one was installed. Like everything else, phones were in short supply and, as was the custom of the country, it would happen in its own sweet time. As she entered the small, dimly-lit office, Esme reflected that she no longer railed against the tempo of life as she once did, realising that it would hasten nothing but a heart-attack.

Distantly, from the other end of the crackling phone line, a hundred miles away in Dar es Salaam, came the lilting tones of Ilse, her programme officer in the funding agency, 'Halloo, Esme. Sorry to call you away from your work, I know how busy you are. We have here, newly-arrived from Sweden, an expert in pottery to work in a new project in the south of the country. He will be visiting some of our projects before he sets off. We have put yours top of his list. When can he come?'

They agreed on a date in a week's time and Ilse added that she would be arranging to visit the project herself soon. Esme felt a flutter of anticipation as she rang off and exchanged pleasantries with the Principal who handed her a pile of mail. As Esme drove the pick-up along the track to their newly-constructed workshop, she felt a twinge of apprehension at the prospect of the imminent visitor: a real potter would soon spot her shortcomings.

In the small office in the corner of the workshop, Esme took out the handful of letters and quickly sorted through for anything personal. Yes! She picked out a small white envelope bearing a Tanzanian stamp and a Dodoma postmark, addressed in the confident scrawl that was unmistakably Ali's. And at the bottom of the pile, a well-filled blue airmail envelope with French stamps. Her heart did a little jump of pleasure as she saw that the writing was indeed Paul's. She put the two letters into her bag to savour at home and sat down to deal with the remainder of the post.

An hour later, walking up the path to the front door of their small house, she noted the weeds sprouting up through the flagstones and the hedge closing in over the pocket-size garden. She wished she had more time to keep the place tidy but, never mind, she thought, at least we do have our own little patch of ground. The front door was unlocked; Mosi must be home already.

'Hi, Mosi *mpenzi!*'

'Hi, *Mama.*' Mosi was slumped on her bed, reading her school notes, the radio playing western pop music in the background.

'I got a letter from Ali!' Esme pulled it out of her bag and sat on the edge of the bed. The letter was written on a page torn out of an exercise book. 'Shall I read it aloud?' she asked. Mosi nodded.

'Yeah, good luck with reading that scribble!'

Esme read the first couple of lines with surprising ease then, as her eye ran down to the next paragraph she gasped.

'Listen to this! "We have three new people living with us now. *Baba* says I should call her Auntie Safina and her children are called Robino and Clara. It's better than just me and *Baba* because Auntie cooks really nice food, I even get breakfast cooked. Clara is a ninny but I just ignore her most of the time but me and Robino get on. He's the same age as me, just as well as he shares my room. Safina sleeps in Dad's room but Clara has got the spare room so Mosi will have to share with her next time she comes to visit us."'

Mosi had sat up and clutched a cushion to her.

'What's *Baba* playing at? What else does Ali say?'

'He just says: "I'm looking forward to coming to Morogoro at half-term. Is it alright if Robi comes too?"'

'I might have known it. My father has just gone out and got himself a new family. He won't care about me any more now.' Mosi's voice was shaking with anger, tears filled her eyes.

Esme put her arms round her daughter. She felt a rage rising up inside her but she had to deal with Mosi first: it was Esme who'd got them into this situation.

'Mosi darling, you'll always be *Baba*'s first-born, no matter what.'

'Who is this bloody Safina anyway? Mosi sat on the edge of the bed, pushing her mother aside. Esme forbore the swear-word; Mosi would have learned it from her in the first place.

'It's quite an unusual name, isn't it? It's ringing a bell for me but I can't think where I've heard it before.'

It was in the middle of the night that Esme awoke from a very unsettling dream involving Martin and some woman. Yes, Esme remembered now, it was the day she had first arrived in the country, in the hotel. Safina had a very young baby with her – Esme couldn't recall its name or even if it was a boy or a girl. She had been too confused, didn't know what was expected of her and was surprised by this sister who wasn't a sister really but was a sort of cousin. A sort of cousin or a sort of girlfriend? Esme grew hot at the realisation that if, as Ali said, she was there as a wife she could not be a blood relation at all – not even Martin would transgress such a boundary. But what of this Clara? She couldn't have been Martin's child: he had been in Scotland with Esme when the child would have been conceived. But Robino, he could certainly be Martin's. What had he been up to?

Well, Esme shrugged, what did she think?

She lay wide awake on the bed in the dark for a couple more hours but her churning emotions gave her no rest. For a while she felt an overwhelming sadness for that young Esme. She had loved Martin so passionately and, despite their difficulties, had always believed that he had loved her. And now, what did Martin's duplicity make of their relationship? That was if he really had been involved with this woman all along – maybe he had just met up with her again – maybe she was a substitute for Esme? Well, this revelation had definitely scotched any possibility of her and Martin getting back together. Ever. In the half year since Christmas when she had made up her mind not to follow Martin an ambiguity had prevailed amongst the four of them. Martin had accepted Esme's decision with less acrimony than she had braced herself for. Maybe, she thought at the time, he was confident she would come round in time as she had done after his last transfer – here to Morogoro. Especially as he had been adamant that Ali would leave with him – almost breaking Esme's heart, being separated from her last-born, but Ali was characteristically nonchalant on his departure; only his mother saw the clenched fists and jaw that betrayed his iron control of his feelings. Since then not a day passed but Esme's heart ached for Ali, and she guessed it was the same for both her children. Mosi's remaining hadn't been an issue for her father though – patriarch to the last - he had sternly warned Esme to guard his daughter closely. Mosi had been distraught at the departure of her father and brother, tearful for days, and for weeks had clung emotionally to Esme. But through monthly trips, the kids had managed to spend a weekend with each other and their missing parent.

Now Martin had destroyed everything. What a bastard! And in a welter of self-pity, regret, loss and anger she let herself cry; tears streamed and sobs wracked her until she feared Mosi would hear her.

At the first call of the muezzin, with dawn faintly seeping through the curtains, she got up and made some tea. She had to acknowledge that she had already moved out from under the spell of Martin, even before Paul had entered her life; gradually she had come to regard Martin only as the father of her children. And no matter what, that fact would remain. How was this was going to affect Mosi and Ali? What was most important now was the present and the future: she was going to have to try and leave the past behind. She set her cup on the dining table, sat down with a writing pad and pencil and tried to pull her thoughts together for the project's first annual report. When the alarm clock rang in her bedroom an hour later there was nothing on the page except black, jagged doodles.

It was only later in the day, when she came across it in her bag, that she realised that she still hadn't read the letter from Paul. For the second time she kept it to read in the evening but this time it stayed in her consciousness as she and Karima went about their work: snatches of the last few months before Paul's departure kept flitting through her mind. Esme had still seen him, usually in the company of Solange and Devin. They had reverted to the friendship they'd developed after their first acquaintance - nothing more physical than the four kisses on the cheeks - but delivered with such tenderness that she had to steel her body from responding to his touch. Until this moment she'd had few regrets but now, suspecting that all the time she had felt guilty for being with Paul, Martin could have been carrying on his shenanigans with that Safina woman, she began again to wonder what might have been possible with her and Paul.

That evening Mosi was still angry and upset. The topic of Martin's new family dominated the conversation; they both wrote letters to Ali. It was going to take time for Mosi to come to terms with the situation and Esme wondered if Mosi's glowing image of her father would stay intact: over the past few years, as she had become old enough to be aware of the tension between her parents, Mosi had excused his every action.

It was late by the time she settled down with Paul's letter. She carefully slit open the envelope and extracted its contents. In the middle of the folded letter was a photograph of him - his dear face beaming out - and beside him a young woman - practically a girl - blonde like him and strikingly attractive. Esme was aghast: first Martin and now Paul - she had been replaced! She threw the photo aside, put her face in her hands and wept.

The outburst lasted only a few minutes before her rational mind took control: it had been her decision to rule out a long-term relationship. She had told him that she would never again up sticks to follow a man to another country. So what did she expect? That he'd pine for her for the rest of his life? Of course not: but a year or two would have been reasonable. She counted back the months and seasons. Incredibly, she realised, it had been about a year. Esme found then that she was miffed more than wounded. She dried her eyes, blew her nose and reached for the letter, curiosity getting the better of her. Well, sure enough, this was Paul's new girlfriend: they had only met recently but they had so much in common, he gushed, having grown up within forty kilometres of each other, both from farming communities and he felt she was the 'real thing'. Esme couldn't help but smile at this typical Paul expression. And no doubt, thought Esme, she hadn't come with two teenage kids and a husband in tow.

Esme thumped the pillow vigorously, put out the light and soon fell asleep thinking of what she had to organise before the Swedish potter arrived for his visit.

On her next trip to the village with Karima she got the stove-makers' approval to bring along the potter from Sweden on their next trip, clarifying for them that Sweden was indeed in Europe. Tanzanians always welcomed visitors who – without phones – would normally arrive unplanned but Esme felt that as this was not to be a social occasion it was only fair to prearrange it. The women were highly amused at the notion of a strange European actually wanting to visit them. They occasionally saw *Wazungu* walking up the mountain but it had been a long time since a researcher had made the effort to reach their village. Esme could understand their excitement, bearing in mind that apart from the festivals for the 'coming out' of girls reaching puberty, not a lot happened round there.

It was as if the stove-making had filled a void: a few months earlier, as soon as they had taken possession of the new forest-green pick-up, a sturdy high-base, four-wheel drive, Esme and Karima had started a stove-making group in Songea hamlet. Once again, Mariamu had come to their aid and rallied some of the same neighbours Esme had accompanied on the firewood foraging expedition. To reach the village meant Esme and Karima driving along the track from the Centre, back through town; not only did they exchange looks with the locals, after a few weeks it was smiles and waves of recognition. Often the locals hitched lifts to town and Esme was frequently hailed as '*Mama* Majiko': an improvement, she thought, on Mama Yusufu or Mama Mosi, whatever way you translated it. Having reached town they turned left and jolted for the best part of an hour up the steep, rocky track to the diminutive plateau where the huddle of huts lay.

The women worked between the houses under the sun - no hardship to them or Karima but, after several hours, taxing on Esme. On their first day, a few weeks earlier, only four apprentices had turned up; each brought their own wooden mortar, well-worn maize cobs and mango stones. Soon a small circle of onlookers from teenagers upwards had gathered, the younger women wearing, as usual, dresses with *kanga* tied round their waists, their hair plaited in corn-rows or more elaborate works of art entailing strands of hair wrapped round with thread, whereas the older women had their hair cut close to their heads. It was common for a woman to have a baby tied in a *kanga* on her back, especially when the child-minding older siblings were at school. Soon a format for these sessions established itself: Karima demonstrated, while Esme encouraged and guided their efforts. Week by week more of the onlookers became participants.

As they worked they chatted and joked. Esme learned that pottery ran in families amongst the Waluguru. Most girls would learn kufin*yanga* - to make pots - much as they would learn to cook and cultivate while growing up but, unlike those activities, there was an element of aptitude and - unusually for girls - choice.

'But these days there isn't the demand for pots that there used to be', commented one of the older women. 'I taught my daughters and my granddaughters to be potters but only Salome here,' she nodded in the direction of a very young mother, 'has kept it up. It's not worth the trouble. But if these stoves are going to catch on, well, please God, we'll be back in business!'

Esme fervently hoped this would be the case. She occasionally attempted to make a stove, or a even a pot, just to show she wasn't afraid of getting her hands dirty. She was slow and cack-handed and the women would fall about laughing at her efforts. Mostly, though, she concentrated on supporting the potters with their own stoves. Although unable to replicate them herself, Esme developed a discerning eye for the details - for the correct dimensions, the thickness of the walls, the height of the pot-rests, and the position of the handles - and could draw attention to any discrepancies. All the time they worked, they chatted.

'This is one of the ways we women can earn some cash,' this was said by Zawadi, a thin bent woman with few teeth. 'And this isn't as hard work as cultivating.' The other women agreed and it was obvious that they enjoyed the social side of the activity, much as they did when collecting firewood.

'So these stoves that we're making, who's going to buy them?' asked another. They're so much heavier than the metal stoves. And if anyone drops them, they'll break.'

Esme and Karima did their best to explain the tests they had carried out and their findings that the ceramic stoves used a third less charcoal than the traditional metal brazier-type. The potters, of course, did not use the stoves themselves – either those they were making or the metal ones - as they didn't have to buy charcoal, having access to abundant firewood. In time, Esme hoped to promote their pottery firewood version but Esme could see it would take a real shortage of free firewood to convince rural women to forsake the traditional three-stone hearth on which they had cooked for millennia.

'We're going to have to make sure townsfolk know about the new "Morogoro Stove" and buy one to try. Once they see for themselves how much cash they can save, they'll be careful of it,' Esme said and added: 'Then, of course, they'll tell other people about it.' Well, that's the theory, she thought to herself and exchanged a smile with Karima.

Ilse had suggested that Esme meet Jens, the Swedish potter, at the small hotel where he would be staying for three nights, apparently unaware that this would be compromising behaviour for a Tanzanian woman. In agreeing, Esme was aware that she was cocking a metaphorical snook at the strictures of society. So it was very self-consciously that she met Jens that first evening. He was a bit older than Esme had expected, maybe fifty, but weather-beaten and he looked physically tough enough for the challenges he was bound to encounter in the countryside. As they shook hands, she felt he looked at her approvingly and flushed. Over a beer he told her that he had travelled extensively in Asia, visiting potters. Her diffidence in the face of his professional expertise soon melted away as she discovered that he was unassuming - shy almost - but humorous. And his eagerness to benefit from her superior understanding of the country, indeed of Africa, buoyed her confidence. He asked how she had come to Tanzania and she gave him a potted version of her life-story, ending with the fact that her daughter was, at this moment, on her own at home and she needed to go back to her.

As she made her way home, she reflected that it had been the most enjoyable evening she'd had in a long time.

After a brief visit to the training Centre the next morning she, Karima and Jens made the journey up to Songea village. As the pick-up climbed the old tarmac road, the massive teak trees planted in colonial times and still protected by the government of the day made a dark tunnel. Emerging into the fierce sunlight their surroundings changed, the mountains loomed up ahead and amongst the abundant bushy vegetation, rose a tall tree bearing large fruit which Jens asked about. Esme pulled a wry face, she often noticed it too at this time of year – the fruit, many of them lying on the ground rotting, were avocados. Esme looked back at Karima, and asked her why local people didn't eat them.

'People round here don't like them, they're considered goat food.' Esme laughed at Karima's reply and translated for Jens and added 'You can buy them in the market for next to nothing but obviously there's not enough demand for them.'

As they lurched off the end of the narrow tarmac and the ancient sLuka track rose before them, Jens let out an involuntary gasp.

'I don't suppose you have a problem with traffic here!' he said.

'Only that occasionally' Esme replied as they caught up with a young man pushing a bicycle.

'Christ, they bring bicycles up and down the mountain!' Jens shook his head. Esme drew to a halt and waved at the cyclist who grinned back and loaded his bike and himself onto the back of the pick-up. She needed to engage low range to move off at this gradient. Esme noticed with a smidgen of satisfaction, that Jens clung to the overhead strap as they lurched over rocks and round bends.

As they climbed and the vista widened, she pointed out the university and its various offshoots in the countryside below. Soon, however, they found themselves hemmed in by hill-sides and Jens was impressed with the gradient of the cultivated slopes.

'Yes, the villagers mostly grow beans and maize, their staple diet. Attempts have been made by authorities in the past to encourage the use of terraces but it has never caught on.'

'Why do you think that is? There must be a lot of soil-loss with the rain.' Jens asked.

'Oh, yes, the university is always writing papers about the erosion and all that but I think that those people who have chosen to stay here, rather than to go off and seek their fortune in the towns, stay because they're pretty content with what they've got. They value their leisure time and actually don't especially want loads of things, material goods.'

'Yes, you're probably right. I've seen that too. Not everyone wants "development".'

'Anyway, none of the developers makes the effort to come up here much so the locals carry on doing what they like.' Esme laughed and pointed out a leafy crop close to the roadside. 'You know what that is?'

Jens peered at it and grinned back, 'That looks like marijuana!' Esme shrugged and answered, 'Well, I never saw it before but that's what I was told,' and she threw a glance towards Karima in the back seat.

By the time they reached the village, the group of women had begun the stove-making session. As Esme and Karima walked up from the pick-up with Jens in their wake, Esme was slightly put out to notice that the potters had all stopped working and were staring open-mouthed at Jens: it wasn't as if she hadn't warned them she'd be bringing a visitor.

'*Karibu*ni, welcome!' at least Mariamu was smiling. She extended her right arm, wrist bent downward so that it was the back of her hand she proffered. Jens smiled but stood looking awkward, not understanding that this was a substitute to a hand-shake as Mariamu's hands were covered in clay. Esme stepped forward and touched the back of her hand to Mariamu's. Jens uttered a quiet 'Ah!' and followed suit with an amiable smile.

Esme noticed that now all the potters were tittering and one of the teenagers spoke up: 'Dada Esme, how come you have brought a man? Is he a special friend of yours? Where is the potter you said would be coming with you?'

Esme, feeling irritated by this less than courteous welcome, spoke to the group, gesturing towards Jens: 'Akina *mama*, this is the potter I told you about. His name is Jens and he's very grateful that you agreed to him coming to see your pottery. It's his first time in the whole of Africa so he is hoping to learn from you.'

This was met with gasps, and expressions of surprise. Then they all started talking at once and some of the girls were laughing so much they could hardly stand up.

Esme was at a loss. Mariamu, to her credit, looked rather embarrassed.

'Dada, excuse us laughing. It's because you have brought a man who you say is a potter! We have never heard of a man who makes pots, it's like having a baby: it's something we thought only women could do!'

'Oh!' Esme was both relieved and mystified. 'But didn't I say he was a man?'

'Hata! Not at all,' replied Mariamu. 'You just said a potter.' And as Esme thought about it, she realised that no, it wouldn't have been evident since Swahili had no distinct words for he, she, him and her.

'Jemani, yes,' said Esme emphatically. 'In Europe, men do more pottery than women. And in some countries, it's only men who do it. Isn't that right, Jens?' She turned towards him and translated the discussion of the last few minutes. It was his turn to be amazed and amused. Despite his evident self-consciousness, he spoke directly to the group giving them the foreigners' greeting 'Jambo! '

'In India I saw only men,' he pointed to his genitals, 'making pots.' He mimed moulding a pot. 'Women' here he cupped his hands under imaginary breasts, 'No!' shaking his head emphatically. This was greeted with an uproar of hilarity and the ice was well and truly broken. Esme made a mental note, however, to warn Jens that although the pantomime was apt for the villagers' ribald sense of humour, anything of that nature would horrify the more godly staff and trainees at Saint Martha's. The Principal had already raised an eyebrow at Esme when she had introduced Jens the previous day at the Centre. Not that Esme was going to let that stop her doing what she wanted, whatever *that* was.

The rest of the day went better than Esme could have hoped with the younger women acting coy and generally flirting with Jens while he gave as good as he got, helping, hindering and generally mucking in.

On the journey back down he thanked her profusely and added. 'I would like to buy you dinner this evening. Are you free?' She thought about it for some time before she answered.

'No, thank you all the same. I don't want to leave Mosi on her own again.' Mosi was, of course, old enough to be left but she so missed her father and brother and she was especially in need of company since Ali's shocking news. If only she could have a friend round to stay the night or at least the evening but it seemed no responsible parent would allow their school-girl daughter out of the home after dark. 'But you're spending the day with us tomorrow at the project, aren't you?'

'Yes, I have a lot of questions.'

Next day Jens arrived early, carrying two books. Esme was sitting on the office steps in the morning sun, reading through a pamphlet from the UK. Jens proffered one of the books, saying, 'I think you will find this useful, I've always referred to it over the years. I'd like you to keep it, as a thank you.' Esme was touched. She took the book and looked at the title: A Potter's Book by Bernard Leach.

'Are you sure? Thank you.' She flicked through the pages, taking in some of the diagrams and photographs showing the beautiful results which could be obtained using methods almost as basic as theirs.

'I know you'll find this interesting also but it's too precious to give away. You could look at it today, if you have time, and then again when you come to visit our project?'

'So, I'm visiting your project am I?' she squinted up at him through the sun. Jens sat down on the step below her.

'How could you not? I hope we can have some exchange visits when I get my project off the ground, your potters and mine.'

'Oh! Well that's certainly something to think about.' Esme carefully leafed through Jens' dog-eared paperback, On Life in Africa and Life as a Craftsman-potter by Michael Cardew. Her heart lifted: she was truly not on her own. She pondered for a few moments, weighing up the conflicting calls on her.

'I'll give it back to you this evening, at dinner, if the offer still holds,' she said smiling at Jens. 'But it will cost you two dinners, I'll bring Mosi, it will be a treat for her and I'd like you to meet her.'

'OK, deal!' he grinned back.

It was evident to Esme that Mosi was won over by Jens that evening, despite her earlier grumblings about her mother looking for a boyfriend because her father had run off with another woman. Quite apart from eating out being rarer than leap years for Mosi, Jens treated her like an equal - even offering her beer which Mosi graciously declined. Jens quietly spoke of his regret that he seldom saw his own two teenage boys since his separation from his wife. Esme could see that Mosi was processing this information.

'Do you think you and your wife will ever get back together again?' she asked. Jens shook his head.

'No,' was all he said before asking Mosi to tell him about the subjects she was studying for 'A' Level. Esme felt proud of her daughter as she told him about her achievements in science and maths and her ambitions as a researcher. Esme judged the evening to be an all round success. She and Jens said goodbye that evening since he was leaving at first light next morning, promising to keep in touch and to arrange for Esme to visit.

The following Monday, knowing that Karima wouldn't be in for another hour, she arrived early at the project base determined to make a serious start on her report. But first, she sat on the step with her flask of tea to enjoy the beauty of the hour: at eight o'clock the sun was already climbing in the sky but, as was frequently the case in kiangazi - the cool season - there was a thin veil of mist over the mountains to the west. She savoured the lingering crispness in the air and that special sense of something to come which unfailingly took her back to summers in Scotland.

Out of the corner of her eye she glimpsed Abie, the new Tanzanian employee who had taken over from the Swiss volunteer couple to run the Centre's small-holding. A couple of days ago he had strolled over in his muddy work-clothes to introduce himself to her and Karima and offer to help them unloading firewood. He had been very courteous towards Karima, much his junior, and spoke Swahili throughout the conversation but it had been to Esme he had addressed himself – or so it seemed to her. Abie had expressed great interest in their project and Esme had told him he was welcome to come and find out more when he had settled in. Afterwards, Esme found herself remembering the way his eyes had kept returning to her and each time shook her head and told herself she was making too much of it. At that moment he looked up from his checklist and their eyes met. He gave her a large wave which she returned with a flush of pleasure.

She tried to marshal her thoughts for the report. The three days with Jens had been a real feast – socially and professionally – and through it she realised that she had been proud to show him her work. Esme acknowledged to herself with an inward smile that she really enjoyed what she did. The stove-making group in Songea was going from strength to strength: the potters were producing skilfully-moulded stoves. The big drawback was that the firing in the open bonfire was cracking many of the stoves so, after a trip to observe the project kiln in action, the Songea women had agreed to build a kiln with Esme and Karima's help. The sessions with the trainees at St Martha's Centre were less successful; in Esme's view this was inevitable, restricted as they were to a few hours with each intake. These sessions couldn't compare with the sustained relationship they had with the villagers but it served a purpose in that it secured their foothold at the Centre and, after all, life was often a series of compromises. Her mind wandered off to the compromise which had enabled her to keep her beloved Mosi as her ward and companion while Martin had taken Ali whom she missed achingly. However, there was no denying that the absence of Martin and of tension in the house, in her life, was invigorating. Inevitably her gaze returned to the mountains; the mist had evaporated revealing the dark forest-swathed peak of Morningside. That day years ago when, in an effort to find some joy in the place, she had dragged poor Mosi and Ali from their flat half-way up the mountainside she could never have envisaged that she would drive up that track as part of her weekly work. She had taken Jens to sit on the parapet of the abandoned hotel to admire the view of what had now become her home turf. Sitting on the step, Esme decided that she would take Ilse there too when she came to visit the project.

Feelings of contentment vied with anticipation as she sat down in the office to write the opening section. She knew she would end up taking home the report to write in the evenings in company with Mosi doing her homework. And then there was Ali's visit to look forward at half-term, only four weeks away. And meeting Robino, Ali's new-found friend and possible half-brother.

And who knew what else lay around the corner?

-oOo-

Acknowledgements

I would like to acknowledge the invaluable support, advice and friendship of the members of the writing group with whom I have met regularly since May 2005: Fiona Allan, Patricia Williams, Wendy Maples and, until his untimely death on 10 January 2011, Nick Cole. I would also like to thank author and poet Kay Syrad who, as my tutor in creative writing, inspired me to embark on the novel. My partner, Adrian O'Brien, my daughters, sons-in-law and friends have always given me morale support. But most of all I want to thank my friend Anne Burrowes for proof-reading the typescript and unfailingly supporting my efforts in so many ways.

Glossary

acha!	leave it!
asante	thank you
baibui	a long black cape worn by Muslim women
baado	not yet
baba	father
Babu	grandfather
Bibi	grandmother
bwana mkubwa	an important man (literally: a big man)
chakula	food
chungu	a clay pot - plural vyungu
dada	a sister; form of address for a young woman
daftari, pl. madaftari	exercise books
daladala	minibus used as public transport
Dar	Dar es Salaam
duka	shop
fundi	a craftsman/woman, artisan, an expert in his/her field
ghimbi, pl. maghimbi	arrowroot, hairy root vegetable
habari?	news?(a greeting)

hatari	danger
hodi	knock knock; may I come in?
hoteli	small, informal guest house
jemani!	literally: hey folks!
jembe	heavy hoe used for agriculture
jiko, majiko	stove, stoves
kabila	ethnic group, tribe
kanga	brightly patterned printed cloth worn by women
kitenge, pl. vitenge	brightly patterned lengths of cloth , heavier than kanga
Kanzu	full-length white cotton garment for men
kapu/kikapu	a basket woven from palm-leaf
Karibu, karibuni	welcome
maandazi	small doughnuts
majiko	stoves (singular: jiko)
mama	a mother; form of address used for a woman
marahaba	response to greeting 'shikamoo'
mfanyakazi	a worker

mgeni, wageni	guest, guests
mkwe	in-law, relative by marriage
mlinzi	night watchman
mpenzi	beloved, dear, darling
mwafrika	a black person
Mzungu	a white person
ndugu	a relative; form of address denoting an equal
nzuri	(response to *Habari?*) - good
safari	a trip, journey of any duration or purpose
samahani	- excuse me
shamba	plot of land planted with crops
shikamoo	greeting to an older person (response 'marahaba')
simba	lion, lioness
sufuria	ubiquitous aluminium saucepan without handle
Ulaya	Europe
vyungu	pots - plural of chungu
Wazungu	white people
yaya	a nanny